FOR BRITO!

RD MORRIS

UNPERSON
PRESS

First published by Unperson Press, 2021
www.unpersonpress.com

Cover design by Unperson Press from original
photographs by C D-X (front) and Gabriel Caroca (back)

ISBN 978-1-8383750-0-3

www.forbrito.com

FIRST EDITION

For Paul,
who provided the security for my creativity,
gave me inspiration when I had only trepidation,
listened to my nonsense as I sought plot points for suspense,
read it all four times or more (telling me he was not bored),
and taught me to believe in my ability to weave
the story within these pages.

Also for Everley,
who became more human with every word.

PROLOGUE

This story is based on a truth to come.

Selby entered his tiny, underground office and tossed a bundle of papers across the desk. He sat himself down with such heavy disappointment that the chair's wheels rolled backwards a foot or so before coming to a quick stop against the adjacent wall.

With the front of his thumb, he rubbed his thick and dark eyebrows in an attempt to soothe himself after the failure of his latest venture. He had been so sure of success this time but, once again, it had all ended horribly. Another Operative was dead, another near-friend was lost and another report needed completing. He wasn't looking forward to facing his manager either, hat in hand and hoping he wouldn't be demoted.

After getting the hopeless huffs out of his system, Selby slid forwards and wiggled the computer mouse until the screen came to life. He clicked an icon on the desktop and, whilst waiting for the contents to load, felt glum at the regularity with which he had to click on the 'Closed Cases' folder.

Loading a template, he began filling each field. He slowly typed the name 'Operative Derby' by hammering each letter's key with his forefinger while blowing a brooding air from his mouth at the same time.

'I hear it didn't go well?' said a co-worker as the office door swung open.

'Ever heard of knocking?' Selby snapped.

'Oh, come on! You need a break. Do you want to play cards?'

'I lost her... She entered a state of shock. Shock! Can you believe that? We were so close with this one. It was like her mind...' Selby looked away from the screen and picked up a photo of the lost Operative that was stapled to the top paper in the stack. Staring at the face, he attempted his sentence again, 'Her mind collapsed inwards.'

'It's not your fault. It happens, you know that. I'll get us some nutrition shakes and grab the cards. Let's have a game, eh?' Without waiting for a reply, the co-worker disappeared down the corridor and called back, 'I'll meet you in the break room!'

Selby hurriedly entered relevant information into the remaining spaces on the template, as though to type quickly might minimise his hurting. As soon as he had finished the form and saved the file, he delicately prised the photograph from the paper by bending the legs of the staple outwards and pulling the two apart. Standing up and leaning over his desk so that he could reach the wall behind, he found a vacant space in the very full collage of otherwise-forgotten faces and pinned the picture to the board.

Selby paused for a moment to remember the many individuals that he had found, nurtured and then put to the test, only to lose them somewhere or somehow along the way. He had never become accustomed to the heartache, despite it being a common part of his work, but it wasn't going to make him quit. He was determined to continue, for he knew that if he could spot those Operatives with the strongest minds in the country, he could free them.

In the centre of the mixture of pictures, Selby had previously written and pinned the mantra of the hidden Organisation he worked for. It had been there many years and was largely covered by the collection of faces. All that now peeked out from beneath the photos were three words. He read them aloud while tracing them with his hand and felt his melancholy lift.

Stepping away, Selby grabbed the papers from the tabletop, shoved them into a cardboard folder and dropped it into a tray labelled 'For Archiving'. He drew a new sheet from the top of a stack in the tray tagged 'New Candidates' and studied the name. Though the eyes were as lifeless as those of any other enslaved mind, the photo affixed to his next case was that of a man with a friendly face.

Selby placed the page carefully in the centre of the table. After a brief break to clear his thoughts, he would turn his attention to this new lost soul. Turning to leave for the game of cards, he took one last look at the penned phrase on his wall and reminded himself that he had an important role to continue. He had a purpose.

'Find open minds.'

I

'Wastefulness is the disease that compromises

the survival of our whole.

Wastefulness must be eliminated.'

- Command Operative Raines

Another body belonging to the homeless and purposeless class was stretched out and in the way of the arched entrance at Point A. The chest was compressed against the concrete platform floor under the weight of a rectangular white machine that had been indelicately placed on the spine. With neck twisted, the front of the face was cleverly facing the back of the body and the open eyes were hooked onto a fixed point in the sky. The image did not tell the story of a soft departure from the living world. Instead, the eyes were wide and filled with horror, which was pleasing.

Operative Everley had arrived at the station his usual thirty-eight minutes before the morning train and was standing over the corpse of the InOperative. In their choice to not work, these pointless people made themselves candidates for killing, but there was much to be admired in the extra effort that had been made in this case. One (or more) Britons had been sure to squeeze some small value from the being by displaying it so deliberately. In death alone, the body served Brito. There, in the entryway passed by all Operatives starting and ending their working shifts, was as clear an example as any of the consequences of not contributing.

Everley took a last and satisfying look at the face of the dead waste and then stepped over the obstruction, for there was nothing he enjoyed more than being first in line for the train. First in line meant he would be first to board the silver Speed Line. It also meant that he would be first to alight, which gave him a slight head start on his working day. Besides, Everley wanted to watch the platform fill with his fellow Operatives. Their united presence and shared purpose could be silently absorbed, and he liked to savour every second of it.

It was unnaturally warm for day seventy-six of the year with just a little snow still settled on the edges and ledges of the station. Within ten minutes of Everley's arrival, the snow on the platform had been trampled away beneath the marching feet of the four hundred in his group. There were no information boards, no loud announcements and no painted signs or markings, yet the Operatives queued in orderly lines for a train they knew would come on time.

There was something symmetrical in the way the Operative body stood on that platform. Male or female, each one had the same efficient hair and was perfectly presented in black trousers with crisp shirt collars peeking out from a black fleeced coat. Purposefully, the blackness would differentiate them from the white windmills where they worked, and the layers would keep them warm.

With so many waiting so patiently, it was neither silent nor loud. A murmur of occasional acknowledgements could be heard (and were allowed, of course) but chatter was not needed. The Operatives smiled enigmatically at each other or to themselves with anticipation, self-fulfilment or contentment from a life usefully lived. And all was calm.

There was one clock. It was a large and old-fashioned thing from the earliest part of the twenty-first century. It had been refurbished, repurposed and efficiently tied to a post in the centre of the platform using what appeared to be a twisted green cable of small lights (bulbs removed). With such calmness, you could hear it tick.

The beautiful peace of the moment was wasted, as always, by the ruinous faction. An InOperative child ran diagonally across and in between the Operative queues while giggling, which displaced their structured lines. A female InOp (seemingly the child's creator) ran after it with arms flailing, trying to grab it.

Amongst the Operatives, these InOps looked so untidy and thoughtlessly inefficient by comparison; the coloured clothes disrupted the presentation of the otherwise uniformed congregation. They must have found some valuable carpet pieces from somewhere and were using them to cover their own useless backs rather than offering them up to Brito. How shameful!

InOperatives always acted-up on the colder days. Perhaps the unruly behaviour served to warm them. Whatever the reason, it would not be tolerated. Seeing the little one run towards him, Everley struck his foot forward, taking the legs out from under the child and causing it to clatter to the ground with a squeak. As Everley stood still, not wanting to dirty his hands by touching it, the mother bundled the child into her arms, silenced the crying with a firm hand over its mouth and backed away fearfully until the two could no longer be seen.

Surrounding Operatives nodded approvingly at Everley and the queuing lines straightened. With faces forward, harmony resumed and the clock's tick-tock could be heard once again.

A poster was hanging from one horizontal and two vertical upright posts of white wood (salvaged from some historical use) on one side of the platform. It filled the available space, as wide as twenty sitting InOps and as tall as two standing. On the poster was drawn the naked body of a young male Operative with a strong jawline, sensible hair, dark brows and intense eyes looking outwards, at you. A muscled arm of such definition raised a pointing finger directly forwards, and the words 'BRITO NEEDS YOU!' were written underneath.

Everley faced the poster and stared at the male image as it stared back at him.

'For Brito!' he roared aloud suddenly.

'For Brito!' was returned by one voice after the next, after the next, as fellow Operatives joined in appreciation.

Everley clapped his hands together from the joy of their echo, but did not move from his queuing position.

'Fuck Brito!' came a throaty bellow from a bedraggled figure that had emerged from the reverse side of the poster, having likely used it as some sort of shelter.

In immediate and unified response, a small army of Operatives left their lines and wrestled with each other to get to the InOp first. There was no doubt that those criminal words would be his last. The Operatives, using both muscle and determination, effortlessly dragged the InOp feet-first towards the edge of the platform. Flinging him into the air and onto the tracks, the group turned away without a second look and brushed themselves off, just as one would toss a bag of rubbish into a bin.

Throughout the scene, Everley did not move. He could feel the familiar and exhilarating vibration beneath his toes that electrified his whole body. The Speed Line was coming. Everley closed his eyes and listened for the growing roar and rumble to get closer and closer. The screech of the brakes overpowered the final scream of the old tramp on the tracks as the train flattened him. That was the end of the matter. And abruptly, all was silent.

With a swoosh of air into his face and a deep breath out, Everley's eyes opened and focussed on the silver door in front of him. He was sure that his heart would beat itself clean out of his chest if the train's doors didn't open soon enough. He would have to wait a moment more; the Night Shifters needed to step off the Speed Line first. As soon as the front door opened, a cascade of black suits and work boots poured from the first carriage. In a continuous line that stretched from one end of the hollow train to the other, the workers marched from the front compartment and left Point A by the only exit.

While waiting, the queuing Operatives on the day shift clapped to applaud those departing, who smiled, nodded, waved or exclaimed 'For Brito!' in return. Everley was still silent and motionless; the anticipation was so great for the journey to the windmills that the minute or so felt like the longest and most painful of waits.

At precisely eight o'clock, the silver door slid to the right and was open. Everley stepped on, turned to the left and was immediately at the front. He reached upwards for the handle above him. The coolness of its metal on his sweaty palm set a frisson of thrill from stomach to chest. He was ready.

With no seats in the way, a queue formed in alignment behind him. Each hand took hold of a handle and each stance was poised. All aboard, and the doors closed. With one jolt, they were away.

It was the best of times. It was the age of wisdom. It was the epoch of selfsame beliefs and the season of solidarity. It was two hundred years since Charles Dickens wrote *A Tale of Two Cities*, but now all that mattered was one land, one place and one body: Brito. With every breath, the Operatives would work for it. With their blood, they would feed it. All believed that perfection, such perfection, needed protection. All thought that they were truly enlightened.

Brito had been booming for some time. The productive populace had mobilised to maintain the country and gave their lives for the whole: mere cogs on sprockets within the machine.

But Britons hadn't always been so united. Before Great Britain died, anarchy was on the rise and lawless acts increased in number and severity until the people could take no more. Turf wars, knife crime, acid attacks, body shaming and negative social media comments all saw the Brits turn to fight themselves. Society was shattered by infinite reasons for division, whether it be from a difference of class, gender, sexuality, ethnicity, race, religion or culture; or a disparity in health, wealth and public displays of happiness. Everybody had become an outsider; every being had become an opposition. The world had become more violent and less predictable, and the Brits were exhausted.

By the time that a sixth wave of a fatal virus had swept through the country, overwhelmed the health system and taken hundreds of thousands of British lives, difference was forgotten. The public were contained by their mutual fear of an invisible enemy and were determined to survive. The only way to succeed was to join together as one. And, if that meant closing the country to other lands, then so be it.

Then, of course, there was Brexit. The very first page in modern Brito books begins with Brexit. After much dither, delay and political play between Britain and Europe (and the rest of the world), the old government weighed the European anchor and the British Isles set sail into the sea. When the Brits realised they were truly alone, it was certainly all hands on deck.

With Britain struggling to save itself from drowning, many bad and truly terrible decisions were made. Determined to keep basic public services functioning, such desirable criteria as qualifications, experience and politeness were forgone to fulfil job roles, and Command Operative Raines was one of the first to benefit from the nation's desperation.

Now sitting in the glory of an office on the highest floor of the second-highest building in Brito, Raines smirked with satisfaction. From a hard start in Great Britain, he had grown into a somebody in Brito and though he was now old, he was comforted by his own self-importance.

With both elbows on the desk, he rested the thick and sagging skin of his chin into both opened palms. Despite the mean grin of his mouth, the space between his white and wispy brows held a permanent frown. The deep crease between his exasperated eyes had been caused by so many years of scowling that it looked as though it had been scooped with a butter knife.

'I made it,' thought Raines as he gazed around the efficiently bare room with a view onto the wasteland of a bygone era and compared it against the memory of his basement flat in Roe Alley, "Old Liverpool", where he used to press illegal uppers and downers before selling them to a customer base of frantic junkies.

Raines was still able to vividly recall the hand-scrawled advertisement for police inspector job vacancies that had been sloppily stuck to the door of a government building, only to change his future forever. By chance, he had noticed the sign on his return home from a commercial exchange in town. He had paused to adjust a bag of powdered steroid that he was hiding in his underpants (and planning to mix into imitation Xanax later), and noticed the advert gleaming out of the greyness like some sort of significant suggestion that he was destined to follow.

Inside the heavy door was an empty reception area without a receptionist. A paper notice scribbled with 'Law ~~Inforcement~~ ENforcement ~~Interview's~~ Interviews This Way' was taped to a post and pointed down a corridor.

'Come in!' yelled a woman from inside one of the rooms as Raines wandered through the hallway.

'Erm... I'm here for the interviews.'

'Sure thing.' The woman, dressed in plain clothes and with flowing red hair that waved past her shoulders in a style that would be unheard of today, gestured towards a metal chair on the other side of her desk.

Taking a seat, Raines began apologetically with, 'Sorry I'm not in my suit. I just popped out and saw the sign. I've been wanting to start a career in–'

'No problem,' the woman interrupted, looking down at a piece of paper. 'Any qualifications?'

'No. Sorry, I didn't catch your name.'

'Convictions in the last two years?' the woman continued, following the next question printed on the sheet.

'Not two years, no. Before that though... Well, I was young and–'

'Previous employment?'

'Erm... I worked as a security officer for the Walker Art Gallery for a year before it was raided,' Raines said quickly and convincingly, which surprised even him.

The woman's head lifted for the first time. She scanned Raines from top to untidy bottom. They both knew that she couldn't check whether he was telling the truth.

'You left *before* the raid? What security system was in place?' she quizzed.

'Well... The Walker had security cameras... yes! Also, we installed a series of magnetic sensors attached to each of the paintings that would trigger the alarm if moved even a millimetre,' Raines began, not knowing if any of that was true. What he did know was that there was something attached to the side of the painting he had stolen during the raid. He had later struggled to remove it with a bent spoon. 'It was the MaxGuard system. I don't know if you've heard of it?' He added fictional details with ease and spoke them with an air of cocky confidence.

'Okay.' The woman looked back down and ticked another section on the sheet.

Raines was almost disappointed at the lack of follow-up questions, taking joy in the comedy of the conversation.

'Look, the country needs workers. Do you want to work, and work bloody hard?' the woman said directly. 'If you would rather stay in bed all day and scrounge for your dinner at night, then you may as well go back into the foulness out there!' Raising her voice, she pointed at the door.

'I want this, miss, please! I refuse to get eaten up by the terror out there. I want to be part of our country. I want to give myself fully to it. I'll do whatever it takes. I don't want to be lost anymore. I'll work every hour I have. Please!'

Raines hadn't realised that he needed a purpose until the very minute he had to beg for it. He felt himself quiver with emotion. It was true, too. He knew what would happen to the non-workers and he wouldn't let that be him.

12

'Okay. That's what I wanted to hear.' The woman ticked through a number of other elements on the paper form and then asked his name.

'Bunky Baines. I mean Kevin Baines, sorry, everyone calls me Bunky.' He must really have felt vulnerable for that to slip out, and he immediately worried she would recognise the name and either reject him or arrest him.

'Well, Bunky, you'll need to take one of these names. I'll pick for you...' She reached for a book on the desk and thumbed through the pages. 'Ah! This will do: *Raines*. It's like your last name anyway!'

Before Raines had chance to ask why his name had to change, she had written it down on a piece of paper, rubber stamped it, folded it over and handed it to him along with a train ticket and map.

'Monday. Five in the morning. Lime Street train station. That will take you to London. The directions for where you must go are here. Don't be late. Good luck!'

With that, she dismissed him, and Raines couldn't have left any quicker. Stepping outside, the feeling of relief was overwhelming. He shoved the train ticket between the elastic of his underpants and the hidden powder for safe keeping. He unfolded the paper, skimmed the stamp that read 'Law Enforcement Entrance Exam: PASSED', let out a bark of wicked laughter and walked briskly back home.

That was thirty-four years ago, when Raines had just turned twenty-nine, but he would never forget it. Remembering to set an alarm on that Sunday night so long ago, crawling out of bed early the following morning, running to the station and waving his ticket at the conductor as he jumped onto a closing door of the London train became the most momentous sequence of events of his entire life.

Back then, old Britain after Brexit and the Sixth Wave resembled wartime Blighty: homeland agriculture, domestic food production, national self-sufficiency, recycling and rationing. All the while, morale was maintained through the common purpose, and the common people became good citizens through their practical help towards the survival effort.

Naturally, the country feared it would never weather its divorce from the rest of the world. The population was petrified: a nation depressed. But this gave way quickly to extreme patriotism, which grew at an astronomical rate. Before long, all truly felt that they would give their lives willingly for the rest, and cast out anyone who wouldn't.

People no longer chose what food to eat, but would collect an appropriate amount. People no longer chose which clothes to wear, but would be issued with a necessary stock. People no longer decided what to do with their time, but would give it to the country. They would do all of this without question because survival was essential, purposefulness was paramount, and any aspect of waste was to be removed. Cash became useless as all resources were pooled and only food, tools, materials, knowledge and sex were traded.

Those believing in the cause became a modern Land Army. Any and all notions of difference disappeared until all that was left were *those that would work and those that would not*. It was a hard line.

One of the Hard Line policies that tipped the balance was the removal of any and all benefits. Jobseeker's Allowance was the first to go, followed by Statutory Sick, Housing Benefit, Child Benefit, ESA, DLA, allowances, credits and grants. The old government made it clear: *Contribute and together we are protected. Refuse to contribute and the nation refuses to protect you.*

Believing their human rights were compromised, many chose to expel themselves. In fact, it was an opportunity for anyone to leave who did not approve of the survival effort, the Land Army, the Hard Line or Brexit in the first place. And many did leave. Those with family in other countries emigrated to join them. Those with strong experience in a profession sought settlement in any country that would take them; Australia and America were primary choices due to the shared language and open-door offers for the skilled.

Huge hordes of the population migrated in swarms, like a biblical plague of flying ants so large it could be seen from space.

Those Brits preparing to leave were treated with the mockery that their cowardice deserved, and those that remained without contributing were ridiculed (and later attacked) with such maliciousness that they soon found any means of escape. Some joined others for parts of the journey and requested asylum in countries along the way. Some stowed away and did the same. Those without a skill who thought the grass greener elsewhere were accepted into the hands of Eastern European countries, only to find themselves gobbled up by organised crime, forced labour, drug rackets and sexual slavery. It was prime propaganda material. 'What of your human rights now?' taunted the tabloids.

Some defied the new way of things but still refused to leave. On many occasions had these work-shy citizens been purposefully killed. These acts – later considered 'waste management' – were either disregarded due to a convenient lack of evidence or simply not investigated. The year 2029 became a landmark when a very public murder of a non-worker went unpunished. It set a precedent.

Raines was proud to say he was there that day.

A gross group of jobless and unoccupied guttersnipes had gathered around parliament in "Old London" to protest the lack of support provided by the British Government. As riots go, this was fairly tame with more verbal dissent than flaming cocktails and pepper spray. Raines remembered thinking it was quite incredible that these sofa-sitting sloths refused to work for the survival effort but would drag themselves out to protest. As all workers thought like Raines, anyone available turned out to mock the slobs and defend the Hard Line.

Understandably, one female worker couldn't listen to the nonsense any longer and fetched a man out of the protesting crowd. Tall, strong and athletic, her powerful arms heaved the hapless man across the muddied garden grounds until she reached the "Burghers of Calais" sculpture. People were shouting (the workers with encouragement, the others with concern), but all watched without interfering.

Upon reaching the pointed edge of the cast, she held the head of the man with one hand around the neck as his arms thrashed about in defence of his life. With harrowing rage, she struck him over and over with the clenched fist of her free hand. The hammering noise of human against bronze was repetitively regular, like a woodcutter against a tree in an otherwise still forest. With the crowd silenced, the rhythmic punches became the only sound. Eventually, and with her own hand bloodied, she stopped.

Those standing closest to the scene went towards the man and, without conferring, showed their mutual support for the act by working together to lift and drape the lifeless body on top of the figures in the statue.

Staring at the body from where he stood a little distance away, Raines was certain he could see the chest move as it struggled to take a final breath. All these years later, Raines reflected on the symbolism of the placement of the man across the sculpture and half-smiled meanly at the memory.

With media reduced to a single television channel and one newspaper, the violent death did feature in the daily round up, but with a simple statement: *'The Operative responsible is free without penalty. Future eliminations of waste will not be reported.'* That was that. Importantly, the report also coined the term "Operative". The label of the "InOp" soon followed.

The Hard Line policies continued to grow aggressively at that time. The old government made it very clear what kind of country Britain needed to be and gave notice of "Embarkation". This was to be the final act of jettisoning the rest of the world and sailing Britain on its own. On the date of Embarkation, all borders would close, walls would be raised, fences erected, security in place: no entry or escape.

A generous five-year warning was given to enable anyone not wishing to participate to leave, and all others to prepare. Embarkation promised a new world for Britain that would be one all of its own. New Britain would be self-governing, self-sustaining and self-centred. Crucially, there was to be no looking back.

Everything that reflected the past was either recycled or sold to the highest bidder to fund the new infrastructure. America took most items of previous value, from cave art, Anglo-Saxon metals, embroidery, portraiture and literature to modern technologies. Before the fifth year was up, even Stonehenge had been sacrilegiously relocated to Cambridge, Massachusetts, where Harvard students researched the effects of fallen empires as part of doctoral programmes. Big Ben became a theme park attraction in China, France bought the top of Nelson's Column for the Louvre, and no-one knew what happened to the Crown Jewels.

Wind and solar power were selected as Britain's prime energy sources, and efficient trains its only transport. All money raised was used to procure materials to construct the wind turbines from Germany, China and India, as well as to purchase high-speed railway tracks and trains from Japan.

It was the dawn of a new age and it was exciting. As time grew closer towards Embarkation, the depleted population celebrated by actively destroying the conventional iconography of Britishness. Representations of historical Britain were torn down by hand, hammer or fire until British identity existed no longer.

Someone, somewhere had used the term "One-ism" to describe the joint belief in national self-interest that was expected to underpin every element of new Britain. The term, as apt as it was, persisted and it was felt that other new terms would be needed to signify the change. New Britain soon became "Brit-o", and with the fresh new name came an even fresher patriot that eagerly awaited the death of the old country.

Thirty days before the borders closed, the government held a final democratic vote: for or against Embarkation. Only Operatives could vote. The results were clear with the ayes at one hundred percent. Oneism had prevailed, the doubters had been dealt with and those that were left in dying Britain would raise Brito from its ashes and militantly protect it.

In 2030, the final moment of Embarkation was marked with the filling-in of the Channel Tunnel. Such an extreme event could only have been joked about in previous years, but became the ultimate demonstration of Brito's birth. Non-recyclable or non-reusable refuse stuffed a large proportion of the one-hundred-million cubic foot hole (without question, a collection of disturbing things found their way down there, too).

The final act was to pump concrete into the void. With all the excitement of a New Year, the remaining population gathered to witness the event and join in national celebration. The atmosphere was that of the most peaceful festival imaginable. There was a lot of hugging and singing, dancing and face-painting with soil. The mood was magical, almost neopagan, as people celebrated the nature and the land on which all stood. Soon, all that would exist and be known was Brito, so every particle of ground and air was to be cherished.

Raines couldn't make it to "Old Folkestone" on Embarkation Day. He was busy in the Watch Room of a Command site. With a small team of other worthy Operatives, he had been called upon to monitor the security drones that patrolled the borders. "Borders" meant every fence and any cliff edge, seaside, waterfront, past port and marked coastal zone defined by an offshore wind farm. It was an honour to be viewing the live camera footage that ensured Brito was closed and without threat of invasion (or last-minute scarpering).

Thankfully, Raines and the team were able to experience Embarkation at a distance, as it was televised on the one channel and screened on a large projector in the Watch Room. With such an historical event, every inhabitant of Brito watched the finale along with the rest of the world.

As the concrete began to pour, the thousands present quietened and observed in a shocking silence. Out of the quiet, a woman in the crowd began to sing. With the most harmonious voice, she sang the same line over and over. The two or three people standing next to her began to clap a very regular clap. One neighbouring man stamped his foot and then smacked both hands on one thigh as the foot landed, so as to accentuate the action. The cameras televising the scene focussed on the small group to allow everyone at site or on screen to see them.

Some in the assembled mass may have been nervous to join, but were soon in the minority as one person after the next followed by imitating the initial trendsetters, singing, clapping, stamping, thigh-smacking or doing all of these things simultaneously.

The volume raised to such a level that even the stream of concrete seemed to shake. The sound carried and crescendoed with increased passion, togetherness and joy. Every Briton was united.

'We-e-e are,'

CLAP THUMP THUMP

'To-o-gether just one!'

CLAP THUMP THUMP

It took a few seconds of staring at the screen from the Watch Room for Raines to recognise the tune. Of all the music from British artists to transcend the old world into the new dawn, it wasn't Beatles or Bowie, Queen, Clash, or Cliff. Instead, it was an indie pop-to-dance band famous for alternative and mesmerising sounds, psychedelia, drinking, having a good time and getting loaded. Although the words had changed, Raines had to admit the song was apt in its mantra-like expression of Oneism.

All these years later, and in his own office, Raines replayed the experience. His singing may have been out of tune but his drumming was in time as he tapped his knuckles on the table in recollection. Raines wondered whether any of the band imagined that their song would become the war cry of a nation, and whether the more celebrated (but since forgotten) old British bands were jealous.

A knock at the door snatched him from the daydream of the death of Britain and dropped him into the here and now, where his skin was thick with age, his hands were worn with time, but his militant love of country was unchanged.

'Yes?' he called out and stood up.

A young Operative entered the room, stopped a foot from the table, rigidly raised one open hand, placed it on her own chest and waited for permission to speak.

Raines nodded in response.

'Command, we have assessed the capabilities of the selected Operatives, as requested. All are InOperative.'

'Expunge them,' Raines replied without a pause.

'For Brito!' came the reply. The Operative removed her hand from her chest, turned and left the room quickly.

Raines didn't bother replying. He took a paper folder from the tabletop and fed it into a hole in the wall, down a chute and into the incinerator below.

INOPS COST BRITO

OVER 144,000 HOURS EACH YEAR

IN DAMAGE TO THE SPEED LINE.

VOLUNTEER SHIFTS ARE EXPECTED.

REPORT TO THE MAIN DESK.

- Foyer Noticeboard, Building 7

Everley's eyes popped open the instant he awoke as though in response to a clicking finger. He turned his head to the gap between the bottom of the blackout blind and the windowsill, through which he could see the large clock face on the building opposite.

Yet again, it was five to six.

For as many days as he could remember, Everley's body had forced him to rise and realign at precisely this time. It happened so often that he now expected it. The inevitability had become as comforting as the regularity with which the rest of his life was governed.

His daily practice was to use those five free minutes to dream of 'The Other Place'. He imagined taking the Speed Line to the end of the line in North Brito. He could almost hear the silver doors of the train swish open to reveal a vibrant new land. His feet twitched with the anticipated tickle of stepping onto green grass for the first time. He pictured flowered fields of all colours, quaint buildings and people dancing and singing. Mother would be there, too. His fancy was shrouded in a soft air. A haze of smooth blues lingered low in small clouds that he imagined, if touched, would feel much the same as the inside of a fresh pillow issued by Brito on Day One of the year. It was the serenest of dreams.

BUZZ BUZZ BEEP BEEP BEEP

The building alarm sounded so loudly through speakers in the corridor beyond his room that Everley jumped out of this daydream with an audible intake of shock. Nonetheless, he was immediately grateful for the interruption so that he could begin the satisfying monotony of his morning routine.

Getting up and out of the bed without delay, Everley took the cover sheet by one hand and pulled it straight upwards to make the bed in one movement. He patted down any folds in the fabric and, once contented it was crease-free, went to the window. With a quick jerk on the material, the blind clattered upwards and was fully open. He squinted to shield his eyes from the morning light and peered down to the ground, twelve floors below.

Although a mere dot from this height, Everley could see the Night Watch Operative leaving after completing the six-to-six shift. The figure crossed another Night Watcher walking from the neighbouring building as they both left their posts perfectly on time. Despite not being able to see them clearly, Everley smiled at the thought that they had exchanged a 'For Brito!' as they passed each other.

Turning to get on with his day, Everley took a moment to notice how beautifully the morning sun lit the picture that decorated one wall of his otherwise bare bedroom. The image was a hand-span in size with a ragged edge that showed it had been torn from a small and very old book (these things only existing in schools nowadays). It had been left by the previous lodger of room B12.13 and, it being an illustration of The Other Place, Everley did not want to remove it.

The poster was a colourful advertisement showing a countryside full of smiling people and had a headline that read

'Operatives! This is Brito's thank you to YOU!'. Everley believed that the picture could only have been painted by someone who had personally been there as it would be impossible to invent such beauty from an Operative perspective. He studied the detail in the image morning and night as a reminder of what the reward would be for a lifetime dedicated to Brito, just as the tag line suggested: 'Your devotion will not be forgotten!'

Without the picture, the room would be without character at all. It was a rectangular box with a window on one wall, a small bed against the second, a pole for hanging clothes on the third and a door on the last. Everley had also found and fixed up a small shelf next to the door to place his only belongings: a toothbrush and soap.

The building itself was a similarly regular square box designed with efficiency in mind. Each side had twenty floors and each floor had twenty bedrooms (with windows pointing outwards). The walls between were created from unpainted boards so thin that Everley could often hear both neighbours snoring. The centre of the building was not for bedrooms, but rather for two toilets, two shower rooms, a lift and a stairway down to the entrance and exit. You often had to wait in line for the loo.

No sooner had the alarm sounded, Everley heard movement from the Operatives in the adjacent bedrooms. Wanting to be first to use the facilities, he grabbed his toothbrush and soap from the shelf by the door, darted out in a flash and skipped naked down the length of the hallway.

The toilet room was made entirely from cream plastic. Everything from ceiling to invisible cistern had been moulded into one solid shape with no moveable parts. When Everley stepped out of the small space, the spring-loaded door closed itself behind him and locked automatically. A one-minute steam cycle sterilised the area after each use.

'Blame it!' thought Everley, noticing that both shower rooms were engaged and he would have to wait in the cold corridor with no clothes on.

'Best Morning, Everley,' came a voice behind him, where a queue had formed.

Twisting to see which neighbour was there, he scanned his mind to find the name of the naked woman who was waiting for a reply. Her body seemed familiar and he knew that he had admired it before, but, try as he might, he couldn't remember her. He threw back a forced pleasantry before quickly returning to face the shower room door.

With a sound of unlocking, a fellow Operative appeared and vacated the cubicle. After waiting patiently for the clean cycle to finish, Everley rushed himself inside and locked the door. Again, it was just a cream plastic container, but this time there was a plastic sink protruding out of the plastic wall that had a mirror attached above.

Throwing his toothbrush into the sink but keeping hold of the soap, Everley stepped beneath a circular pattern of holes in the ceiling. Sensing him there, water sprayed through the holes with high pressure. The temperature was just right for Everley: tepid. Any hotter and he would want to stay there for longer than the one minute the water would run for. He dragged the soap block up one leg and down the other, then the same with his arms. After a swoosh on the face and a smear through the hair, he threw it into the sink. He used the remaining forty-eight seconds to enjoy the water run across his skin and cleanse him ready for a utile day.

The water stopped with a click. Through those same circular holes in the ceiling, powerful jets of air pumped so forcefully that they pushed shapes into his skin as he moved beneath them. Sixty seconds later, the air stopped. Every part of him was dry.

After two whole minutes in the cubicle, Everley felt self-conscious. He had to be efficient and didn't want to keep his neighbours waiting. He seized his toothbrush and held it below a sensor in the mirror. A fingernail-sized amount of clear gel churned out of a hole and onto the brush. It never took long to brush teeth in Brito, them not being used much; everything a Briton needed was provided in drink and tablet form.

24

Everley took a facial hair remover that was clipped into a holder beside the sink and tethered to the wall with an elasticated wire. There were only a few hairs growing on his chin and cheeks, but he still winced as the electric machine ripped them out from the root. A quick check in the mirror as he replaced the little tool, and he was done.

Everley took the longest route to Point A station. It wasn't the most scenic of walks, but it was the most interesting because the diversion steered him through an InOperative district.

Set upon the flimsy and fragile foundations of demolished constructions and dismantled commodities, the InOperative area was a wasteland filled with curious items from a forgotten era. Everything of use should have been collected and donated to Brito for recycling, but there was so much waste and so little free time in an Operative day that the InOps had the run of things there. They had shaped shelters from old concrete pieces balanced on top of brick. They had found hard plastics and stacked them to form huts. They had gutted large machines of their components and left the shells of these objects lying bare on the land. Who knew what they did with the contents.

Walking through the area gave Everley an insight into how the InOps spent their wasteful time. Without purpose or work to do for dear Brito, these persistent InOps were forever foraging. They could also be found sleeping, drifting about confusedly as though detached from reality, or chatting together crassly in clusters.

Striding through an open area, Everley observed from a distance a group of at least five InOps involved in some kind of unproductive activity. They were raucously jeering with arms interlinked as they hopped around each other. Everley watched as they each seemed to take something from the centre of their circle, hold a hand in the air then move it towards their mouths and eat something.

'Filthy worm-eaters,' thought Everley.

25

As he walked around a small mound of rubble and ruins, Everley spotted four legs sticking out from underneath a vast sheath of black plastic. Beneath it was much groaning and moaning. Everley was sickened by the idea of being so close to another's body that it would compromise his own cleanliness. School had taught him about the gamble of sexual mixing and Brito forbade it, but those dirty InOps didn't care about such things.

Wary of inhaling the InOperative disease that they passed to each other during such depraved encounters, Everley slipped past whilst holding his nose and mouth. He marched away quickly to create a distance between himself and the degenerates.

'Disgusting!' came a shout from close by, behind him.

Everley stopped and watched a male Operative (in Brito-issued wear) approach the couple. He reached loudly into the depths of his own throat, brought up a cloudy ball of drool and spit it across their exposed legs. He then stomped straight towards Everley.

'Best Morning, Briton,' said the Operative as he drew closer. 'What brings you to this lost land?'

'Best Morning! This is the longest walking distance from my lodgings to Point A,' Everley replied.

The Operative returned a quizzical look then raised one palm and placed it on his chest. 'Capital Selby,' he said, introducing himself.

Everley hadn't noticed the circular bronze pin that was positioned on his outfit, and was now peeking from beneath the Capital's hand. He straightened his stance immediately, raised his hand and strongly planted it to his own chest.

'Operative Everley' he responded formally and waited for permission to speak or move.

'Well, Everley, let's walk to Point A together shall we?' said Selby, signalling to move and starting on the same path to the station.

26

Everley and Selby were of a similar age: early 20s. They certainly had the same sensible hair in the same black colour and, except for Selby's bronze pin, they had the same uniforms too. They held themselves in the same manner and were equally muscular in all of the places that demonstrated a dedication to strength training and exercise. In many ways, they mirrored each other. Although they were of a similar height, Everley felt as though Selby towered over him. He respected him immediately.

'I am not being wasteful with my energy by walking the long way, Capital Selby. I have calculated that I will arrive at exactly the same time as the shortest route if I power at my quickest pace. I'm building my stamina and travelling to work in the most efficient way, sir.'

'Very good, Briton. Methodical thinking indeed!'

The two marched in step with each other along what had historically been a road for vehicles. There was no chatting at first. Everley was a little nervous in the Capital's presence and, searching his mind for topics of discussion, he rejected every conversation starter for fear of talk improperly in front of a Higher Operative.

'What say you of those despicable InOps back there, Briton?' Selby began, 'So brazen in their wastefulness, aren't they? Why do they persist in living?'

This was something that Everley had considered many times. All Operatives had questioned this, no doubt.

'They need to be forced to operate, instead of being left there to spread disease,' he replied confidently.

'*Who* leaves them there, Briton?'

Everley paused. He knew his reply had inferred that there was something other than the Operatives in control. After a pause he responded, 'We do, Capital.'

'And what are *we* going to do about that?'

Everley wanted to give a perfect answer. Hesitating for a short while, the pair had taken at least ten strides before he offered his reply.

'Nothing, Capital. They choose not to Operate. They choose not to join together with us. *We* will leave them to die. We will not drain our resources to feed them, as they do not feed Brito. We will not help them, as they do not help us. They are not part of our One, and they will not be rewarded in The Other Place.'

Selby nodded in a way to recognise that while the response was satisfactory, it was too taught. 'Yes, yes. But what say *you* of the InOps?'

Everley had tried to be emotionless. He had not spoken to a Capital before about anything except Operative activities and he didn't know what Selby wanted him to say.

'Well, Everley? Don't think about it, just say it!'

Everley took one look at Selby and decided that he had to be honest with his answer. After all, Selby was just like Everley; there was only a bronze pin between them.

'I hate them, Capital!' Everley exclaimed as the two continued to march onwards. 'How can they choose not to help our Brito?! I hate their selfish choice! Every time I see an InOp it raises an anger in me. It feeds my passion and makes me want to work harder, be a better Operative and use my life to serve our Brito. We'll show the InOps that they are nothing... And if they die by their own hands or by ours then so be it!'

Everley breathed out a massive sigh as he finished the statement and released his feelings aloud. Remembering that it was a Capital he was talking to, Everley's eyes widened and he slapped a hand against his mouth. He wasn't sure whether his answer was correct and instantly panicked. He turned to Selby to see the reaction.

'Indeed, Briton!' Selby smiled and clapped his hands together in agreement.

Everley was relieved.

'That's the spirit!' Selby continued, adding, 'We need more like you!' as he patted a hand strongly on Everley's shoulder while they continued to walk.

'Thank you, Capital. If you ever need an Operative for additional duties, please consider me.' Everley was overjoyed. Selby's response had provided an affirmation for his own beliefs.

'Well, actually, I have been considering you for some time.'

'*Considering* me, sir?'

'I have seen you walking through the InOp wasteland before. I have watched you at Point A. You're always early and always first in line. And now, *Everley*, I know your name!'

The pair approached the archway at the entrance to the station.

'Keep doing what you're doing, and next time we speak it may be about a Special Project!' With that, he saluted to Everley, said 'Have a utile day!' and turned to leave.

'For Brito!' Everley called out hopefully to Selby, who merely waved with the back of his hand.

Everley took up his standard position on the platform. Rather than the environment around him occupying his attention, now his mind was filled with the prospect of a *'Special Project'*. The fire inside him raged. He knew that everything he believed was right. The way he operated was right. His hatred of the InOps was right. He was being recognised by a Higher Operative, a man just like himself, and if he continued to exemplify what they were looking for then maybe he would be promoted to Capital, too. Maybe one day.

After a time, Everley blinked himself out of his fixed stare at the tracks. While his thoughts had been running away with themselves, the platform behind him had significantly filled with other Operatives waiting for the train. He scanned the platform for Selby and looked into every face, just in case. He wasn't there. Perhaps Selby was working on a Special Project of his own.

That giggling InOp child was back again and loudly interrupting the peaceful queuing. Everley assured himself that if the child came near him this morning, he wouldn't trip it over. He would ring its neck.

'I dare you to come here,' he muttered under his breath, feeling his hands get sweaty and his shoulders tense with the lust to kill. But with the ground beginning to shake and the train whistling to view, he was distracted.

It was fortunate for the child today, but Everley would be back again tomorrow.

If one Operative were to stand at Brito's most south-westerly edge with another at its most south-easterly, and both were to start walking at the same time and pace, they would meet in the middle at Point A.

In history, this place was "Old Salisbury". It had been a small city with five rivers running through it, pretty buildings and parks above ground and a network of military bases below it. The site was chosen as the optimum place to establish Point A due to its geographically central position, its distance from Old London (not too close to build the new infrastructure, but not too far away from the old government), and its emptiness.

Three years before Embarkation, foreign agents from countries that wanted to stop old Britain's parting from the rest of the world infiltrated Old Salisbury and painted nerve-attacking poisons onto door handles, chair backs, coffee cups, handrails and help buttons. Though it wasn't the first time for such an attack, it was the most destructive to a population already dwindling. After the contamination caused forty-five thousand deaths in the city alone, the Armed Forces purified the entire county. The desertion that followed the "Salisbury Cleanse" made it a prime choice to set new foundations.

Reborn as Point A, the old city and beyond became the vast metropolis of Brito. The train station was positioned at the very core, from which a network of Operative lodgings sprawled outwards in every direction. The required number of purpose-built quarters had far exceeded the original dimensions of the city, eating up the suburbs, historical parts and rural areas, too. All Operatives started and ended their working days in Point A, making it the beating heart of Brito.

The central track of the Speed Line ran like a spine through the middle of the country. From Point A in the South, the tracks tore vertically through the whole body of Brito to end at The Other Place in the North. From this spine, five train lines extended like ribs to both sides. Each rib was a direct cut from west to east, like Point B (previously "Old Penzance") to Point C ("Old Margate"), or Point H ("Old Windermere") to I ("Old Whitby"). Though there were occasional stops along each route, The Speed Line ran fast and straight from Point A to any end station, and back.

Everley worked on the waterside windmills, one stop short of Point F ("Old Holyhead"). This meant that he had what he thought was the best of the routes with an hour zipping through the core of Brito followed by a five-minute sea view to the right.

As he stood there (first to board, so first to the front) holding the handrail and swaying with the movement of the train, he had a mostly clear view out of windows. He adored turning his head from one side to the other and back again so that he could see the difference in Brito's evolution.

While the Speed Line's track and train infrastructure had been established before Everley was born, Brito had evolved around it at a much slower rate. The Operative population assigned themselves to clear each sector at a time, and so far only the South West of Brito was fully effective. The middle lands and above were in development and everything to the East was vacant, bare and without purpose.

As the train departed from the station, Everley watched the tall buildings pass regularly, with one grey rectangle after the next flashing past the left-hand window. After not five minutes, these shapes disappeared and were replaced by a wash of greens and yellows that filled the scene in bright and blurry lines. Everley's eyes watched the endless sweeping strokes of colour, unable to fix on any part of them. He wished to pause the train – just for one second – so that he could see the view in true definition. He was sure that the colours were that of vegetables growing in the sun to be used for nutrition tablets and drinks. That's what Mother had told him, anyway.

Everley had never seen a vegetable and could only imagine what one might look, feel or smell like. He had seen flowers before (in pictures), so wondered whether vegetables were simply big flowers that only grew in yellow. Perhaps they felt slimy and smelt of sweaty feet, just like the gritty liquid he drank every day at noon.

The colour became a spray of different greys. The greys seemed to swirl around each other as the train shot up Brito's spine at two hundred miles an hour. Everley couldn't see any detail until the part of the journey when the speed slowed to enable the train to turn towards Point F. At that moment, he always looked to the left to see whether the vegetables were visible but, as usual, the view was obstructed by a wall of enormous posters promoting Oneism. The pictures depicted Operatives with perfectly-sculpted physiques pointing into the train. These images changed rarely.

Turning right, an immense expanse of emptiness could be seen. There were empty old buildings, barely standing. Old vehicles were stacked and balanced on top of other empty things. Scrap machinery, strangely patterned objects and towers of surplus technologies were visible as far as the horizon line. It made up one giant pile of things that had no use in their current state and had not yet been recycled. There was so much waste there that Everley doubted it would reduce in his lifetime.

It was difficult to distinguish a lot of detail with the train still moving, but it was normal to be able to make out the figures of InOps atop mounds, rummaging.

As the train tilted into the corner, a ruckus of shattering and rattling and smashing sounds shook the commuters. A hand grabbed Everley from the side and pulled him to the floor. With both of his hands and both of his knees pressed hard against the cold metal, he peered up and watched every other Operative around him drop down, raise their hands over their heads and hold one another. The crashing and banging continued loudly down the length of the train and then stopped.

Everley was petrified. The Operatives around him were terrified, too. Everley noticed that he was gripping the hand of a man to his side, who was squeezing the tummy of a woman to his side, who was herself clenching a pole by the door. Everyone was confused by the commotion and did not move. The train continued.

Everley could see an Operative walking the length of the train and pulling people up to their feet. Though he couldn't hear what was being said, everyone appeared relieved and resumed their travelling positions.

The man approached Everley's group at the front of the train.

'Everything is well, Britons,' he began, peeling open the fingers of the female to release her from the pole, 'To your feet, to your feet!'

This time, Everley noticed the pin on the Operative's chest; it was silver to signify the superiority of a Command Operative. Everley jumped to his feet and placed his palm to his chest. The train, regaining full speed, jolted him off-balance and caused him to use his saluting hand to grab the handle.

The Command nodded at Everley and said, 'It's only those degenerate InOps throwing waste at the train to frighten us,' before turning to face the Operative group and shouting, 'Britons! Are we be frightened by the InOps?'

'NO!' came the reply from the Operative body, en masse.

'Why do we operate, Britons?' asked the Command.

Fired up, they answered, 'FOR BRITO! FOR BRITO! FOR BRITO!'

Capital Selby was back in the InOperative area. Taking a glance over both shoulders, he jumped down from the road and onto an old walkway beside a river. Making sure there was nobody behind him, he continued to follow the path as it trailed beneath a brick bridge. At the very end, obscured by a large metal post (holding one of many cameras in the zone), there was an old wooden door with an "0" pinned to it. It was hidden from view to all who didn't know it was there.

Selby paused to assure himself that there were no watching eyes, then rotated the round handle to the left while gently kicking the bottom of the wood. The door opened.

Stepping into a dingy area inside, Selby let the door swing back slowly into its original position. With it, the daylight gradually disappeared until the click of the door's latch sank the area into absolute darkness. He stood a minute or so, with only the sound of his breath for company, as he waited for his eyes to adjust and the pathway to become clearer. He placed one hand on the cold wall and used it as a guide as he walked around a tight corner.

Up ahead, Selby could faintly see the outline of a control panel. It sensed him as he approached, causing the screen to light with the image of an "0". He reached forwards and pressed his thumb to it, at the same time looking straight into the camera that he knew was above the panel but could not see.

With a loud clang, a metal inner door opened ahead of him and revealed a brightly-lit stairway. As soon as he reached the first step, the same heavy door clunked closed. Selby threw his hand to his brow to shield his squinting eyes from a channel of spotlights and descended into the old military base that was home to "The Hidden".

'Servant, you are late for this briefing,' asserted the Official at the head of a huge table as Selby hurried into the boardroom.

'Please accept my apologies, madam,' Selby began as he reached for the one empty chair and pulled it out to sit down. 'I found another candidate for our organisation while in the InOp area and had to take some time to befriend him.'

'An InOp?' the Official questioned, surprised.

'No, madam,' Selby continued. 'An Operative fully indoctrinated and at the edge of extremism.'

'Shouldn't they all be so!' jeered one of the ten or so other Servants sitting around the table. 'Yet another lost soul you're going to save?' the Servant taunted as the entire group fell into laughter.

Selby could feel himself squirm at the public mocking. 'This one is different,' he defended.

The Official, standing while all others sat, commanded order by tapping her index finger down on the table. 'Settle down everyone!' she called. 'Servants, back to the agenda please!'

ITEM 06:

BOOSTING PRODUCTIVITY WITH

NEURO-LINGUISTIC PROGRAMMING

III

Gelatine, Adipose Tissue, Rendered Tissue Fats, Offal, Caffeine, Carnosine, Creatine, Cobalamin, Taurine, Iron, Phosphorous, Magnesium, GnRH agonist, Vitamins A, D, E and K, Amniotic and Fetomaternal Organ Compound, Micronutrients and Minerals

- Ingredients (Nutrition Tablets)

It had been a particularly challenging day at the windmills with the weather so bad, but thankfully Everley's body had been protected by the thick clothing provided by Brito. Now, back at his lodgings and standing under the powerful jet of water in the shower (warmer in the evenings, with 90 seconds allowed), he felt rewarded.

After the air dryer stopped, Everley faced the mirror and ran his fingers through his thick, straight hair that held itself upwards in spikes. It grew so quickly and was getting longer than appropriate, which told Everley he was healthy. It also meant going to the Service Room to cut it right away and before being reprimanded. It was a good excuse to go down to the room and speak to the main desk; he was so eager for news of the Special Project after five full days of waiting.

For five days, Everley had walked that same route to Point A in the hope of bumping into Capital Selby again. Each day, he had looked into the faces of the queuing crowd on the platform and yearned for the vision of his future self that he believed the Capital to be. But, for five days, there had been no sign of Selby.

Everley dressed in his indoor clothing, headed down the long corridor and waited for the lift. As soon as he pressed the button marked 'S', the lift shot straight to the basement. The velocity with which it dropped, followed by a sudden still and silent stop, left Everley grasping his throat to stop his stomach from jumping out. It was a real thrill.

In the Service Room, speakers on all sides blared with the announcements of the television broadcast that was projected onto one tall wall.

'North Brito reports our nutrition tablet supplies are limited but replenishing. Your blood helps Brito to test new ingredients. Feel the added purposefulness you will achieve, Britons, because you are welcome to visit your Health Centre and give your blood to Brito. The time is half-past ten after dark. Your entertainment now follows.'

The News Operative saluted and the image on screen faded. With the *PA PA PAH* of exciting sounds, the next programme started. An enigmatic Entertainment Operative was sitting casually on one of three steps next to a caged stage. He was wearing a smart blue suit, holding a microphone and talking directly into the camera, to the audience that watched across Brito.

Everley was mesmerised by the television. The opening music had grabbed him and he couldn't tear his eyes away from the bright colours that opened the show.

With excitement, the host introduced an InOp who was hauled through a door into the caged area. The dishevelled man was abnormally large, with all folds of skin exposed at the sides by a peculiar cape made out of foraged plastic.

'How do they get so big?' called one Op to all others in the Service Room.

'Theft of our resources,' replied one.

'They eat each other!' shouted another.

This resulted in a wave of disgusted groans across the room with various insults shot at the screen. 'Sick creatures!' 'Foul beings!' 'Save our Brito from these purposeless insects!' they shouted, along with several other statements of hate.

Though Everley could no longer hear the television over the heckling, he continued to watch the screen. The Entertainment Operative moved his microphone between himself and the bars beyond which the caged InOp was speaking furiously and spitting all over the place. Two burly Operatives thrust a second InOp into the cage from one side: a scrawny woman who was wearing plastic around her middle and a look of horror on her face. She pushed back at the door she had been forced in from and then pleaded on her knees to be released.

Everley turned away just as the big one took a running bound towards the woman with both hands open and fingers bent into claws, ready to scratch and attack. He didn't need to watch the rest; these things always ended the same way.

Everley moved to an area of the room that had a table, stool, mirror and a number of necessary items for sharpening a Briton's appearance. There were framed posters with guidelines to follow, too. Holding his hair out at the front, he took the scissors and chopped a fair amount from the ends. He did the same around his head until it was neat and Briton-perfect, just like the people in the posters. With a forearm, he wiped the hair from the table into an adjoining bin labelled "Hair and Nails ONLY". He did miss Mother doing his hair in the early years, before he went to live at school and she went to The Other Place.

Behind him, Everley could hear the cracking, crunching and bone-crushing sounds of the entertainment programme over the roar of watching Operatives. The volume had been increased and the crowd of viewers were excited. As he moved through the madness to get to the main desk, Everley avoided looking directly at the screen so as to not be drawn into watching the violent routine.

'Best Evenin' young Everley,' croaked the Night Watch Operative from the desk. His raspy voice alone revealed that he was past his best years.

'Best Evening, Night Watcher. I wondered whether–'

'No Everley! No messages!' As he replied, a pair of glasses fell from his head and onto the bridge of his nose. The thick glass enlarged his hooded eyes in an unusual way. 'Everyday y' ask me! PRORA is in one day, okay?! Y' only get a personal invite if yer productivity is over 99.9%!'

'Apologies, I was hoping for notice of an award this time,' Everley lied. He was getting impatient for a message from Selby. That's if Selby knew where his lodgings were. Of course he did, he was a Capital, Everley reminded himself.

'Y' must have really been *doin' your Brit!* Look, I will let you know if anything comes in, okay?'

'That would be most kind. Best Night,' smiled Everley.

'Best Night... and remember yer nutrition tablet!'

Everley nodded as he turned away from the desk and walked back through the lively lot of television viewers, who were now off their seats and applauding the screen.

'You missed it Everley!' his neighbour said, nudging Everley in the arm as he walked past. 'That bony one tore the cheek off that rabid one while he squeezed her throat! She killed him! How unexpected! What great entertainment for us!'

'Good riddance,' Everley responded unenthusiastically. He would have preferred the demise of both.

Next to the door of the Service Room was a rectangular metal box with a hole at the front and a touch pad on top. Everley placed the index and little fingers of his right hand to the pad at the same time. With a tap, a little grey tablet hopped out of the box and landed on a tiny tray in front of the hole. He picked it up and, instead of swallowing it immediately, saved it in the crease of his hand for later.

'If Brito needs more nutrition tablets,' he thought, *'I will save mine for when I really need it... When I am starving.'*

Knowing that sleep would stave off the hunger this night, he marched straight to the Health Centre to give his blood to Brito, then back up to his quarters and into bed.

Come morning, Everley awoke feeling weary. The building alarm had woken him at six o'clock; his body clock had failed him, which disappointed him immensely. After struggling to drag himself from the comfort of the hard mattress and single sheet, he was so far down the queue for the toilet that he nearly didn't make it in time.

Before leaving the building, Everley collected his daily drink from the dispenser in the Service Room and placed the squidgy, liquid-filled pouch in a deep pocket in his coat to save it for his midday rest minutes. He had reached the corner of the InOp area before realising that he had forgotten to pick up the nutrition tablet from last night.

'Blame it!' he said aloud, as he halted immediately.

Feeling unnaturally exhausted and already hungry, Everley didn't doubt his body would need the nutrition at some point during the eight-to-eight shift. He shook his head to and fro and questioned whether he could get through the whole shift without it, and what risk it would be to Brito if he was unable to operate efficiently. Not knowing the consequences of being without his nutrition tablet, he sprinted back to his quarters to collect it. It would mean taking the quickest route back to Point A, but, feeling inexplicably miserable, he was less optimistic about seeing Selby today anyway.

Everley almost fell into his bedroom, bungling over his own feet in haste. He was certain that he had kept the tablet safely on the shelf next to the soap. It wasn't there. He fumbled around on the floor beneath the shelf in case it had fallen, but there was nothing still. Thinking it may have been in his hand when he made the bed, he ran over to it and threw the sheets back. His hands patted every part of the mattress as his panic grew. Finding nothing, he dropped to his knees and scoured the area with his face close to the bed and eyes peeled wide.

He jumped back to his feet and began rubbing himself down, hoping he had remembered to pick it up after all. He removed the drink sachet and turned his pocket inside out. There was still no sign of the tablet. All that was in there appeared to be a small clump of hair. He rubbed it between his fingers for a second then forced it back into his pocket, knowing it instantly to not be his own but not having the time to consider its origin.

Everley knew that if he didn't leave very soon, he would miss the train (as it was, he would have to run). If he missed the train, he would be punished and likely refused his PRORA tomorrow. He let out a loud huff at the thought of sacrificing his Operative reward over something so foolish and threw both arms down to his sides. He would have to leave without it and do his best to perform productively.

As he moved to the door, he glanced back at the little shelf. In both anger and relief, he snatched the soap. There, on a wet and frothed edge of the bar, the tablet was stuck. 'Thank Brito!' he proclaimed gratefully, peeled it off gently and left the room right away.

Halfway through the less-than gentle jog to Point A, Everley realised he had left his midday drink on the bed. Never before had he been so forgetful. There was no time to go back for that now, but it meant that he would have to wait as long as possible before taking the nutrition tablet, as there would be nothing else to keep him going all day.

With six minutes to go before the train arrived, Everley felt infuriated at what he believed was a very late arrival. He was sweaty, breathless and, most disappointingly, not at the front. He felt a wave of strangeness come over him while he waited there. His vision blurred and focussed, then blurred again. He rubbed his eyes but that didn't help. His ears felt like they were vibrating; he could hear a high hissing that seemed to get louder and louder until it rang like an alarm in his head. He bashed at his ears with an open hand and prodded his little finger in the hole. It was a dizziness he hadn't experienced before. He closed his eyes and held his head, waiting and wishing for his legs to stop swaying, his head to stop throbbing and balance to resume.

There was a tugging at his trousers that pulled him back into focus. It was *that* InOp child. Instantly enraged that it had dared to touch him, Everley flung a flattened backhand down to swat the boy like a fly. With a clap, the child was knocked to the hard platform floor. It had an arm outstretched and was shouting something to Everley that he couldn't hear over his own ear-ringing and rage. In his peripheral vision, his fellow Operatives were animatedly encouraging Everley as he seized the little being into a bundle and prepared to throw it in front of the next train.

The child's mother appeared out of nowhere. She scratched at Everley's hands and was screaming at him to let go of the boy. With one movement, she had gotten something from the wriggling child and held it directly in front of Everley's eyes. It was the nutrition tablet.

'You dropped it! He was giving this back to you! LET HIM GO!' she shrieked.

Everley lurched back and released the child instantly. The child bolted, leaving only the mother standing there, still holding the tablet.

'Are you so inhuman?!' she said as she turned to the Operative body, which was slowly closing around her. She launched the tablet an Everley's feet and yelled to the gathering, 'I used to be an Operative, just like YOU!'

As the crowd looked confusedly at each other, Everley delved down to get the tablet from the ground. Gratefully grasping it, he threw it into his mouth quickly and swallowed. He hoped it would fix his light-headedness and chastised his unwise behaviour. He felt a fool for thinking he should decide when to eat, rather than following Brito's guidelines; he should have done as directed. It was a lesson learned.

As Everley lifted himself back to his feet, the rumble of the train started to vibrate the platform. The child's mother, who had been so defiant until now, was distressed. She was trapped between the Operative mass and the oncoming train with both bare heels teetering over the edge of the platform. The train would soon be zooming into the station and one slip would leave her on the tracks, but the crowd were closing in. She was surrounded by a ring of expectant eyes and salivating smiles; the inevitable predicament was much to the satisfaction of the Operative mob.

As the grumble of the train grew louder, a sudden scream distracted the group and caused all to turn towards the post in the centre of the platform. By an unknown other, the twist of cable that held up the station clock had been unravelled. The glass face had fallen and smashed into hundreds of sharp pieces all over the floor.

But Everley hadn't turned away; he was watching the InOp. She looked back at Everley, hesitated for only a second before using the disarray to dart along the platform edge and hide behind the large poster that was hanging on one side.

Everley felt frozen to the spot. '*How could she have been an Operative?*' he questioned as the train screeched to a halt.

With all the disruption, Everley found himself at the front of the queue again, which was delightful. The nutrition tablet had started to kick in and he was looking forward to a final day of productivity and purposefulness before his two-day reward at the PRORA.

Command Operative Raines had taken the eight o'clock Speed Line to the waterside windmills, just one stop short of Point F. It was the closest stop to his newly refurbished PRORA, which was due to reopen tomorrow.

There was a disturbance from a group of InOps who had settled in an area close to the line and had taken to throwing things at the train as it passed. Raines enjoyed these dramatics. By riling up the Operatives in response to the InOps' futile gesture, he could directly influence the divide between worker and waster. For once, the InOps were unknowingly serving a useful purpose.

'FOR BRITO! FOR BRITO! FOR BRITO!'

At the station for the windmills, Raines alighted with the rest of the Operatives. He stood to one side while each collected a bicycle with a map attached to the handlebars and set off for a hard day's work. Many noticed his presence – and that of his silver pin – and saluted before departing.

Raines had gotten used to the salute over the years, but was in a rather reflective mood this morning and felt a warm gratefulness at the respect he now commanded. He responded to each with a smug smile.

After the platform emptied out entirely, Raines took a bicycle from within a separate storage area that had a wooden swing-door with one broken half of a plastic "Reserved" restaurant table sign glued to it. Mounting the bicycle, he took a long look at that sign and a big sniff in. If only he could really smell the garlicky and rich tomato sauce that was thickly drooled over dense meaty balls and spaghetti pasta from the menu in his local Italian restaurant. That was pre-Brito, of course. He took a couple more sniffs until he could almost recall the smell. With the top of his thumb he rubbed the saliva from his bottom lip; his taste buds wished the memory to be true.

'Lucky young Britons,' he thought, knowing it far better to never experience the wonderfulness of every imaginable type of food, than to have tasted its infinite flavours and be without them forever more.

He *had* to shake these musings, Raines told himself. These memories served no purpose except to torment him, yet they seemed to occur ever more frequently. He wondered whether it was his growing age that was causing them, or the monotony of the predictable rhythm of Brito.

Before, when Raines was at the forefront of change and the architect of much transformation, there was such exhilaration in the reshaping of the new land. Now, everything functioned efficiently and without the need (or means) for further significant change. The goal had been achieved and Raines was bored.

At least the redesign and reopening of *his* PRORA had given him the opportunity to make improvements, try new techniques and remodel the area to ensure it was perfectly purposeful, he reminded himself. So, without pausing any longer, he pushed the bicycle to the edge of the platform, let its wide wheels roll down onto the soil, awkwardly clambered onto the seat and began to peddle. He knew the route well indeed.

Tomorrow, the train from Point A was going to stop at the PRORA, but to do so today would have caused unnecessary excitement and curiosity in the Operatives. Instead, Raines would need to double-back on the train track and cycle a while to reach it.

After a time on soil alone, he reached the tarmac of the old coastal road. At once, the view out to sea from the "Old Wirral Peninsula" took his breath away. With quite a distance still to travel, he continued powering forwards against the wind. The air flung what was left of his mostly-white hair backwards and sent his eyelids blinking involuntarily. He wasn't enjoying it; *'Not like when I was a lad.'* And with that thought, he found himself halfway between reality and his own memory.

Too many years ago to count, Raines would bunk off school, acquire a bike, dodge the fare for the ferry over the water by slipping through the queues and past the ticket inspectors, and then go for a ride along the Wirral coastline. He scrunched his nose up and smiled secretively at the thought of *Bunky*, his inner rebel.

There had been some wind turbines on the skyline back then, but a small fraction compared to the number today. Raines remembered the boats that used to be in the water and could picture them there now. With vivid recollection, he could see the runners, the dog-walkers and ramblers that used to trudge the sand or wander the walkway while his younger self would race past. Over the whistle of wind through his ears, his mind replayed those long-gone sounds of life. Embodying the carefree teenager within, he lifted his hands and let his arms blow out to the side in the air.

Regaining his clasp on reality – and the handlebars – Raines realised he had reached such a speed that he was barely in control of his spinning legs. He gently squeezed the brakes and brought the bicycle to a much more comfortable pace, and then a stop. He had scared himself a little there and decided to walk the remaining mile. Dismounting, he completely misjudged the position of the central bar, lost balance and grazed both palms across the concrete edge of the walkway in an attempt to steady himself whilst falling forwards.

Calling out a barrage of definitely not Briton-like swear words (most of which would be incomprehensible to the Brito-born population), he kicked the bicycle over, kicked it again in frustration and then insulted the inanimate object with one last unrepeatable but perfectly vulgar phrase.

With the sides of his fists, Raines lifted himself onto the top of the wall that bordered the old road. Sitting there, he stared back at the treacherous bicycle, down at the scratched skin on his hands, forwards to the view across the "Old Mersey", and then down at his palms again. As he rubbed some black debris carefully from the minor wound, he traced the beginnings of a tattoo that started near his wrist, ran around to the back of his hand and down all fingers (except the thumb). It used to be black but had melted over the years into a bluey green.

Only in the olden times could a person decorate the skin with pictures. Creative expression could have never survived in the purposeful land of Brito. The only Britons with tattoos were those of an age to have lived in the old world; a world of waste and inefficiency where it was popularised to permanently mark the body with meaningful or meaningless words and images that 'celebrated your individuality'. In hindsight, and with most of the population branded in some way, the act of tattooing oneself had not been individual at all.

The Brito-born generation knew only of a utilitarian way of life. To the young Operatives, 'skin pictures' were mystical remnants of a historical time that they could hardly imagine. Tattoos on elders and Highers were regarded as badges of honour; these individuals had witnessed and participated in the death of Britain, chosen the Hard Line and come together to build Brito. While this was true for Raines, he found it ironic that the tattoos he acquired while serving time for his sins in prison now afforded him respect. He could remember the trade exactly: 4 cigarettes, 12 minutes' phone time and one pair of socks. The symbol, taking a circular space across his chest on the left, had been surprisingly well-administered using a staple as an improvised needle and ink from melted plastic.

Looking out across the water, he pressed his grazed palm to his heart. Beneath his jacket and there on his skin was a swastika. He could feel its power radiating even after all these years. A lifetime ago, when he was Bunky, Raines would rip World War II images from history books and plaster them over the walls in his basement flat. The single room had a bed to one side, a kitchenette on the other and the perpetual mess of drug-making and dealing paraphernalia on a table in the centre. Without a window, the space was as dingy as one could imagine. Raines had used red paint and a multitude of photographs showing the Nazis in lines to decorate it, along with one large swastika made from six wooden planks he had painted black and nailed to the wall. He was fascinated by it all.

'Don't you ever get sick of this life?' Raines remembered asking a friend and fellow dealer who visited every now and then to muck around with the recipes.

'What do you mean? We've got it good, mate. We aren't as low as the scum we serve this shit to!' said Dippy, whilst crushing paracetamol tablets with a spoon and scraping the debris into a mixing bowl.

47

Dippy's nickname was thanks to his obsession with tie-dye t-shirts; his hands were permanently multi-coloured from the dyes he daily dipped clothes in. You could tell a customer was Dippy's not only because they would be strung out, but also because they would be wearing a top of swirling colour. So prolific a dip-dyer and dealer was he that a walk around the local area would mimic a day at a festival in the Sixties.

'It's the disorder of it all. Sometimes I get so angry about the country we live in, the people that are in it and the way it is run. Do you know what I mean?'

'Sort of,' replied Dippy as he sprinkled talcum powder into the bowl and stirred. 'What, like you're angry at the government, mate?'

'No, it's more than that,' started Raines, wondering whether to even try to explain his disillusionment to Dippy. 'The country is going to fuck all. We used to be strong, right? We used to be *Great* Britain. Now we're just a shitty little island with no power on Earth. We don't achieve anything anymore. Instead we have to answer to the big'uns: America, Russia, China, L'Europe-Uni. *They* are creating the technology. *They* have their military. *They* have a sorted economy. *They* are in charge of things.'

'What's it matter?' Dippy asked. 'We're alright, mate. We've got our own economy, eh?!' he teased, nodding at a ball of white dough he was now kneading on the table. 'You and me, we're okay. We aren't the lowest, you know. The worst are the scum on the very bottom.'

Raines didn't reply, knowing it absurd to attempt to discuss the topic sensibly with Dippy. He did have a point, though; the lowest lives in society were dragging down the rest.

'And by the way, you know all this history stuff you're into?' Dippy continued as he stood next to one of the German propaganda posters that Raines had pasted to the wall. 'That's all racist right there. I'd be hulled out by your *Nazzi* friends if that were still going on!' He blew out his cheeks and looked down at them, to accentuate the soft colour of his mixed-race skin.

'That's not what it's about Dippy, honest!' Raines shook his head. 'Those pictures are about *order* and *perfection*.' He really enunciated the words, continuing, 'It's about not tolerating anything less than the best. *That's* why I'm into it.'

Raines was impressed by how much of that early conversation he still held in memory. At that time, Raines was addicted to the order of Nazism alone. It was the idea of a productive people that didn't tolerate the idle end of society that had seduced him. Ever since, he had held the policies and slogans in his mind with all the obsessive passion of a teenager able to recall the entire back catalogue of a favourite band, or quote every line of a film scene. They had stuck with him since.

Even pre-Brito and before the term 'InOp' had been created, most believed the scum of society, the algae, grime and dregs, served no purpose. In past years, charities and support groups had tried the help. In later years, and with old Britain dying, this could not be maintained. So, Raines had always felt fully justified in abusing, exploiting and cleaning away the dirt. And he did, even in those early years. Bunky and Dippy profited from the pitiful and insignificant addicts in the area by making money from highly priced, low quality drugs. Raines remembered manipulating their desperation by offering 'deals' and handouts, knowing they would be back for more when the withdrawal symptoms started. And when they couldn't pay, they would steal and sell everything they had. Either way, Raines would get his money.

One time, a regular had appeared at his door rattling like a lunatic with a tambourine. He thought back to her pleading and remembered how obliged he felt because it was clear she would have been a pretty girl, but for the effects of the drugs. His supplies had been reduced thanks to a festival in town and all that was left was some severely degraded powder that he and Dippy had been weakening with any cutting agent they could improvise with.

He had offered the concoction to her and, desperate for the hit, she ferociously administered it right there in his room. After not long at all – maybe less than a minute – she started struggling with herself, jerking about and thrashing out. Her eyes had all but disappeared into her head as she lay convulsing on the carpet. Raines recalled watching for a bit and wondering, *'Would it matter if she died? What would he do with the body?'*

He had stood solidly, playing out potential scenarios in his head while her violent convulsions continued and caused her head to bash the table leg over and over. The repetition of these contractions stopped and, with fingers awkwardly bent, back arched and neck curved unnaturally, it was only her chest that moved with the intake of breath. The only course of action for Raines was to disassociate himself with her inevitable death by getting her out of the building, slumping her on a bench somewhere and making it look like just another junkie who had over-done it. It wouldn't be a loss.

Using the strength he gained through a combination of weights and steroids, Raines easily lifted her into his arms (she weighed very little anyway). Up two flights of stairs and out of the front door in the middle of the day, he had dashed whilst cradling her like a baby as her body lay limp. Anyone around wouldn't have been surprised by such a scene in that area, but he wasn't going to stick around just in case. It was a choice between left to the hospital or right to the park. He went left; his conscience had gotten the better of him.

Despite the last-second attempt to save her life, she died. The police had nabbed him at the hospital and the courts later handed him a five-year sentence for involuntary manslaughter. If that were now – in Brito – Raines would have been celebrated for taking out the rubbish, rather than punished. But prison was not really a punishment to Raines; he appreciated the strict regularity with which meals, showers and sleep were planned. Prison was warm. Prisoners were fed, clothed and safe. After five years, Raines was sold on the lifestyle and reoffended upon release so that he could *get back in.*

Raines would forever thank the experience of prison, for it had given him ideas that got him noticed in Brito's early years and led to his position of power. After Bunky Baines became Raines and he was given his first Operative job, he was encouraged to offer up any proposal or even semi-sensible suggestion for the running of Brito. He had thought for some time on the topic of how to keep

Operatives motivated towards the common good of Brito, then approached his Capital with *a solution to keep Operatives imprisoned by Brito's way of life, whilst feeling free.* The solution was the PRORA.

Raines had been programmed in Great Britain's prison service. He knew how to use that experience to ensure each Operative's acceptance of Brito's principles was reinforced and maintained. It was Raines alone who designed the Hitler's Holiday Camp-inspired sites that became the ultimate solution for indoctrinating the nation.

After the first of four PRORAs had been successfully implemented over twenty-five years ago, Raines had been honoured with the 'Best Order of Brito' and catapulted from Operative to Command, bypassing Capital altogether and with a secure standing in the new society. Ever since, his role was to monitor the success of his invention in its function to *remind* Operatives of their purpose.

'That's how you keep someone in a prison willingly!' said Raines aloud, as he stopped daydreaming of times past, grabbed the handles of the bicycle and set off for the refurbished site he was due to inspect.

As he approached the gated entrance, Raines looked upon his creation with a sinister grin.

IV

NIL SATIS NISI OPTIMUM

- Inscribed across the golden gates

Operative Everley had woken far more than five minutes before the alarm this morning. He was due to go to the PRORA today and was too excited to sleep properly. He had washed and dressed so early that there hadn't been a soul in the corridor, and he was now sitting stiff upright on the side of the bed while watching the clock tick time away on the face of the building opposite. Everley stared angrily at its hands, believing that they were tormenting him by moving so slowly. Frustrated, he rapped his fingers on his knees and sniffed out at the clock with teeth pressed into his bottom lip.

'What did she mean when she said that she used to be an Operative?' Everley questioned as he sat waiting on the bed. *'Maybe she chose to not Operate. Maybe she hurt another Operative. Maybe she broke the oath."*

It was so abhorrent to Everley for anyone to reject Brito that he could barely consider that an option. He was intrigued though, and the idea of her being an Operative *just like him*, even in her past, made him less angry towards her. Perhaps he should ask her, if he could bring himself to talk to an InOp. But he knew that if he didn't ask her for answers then these questions would whisper endlessly through his thoughts.

There was so much time to spare that Everley left the building as soon as the alarm sounded. With the early morning sun lighting his path, he took the longest walking route to Point A.

'Capital Selby! Sir! Capital! Capital Selby, sir!' Everley shouted across the wasteland, immediately recognising a figure emerging from a darkened passageway. Waving a hand in the air, he ran quickly in the direction of the man.

The figure moved promptly to one side, out of the passageway and into the light. He seemed to call back to someone hiding in the darkness and then walked away quickly whilst patting his hands together as though to remove dirt or dust. He did the same to his knees and then used the back of his hand to wipe his brow.

As Everley drew closer, he could see that it was indeed Selby and excitedly wondered whether the day could get any better.

'Why, if it isn't young Everley!' said Selby calmly, although his face was flustered.

Everley couldn't respond straight away. He had run across the InOp quarter so fast that it had taken his breath away. He found himself in front of Selby, saluting but coughing, spluttering and bent in the middle with stitch.

'Blimey Briton! You take a breath there, son!' laughed Selby.

Everley found it strange to be called 'young' and 'son' by an Operative of the same age, but knew that these were simply signals of Selby's authority. He wanted to be able to call his peers 'son' one day too.

After a silent minute, Selby patted his hand strongly on Everley's shoulder. The sensation sent a spark through Everley's body and he stood bolt upright.

'Best Morning to you Capital Selby!' said Everley, still saluting.

'Ah! You have your breath back, dear boy!' Selby responded, his hand still on Everley's shoulder as he led him away from the area and back to the familiar path. 'Shall we walk to Point A together again?'

'That would be positively wonderful, Capital!' responded Everley, unable to conceal his eagerness. 'I have been enquiring at my building's Watch Desk for any messages from you, but then I remembered I had not given you my lodging details. Apologies, Capital.'

'I know your lodging details, Everley,' Selby smiled.

'I knew it!' thought Everley without responding.

'I do want to talk to you about a Special Project, but I have to know you can be trusted,' Selby continued.

Everley stopped walking and turned to face Selby. He placed his hand to his chest again, stared with serious eyes and said, 'I can be trusted. I live for Brito.'

Selby patted Everley on the shoulder again and the two continued to walk.

'I am going to the PRORA today,' Everley continued, 'but when I return tomorrow after dark I will do anything you require.'

'PRORA today?!' Selby laughed. 'Oh... I'd forgotten about that,' he added quietly, to himself.

Everley wasn't sure why Selby was laughing.

'In that case then, I will tell you more when you return,' he said.

'As you wish, Capital,' Everley said in disappointment. He would have to be patient for two days and wait again for this exciting information. He hoped the wait wouldn't ruin his time at the PRORA. 'When will I see you again?'

'I'll find you,' said Selby, removing his hand from Everley's shoulder as they reached the station entrance together. He turned away, then, seeming to have an idea, called back to Everley, 'I have a thought.'

'Yes?' said Everley desperately, thirsty for scraps of anything more.

'When your return train arrives back tomorrow, I will be waiting next to this picture, here.' He pointed to a protruding ledge, above which was pinned a sizeable picture of The Other Place in a hard plastic frame. 'Come to me then and I will tell you all about the Special Project.'

'I will surely be there, Capital, you can count on me! For Brito!'

'Enjoy the PRORA Everley.' Selby nodded and marched back towards the InOp quarter.

Everley was beside himself with the anticipation of it all. There were over eighty long minutes until the Speed Line, but at least his brain was busied with thoughts of three exciting things: Two days at the PRORA, his own private mission to discover the InOp woman's Operative past... *and* the Special Project.

As the train stuttered to a halt, Everley was the first of four hundred to step onto the renovated platform of the station, one stop short of Point F. A number of differently-dressed Guide Operatives ushered everybody across a grand new bridge that led from the platform to a wide and perfectly-flattened walkway. The walkway stretched down the hill to an enormous golden gate that stood proudly at the bottom.

The four hundred waited in lines of ten at the closed gate, above which large capital letters on the archway read:

PURPOSEFULLNESS REWARDED:

OPERATIVE REPARATION AREA

One Guide stood at the head of the first waiting ten and shouted, 'You are welcome at this new PRORA. You are welcome to enjoy your reward.' This was repeated, line by line, and all Operatives saluted to receive their greeting.

As the final line of Operatives were addressed – and the welcoming statement had been called forty times – the golden gates opened. The Operatives maintained their linear arrangement as they began to march beneath the arch and into a square piazza, behind which was only sea, sand and windmills.

Everley found himself still at the front. He looked upon the newness of the polished black piazza floor with a wonderment that made him smile widely. He noticed that he was not the only Operative to be all teeth and open-mouthed in elated awe. The sound and smell of the seaside swept over a low wall and into the piazza, and Everley shuddered a little as the sea breeze tickled the already-raised hairs on the back of his neck. He felt electric and found it difficult to stop himself from jumping up and down in joy.

The Guide Operatives moved between the lines and served long drinks in metal glasses to each attendee. When Everley received his, he held it proudly at the base with his left hand, while saluting with his right. He looked down into the glass, noting how the blue colour of the liquid that fizzed at the edges almost mimicked the sea itself. He knew not to drink it yet; it was for the oath.

The sunshine bounced light over the shined surface of the piazza, the metal glasses and the silver badge of the Command Operative that had assumed a position on an elevated stage in front of Everley. Everything about that moment was blindingly bright, but Everley did not want to shield his eyes from such astonishing sights.

'Dear Britons!' the Command began into a microphone that was pinned to his collar. The sound of his voice boomed out of big speakers on all four sides of the piazza, vibrating, ricocheting and surprising even the Command himself.

Everley squinted to sharpen his focus of the older man with white hair and skin pictures on his hands. It was an honour to hear a Command's address and Everley wanted to remember every word.

Turning to a Tech Operative to one side, the Command paused a moment before starting again. 'Dear Britons!' he said, the speaker tone less forceful than before. There was another pause. 'Dear Britons!' he repeated a third time, as though he was waiting for the crowd to silence (although no other was making a sound).

He shakily removed a piece of paper from a top pocket, unfolded it, coughed, patted his chest, coughed again, then raised his head to look into the four hundred expectant faces. From where he stood, Everley could see the Command's cheeks redden and flush. There was another not insignificant pause, but all were patient.

'Britons, in your number and strength, I admire you all. You have taken the words from my lips. Your dedication and purposefulness is for all and for Brito to applaud.'

Everley and the crowd erupted spontaneously, with a responding chorus of 'For Brito! For Brito! For Brito!'

The Command smiled and seemed to ease in his stance. He raised the piece of paper nearer to his eyes and began to read.

'Dear Britons, you are welcomed here today for a special reopening of this *Purposefulness Rewarded: Operative Reparation Area*. In your honour, Brito has resourcefully improved these PRORA buildings and this facility to ensure you will benefit from your time here. It is for your efficient service to each other and to the future of Brito that you are praised and provided with this reward. Today and tomorrow you will all be commended for giving yourselves to Brito. For your pleasure, you have access to the best Brito can provide.

'Through your productivity scores, you have each chosen a programme to serve you best. These activities include, "Collective Contemplation", "Best Body Building" and sessions on "Oneism Wisdom", as well as many, many more. You will also be the first Operatives to experience new nutrition solutions. Be exhilarated, Britons, because your rewards are exceptional! Open your eyes and minds. Receive all that is given because your time here will pass quickly. This is your gift.'

The Operatives responded with a lot of loud praising 'For Brito!' and cheering. Everley could hardly wait to see what he had chosen.

The Command raised his saluting hand to signal the Operatives to quieten, and then replaced it on his chest. 'Now it is time for us all to pledge our Operative vow.'

We swear to each other this everlasting oath:

We do solemnly and truly declare that we faithfully give unconditional and absolute allegiance to Brito, the safe land that gives us life.

We, by willing choice, duty and responsibility, give ourselves efficiently, productively, for the good of all Britons and in defence of our Brito against any individual InOperative.

To this purpose we pledge our lives and give ourselves entirely for our One, for Brito, for Brito, for Brito.

In unison, all present had spoken the vow. On the final word, glasses were lifted, lowered and drunk. With the last sip surged the sound of whoops and claps and singing "We Are Together".

'Enjoy your PRORA!' called the Command as he left the stage and was replaced by a Guide Operative.

'You are welcome to enjoy your social time now. When you feel the need to rest, please go to the information board to receive your room allocation and programme choice.' The Guide then hurried from the stage.

Everley had wanted to introduce himself to the mighty Command, but he was already surrounded by a group of fanatical young Operatives quizzing him about his skin pictures and life pre-Brito. Everley didn't want to join in with the social time, although he noticed that everyone did look joyful whilst talking to each other. Instead, he headed straight for the information boards and shuffled through the loud and busy crowd, eager to receive his room and itinerary.

Making it to a large screen, Everley pressed the open palm of his right hand to a part of the display marked with the image of a handprint and the words "Start here" flashing green above it. As he did so, an image of an egg timer rotated once or twice, before a message appeared: *'Congratulations Operative *EVERLEY*! You have been awarded the Superior Lodging *BLOCK 3 ROOM 56*! With Your exceptional productivity score, You have chosen the "Perfect Briton Programme". Details of Your personal programme is awaiting You in Your room.'*

Everley span around quickly on one heel, ready to run to the block, but another Operative was directly behind him and blocking his way.

'Good news, Briton?' smiled a friendly face.

'Block 3! Superior Lodging!' Everley squealed in excitement. He was so overjoyed at his own performance awarding him a top room and "Perfect" programme that he couldn't contain it.

'Well done! For all Brito, congratulations! Best day!' the female Operative said, seizing him by the hand and clapping against it. 'Shall I see what I have?'

'Oh yes!' replied Everley sincerely. He was less impatient now that he knew his own room and programme. Besides, the female's delight at his achievement had exaggerated his own excited feelings and he felt warmth from the praise. He waited next to the machine to see whether she had done well (but doubted she would have been as high-scoring as he).

'Block 3! Superior Lodging! Superior! Superior!' the female squeaked repeatedly.

'For Brito! Fine work you must have done!' Everley found himself as happy for her as he was with himself. 'Think of the good we are doing for our One!'

'We are! Shall we go now? I can't wait!' she said, extending a hand to salute and introduce herself. 'Operative Wilton.'

'Operative Everley. Pleased to meet you Operative Wilton!' he responded formally but excitedly.

The two wasted no time in racing towards Block 3 by forging a route through any available gaps between those who were socialising on the piazza. It was packed with people and buzzing with conversation. Wilton had taken his hand so as to not lose him as she ran ahead, and, at one point, Everley felt his hand tingle and a shudder of sexual anticipation race up and down his body.

Halfway to Block 3 but still in the middle of the crowd, music began to play through the large speakers on all sides. Wilton stopped running suddenly, causing Everley to fall into the back of her. The two caught each other's arms to steady themselves from toppling over.

'Let's dance!' grinned Wilton, chuckling.

Everley didn't know how to dance, but found himself carried away by the tantalising touch of Wilton, the sound of song and the atmosphere of it all. There, beside the natural seaside, he felt he was floating in a sea of other swaying Operatives. Nothing could remove the smile from his face. In front of his eyes, the sky melted into the ocean in a backdrop of beautiful blues, and even the music seemed to spit rainbow colours from the speakers. Everley felt he had been eaten up by a strange but wonderful euphoria that pricked at his senses like a thousand tiny needles that brought no pain.

"We Are Together" was played, of course, and then a mix of other tunes. Everley wasn't sure if he recognised these or not, but they mesmerised him nonetheless and he became aware that he was moving about in a way that could be described as dancing.

After an amount of time he couldn't quantify, Everley noticed he was standing right next to one of the large speakers. The massive electronic box vibrated with every beat. He looked into its front and stared intently at one of a million black holes that the sound was flowing from. He couldn't remove his gaze. He was sure he could hear the grumble and judder of the Speed Line coming from within, somewhere behind the music. He could feel that familiar rumble through his toes, just as the train does at Point A, and he could hear the growing screech of brakes getting louder and louder until it overpowered the music.

As the sound grew to an almost unbearable level, Everley felt his heart ache, his whole body arch involuntarily and his arms stretch high into the air. His fingers widened apart as though his palms were stopping sky from falling down, and he watched flickering sparks of lightening cross the gaps between his digits. Bright electric bolts popped in front of his eyes as the ground bounced beneath him.

A thought burst into his mind. For a moment, he believed the energy from the floor was entering him at his feet, carried by his veins as it moved up his legs, tingled through his tummy and was absorbed by the sponge of his lungs. With his next breath out came the uncontrollable culmination of all the energy that had raced through his body.

'FOOOR BRITOOO!' Everley let out in one long, drawn-out shout. He was aware that others were exclaiming things too, but all was muffled around him.

And with that, the sound of the Speed Line stopped and the music was just music again. The tempo of it had changed and Everley felt a wave of a new type of energy grow in the central point between groin and upper thigh.

'Wilton? Wilton?' Everley called out as he searched the piazza for that female face. He dabbed his cheeks with the sleeve of his uniform, feeling himself get hot and desperate for her in a way he didn't understand.

Through a gap in the gathering, Everley saw her. She was dancing with one Operative, then weaved to one side to dance with another, and then another. She moved in smooth sensual swings, more alluring than before, and Everley was transfixed. To him, she was dancing in slow motion, allowing him time to notice every part of her: the shape of her female body, the way it leaned and waved as she danced, the delicacy of her movements, the suppleness of her skin and the softness with which her eyes blinked. Her short hair was a nearly-white blonde and the apples of her cheeks were pink, as though they had been pinched. Everley watched her with a desire he had never known before and eased himself through the crowd to be with her.

In a haze, Everley had fallen forwards. As he regained his balance, he found himself standing in front of her. The world around them had faded into nowhere and, without a thought, Everley raised his right hand to her neck and held it at the back so that only the pads of three fingers touched her skin. He meant to look into her eyes, but instead was solidly focussed on the stretched skin of her plump lips. It made him think of nothing else than her nakedness. He wanted her. It was a hunger. He had to have her.

Everley ran his thumb down her cheek bone, following it to her chin. He paused briefly to take in a deep breath before using the position of his thumb to lift her head so that her face turned upwards. He pressed his mouth against her soft smile more forcibly than he had intended, then pushed his body against hers. Opening his mouth wider to thrust her lips apart with his tongue, he sensed her quiver in his arms.

Everley felt wobbly. Though continuing to kiss her, his legs could hardly hold himself up. With eyes inescapably closed, all was as black as though he had dropped into the very depths of his own body. He couldn't be sure whether he was still present on the piazza, or whether the intoxication of her kiss had caused him to die and float into the vastness of the night sky, only to bob along without gravity for an eternity.

He awakened from the euphoric daydream with Wilton pulling away from the sloppiness of his kiss. She put her hands on his, which had remained around her waist, and pulled them away.

With a strange but sultry half-smile, she mumbled something incoherently and tugged at his arm while pointing over to the Blocks.

'Your room!' she finally blurted out.

Before Everley realised he had agreed, the two were entering the lodgings.

Everley awkwardly pressed his palm to a control pad beside the door of Room 56.

'Welcome all guests to use the control panel,' came a voice from at or near the door.

Wilton slid her palm onto the pad and the door opened.

The curtains had been drawn inside the small room and the lighting had been dimmed to a pink tint. More music was playing from a speaker above the bed and the repetitive beat made Everley feel oddly aroused. There was an opened bottle of drink resting in a cooling bucket and two empty glasses waiting on the bedside table to be filled.

'One minute,' muttered Wilton as she stumbled into the private shower room.

Everley picked up the bottle of drink but, being unable to steady his hand, accidentally poured it over the lip of one glass and all over the table. He tried again, but the task seemed too difficult, so he raised the bottle to his mouth and took a huge gulp. Then a few gulps more. Then, not knowing why, he threw the bottle into the bin, where it missed and smashed against the side with a crash. His excitement was getting the better of him, he thought, while telling himself to calm down.

He removed his shoes and placed them at the bottom shelf of an open clothes rail. He pulled off both socks and dropped them into the wash bin, and began to unbutton his top. With shaking fingers, he struggled to get a proper grip, so tapped at his chest to calm his heart. It was beating so hard that it made his stomach muscles contract with every pulse. Once off, he folded his clothes neatly and placed them on top of his shoes with care. Then Everley stood next to the bed, waiting.

A couple of minutes later, the door to the private shower room slid backwards slowly. Wilton peered around it at Everley.

'Best Evening,' she said enticingly, leaning against the door frame entirely naked and holding an untidy ball of her own clothes and shoes in both hands.

'Best... Evening,' Everley returned slowly, unable to get the words out. All he could think of was touching her. He licked his lips over and over, he just couldn't control his tongue. As he started to feel dizzy and the world dipped from focus, he wondered whether he should have drunk straight from the bottle.

Wilton dropped her clothes onto the floor and flung herself onto the bed. Beaconing urgently for Everley to join her, he had no urge other than to comply.

V

The first order of Brito is to maintain control and conformity

through autocratic management.

- The Cardinals

A high-pitched noise shot through the speaker over the bed with no warning, waking Everley with a startle. It was a long, piercing and uncomfortable tone that had him holding his palms to his ears and pressing his head hard into the untidily scrunched sheets beneath him. Even once it had stopped, his nose was crinkled and brow wrinkled from the reverberation through his head.

'All Operatives are welcomed to return to their assigned quarters. All Operatives to assigned quarters. Assigned quarters. Assigned quarters. Assigned quarters,' announced a voice from the ceiling speaker.

Everley delicately opened one eye the tiniest bit and, scanning the strange PRORA room, he wasn't sure whether he was in his own assigned quarters or not. A late-afternoon sun was breaking into the room from a gap in the curtains and Everley wondered how much of the day he had been asleep. He groaned and rolled himself over so that he could bury his whole head into the bedding. His head pulsed with the thumping echo of his own heartbeat, and it hurt.

Everley became aware of a person next to him. Someone seemed to slide out of the bed, take something from the floor, open the door and leave. He didn't have the energy to move to see who was there.

Another sound made Everley jump and lift his head to look; it was the shower. With the door to the private shower room open, he watched water spontaneously fire from the holes in the roof and strike the plastic floor loudly. Without a thought, he heaved himself upwards and onto all fours. He grumbled as the daylight infiltrated the narrow crack between his eyelids, and his whole body shook as he lifted each leg at a time and planted them on the floor. Every part of him felt weighted. He wobbled towards the shower room with his legs dragging heavily underneath him.

As soon as the stabbing force of tepid water hit his naked body Everley winced but was more awake. He stood still beneath the jet, waiting for and wanting it to bring him out of this painful drowsiness. The spray continued far longer than the standard single minute he was accustomed to at home, but he enjoyed all of those extra seconds. He lifted his head upwards so that the water smacked his cheeks; at the same time he strained to remember what had happened in the hours previous and why there was a person in his room. And in his bed.

With a click, the drying cycle started. Everley ran his hands through his hair and opened his eyes. He grasped for a fading memory of the day that couldn't be gripped before it left his mind altogether.

When the dryer stopped, Everley attempted to look at himself in the mirror to confirm he was alive and okay. With vision still foggy, he could only see the undefined outline of his face. A sickening surge overtook his muscles and hurled him forward. He threw up in the sink.

'Your chosen session begins in five minutes. You are welcome to proceed to "Collective Contemplation" in the Golden Room,' came another announcement.

Everley was certain he remembered folding his clothes, but they were lying in rolled lumps, creasing on the floor. He tutted then

66

clumsily dressed, missing the leg hole in his trousers not once but three times. With a deep breath, he left his room.

The corridor was busy with Operatives, though there was no conversation or acknowledgement of each other. All seemed scarcely awake as they stumbled their way to the neighbouring building.

The Golden Room was a vast space in which more than a hundred black plastic seats had been carefully arranged into lines. Ahead of the seats was a raised stage. A tremendously large, thick and ruby red curtain hung down from an area above the visible ceiling and gracefully grazed the stage floor. On the stage and in front of the curtain was a white podium, and from the podium protruded a microphone.

Everley trailed an orderly queue of Operatives into the room. Unspoken but understood, each seat was filled one after the next and without any gaps. Everley looked up at the curtain, and up further still at the gold ceiling that was decorated with a number of little lights that twinkled like stars. He rubbed at his eyes and tried to focus on the podium, conscious that he wanted to be back to his normal self to enjoy the reward he had chosen.

Once all seats were filled, the ceiling lights dimmed and a door to one side closed with a heavy thump. A Capital Operative entered the stage from the left and all Operatives stood to salute.

'For Brito!' saluted the Capital from behind the podium, signalling with her hands as she said, 'Please be seated.'

The ceiling lights faded a little more (which only worsened Everley's fuzzy lack of focus) and the white podium illuminated with a blue hue. The blue dissolved into a green, which stayed a moment before blending into yellow, then orange, and then red, pink and purple. It returned to blue again and continued to revolve in a way that made Everley's eyes spin, magnetised to the stand.

'Please make yourselves comfortable young Operatives and relax, and take some deep breaths as you enjoy now relaxing and descending into this relaxation.'

There was something in the way that this softly spoken Capital said those words that made Everley feel incredibly serene.

Music started to pour into the auditorium from somewhere unseen. Seemingly electronically-created beats bounced in, one at a time and at a regular rate. At first it was a high *ding* followed by a low *dong* that continued over and over in this way. A deep, bass vibration gradually emerged behind the repeating notes, gaining strength and volume only to swerve away again. The humming tone came and went; it rose and fell just as the drowned sound of waves might do from a listening place at the bottom of the sea.

Next began a *click-click-clap, pause, click-click-clap* that maintained a rhythm constantly. To that was introduced the kind of hiss that flowing air through a tube might make, and then the kind of high-pitched clash that tapping metal with metal might make. There was a synthesised shiver of strange noises for which Everley couldn't even imagine the origin. He felt as though the sound was unavoidably wrapping itself around his mind and taking a hold of his heart so that its own beat fell in line with that of the music. It was slow.

'Are you feeling relaxed?' asked the Capital. 'Nod with me, if...' she paused for longer than was natural mid-way through a sentence, '...you are.'

Silently, Everley and the crowd nodded heads up and down in agreement.

'This reward is for *your* pleasure. Are you pleased? Nod with me if...' she paused again, '...you are.'

Everley and the crowd nodded. The bow of their heads perfectly coincided with the *click-click-clap* of the music.

'You give absolute allegiance to Brito. Nod with me if... you are purposeful.'

Everley and the crowd nodded.

'Together we are the ultimate society and... you have a role to perform.'

Everley and the crowd still nodded.

The thick red curtain began to open from the middle and was pulled apart from both sides. It revealed the biggest of windows facing the coast. It was as though the front of the building had been removed and what would have been a giant television screen had been replaced with a sublime reality. At the view, Everley inhaled a filling breath and gulped down a wave of emotion that had caused tears to appear in his eyes and the heaviest of pressures to push at the back of his throat.

'Behold the beauty of Brito! For this... you give your life.'

They nodded.

Windmills stood tall in organised lines that stretched from the sand and into the sea, where natural ripples created a multitude of blue lines that crinkled the water around them. Behind the stunning sight, the sun was setting. The brightest of pinks bled into luminous oranges and the sun was aglow as it lowered itself tenderly into the sea.

In The Golden Room, the music was continuing, and Everley was still nodding.

'Take your right hand and place it on the shoulder of the Operative next to you,' the Capital instructed the willing crowd, who immediately obeyed.

With that touch, each Operative's eyes closed. All heads hung motionlessly. The nodding had stopped. All were asleep.

Raines was talking loudly into a speaker phone on the desk of a temporary office he had taken at the PRORA.

'The reopening was a complete success, Cardinal. I believe we have refined many of our techniques. Were the results clear from the Watch Tower's feed to Head Quarters?' he asked.

'Indeed we did, Command Raines. We are very pleased,' came a female voice from the phone.

'As am I. I have asked the Administrators to record more notes than they would normally, so that we can compare the results of this group with that of the next. I will now return to HQ,' Raines said, then hesitated and added, 'if I have your approval?'

There was a pause on the end of the line.

'Cardinal?' Raines moved closer to the phone on the desk and could hear some mumbling as the female voice conferred with another group.

'The Cardinals would welcome a full written report after the next cycle,' finally responded the official voice.

'Sure. May I now return to my office and quarters on Floor 72?'

There was another break in response while a lot of quiet murmuring was audible through the speaker.

Raines huffed and rolled his eyes as he waited for a reply. He waggled his toes in his shoes and held his hand to his knee to stop it fidgeting up and down. *'Why was there so much fuss and dither about every decision?'* Raines thought. *'Everything in writing, in triplicate, awaiting approval!'* He wanted so desperately to change things up, and bring a bit of sense and agility to the running of things.

'Cardinal?' Raines called out again, unable to wait. *'One day it'll be me in that room!'* he said to himself, shaking his head in annoyance.

'Command Raines, we would welcome your presence in that area until your report is completed. We would like you to observe this group closely; at rest in their Point A quarters, at work at the waterside windmills *and* at their next PRORA cycle.'

Raines stood up and threw the chair backwards. It hit the wall behind him with a bang. Not one second later a concerned Capital ran into the office (without first knocking on the door) and began looking all about the room for any cause of the noise or any hazards to his Command.

'GET OUT!' shouted Raines at the worried Capital, who saluted and left as quickly as he had entered.

'Command Raines? What is happening there?' came forth from the speaker.

'Apologies, apologies,' said Raines as he clambered for the phone, turned the loudspeaker off and held the handset to his ear. He wiped the sweat from his top lip and continued, 'I am very happy to delegate this to my capable Capitals.'

'No. This is a job for you, Raines. We understand that a further twelve days is some time... plus another five to complete your report. But this would surely demonstrate your commitment. *And* it would illustrate to the Cardinals your wish for your efforts to be recognised. Your appraisal is coming up, Command, and we are aware that you are seeking a Higher position in your older years.'

Raines pulled the phone away from his ear and pressed his forehead against the cool glass of the office window. He banged it a few times as the words *'I've been seeking a Higher position for nearly thirty fucking years!'* screamed through his mind.

'Command? Command?' came the voice quietly through the receiver.

He raised the handset back to his ear and, with his head still against the window, said the words, 'Okay, I'll do it.'

Raines had resigned himself to the inevitability of it all. Despite this, he was more aware than ever of how old he felt. As he had aged, so too had his defences against his true character; he didn't know how much longer he could live this pretence before the volatile ego of Bunky broke through. He couldn't imagine what detrimental effects would be caused by his own personal eruption of chaos, but he knew it could be bad for everyone. What he needed was a change, a taste of excitement and a bit of old-British fun. But all of that was wanting in Brito.

'Command Raines, we thank you,' replied the Cardinal with an almost-condescendingly gracious tone.

'I request that The Cardinals accept my wish to be considered for a promotion,' Raines asserted, knowing that they needed him, for there was no disputing that he was the best and most brilliantly ruthless at the role.

There was no response.

'Cardinal? Cardinal?' Raines said with the receiver crushed to his ear.

The line was dead.

'Bastards, bastards, bastards!' swore Raines aloud as he bashed his head against the glass and let the phone fall to the floor. Feeling a tantrum rising, he had the immediate urge to smash something, but found himself distracted by the view.

Beneath the window and down on the glossy black floor of the piazza, a child was swinging a hosepipe from side to side to clean the surface with water. Another child was hopping about happily and splashing her bare feet into a pool of rich liquid in the centre. Though Raines couldn't hear them, he watched the second child signal to the one holding the hose, who then fired its flow at puddle. The force of the spray displaced the dark pool to the edges of the piazza floor, and, as the child continued to chase it, the thick liquid spilled onto the grey concrete beside. As it drained down, the red colour and congeal was immediately visible. It was unmistakeably blood.

The children were Raines' idea. Whether the lowest performing pupils of Brito's schools or harvested directly from InOp homes, there were plenty of children available. As soon as each PRORA round ended and the Operatives left on the Speed Line, a group of tiny tots were set to work as cleaners. Watching them from the window, Raines was impressed to see how efficiently his designs

72

had materialised and knew that, with a regime impossible to improve, he was at the pinnacle of his second-life's career.

'Just one more report!' he thought, as he snatched his notebook from the table and opened the office door, behind which was diligently waiting the Capital he had shouted at moments earlier.

'C-Can I get you a-a-anything, C-Command?' asked the Capital, nervously.

'Come with me, son. You might learn something,' said Raines as he bound past and down the corridor with the Capital jogging quickly behind him.

They stepped outside and marched across the piazza, past the lodging blocks on the left and The Golden Room on the right, then through an alleyway between the two buildings.

'We are going to that cabin with the red door,' Raines pointed as he emerged from the alley with the Capital trailing behind him. 'Things don't always work out how you plan. You can't control everything, but you can minimise the variables. To maintain order, a manager has got to keep his eyes open!' He stopped walking, looked round at the young lad and tapped his finger right in the middle of his forehead. 'Get it?' said Raines, into the Capital's face.

The Capital's eyes were at first fixed at Raines, then wandered to the side as something else had caught his attention.

'You will look at me when I'm talking to you, SON!' raged Raines.

'B-but C-Command... there,' his voice tailed off. He gingerly pointed over Raines' shoulder to a small cluster of Capitals that were crowded around something on the sand.

'What is going on here?!' Raines demanded very fiercely.

The group – three female and three male Capitals and Administrators, all in their twenties and making up a small quarter of the PRORA team – turned hastily with faces horrified that they had been found out. They saluted.

Still fifty yards away, Raines waded gracelessly through the wet sand. He intended to sustain an air of authority, but instead embarrassed himself by bumbling about, sloshing in the sand and splattering his trousers. They still saluted, but held their lips together tightly to contain their laughter.

'Bloody hell! Fuck it! Shitting b—' he was muttering as he trudged closer to the group. He reminded himself that he was amongst youngsters who wouldn't understand what he was saying but would know that these were illegal words, so hushed.

'Command, we were only looking at this InOp,' said one as all stepped aside to reveal a badly beaten body on the sand.

'Well? And what of it? *It* is to be thrown into the reservoir with the rest!'

'But... Command... it's still breathing!'

Raines crouched down to get a clearer view. Although naked, he wasn't sure whether the body was male or female because it was curled so tightly into a ball with arms squeezing knees to chin. The face could not be seen at all through hair that was matted with dirt and blood and mud. The body was so bloodied that sand was sticking to every part of it in blobs of burgundy. There were cuts all over its back and a wound was oozing from a deep tear as one of the Capitals prodded at it with a stick.

'Stop that!' said Raines as he pushed his hands on his thighs to stand upright again. Unusually, he felt quite queasy at the repugnant sight.

'It *is* alive! Look!' said the Capital who had arrived with Raines.

The body was moving. Only ever-so slightly and gently, but the arm was rising and falling as the chest beneath it moved with the slow intake of breath. Then came from it a quiet and pained whimper.

Raines gritted his teeth together. It was only an InOp, after all. 'Well, what are you waiting for?' he scorned to his subordinates. He would have to lead by example, or else all would fail. ''Tis no

74

different alive or dead! They have no purpose,' he stated plainly, and continued, 'They are not Britons. Get rid of it in the reservoir.'

Three of the Capitals dragged the body away without delay, while the others lingered, wanting to converse with such a notable figure as Raines. He was a shining celebrity in Brito, and although the sun's rays of responsibility burnt him until he ached, he did bask in it once in a while.

'Command, may we know more of your skin pictures, if you please?' asked one, shyly.

The images on Raines' wrists and hands had been permanently penned on his skin after a third stint in prison, and in exchange for a three-month supply of benzodiazepine downers. The pictures were of flames on one hand and waves on the other. They had very little significance to him and in all honesty he couldn't remember why he had chosen these designs, but he had certainly enjoyed inventing new meanings for curious and eager Operatives ever since.

'Well, there is a great story behind these, but it might scare you to hear it. Are you strong enough?' he teased.

'Yes! Yes! Tell us!' came the chorus of all the young Capitals, including those that had so simply done away with the dying InOp and rushed to rejoin the group.

'For Brito, then,' Raines started, as he bent down slowly and sat on the sand, facing the sea and with his back to the site where the bloodied body had been.

The Capitals sat with him, and, leaning forward with eyes open wide, they waited for the incredible story to start.

'It was a long time ago and many years before you were brought into this wonderful world of ours. Brito was only just being born. You remember your history, right? Well, at that time, at the earliest beginnings of Brito, all of the other countries on our planet each had one person that ruled them. Every country's *overlord* had a government – a group of people who helped the overlord to tell their subjects how to live. While these chiefs sat happily high in their castles, making their rules, the people of their countries lived purposeless lives. The planet was a *very scary* place.'

Raines looked at each in the eye and continued, 'In these countries, the people, humans like you, and you and you,' he pointed, 'selfishly chose *themselves* before any other. They competed with their fellow countrymen and women for food, water and belongings. They served only themselves with lavish lodgings filled with decorative objects that had no use, peculiar clothes and personal vehicles that polluted the air with deadly gases. The people were self-serving. They *chose* themselves and cared little about the health of the whole. Can you understand?'

The Capitals were shaking their heads not with a lack of understanding, but with a disbelief that any person could have individual, selfish wants. It was difficult for the youngsters to imagine.

'The overlords of the other countries watched what Brito was becoming: A self-sufficient society where *every* human that contributed was rewarded equally. *We*,' he pointed to himself, 'understood that life was not about ownership, but about purpose. We took care of our country, our countryside, our pollutant-free air and our healthcare. Those foreign overlords could see that in Brito every person had a part to perform. *We* operated together, and *they* couldn't bare it. They knew that if their people found out about our beautiful Brito, they would desert their own countries and come to live with us. You would too, wouldn't you?'

The Capitals gestured 'yes' with nodding heads and humming sounds.

'So, scared of Brito's beginnings, the overlords of every country on the planet got together and had a big meeting. At this meeting, they decided to tell their subjects that Brito was bad, and that all the people of the world should come together to invade our island. For this, they promised their subjects that they would be richly rewarded with more useless belongings.'

The Capitals gasped with the fearful thought of a breach of Brito's borders.

76

'We wouldn't let Brito be broken!' Raines continued with a waving fist. 'We were prepared. We decided to use the *natural beauty* of Brito to overcome our attackers... Brito is an island. What does that mean?'

They looked at each other, not one daring to interrupt the Command's story. Raines pushed forward his left fist into the middle of the sitting circle to show the tattooed navy blue waves spreading down the back of his hand. As he rolled up the sleeve of his shirt, the Capitals leaned in further to look. The artwork continued up his forearm and disappeared underneath the crumpled shirt at his elbow, where the material was too tight to roll any further.

'What defence does an island have? Come on, come on!'

'W-w-water?' replied the nervous Capital he had arrived with.

'Yes! It is surrounded by sea! This was our protection. We vowed an oath to defend at the seashore. We heard word from our spies that the other countries would start their attack at our narrowest coast: The South. We made a plan to take the waste of old-Britain – the no-longer needed paintings and pictures and material possessions – and we used *nature* to turn them into weapons! What do you think we did?'

There was again no response from the captivated Capitals. Raines thrust forward his right hand into the sand in centre of the circle and pushed up his shirt to reveal red flames with orange flicks and yellowing borders, though the colours had gone murky over the years.

'You set fire to everything!' roared one of the Capitals, clapping in enjoyment of the tale.

'Yes! Yes! You took the waste that Brito didn't need, and you burnt it!' exclaimed another.

'And when the attackers tried, you threw all of the waste over the island's edges while it was on fire, so that they got burnt!' said another as all applauded.

'Yes, you are all correct! We did all of those things and more besides.' Raines giggled, enjoying a small opportunity to be a storyteller. 'That's enough story time for one day,' he concluded, lifting himself to his feet, 'We must get on!'

'But what about the countries? Tell us more! Did the attackers all die?' came questions from the group.

'Some died. Some didn't die,' he said whilst wiping sand from his bottom. 'Some found a way to hide in Brito and became InOps. Some of today's InOps are descendants from them.'

The Capitals cheered and booed and clapped as they rose to their feet.

'What about your skin pictures? *How* did you get those?' called one.

'Yes! Tell us! please!' pleaded the rest.

'Well now, I'm not sure that you're strong enough to hear that part!' Raines toyed with them. 'Alright... I'll tell you... but,' he paused, 'you'll never look at the sea the same way again!'

'Go on! Go on!' they begged.

He searched his mind for a moment then began, 'I was setting fire to a stack of books and tossing them into the sea. Then one of the books opened all by itself! It was a book about... oh... Hobbits! I mean, a small race of people that mostly lived in the countryside. Like a rabbit, I suppose... Do you know what rabbits are?'

They all looked at each other and shook their heads.

'Well, I had read this book before, and there was a *dragon* in it! I mean... a creature that you won't have seen or heard of before because there aren't dragons in Brito. Not anymore. But there used to be. Okay? Dragons were wild creatures that breathed fire! Anyway, all by itself this book opened on a page, so I went to have a look and pick it up. And as I did...' he stopped to add dramatic effect.

'Yes? Command, tell us!'

'A dragon reached out and grabbed my hand! It breathed fire on me and burnt my skin. I pulled my hand away and kicked the book closed,' Raines replicated the action on the sand, 'and then I picked the book up and jumped into the sea. I held the book tight as it wriggled in my hand, but I drowned it in the deep water and then swam away. The sea grumbled and there was a huge wave, and then the sea spat me out! I went flying through the air and landed back on the sand! When I got up, I had these skin pictures. The dragon made the flames and the sea made the waves... The end.'

Each of his young audience had a hand over their mouth and was exclaiming 'Wow' through the gaps in their fingers.

'Come along now, we've had a long break there!' Raines said authoritatively.

'Tell us about Hobbits and rabbits and dragons! Where do they live now?'

'Another time, another time, young Britons! We will have to operate extra-productively to make up this lost time! Back to your tasks, now!' Raines half-smiled as the Capitals saluted and scattered in a number of different directions.

'Right you, we have work to do in the cabin,' Raines asserted as he led the way.

'C-Command? That w-was an un-b-believable story!'

'Unbelievable?! It was entirely factual, son!' blasted Raines. *'Gullible fools,'* he said to himself, tutting at the brainless ignorance of the Briton-born race.

Selby was waiting at Point A for the Speed Line to arrive. Although he was under no illusion that when Everley stepped off the train he would have forgotten him after the stint at a PRORA, there was always a chance. There was something about Everley that seemed different and particularly special, and Selby was confident that The

Hidden should explore it. Now was the time to see how strong Everley's mind was.

Selby leaned casually against the wall upon which was pinned the framed picture of The Other Place. He picked at his fingernails whilst waiting for the rumble of the train and pondering potential outcomes. If Everley *didn't* remember him after two days at the PRORA, then it would be clear that his mind was malleable, easily influenced and obedient. If Everley *did* remember Selby, then it would reveal a mind that was strong, wilful and defiant.

With a loud screech of the breaks, the silver train arrived into the station. Selby pushed himself away from the ledge to a more formal standing position and watched as the front doors opened to let off the passengers.

In a patient, efficient line, they alighted one by one and trailed their way out of Point A. Selby moved his head to try to catch the faces and find Everley. He would usually be at or near the front, although anything could change after a PRORA. There was no sign of him at all.

The platform had become busier with other Operatives waiting to board, so Selby took a few steps forward. He made sure not to stray too far away from the designated meeting place and continued to scan the marching line of leaving Ops. His darting eyes searched desperately for Everley.

Out of the line, one Operative stepped and swerved across the platform. Selby saw Everley's confident stride and immediately knew it was him. He stood still and waited as Everley continued through the crowd and headed straight towards him.

Halfway, and as though he had hit an invisible wall, Everley stopped. His eyes were locked on Selby but, at ten paces away and with people in between, neither moved.

'He must recognise me,' thought Selby, *'which means the PRORA's mind-programming didn't work!'* Selby was so excited and signalled with a hand for Everley to come closer. Still he didn't

move. *'Keep coming. That's right, you DO know me!'* Selby willed in his mind.

Everley blinked a few times, shook his head and looked away. He turned and marched out of the station exit.

Selby held his hand to his head and huffed. He couldn't fathom how Everley could partially recognise him, then instantly forget. It was a sign; Selby was right all along. Everley was *particularly special.*

VI

In summary, from an estimated population of 4.7 million, of which 3,937,298 are operational, we were only able to identify 337 candidates last year. From those, only a minority successfully passed all tests and were deemed suitable for the Organisation. These 21 individuals represent the small proportion of Brito-born subjects whose conscious minds are less susceptible to the means of influence practised in PRORAs. This year, we hope to raise this percentage from 0.0005% to 0.0010% of the Operative population.

- Annual Report, The Hidden

Everley rose right on time: five minutes before the alarm. He daydreamed of The Other Place until the alarm sounded, was first for the toilet, third for the shower, dressed and downstairs in quick time. He had woken excited but wasn't confident why, so attributed it to the fact it was Day One again. There was only another ten days before his next PRORA, and he was aflutter already.

'Best Mornin' young Everley!' said the Day Watch Operative, who was sitting at the front desk. She had attempted a standard Brito haircut, but her thick grey hair had natural curls that flicked upwards rebelliously above her wrinkled eyes.

'Best Morning, Day Watcher!' replied Everley, far more joyfully than came naturally to him.

'Did y'av the best time at PRORA?' she asked with a tongue that showed she hadn't been educated by Brito.

She eased herself gently from her seat with a groan, and then leaned forwards to place her ashen and work-weakened hands on the front of the desk. Even standing, she was much shorter than Everley.

'I certainly did! I have felt full of positivity, purpose and efficiency ever since!' Everley replied with a smile whilst turning to take his nutrition tablet from the machine.

'Oh! Well you do sound 'appy! It has been made more newer, ain't it? Refurb'ed, I 'ear. Is it the best kind a place? I has been waiting for one of you ta come downstairs an' tell me a bi' about it! Was it better than I could imagine?' the Day Watch Operative quizzed as she scuttled around her desk to be next to Everley.

'Yes, better than you could imagine! And yes, it was the best type of place! It's right next to the sea.'

'Tell me more! What were the rooms like? And your rewards, what were they?' she continued to probe breathlessly.

Everley looked down at the old Day Watcher and wondered how to express that although the last two days were the best of his life, he was entirely unable to remember the finer details. Or any details at all.

'I don't want to spoil it for you,' he said, hoping that would free him from having to answer. 'When are you going?'

'Oh, I'm too old for PRORA, son,' she said, pouring Everley a cup of water from a spout that protruded directly from the wall and offering it to him. 'I has got The Other Place to look forward to now. Tha's my ultimate reward! So, please, tell me more!'

'Thank you,' Everley said as he accepted the water and took a series of slow sips.

Frozen and wide-eyed in anticipation with both haggard hands held together, she waited for him to drink.

'Well,' he began, unsure of where it would lead, but hoping it would jog his own memory, 'there was a large black floor, and a Command Operative gave a speech, and the gates were golden. Yes! The gates were golden! And I was given a Superior Room because my productivity was so high, and my room... my room...' he tailed off.

'Yeh?' she tapped him on the arm as though to bring him back to reality.

'Being beside the sea brings with it a soft wind that tickles the back of your neck,' he said wistfully, and looked down to smile at her.

'Oh!' She grinned and wiggled her aged fingers.

Another three Operatives entered the Service Room, calling 'Best Morning!' as they passed Everley and the Day Watcher and turned on the television.

On screen, the Entertainment Operative in the smart blue suit was sitting on the steps of the caged stage again. Two warring InOps were clawing at each other's faces, pealing skin and ripping hair.

At once and involuntarily, the three Operatives and Everley yelled furiously at the screen.

'InOps we hate! InOps we hate!'

The old Day Watcher scurried quickly backwards and recoiled to her position behind the desk.

'Waste we will cull! Waste we will cull!' they continued in a mad anger that was directed at the screen.

The InOp images on the television faded out with a *PA PA PAH*, and a saluting News Operative appeared. Without hesitation, all three Operatives and Everley ceased their shouting and returned to their previous conversations, as though the bizarre moment had not even occurred.

'I'll tell you more another time, Day Watcher. Have a utile day!' Everley said merrily, leaving the Service Room with a bounce in his step.

She didn't respond, but timidly nodded and saluted as he left.

Predictably, Everley was first to arrive at Point A station. He marched slowly from left to right, alone and reciting the oath.

After a little time, he found himself stationary and staring at a recent replacement of the large painted poster that was draped over the horizontal poles at the edge of the platform. The new image had a yellow background. Four naked and perfect-bodied Operatives were standing side-on with bent arms and fists in the air. From a blue speech bubble their shared words read, "WE DO OUR BRIT!".

Everley became aware of the other Operatives that had filled the space around him. The sounds of their movement and morning exchanges reached his ears gradually, like steadily turning the sound dial on a television from mute to max.

'For Brito!' he shouted at the poster, and sighed with satisfaction at its release.

The poster crumpled from the bottom upwards as a child emerged from underneath. It was an InOp, and it rushed past Everley with a skid. He turned to see the child zip through the crowd, and watched it weaving in and out of view. He decided very quickly that he would grab it and throw it on the tracks as soon as it returned.

The poster crumpled upwards again as a female InOp pushed herself to her feet and called to the child urgently, 'Little Lyndon, no!'

Everley turned and grabbed the woman with both hands, squeezing her upper arms. His teeth gritted together as he pulled her closer violently and hissed in her face; his grip was so tight that his nails sunk into her flesh.

'Stop it! Please!' she begged as she squirmed.

As her fearful eyes looked at Everley, there was a flicker of something he recognised. He couldn't be sure what it was, but something made him feel instantly sick at his own behaviour. It was as though a poison had hit his stomach, and it made him wince and swallow and heave. He softened his grip but did not release it altogether.

'Please! I beg you,' she pleaded forlornly, looking up at him. She sniffed and said, 'I can't fight anymore. Please let me get the child and I'll be out of your way.'

The sick feeling came again and his stomach cramped as though it had been wrung out like a wet cloth. At seeing a tear drip from a crease at the bottom of her beautiful button nose, Everley's hands dropped to his sides.

'I'm sorry,' he said, and then wiped his eyes and shook his head in confusion that he was apologising to a despicable InOperative. Though his 'sorry' had not been heard by others, his mercy in releasing her had been noticed by those around him. A group of Operatives rushed toward the scene.

'What's going on, Everley?' called a voice he recognised to be a neighbour.

Everley was cemented to the spot and still looking at the InOp. He held his hands to his temples while searching his mind for a reason why she was interesting, familiar or special.

Astonished at the apology, the InOp looked mystified while rubbing the parts of her arms that he had pinched.

Breaking the concentration of both of them, the child swooped to her side, grabbed her hand and was pulling her back towards the poster. At the same time, the Operatives crowded threateningly and were moments away from pouncing on the woman and her child. She took one look at the mob, one last look at Everley, then lunged underneath the poster and was away.

'You used to be an Operative, too!' Everley whispered as he stared at the spot where she had been standing.

A harsh shove on the shoulder forced him from his wondering.

'Why didn't you stop the InOp?!' came angrily from an Operative at his side.

'Traitor!' was shouted from another a little further back, which initiated a tirade of insults about breaking the oath and defending the InOps.

'No, no, no! You are wrong!' asserted Everley, knowing he would have to think fast to appease the horde, but not knowing what had compelled him to release her.

'Break it up Britons! Break it up! Order! Order!' called a voice through the crowd. 'What is happening here? It is very disappointing to not see your orderly lines waiting for the Speed Line.'

'Capital, this Op saved an InOp!' said the Operative nearest Everley fervently, while saluting with one hand and shaking a pointing finger at Everley with the other.

'Yes!' echoed the crowd, repeating the accusation, 'Traitor!'

'A traitor to the oath is not one of us!' blared one from the back.

'Decorum, Britons! You are now calm,' began the Capital. He shushed the group with a waving hand and continued in a cool and confident tone. 'That is not what I witnessed. This strong Briton took hold of the InOp to throw her to the tracks, but she spat in his face! InOps carry diseases, you know! This fine Briton only released her so that he could wipe his eyes.'

The Capital unbuttoned the cuff of his coat and pulled his hand into the sleeve so that a little material hung free. He reached forward to Everley's face and rubbed his temple with the cuff while tapping him reassuringly on the shoulder with his other hand. He smiled at Everley, whose face showed only confusion.

'That's better, young Briton. You're alright now,' the Capital spoke loudly enough for the group to hear, 'and it didn't get in your eyes after all. Fine work young Briton. Fine work indeed.'

'S-S-Selby?' whispered Everley, not understanding how he knew his name.

The Capital winked at Everley, withdrew his cuff, pushed his hand back through the hole and buttoned it up again. He turned to the group, saluted and said, 'You are all One. Join together for Brito!'

'For Brito!' was returned by all. And, with that, the Capital left.

Everley still hadn't moved from the spot. The entire event had baffled him, but seeing the Capital – Selby – had made him feel safe.

The platform started vibrating as the Speed Line approached. It was enough of a distraction to cause the crowd to break the circle around Everley and create neat and tidy lines from the platform's edge backwards, in preparation for boarding the train. Everley joined the nearest queue.

From behind, a hand tapped him on the shoulder. 'Well done, Everley!' said the Operative Everley recognised to be his next-room neighbour.

Everley nodded and returned to face forward, breathing deeply with a *'Phew!'*

As the train shot up the spine of Brito, Everley didn't look out of the windows and contemplate the view as he would normally do. Instead, he thanked Brito for Selby and asked himself how he knew the Capital... and the InOp too.

BUZZ BUZZ BEEP BEEP BEEP sounded the following morning's alarm so loudly that Everley was snatched from his sleep with a sharp gasp. He sat himself up and held his throat while panting.

This morning he knew why the alarm had been the one to wake him, rather than his body clock; he had only just fallen to sleep. All of those questions had kept him awake, and now he was exhausted.

Those questions had interested him at first, and he enjoyed hearing himself consider the answers. But as the night continued and he grew tired and desperately wanted silence and sleep, the voice inside his mind tormented him. Never before had he considered a subject so deeply that it had consumed him. Never before had he a subject to consider! Before last night, the voice inside had been there to simply instruct him: *'Brush your teeth. Cut your hair. Wake for work. Work for Brito. Hate the InOps.'* Yet, last night the voice chatted incessantly. It spoke of many things at once; many questions and many answers were all spoken at the same time, like a chorus of six singers singing six separate songs. Maybe more.

At times, he could make no sense of the blather, which argued even with itself. At other times, and amongst the noise, something would chime in a way that made sense and was the start of an answer. Everley wanted to follow those thoughts, but by approximately two o'clock he found himself slapping his own head with both hands in an attempt to silence the relentless noise and get to sleep.

By four o'clock, everything that Everley could confidently recall was that (1) the Capital that helped him was called Selby, (2) Selby wanted him for a 'Special Project', and (3) he was supposed to meet Selby by the big poster at Point A, but he had forgotten. (4) There were a lot of things he was forgetting, but (5) he didn't know why. (6) The female InOp at Point A had once been an Operative too. (7) He liked her, and (8) liking her made him feel sick.

Everley had still been awake for the morning sunrise, and knew that to be the case when he saw the orangey light tip-toe into his room through the gap between the bottom of the blind and the windowsill. He must have dropped off not thirty minutes before the alarm so now felt as though he had been attacked by an army of InOps. His head thumped, his eyes stung and he wondered how he would get through the day.

Naked and before going to the toilet or showering, he hurried down to the Service Room to collect his nutrition tablet, hoping that it would give him a burst of strength. Naughtily, he tried the machine a second time to see whether it would dispense another for him, but it only made a clicking sound. He hoped the energy from this one would sustain him.

When he got back upstairs there was a queue of at least four for each toilet. He was not the only one that was standing cross-legged, purse-lipped, holding his parts and jigging up and down, but the few before him could see the panic in his eyes and let him go next. After showering, he dressed as quickly as he could and briskly walked out of the building in plenty of time to seek Selby in the InOp area, speak to the female InOp at Point A and still be first for the train.

Everley circled the deepest part of the InOp area. Frustratingly, Selby was not there. He waited a short while on one corner of the wasteland, but felt increasingly uneasy. Some InOps had noticed him loitering in their domain and roused others from their shelters to assemble a growing group of dirty deserters that eyeballed him from forty foot opposite. Outnumbered, he resolved to try again tomorrow and ran to Point A.

'Lyndon? Lyndon? Lyndon!' Everley called out across the empty platform.

He waited alone, patiently and with only a bracing morning breeze for company. He continued to call out and search underneath the hanging posters for signs of the female InOp or her child.

'LYNDON!' he shouted one last time while standing on the platform's edge so that his voice echoed down the train tracks.

'How do you know my name?' came a soft voice from behind him.

Everley twisted around swiftly and saw it was her. He smiled and took a step towards her.

'Don't you come any closer!' she said curtly, with an arm and hand stretched out and a back that was arched away.

Everley noticed his tummy tumble at the sight of her again. He didn't understand the feeling, but he wanted to pause the moment so that he could paint a mental picture of her standing there; it would be something to remember tonight, when he would be trying to silence the voice inside and sleep again.

She was so different to an Operative. Her appearance was untidy and colourful. Her hair was so long that some of it pooled on her shoulders before falling like water to halfway down her arms. It was dark brown, but Everley noted the light bits in it that made it look stripey. Her eyebrows were dark and dense and accentuated the intensity of enticing eyes that were framed with long lashes. Her eyes were light brown with dark rims that he could see even from the few steps away. Her lips were full and round with a clear V-shape in the middle under her nose. They were pale, and her skin was pale, too, and there was a dirty patch across one cheek. Everley wasn't sure what her clothes were made from, although they appeared to be a patchwork of carpet pieces that had been stitched together messily using plastic cables.

While he could make no sense of it, he thought she was beautiful. A veil had been lifted from his eyes and he saw a sight that sparked his heart.

'I won't hurt you. Sorry,' Everley replied.

'Why are you apologising to me? I am an InOp!' she said, scoffing at the very idea.

Everley shrugged his shoulders and shook his head.

'How do you know my name?' she asked him again.

'Yesterday you called out for your child, Little Lyndon, so you must be Lyndon,' he said calmly.

'Yes, I am. What do you want with me?'

'We have spoken before.'

'Spoken?' she mocked. 'Spoken?! You and I have never spoken. YOU attacked Little Lyndon when he was trying to help you. YOU dropped your nutrition tablet and when he tried to give it back to you, you hurt him! I had to stop you!'

'I don't remember that, I'm sorry.' Everley was confused. This was yet another thing he had forgotten.

'Why are you apologising to *me*? Have you forgotten I am an InOp?'

'You were an Operative, too,' he said, 'I remember that.'

Lyndon looked at him solidly. There was a long pause between them.

'Didn't you go to the PRORA?' she asked, more gently now.

'I did.'

'Then why don't you hate me? Why don't you hate me even more than you did before?'

'I don't understand. Why would I hate you more after going to the PRORA?' asked Everley, thoroughly confused.

'Wait,' she said, pointing a finger at him and half-smiling, 'how can you remember me at all? You saw me *before* the PRORA.'

'I don't know what you mean. I don't understand. Why don't I understand?' Everley felt fearful. He thought he knew everything there was to know about Brito, but all of a sudden he couldn't fathom any of it. He reminded himself, *'The PRORA is the reward. InOps are bad. InOps we hate. InOps we hate.'*

'Did you drink the blue liquid?' she asked.

'I did... I *do* hate the InOps, but...' he squinted his eyes, turned away and said aloud but to himself, 'I must uphold the oath.'

'You hate the InOps, but what?' she probed, stepping closer to him. 'But what?'

'But I don't hate you. And I don't know what the PRORA has to do with it.' Everley turned to look at her again, and saw her smiling. He wanted to remember that smile forever, and hoped to Brito that he would never forget it.

'Operatives are coming.' Lyndon had spotted a figure entering the station, and was starting to widen the distance between them.

'Don't go,' pleaded Everley, eager to speak more so that he could understand what it all meant. And eager to look upon her beauty for a little longer.

'I need to go, or they will hurt me. They will hurt you too if they see you talking to me,' Lyndon whispered.

'I need to know, is there something wrong with me? Am I unwell? Is that why I'm forgetting everything? Why don't I hate you? What is happening to me?' Everley's voice was raised. He didn't care who heard, he just needed answers.

'Go! I will be here this evening when you return.' She lifted the hanging poster and was away before Everley could reply.

The voice in Everley's mind was prattling on louder than ever. One voice shouted a question over another voice, and another, until the sound inside was deafening. He dropped to his knees on the hard floor of the platform, held his hands to his ears and let out a sustained scream of excruciation. The scream was louder than his internal chatter, giving him a short break from its noise. As soon as his breath ran out and the scream stopped, the voices in his head began again. He took a deep intake of breath and let out a second lengthy scream.

Then all went dark.

Everley had fainted.

When Everley's eyes opened, he didn't recognise his surroundings. He was lying on a bed in a room with white walls, a white ceiling and a bright bar light above him. It was all blinding.

'Operative Everley, you are awake! Here is a certificate to excuse you from Operative duties for one day, but you will be penalised your PRORA for this round. You may now leave.' A Medical Operative forcibly put a hand underneath Everley's back and pulled him upwards to a seated position on the bed.

'What happened?' Everley asked as he turned to let his feet hang off the side of the raised bed. Before he could acclimatise, the Medical Operative pulled him to his feet.

'You collapsed at Point A. A fellow Operative brought you in. Said he lives in your Operative lodgings. Said an InOp spat in your face yesterday and feared you may have caught a disease. We took some blood. There's no sign of illness. Go back to your lodgings and get some rest. Back to work tomorrow.' The Medical Operative handed Everley a sheet of paper with a stamp on it and then moved to the next bed, which had another Operative lying upon it.

Everley hobbled out of the room, down a long corridor, past a front desk, through a large door and outside. Still feeling sleepy, he leant against the wall of the building whilst waiting for his eyes to adjust.

What a shame he would be without any reward, he thought. He so looked forward to each PRORA, and today's excuse from duties would mean working until the end of this round (eight more days), then two days of "Social Contribution", plus a further ten days until he would get to go to the PRORA again. Never mind. He needed the rest today and was looking forward to sleeping through it.

Pushing himself away from the wall and starting to walk back to his building, he felt a pang in his stomach as though it had been jabbed with something sharp. He lifted his work shirt and brushed a hand over the area under his belly button. His fingers quickly found a miniscule hard droplet of dried blood, which he instinctively picked away with his nail. As he did, it sent a tiny twinge through his tummy, hurting only for a split second. He looked down at his stomach to inspect it, but found only a spot of red where his skin had been punctured with a needle.

Everley slowly paced home. He didn't acknowledge the greetings of the Day Watch Operative as he returned to his lodgings, but instead got straight into the lift. Back in his room, he fell asleep immediately, face first and fully-clothed on the bed.

Selby stood in front of the management board for The Hidden. He was nervous and next on the agenda.

'Now we have Servant SV23 with the item 'Candidate for the Organisation'. Please step forward and proceed.'

'Thank you, madam.' Selby stepped forward, twiddled the circular bronze pin that was positioned on his outfit at the chest, took a breath and began, 'Officials of The Hidden, thank you for accepting my request to be heard by yourselves today.

'As part of my work in and around the InOperative area, I discovered an Operative that I believe to be of interest. I found him some time ago, but thought it necessary to only bring him to your attention once I was confident that he would be a viable candidate for the Organisation. I have studied him and prepared a report, within which you will find clearly detailed reasons for this nomination,' Selby said as he handed a stack of papers to an assistant, who silently distributed them to every member of the board.

'I have been observing this Operative for over forty days,' he continued, 'and, as we would expect, he has always forgotten me after the PRORA. Until now, each time we met he would greet me anew, as a stranger would. Yet, *after* his last stay at the PRORA, he has displayed signs of remembering me.'

'So?' impatiently asked a member of the board.

'You will see from my report that this Operative can recall memories and feelings, despite the mind control techniques used at the PRORA. However, he also finds himself conflicted and bound by the words of the oath. This means that his mind is both open to suggestion, and strong-willed enough to rebel.'

'What else?' came another annoyingly impatient voice.

'You will also see from my report,' continued Selby, hoping they would let him get to the point, 'that I have monitored his interaction with an InOperative. To date, he has violently displayed his disdain for the InOps. In the last two days, however, he has spoken to a female InOp, stopped himself from hurting her *and* conversed with her. I believe he feels a not forced nor manipulated connection to her.'

'And therefore?' prompted the Madam.

'Therefore, Officials of the Hidden, I believe that this Operative is able to identify his natural emotions. Therefore, Brito's programming of his mind will not succeed. And, therefore, there will be a moment where he rebels!' Selby felt the passion in his own voice and realised he was stating each fact whist pointing a finger at the board. He quickly straightened himself and carried on, 'If we catch him now, Officials, his mind will be open to *our* suggestions... He already responds to the anchor I have placed on him by tapping his shoulder... But, if we leave it too long, he will rebel against Brito. He may be banished or even expunged. This is an opportunity we shouldn't waste and I implore you to accept my recommendation to commence the first stage of suitability tests.'

Selby nodded a self-satisfied smile and waited for the board to respond.

VII

REMEMBER - His quote sets the standard:
"The very first essential for success is
a perpetually constant and regular
employment of violence."
- A scribble in the notebook belonging to Command Raines

Raines drew some water from the basin's hot tap in the en-suite office room he had taken at the PRORA. He splashed his face once, then twice, then left the tap running while he stepped out to the office, took a tumbler from the table and emptied it of pencils by turning it upside down to spill the contents all over the desk. He returned to the flowing tap and filled the pot with the now-boiling water that spurted out in spitting starts. It was so hot that it smoked.

Once full, Raines shyly turned off the tap, which had become so hot that he had to spin the metal handle clockwise in increments, blowing the tips of his fingers at each attempt until the water was stopped. He paced slowly back to the desk and eased himself into the plastic chair that was there. Cuddling the tumbler of hot tap water between both palms, Raines held his face over the steam and let his tired eyes close.

'If only it was coffee,' he thought.

Raines sat there a while, reliving a simple pleasure of old Britain and wishing he had never taken it for granted. He could almost hear the chink of coffee-shop crockery, the distant hiss of a Barista steaming milk and an espresso stream from a machine. He could almost smell it. Could he? No. Finally that memory had left him and he could no longer revive that rich and luxurious scent. He opened his eyes and sipped from the cup.

'Pah!' Raines spat in disgust. Not only was it hot water, not coffee, but it tasted strange too. He wondered whether Brito had toyed with the taps and 'enhanced' the water with a concentration of additives. It was possible. Regardless, Raines continued to caress the container. He was cold, tired, very bored and very miserable that his Highers had demanded he stay at the PRORA to complete the report. Motionless, he held his hunched position over the hot water and looked sulkily upon the office with his bottom lip curled down and out, like a child told to sit silently on the naughty step.

Many minutes later, Raines dragged himself reluctantly away from a series of depressing thoughts that preoccupied his brooding mind and found himself humming. He immediately recognised the song. His pouting lips curved into a smile as he allowed his hum to get louder and then, when he reached the chorus, let out a line from Pink Floyd's classic song of protest against strict schooling.

He laughed aloud, alone in the room, and nodded at the thought that such 'real' music could be as relevant now as when it was written. His moping mouth quickly returned when he reminded himself that "popular music" didn't exist in Brito.

Growing up, Raines was unapologetically snobby about music. He would listen only to that which been released twenty or more years before he had even been born, and would ferociously criticise the noise that topped the charts in his teens by saying things like, 'Brian May would spin in his grave if he heard this stinking substitute for the sound of a musical instrument.' When his friends would say they'd found a new anti-establishment ode, he'd simply reply, 'But it's not "Taxman", is it?'

Raines gazed at a bookshelf beside the office door. It held only official files and folders, but would have been the perfect position for a CD player and two speakers.

Back in Britain, when music did exist, Raines had acquired a vintage nineties stereo. Over the years he had bought (or stolen) as many discs as he could find and had amassed a collection of classics to envy. Of course, it all went with old Britain. Recycled, reused, who knew. He hadn't seen any of his possessions since the morning Bunky left his flat and boarded the train to start his new life as Raines.

If only there was real music in this room, he wished. If only he could press play on a song – any song – and turn up the bass. He resumed his humming and pondered the reasons for Brito banishing popular music.

Beethoven once said, 'Music can change the world.' Bono once added, 'Because it can change people.' Both were right. Perhaps Brito knew that it could never control its Britons as long as song lyrics were there to give power to people, express a loving feeling or shout out about Christmas. No. Pop music, like love and Christmas, had to go.

The hum of one song had inadvertently reminded Raines of all the things he was missing, so he silenced himself. He sat there, still and dejected, wondering whether he should enrol himself in a PRORA to have his own mind erased of the past. It would be easier to not remember these things, he decided.

Raines walked over to the first-floor window and opened it. There was a thick layer of ice glistening on the concrete below. He held the tumbler out of the window and slowly poured the hot water. He watched it smack and crack the ice, which melted into a puddle. The destruction of it gave him some joy at least.

Turning back to the room, he yelled for the Operative that he knew would be standing to attention in the corridor just outside his door.

'Capital?' he called out officiously, expecting an immediate response to which there was none. 'CAPITAL!' he shouted again, more aggressively this time.

Frustrated, Raines whipped the door open. The Capital Operative on duty was asleep while standing, slightly slumped with her shoulders against the hallway wall. Without a thought, Raines launched the empty tumbler at the Capital. It hit her across the face and awoke her immediately.

'Command!' came a confused exclamation from the stunned Operative, who began rubbing her injured cheek and checking her hand for blood.

'Sleeping on the job! That's unacceptable!' Raines began. 'How are we ever to maintain efficiency in Brito if our own Capitals cannot control themselves?'

'Forgive me Command, I—'

'Silence! Get in here! I need you to assist me with my report.' He held the door to his room open and lowered his head, his eyes looking intensely at the shamefaced Capital underneath his thick eyebrows. He continued in a low and definite tone, 'If I find you sleeping in your operating hours again, I will have you demoted.'

The young female Capital rubbed a tear from her eye and stepped into Raines' room. She stood rigidly at his desk, saluted and waited for Raines to sit. With a grunt, he eased himself back into his chair then gestured over to a chair in the corner of the room while mumbling to her to sit down. The Capital robotically walked towards it, dragged it back to the desk and placed it directly opposite Raines.

'Let us begin. I am carrying out some research on the last PRORA group's efficiency at work at the waterside windmills. I need you to—' he stopped short, noticing that her cheek was a blazing red colour, caused by the clap of his cup.

She continued to look across at him with wide and anticipating eyes. Her back was stiffly straight, her hands rested on her lap and she maintained a respectful silence.

Raines muttered something inaudible. He refused to actually apologise, but was aware that he had scared her with his snapping. He pushed himself out of the chair, went into the en-suite and ran the cold tap. He took the towel from a hook, folded it in half and then in quarters, and then held it under the cold water. He stepped back into the room and offered it to her without words. She nodded gratefully and held it against her cheek with an initial wince and then a smile to signify it had made it better.

Raines sat and continued, 'I want a constant report of productivity rates. I also want any differences in behaviour immediately escalated to me. I need you to select a small number of Watch Tower Operatives to assist us. Only tell them that we are carrying out quality assurance checks. Yes?'

'Certainly. I—'

'And I will need access to the Watch Tower today, by myself, for a few hours. I need you to arrange that and redistribute the Watch Tower Ops to a different task for that time. Yes?'

'Certainly. It will be arranged.' The Capital took the towel away from her cheek and looked hopefully at Raines, as a dog would wait for a treat.

'Well? Get started!' He thrust a wad of paper sheets that listed Operative names and locations into her hand and shooed her away.

The Capital stood, tentatively returned the wet towel to Raines and reached for the door handle. Rather than twisting the knob, she paused. She slowly looked backwards at her Higher and breathed in sharply as though a word was waiting to fall from her mouth.

'What is it?' Raines asked, short of any patience this morning.

'I was not aware you were carrying out a report—' she began quietly.

'Why would you be? What is it any business of yours?!' Raines slammed his hand onto the desk in an obvious display of rising anger.

'None at all Command. What I mean to say is that if I had been aware yesterday I would have immediately brought some information to your attention,' she said hurriedly, conscious that she wanted to complete a full sentence before being cut short again.

'What information?' said Raines, picking up a pen and tatty notebook from the desk and flapping through for an empty page.

'One Operative was excused yesterday by the Health Centre.'

'Name?'

'Everley. Male.'

Raines looked up, tilted his head and rolled his eyes from left to right. No, he didn't recognise the name.

'Reason?' Raines continued, writing *'Everley (M) Absent Day One'* in the notebook and then squeezing it in half so that it would fit in his top pocket.

'He collapsed at Point A. It appears there was some altercation between him and an InOperative.'

'What happened to the InOp?'

'I believe it got away.'

'Hmm.' Raines pursed his lips and shrugged. He was unsure whether this was important but wanted to encourage the Capital to keep him abreast of all information (and felt a little guilty for being so harsh with her), so forced himself to thank her.

'Very good Capital, please advise me if Operative Everley does not arrive for work today. Now... to work!'

BUZZ BUZZ BEEP BEEP BEEP the building alarm wailed.

Everley awoke again with a jump. He bolted out of bed, leapt towards the window and tugged so violently at the blind that it almost fell from its fixings as it clattered upwards. He read the time from the large clock face on the building opposite: Six o'clock!

He span around, shook his head and wondered how he had managed to sleep through one whole day and to the following morning.

'Lyndon!' he yelped as he remembered that he was supposed to meet her in the evening, yesterday after work.

'NO!' the voice inside bellowed at him. 'Get to work. Work for Brito. Hate the InOps,' it played in his brain, reminding him that the voice was in charge again.

Looking down, Everley realised he was still wearing yesterday's clothes. He tutted at himself. This was a visual warning that all was not well at all. Order had gone awry and normality *needed* to resume because efficiency and purposefulness depended on it. For Brito and for himself, Everley agreed with the voice; the disruptive thoughts had to end. He decided quickly that he was going to avoid Lyndon. She was, after all, merely an InOp.

To make sure he wasn't distracted by her (and Selby, too), Everley knew that he would have to get to Point A later than usual. He tried to slow himself by having a chat with the Day Watch Operative over his morning nutrition tablet and even stopped to converse with his neighbour over a shortage of bootlaces, but, efficient as ever, Everley was still the first Operative to leave his building. He didn't walk the long route through the InOp area, so, with the set speed of his unconscious quick-march, he found himself first on the platform again.

The morning air felt wet. The coldness of it tickled his nose as he waited in his familiar spot on the platform. Everley didn't mind the cold. He didn't mind the hot either, although it made working sweaty. But there was something about the chilly weather that made him feel more connected with Brito. He had considered it often: the way the crispy air took tiny bites at his fingertips with frozen teeth and made miniature mountains erupt as spots on the skin of his arms. It seemed to Everley that this was Brito itself touching him, speaking to him and thanking him for being a good Operative. And, other than his productivity scores, the whisper of Brito on the wind was the only thing to bring happiness to his purely purposeful existence.

His hands shook. Giving in, he pushed them into the pockets of his coat and squeezed them into fists in a pumping motion so as to warm them up. Something stroked his right hand. He gathered the thing between thumb and two fingers, lifted it out of his pocket and held it close to his face for inspection. It was a small clump of hair. Without a doubt, he knew it was not his own. The cluster of short strands were a hundred tones lighter than Everley's dark hair, and, unlike his sensible straight locks, it was curling.

The coat had been Mother's, but the hair certainly was not. She had very dark, almost night-sky black hair that bypassed any other colours when it turned immediately to grey in her later years. It was straight, too, so the curl in his pocket could not be hers. Unless he was forgetting her after ten years of not seeing her face, he questioned inwardly. Maybe it had been more than ten years. She still wrote to him from The Other place, though. Every year, on the final day of the year, he would receive a telegram from her. She would always say that she was well and happy in the peaceful place. She would always tell him to be a good Briton so that he could join her there one day.

'Hello there Briton? Help me please!' came a shout from an Operative at the station entrance. Everley couldn't quite see what was going on, but scrunched the hair back into his pocket and ran over right away.

A female Operative from his building was bending down and battling with something at her legs. As Everley got closer he could see that an InOperative clothed in nothing other than a small bed sheet was lying on the ground at her feet and pulling at her work trousers.

'Briton, please help me get this InOp away!' said the woman, who was struggling to both stay standing and keep her trousers up while the InOp tugged them.

Everley clasped the InOp's hands, but it shook about hectically and tussled free, only to take hold of her trousers once more. Everley tried again, but again the InOp untangled itself and grabbed the trousers. Possessed by the grip of the cold weather, the InOp was desperately scavenging for clothing... even if an Operative was already wearing it.

Without a thought, Everley lifted his foot and shot it forward. The thick and stiff outer material of his boot caught the InOp's chin, sending it rolling a few feet across the floor. A little line of blood dotted the corner of the bed sheet that the InOp was wearing. Everley noticed that the sheet had been stitched in such a way that something was written within the fabric: "Property of the Health Centre".

'That sheet is stolen,' Everley said matter-of-factly, turning to the female Operative who was readjusting her work trousers and dusting them off. 'Shall we take it back to the Health Centre?'

'Thank you for assisting, Briton!' she said, ignoring his question but extending a hand to salute and introduce herself. 'Operative Wilton.'

'Operative Everley. Pleased to meet you, Wilton,' he responded formally. As he did, he felt the familiarity of already knowing her or living through this present moment before. It was an unsettling sensation that faded as soon as he paid attention to it.

'P-P-Please h-h-help me! I'm f-f-freezing!' coughed the InOp from a kneeling position on the floor.

Everley and Wilton didn't speak. Both simply stared at the quivering heap with a look of disgust about their faces. Everley was drawn to the InOp's lips, which were the soft blue of a summer sky. The rest of its skin was almost as pale as the sheet it was wrapped in.

'We should lie it on the tracks,' stated Wilton. 'Let's wait until more Britons arrive to help us drag it away.'

Everley hummed in agreement, aware only then of movement behind them. He pivoted on his heel and instantly recognised the figure. It was Lyndon.

She wasn't far away, possibly ten strides or so, but it was undoubtedly her. He knew the slight frame, the flowing hair, the button nose, the patchwork clothes and the bolt of lightning that sparked through him at each meeting. He looked fixedly at her face and her eyes shined as they looked directly back at him.

Neither moved.

Her stance was that of disappointment – if it is possible to read disappointment from a distance. One of her arms was wrapped tightly around her own stomach, as though to cuddle herself in consolation. Her free arm held a hand to her own chin, as though to have been on the receiving end of Everley's kick.

Everley swallowed deeply.

Wilton hadn't noticed that anyone else was on the platform and was still speaking of some mode of killing the being, but the beat of Everley's heart drowned her Brito-born opinions out until they were but a muffle.

He *had* to talk to Lyndon. If only he could rebel against the voice inside, then he could tell her how she made his brain weak, his chest hurt and his stomach sick. He could ask her all of the questions about Brito, InOps, Ops and the PRORA that were still hiding in his mind, quietened by a long sleep but still there really, if he concentrated.

Focussed on each other, Everley took one step towards Lyndon.

Lyndon stepped back.

Everley stopped walking, but held out a hand as though to silently say 'Okay'.

'I suppose Brito will kill it with a frost if we just leave it here,' remarked Wilton.

'Pardon?' replied Everley as his attention was torn away.

'The InOp,' said Wilton, pointing, 'will die anyway if we just leave it here.'

Everley turned to see the InOp crawling slowly across the ground, wheezing, shaking and moving in the direction of a sheltered corner near the station entrance.

Everley glanced back and caught sight of Lyndon disappearing under the large hanging poster. It was too late to stop her and too risky with Wilton present. Unequipped to deal with the strange feelings that the sight of Lyndon induced in him, Everley sensed all of the curiosity, happiness, excitement and attraction slip away, only to be replaced with an uncontrollable rage.

He leapt over to the foul, freezing InOperative and grabbed the bed sheet. He yanked at it so forcefully that the InOp, clinging to it with all its might, lifted off the ground as the tug of war went to and fro. Everley punched, kicked, spat and saw red while jerking at the sheet until finally it was free.

The InOperative let out a snivelling moan as it lay there entirely naked.

'It will die now, that's for certain,' replied Everley to Wilton, who watched the occurrence with all the indifference of a fly being swat.

Everley span the sheet between his arms so that it rolled into an untidy ball.

'Here,' said Wilton, 'let's fold it. We can turn the bloody bits inwards so they don't infect anything.'

Everley nodded and released the sheet. Assisting each other in holding the corners and swapping hands over, they succeeded in methodically condensing the dirty sheet into the size of a piece of paper, clean sides facing outwards.

'I'll take it to the Health Centre after work,' said Everley as he unbuttoned his coat, tucked the sheet inside and under one arm, and zipped it back up.

All was silent at the top of the waterside Watch Tower. The tall structure looked like a colossal tee suitable only for a giant's game of golf.

Raines had plodded up the steep, spiral staircase of the seventy-metre tower shaft and was now alone in the open viewing station at the summit. Standing with arms crossed in the centre of the heptagonal room that was windowed on every side, he rotated his body slowly to get a panoramic view of the area in all directions.

The land and seascapes were as staggeringly picturesque as one would expect at such a height, but for Raines it was the feeling of familiarity that excited him the most. This had been his domain, and his first proper job. By working in the Watch Room of a Command site in the formative days of Brito, Raines had been part of putting the initial processes in place that had been obeyed for thirty years since. Nothing had changed, including the technology: a setup of computers receiving signals from autonomous air drones that patrolled Brito's borders.

In the viewing station, all tables, seats and computers were identical and each faced a window. Circling the room once or twice, Raines chose a chair and sat down. The computer display showed the words 'For Brito!' in a yellow, wavy font that floated around the black screen and bounced upon touching a corner. He poked the computer mouse to flick the screen-saver off and display the login page. He entered R-A-I-N-E-S on the keyboard, held his thumb to a fingerprint reader that was attached to the computer with a cable, and then waited the four or more minutes it took for the system to churn a little egg timer around and around before finally coming to life.

With the flair of an artiste, Raines tapped on the keys and swished the mouse about, finding the correct program and settings effortlessly. He had to admit, the action gave him the same sort of buzz as that of bumping into a sexual partner years later: a kind of vainglorious knowing that he had conquered the inner workings and could dexterously master it again, should the mood take his fancy.

He selected a drone number at random and the whole screen filled with the live feed from its on-board camera. It was as though Raines himself was in the air, and he couldn't help feeling lifted by the view. He switched the setting to manual, took hold of the control stick and soared the drone up and down while giggling like a child. It brought back all the fun of his first job; it was the only computer game one could play in Brito, and, thankfully, he had expelled all other Operatives from the Watch Tower for a few hours so that he could lark alone.

He swooped the drone from one turbine to the next and zoomed-in on Operatives as they walked between windmills, entered lower doors, emerged from exposed roofs, readied their tools and carried out their cleaning and maintenance tasks. None of the working Operatives paid attention to the loud whir of the drone's propellers, that being such a common coastal sound. All were busy in any case; each Operative was responsible for a small area of windmills and had a series of duties to complete.

Raines took the tatty notebook from his top pocket and bent it forward and backward so as to flatten where it had been folded in the middle. He placed it on the table and watched it slowly curl and spray its pages like a fan while he searched his other pockets for the pen. He thumbed the pages to find the last note and added simply, *'Day Three: All as expected. Operatives work systematically through their functional routines'.*

Before closing the book, he reflected happily on the robotic order with which every worker performed each task, as though they had been programmed to do so (which, of course, they had). They worked alone, but with such synchronicity that at one point Raines was sure he had accidentally focussed on the same Operative twice. He hadn't. Instead, it was the perfect doubling of their actions that had him temporarily disorientated. They moved purposefully, worked efficiently and had a methodical manner. He was pleased but not surprised that the Operatives continued restlessly, even without the presence of a manager. They worked for Brito compliantly and without question. It was a wondrous trick by Brito, he thought, knowing the laziness and waste that existed in old Britain before.

He added, *'Report result: programmed Operatives perform at maximum efficiency'*, to his note. He circled 'programmed' three times with the pen and then shut the book.

There was a sudden hiss of white noise that made Raines jump and look around the empty room.

'Whiskey Tango One, Whiskey Tango One, this is Sierra Three. Come in. Over,' came a faint voice through the foam headphones that were lying on the desk in front of him.

Raines scrambled to pick them up quickly and untangle the cable that was wrapped around them tightly. Flapping about, he managed to free one of the circle headphones and held it to his ear. There was a moment's silence followed by a second loud hiss that made him pull his head back and swear.

'Whiskey Tango One, Whiskey Tango One, this is Sierra Three. Come in. Over,' the voice repeated the call.

Raines was on autopilot. He pressed a button on the keyboard to activate the built-in microphone, and felt a thrill of excitement as he answered the call, 'Sierra Three, this is Whiskey Tango One. Go ahead. Over.'

'InOperative intruder in Sierra Three. Repeat. InOp intruder in Section. Over.'

Aware that all Operatives would be able to hear the transmissions, and may be distracted from their duties, Raines replied sternly, 'Roger. All other Operatives to continue their tasks. Repeat. All Operatives to continue their tasks. Over.'

'Wilco. Over,' echoed numerous different Operative voices in turn.

Raines continued to take control and Command the Operative who had made the call. 'Operative in Sierra Three, this is Whiskey Tango One. Come in. Over.'

'Go ahead. Over,' came the faint voice of the Operative in Section Three.

'Command order to detain InOp but do not destroy. Repeat. Detain but do not destroy. An Inspection Operative will be sent at the end of the shift. Over,' said Raines, thinking he could use another InOp for a reinforcement session at the next PRORA, so would arrange to have it collected and caged later.

There was a pause from the other end of the line.

'Do you copy? Over.' Raines tapped at the headphone, twiddled with the cable and squashed the foam closer to his ear before loudly calling, 'Operative in Sierra Three, come in! Do you copy? Over.'

'Roger. Over and Out,' replied the Operative in such an abrupt tone that Raines was left open-mouthed in offence.

Raines grabbed hold of the control stick and, following the navigation system, flew the drone directly to Section Three.

As soon as the drone reached the area it was immediately clear to see the Operative in his brilliant black, Brito-issued workwear against the otherwise vibrant yellow of the sand and soft greens of growing grass. Puffs of sand threw themselves into the air as the Operative rolled and wrestled on the ground with what must have been the intruding InOp.

Raines angled the control stick down hard, so as to drop the drone nearer to the scene, but stopped himself short. He knew that the loud sound of the drone's propellers would be heard if he got any closer and it had dawned on him that, for the benefit of his report, he should observe the events without interfering. The adrenaline had made his hands shake but, with them now away from the control stick, the drone hovered in the air as though anchored to the nearest cloud. Raines stood up and leaned tentatively towards the screen. His face was so close that his eyes twitched and his nose was but a whisker away.

The Operative's black clothes were smudged with sand as the two continued the frenzied fight. Raines couldn't make out the age, sex or appearance of the InOp through the tangle of limbs that wrangled on the ground. Soon enough, the Operative had the advantage and Raines watched him jostle and kick some distance between them. The InOp tried to rise but was shoved straight back down as the Operative lunged forward and started hitting. He was hitting and hitting and hitting the InOp with a fist to the face. It was relentless. It didn't stop.

With the hitting the only movement and the InOp lying motionless, the sand had settled and Raines could see a clearer feed from the drone above. The Operative was sat on top of the InOp, with a leg bent either side. His back was arched forwards and his left arm was plunged into the sand. His right arm was still hitting. And hitting. He was hitting just at the place the face would be, although Raines couldn't see it below.

Eager to get a better look, Raines grabbed the stick dipped the drone sharply. He locked it in position again, but this time much closer so that the screen was filled with the image of a fist throwing each rhythmic punch. Though the humming of the drone must have been heard by the Operative, the punches didn't stop.

Although the killing of InOps was an everyday act, there was an anger in this that took it a step further. It was the kind of killing Raines might do. It had more intent and passion-filled perseverance in it than Raines had ever been able to instil in Operatives at the PRORA. Despite his best efforts, they were always so damned efficient in their removal of waste.

The hitting continued until the sand around the site had turned a wet and muddy magenta. With one final punch, the Operative sat backwards and looked upon his work. As he slid from his straddled position over the InOp, the screen filled with the result of the violence. The face was mangled. There was nothing left of what was the jaw, the cheek or the eyes, but from the mess fanned a mane of long and blonde hair that was saturated with blood. It was a female InOp.

Raines had developed a pretty strong stomach for death over the years, but this one got him in the gut. His face contorted in revulsion. He rubbed his eyes and grabbed blindly at the control stick to bring the drone higher into the skies and the image beyond focus. When he looked back towards the screen, the Operative was merely a blob.

From the distance, Raines watched the figure produce a large white piece of material from somewhere unknown and drape it squarely over the red heap. Though it was a blur, Raines could see an attempt to wrap the body before hauling what was left of the InOp towards the water's edge. Despite the covering sheet, the dragging drew a long and straight red streak across the sand. With a kick, the

Operative sent the remains rolling into the sea, then turned back to the windmill and disappeared into the lower door.

Raines was left looking at the line of blood that crossed the landscape. He gazed at it, questioning whether what he had witnessed was good or bad for Brito. *'Was this too far? Had the programming gone wrong? Or was this a perfect solution?'*

'Capital!' Raines shouted into the speaker phone on the main desk of the Watch Tower, while pressing down on the button for the extension to his private office.

'How may I assist you Command?' was the prompt response.

'Read me the names of the Operatives in each section,' Raines demanded.

'Certainly. Section One, Bristow. Section Two, Harford. Section Three, Everley. Section Four...'

The Capital continued but Raines had stopped listening. He snatched the notebook from his pocket and hurriedly turned the crumpled pages to find the note he had written that morning: *'Everley (M) Absent Day One'*. Raines took his pen and scratched a square around the name 'Everley' so hard that it etched the pages beneath it. He underlined it a few more times for good measure.

Some private investigation was required to understand the significance of what Raines had just witnessed. Though the employment of violence may have been the greatest success to come out of the PRORA, he couldn't stop the sinking feeling that the show of deep hatred indicated a critical failure to control free will.

VIII

*'North Brito would like to commend the five
Operatives at Point D for efficiently culling a cohort
of InOps in their area.*

*This is an opportunity to remind all of you to do
your Brit; follow the oath and ensure the survival of
our safe land.*

*To break the oath is to be banished for risking the
lives of your fellow Britons and our dear Brito.'*

- Television News Operative

Everley was curled into a tight ball against the wall on the floor of
his quarters. His knees were pressed firmly against his chest as his
arms squeezed hard around them. His forehead was planted to his
forearms and he looked down into the dark hole he had created by
the position of his body. With his face pushed into his skin he hoped
his sniffs and sobbing could not be heard by his neighbours. Tears
had been falling from his eyes for some time now and were puddling
in the folds of his naked stomach and the creases of his bended legs.

The image of the InOp beneath him as he killed it, one blow at
a time, replayed in his head in such vivid technicolour that he felt
he was watching a television with eyes pinned open, unable to look
away. The ground was golden yellow, the sun lit him from the sky
with a blinding and almost-metallic spotlight, and the InOp's skin
turned pink to white to black and purple and blue. Flashes of

burgundy blood splashed upwards as he watched his own fist pound down relentlessly.

Thwack! Thwack! Thwack!

He could hear it. His muscles pulsated with every recollected smack. He couldn't shake the sound or vision of human bones breaking by his own hand, which was now throbbing.

The *BUZZ BUZZ BEEP BEEP BEEP* of the alarm sounded from the speaker in the corridor. It marked another night without sleep.

Everley rose slowly to his feet using the wall to steady himself. With a big sniff he wiped one eye and then the other with the butt of his hand. Turning his hand over, he then stared at his bruised knuckles and the skin in between that was grazed, torn and feathered upwards.

Marching straight to the showers, he was first in. He had to wash himself first, so there was no time for the toilet. Instead, he peed where he stood and let it trickle into the plug hole. With his left hand, he held his right under the violent high pressure of water that shot from the ceiling. He flinched as the water stabbed at the tender skin, but kept it there to wash the blood out. He had forgotten his soap in his room, but with what he estimated to be another twenty-or-so seconds left under the automated spray, Everley scoured his fingers roughly through his hair and then rubbed up and down both legs and arms just in time before the shower clicked off.

He moved straight to the sink to brush his teeth and avoided the dry cycle, which was whirring away behind him. Glancing upwards, he was presented with himself in the mirror. He dropped the toothbrush into the sink and, with both hands around the mirror's edges, moved his face closed to the reflection until the only things that he could see with any focus were his own eyes.

'Are you so inhuman?' he said aloud, narrowing his eyes in disgust.

The tears came again.

Everley spat into the sink to activate the automatic tap and grabbed at the water, throwing it at his face to drown those tears and wash them away. With wet skin still, he unlocked the door and squelched his sopping feet back down the corridor no more than two minutes after he had left his room.

'Briton! You have forgotten this!' came the voice of a neighbour from behind him, wielding a toothbrush in the air.

Everley didn't reply. He raced into his room, slammed the door of his quarters behind him and then stopped. He held both hands hard around his mouth with all the force his energy could afford and let out a muffled scream.

As Everley headed towards Point A and raced at pace through the InOp area, he could hear his name being called in a voice he recognised. The sound was somewhere in the distance and he dismissed it, not wanting to be disturbed.

'Ever-ley!' came a breathless cry from behind, accompanied by the rhythmic sound of boots crushing rubble underfoot as their owner ran across the InOp wasteland.

Everley glanced back quickly and saw a figure he knew and had been avoiding in favour of simply getting to work, working for Brito and not being distracted by his own curiosity on the subject of Special Projects. He continued his walk to the station.

'Operative Everley, you WILL stop on a Capital's command!' was shouted from behind, causing Everley to stop as immediately as the pausing of time.

With his back to the figure, he could hear running footsteps get closer until he felt the sudden presence of the Capital and a strong touch on his shoulder.

'Capital Selby!' Everley said and saluted, still facing away.

With his hand forward and firmly gripping Everley's left shoulder, Selby rotated himself around to the front so that the two were face to face. Selby began to speak the same sentence a couple of times but was too out of breath, so paused to allow air to reach his lungs.

'Why,' he began, croaking a little, 'why didn't you stop when I called to you?'

Both stood with their stances mirroring and their eyes fixed on each other. With his hand locked on Everley's shoulder, Selby could feel him tremoring.

'Please accept my apologies, Capital Selby.'

Selby watched Everley's pupils shake and lashes blink as a bucketful of emotion hid within his eyes.

'It is forgiven. How are you feeling today, son?' Selby moved his head forward a small amount in an attempt to read more from the watery sorrow of Everley's eyes.

'How is it that I know you, Capital Selby?' Everley asked with a helplessness in his tone.

Selby's touch and the sound of his voice provided all the security of a mother's protective cuddle. This sensation of such certain safety caused a single tear to escape from Everley's eye, run down the side of his nose and sit in its crease.

'We will come to that later,' said Selby. 'Tell me what has happened.'

'I don't know if I am a good Briton or a bad Briton!' As Everley replied, all of the emotion he was trying so desperately to hold inside started spilling out of him. He began to weep and whimper and pant. 'I, I, I—' he tried to speak but his throat was clogged with grief.

'Everley, look at me! I will help you.' Selby moved Everley towards a stack of concrete slabs. He brushed the dirt away with one hand, making sure not to release Everley's shoulder with the other, and said, 'Let's sit here. We have plenty of time until the train. You can talk to me.'

They both bent and sat on the slabs. With not a lot of room, the sides of their thighs touched as they settled there together.

'I murdered a female InOp,' started Everley.

'The one at the station?!' Selby asked, surprised.

'No, not her.'

'Oh, okay. Carry on.'

Realising that Selby had been there that day that he had fainted, Everley said, 'Thank you for helping me with *that* situation... Why did you help me?' He looked up at Selby with more questions forming in his mind.

'We will come to that later,' said Selby, who then smirked as he scoffed, 'Cleaning waste from Brito by getting rid of an InOp is not *murder*, Everley!'

'I did murder her! I was not only getting rid of waste. I murdered her out of anger,' Everley paused, 'and at that moment, I, I,' he looked at his feet and said solemnly, while shaking his head, 'I enjoyed it.'

'It is right and good that you feel good about ridding Brito of waste, Everley! It is right and good that you are angry at the InOps because they drain Brito of its resources. They are *not* part of our One. You *are* a good Briton!'

'You don't understand, Capital!' Everley threw his head into the air. 'I was not operating *efficiently*. I have played it over in my mind and I know that what I did was not true Briton behaviour. I will tell you what I have done, and you will punish me, Capital.'

'Tell me. I will help you.'

Everley began easily. He wanted to vocalise the event so that it could, he hoped, be released from his mind where it had been tormenting him for every second of the thirteen hours since.

'I noticed an InOp in my Section while I was working at the waterside windmills. I called to the Watch Tower on the radio and they sent a command to detain the InOp but not destroy it. *Detain it?* I remember thinking that surely I should destroy it, but I was prepared to comply with Tower orders, so I fetched some rope from my kit bag and headed to where I had seen it.

'As I got closer, I could see the InOp was a female. It reminded me of Lyndon – the InOp at Point A station. I am sorry, Capital, I know how wrong it is to mingle with the wasteful, but I have spoken to the InOp Lyndon on occasion and I find her to be...'

'Go on.'

'Beautiful,' he said quietly, with eyes now closed as though he was picturing her standing in front of him.

'Go on, Everley.'

'I cannot explain it and I do not understand it, but her beauty fills my insides with a burning fire. It's like flames start in my stomach and roar up my chest and down my legs, melting me like one of the candles that Brito gives the Night Shifters for their lanterns. I want her. I know that's wrong. I accept any punishment. I have tried to distance myself from her, though, and when the InOp invaded my Section and reminded me of Lyndon, it made me angry. I was angry that I wanted something that was wrong and that I desired something that was shameful. I directed my anger at that InOp and I couldn't stop myself. Before I knew it, her head had crumbled as though it was made out of sand and I was covered in blood.'

'Everley, you once said to me that InOps cause you anger to feed your passion to work harder, be a better Operative and use your life to serve our Brito.' Selby patted him on the shoulder with the hand that rested there, and pointed into Everley's face with a finger of the other. 'YOU said that *if an InOp dies by their own hands or by OURS, so be it.*'

'I don't remember saying that. There are many things I am not remembering at the moment. Are you not going to punish me for the feelings I have told you about?'

Selby hesitated for a moment. Now was not quite the time to tell Everley everything about The Hidden. But Selby did want to provide some reassurance to end this visible anguish.

'We will come to that later. What you need to know now is that you are special. You have feelings, and those feelings will become

119

more and more important. In time, I will come to you about that Special Project—'

'The Special Project! I have questions about that too,' interrupted Everley.

'But before we get to that,' Selby continued his previous sentence, 'I want you to try to understand those feelings. I want you to think about them rather than stopping them. It is in trying to contain your free will and emotion that your anger has led you to...' he tailed off, thinking carefully about his phrasing before ending with, 'rid Brito of its waste inefficiently.'

Everley nodded. 'When my mind replays what I did, it's like watching it on the television. I hit her in the face thirty-six times. Thirty-six! That's what I've counted. I didn't see that at the time and I don't remember delivering thirty-six blows!' He held his head in both hands and spoke through the gap in between, 'That InOp represented all that has been confusing and worrying and fearful to me recently. I wasn't just hitting an InOp, I was hitting everything that had been hurting my mind, stopping me sleep, making me ill and preventing me doing my duties as a good Briton.'

Lifting his head to looked at Selby with red eyes and wet cheeks, Everley added, 'I live for Brito.'

'Operative Everley,' Selby hushed as an adult does to a child who has fallen and grazed a knee, 'you are closer to understanding what it is to be human than you know.'

'So I am not inhuman?' said Everley with wide eyes so full of relief that his whole face lifted.

'You are special, Everley. Remember these words.' Selby squeezed his shoulder tightly. He could feel an uncontrollable hum of empathy rising in his own chest caused by the sight of Everley struggling with something so confusing to a Briton as natural human emotion.

'I have so many questions. Please will you help me?' begged Everley.

'I will. For now, you need to be calm. You need to allow thoughts and feelings in. Think about them. Try to understand what they mean. We will talk again. Tomorrow. Here. At the same time. Okay?'

Everley nodded silently and looked happy for the first time in some time.

'Now, we must have a utile day and get to work!' Selby smiled, stood, and took his hand from Everley's shoulder.

Both marched in unison to Point A, talking of lighter things: a shortage of nutrition tablets, productivity percentages and, of course, the weather.

Other than the occasional bright light that zoomed past, all else was black out of the Speed Line's windows on Everley's journey home that evening. It was fast approaching eight o'clock and his twelve-hour shift was almost finished. Work had provided a pleasant distraction from all that had unsettled him recently and it had been a productive day. He felt a sense of satisfaction for completing his duties efficiently and surpassing his performance quota. Recalling Selby's instruction, he made a mental record of the feelings: *I have pride in my work. My work gives me purpose. This purpose gives me safety. I feel proud, fulfilled and secure.* He repeated the last statement a number of times so as to memorise it. He would make sure to recite it to Selby tomorrow.

Everley was feeling tired. He had used his midday rest minutes to brush sand over the bloody mark where the InOp had been and erase any sign of what he had done. Although he was sure his Highers would approve of his removal of waste, he had been commanded to detain the InOp and was conscious that in destroying it he had not followed orders. All day he was on tenterhooks expecting to be called to the Watch Tower about the matter, but the call didn't come. Perhaps tomorrow. He did notice the noisy presence of an air drone in his Section for longer than was usual, only to conclude that this was probably due to a rise in calls on the radio about InOp intruders.

The Speed Line juddered as the brakes were applied on the approach into the station. Supported only by holding the ceiling bars, the sudden slowing sent every Operative forward, sideways and into each other's backs or armpits, causing a chorus of humourless apologies. Thankfully, Everley was at the front so was able to steady himself against the sturdiness of the carriage. He beamed, knowing how much he enjoyed the unpredictability of the train's uncontrolled movements and acknowledged the exhilaration: *I feel excited.*

He paid attention to his heart, which was beating a little louder it seemed, as he waited for the train door to slide open. When he stepped onto the platform the cold wind clouted him with all the might of a bucket of water. Wanting to enjoy the feeling of the icy air on his skin, he stood to one side to let the other Operatives past, which took a minute or so.

'For Brito!' came the cheer of the many queuing night shift Operatives who were waiting to board, along with a clapping applaud.

'For Brito!' waved Everley and the other day Operatives in return.

The platform emptied as the day Operatives departed and the Night Shifters boarded the Speed Line. Everley, still standing on the edge, noticed how silent Point A became as soon as the train left and vanished down the tracks. He lowered himself to the floor and sat there with his legs dangling over the edge. It was peaceful.

'Little Lyndon! Little Lyndon!' There was a panicked shout from the opposite edge of the platform, followed by a pained wail.

Everley knew the voice and hurriedly jumped to his feet.

'Lyndon!'

'YOU!' Lyndon cried, stopping in her tracks. 'Stay away from me!'

'Lyndon?'

'I watched what you did to that freezing InOp who had nothing in this world except a bed sheet. He froze to death right there!' She nodded to a doorway.

'I'm sorry I didn't meet you here the other evening. I was unwell and—'

'I thought you were different! You are inhuman!' Lyndon screamed. Her hair was ruffled into a fuzziness that made it look bigger, her clothing was torn and there was a red mark – a deep cut – on her dirty face.

'I am! I am! I have been *feeling* things! I need to tell you all about it! I am different. Capital Selby said I was 'special'...' Everley fumbled for words. 'Please, I just need time to think and to talk to you and I will be human!' He moved forward, wanting to see her in the light and for her to see him. He was desperate for her not to leave.

'Different?! You're all the same. Look what you Ops do!' Trembling violently, she pointed towards the cut on her face, lifted part of her clothing to show an equally deep wound on her stomach. Her face then contorted as she seemed to explode into tears and fall into a bundle on the platform.

'I will show you I am different. I will help you!' Everley ran forward and put his arms around her instinctively, as his mother had once done to him.

'Get off me! Stay away!' Lyndon whimpered while pushing away, only to relent and ease into his protective hold.

'I will help you, Lyndon. I can go to the Health Centre for supplies to fix you.' Everley felt in that moment that he would do anything to make her better.

'I need to find Little Lyndon,' she said, more calmly now. 'If you help me find him, then—'

'We will find him together,' said Everley, tapping her on the shoulder to reassure her. He had learnt that from Selby. 'Do you know where he went?'

'When the Ops attacked me, I told him to run as fast and as far as he could. I thought they were going to kill me, but I managed to bite one of them and get away. He is always playing at Point A so I thought he would be here... but he's not. He won't survive alone. We *have* to find him!'

'We will,' Everley replied, helping her gently to her feet, 'We will. We will do it together, so you don't get hurt again. And then, when we find him, I will go and get medical supplies for your wounds.'

Lyndon whispered a 'Thank you' as she regained her balance and her lips bent into a faint yet uncertain smile.

'Let's start in the InOp area, don't you think?'

'It's this way. We will have to be careful.'

Lyndon pulled Everley's hand to lead him towards the large hanging poster on the side of the platform. She folded it upwards and signalled for him to crawl underneath. As he stepped forward, Everley became aware of his surroundings and took a look around the station to see if they were being watched. Thank Brito, all was still and there was no sign of any other person. He felt his heart leap as he shuffled beneath the poster and into the unknown world behind it.

IX

Beyond the large hanging poster on the platform was an entire world of disorder so different to the efficient and organised Operative existence. Everley had seen it on his long walks through the InOp area and from the windows of the Speed Line, but stepping through it now – hand-in-hand with an InOp – cast a new light on the dark and dreary landscape.

The ground underfoot was uneven and difficult to walk on. Aside from having to spot and dodge any gaps in the rubble where one could fall and twist an ankle, the mass of mounds moved as soon as they were trodden on. These hideous hills were made from the broken remnants of things Everley recognised, like cracked cups or ceramic toilet bowls or parts of chairs, tables and building materials. But there were also things that Everley didn't recognise at all, like little things with little screens (that were smashed) that looked like miniature televisions. Or biggish box-shaped shiny things that had a door you could see through with buttons beside. And there were lots and lots of small-sized cylindrical containers made from a transparent hard material and all with different coloured lids. The more he looked, the more he saw of these things: there certainly was enough for more than a hundred for each and every Briton, whatever they were.

Every single item was so marked and dirty that Everley felt unclean in this close proximity, but it was the terrain that frightened him most. He was sure that the land itself was alive; it moved of its own accord as though it was breathing, causing objects to slide and fall from precarious places. It even seemed plausible that the piles of waste could grab, snatch and gobble a person up without warning.

Until this moment, Everley had looked upon the wasteland as entertainment. It was the place where the worthless class wasted what little of their lives they had on feeding, sleeping and misbehaving. And doing the latter two on top of the rubble or underneath the shelters made from badly balanced broken bricks. Tonight it didn't seem so amusing. *This* was Lyndon's living area, and it didn't appear to be comfortable at all.

'Here, quick!' Lyndon said as she pulled Everley to the shelter of a leaning piece of waved metal. They scurried into the tight triangular space and watched a group of InOps come closer and slowly shuffle past their hiding place, not noticing them there.

'It's dangerous for an Op here,' Lyndon whispered and clasped Everley's arm. 'You should go back. I'll look for Little Lyndon by myself.'

'No! I want to help you. I *have* to.' He took his cuff and dabbed her cheek of the wet blood that glistened in the little light they had. He knew the action would calm her, just as it had calmed him when Selby had done it. He thought how much he had already learnt from Selby.

'But if they see you here in their area, alone without any other Ops, they'll...' she inhaled, 'I have an idea.' Lyndon grinned.

Lyndon reached forward to Everley slowly and began to unfasten his coat. As she moved downwards from one button to the next, the cold of her icy fingers skimmed against his naked chest. The touch sent a flutter through Everley so thrilling that he was sure he had stopped breathing altogether. He shuddered as she reached the final button. She slipped her hands into the opening, flattened her palms on his torso and rubbed them delicately upwards and over his shoulders so as to push his coat open and slide it from his back.

Everley was grateful that the cool air immediately made him shiver, hoping it had concealed the shakes her touch had caused.

Lyndon held the coat between her knees and then removed her own clothing – a patchwork cape of various materials – by pushing it over her head. She held it out to Everley. He didn't take it, so fixated on her naked body that his mind could think of nothing else. He felt himself get hot and sweaty, and his trousers tighten.

'Blame it!' he cursed quietly as he turned away from her and pushed his head into the metal shelter. 'I'm sorry, I don't understand what is happening to me,' he huffed.

'Take it. We can't hide here much longer or we'll be found,' Lyndon said, holding the clothing around and to the front of him.

Everley took it slowly and, without turning, raised it up and pulled it over his head. The assorted pieces of cloth and other, harder materials started to itch his skin straight away. It was heavy, irritating and thorny to wear and it smelt a little funny too. It smelt old.

Everley could hear Lyndon fumbling with the coat, so continued to cower in the corner. He waited, hoping she would hurry to put it on and save him from seeing her beauty again. He knew that he would not be able to control himself if he saw her nakedness. Never had a naked Operative made him feel this way, he thought, and then reminded himself that, more worryingly, this was an InOp.

When the rustling stopped, Everley turned around. Lyndon was wearing his coat, only it was turned inside out.

'It's not perfect, but it should avoid any suspicion,' she said. 'Ready to go?'

'Wait, what else must I do to *fit in*? What do InOps talk like and walk like... and what do they do?!' Everley asked, with a deeply concerned crinkle of the eyebrows.

Lyndon grabbed hold of her nose and mouth, trying to stop the volume of her laugh being heard from outside their hiding place.

'You Operatives are so oblivious!'

'What do you mean?'

'You have no idea! You are blind, unaware robots without minds!' she chuckled condescendingly.

Everley looked both puzzled and offended, but did not reply.

'It's not your fault Brito has made you this way.' Lyndon puckered her lips together to stop herself giggling and continued, 'InOps are just like you! We talk the same as you, we walk the same as you and we try to *do* the same as you – that is to live a purposeful life... Only there is nothing in Brito for us to do, so we scavenge to keep ourselves alive. Imagine you are you, only without the safety of your living quarters and your work. Make sense?'

Everley bowed his head to show he had understood, but his face remained twisted with confusion.

There was another noise from outside the shelter; a crunching on the craggy ground made them both flinch and freeze. Lyndon pointed to Everley with her forefinger and put the same finger to her lips and shook her head to tell him to not say a word. There was a knocking and a pulling at the metal of the shelter and it was obvious that in less than two seconds they would be found. Lyndon whipped past Everley and out into the open, taking him with her by the hand.

'This is my shelter!' she said confidently.

Four InOps were standing in front of them, all a bit older than Everley but much paler and weaker-looking. They were fatter though, which surprised Everley as he had never been able to determine what they ate (except worms). The moonlight illuminated the aggression on their faces and Everley knew that, when the same light lit his face, they would see that he was cleaner and leaner... *and his hair was tidy.* He was certain it was only a matter of time before they looked beyond the InOp cloth he was wearing and detected the imposter in their territory. Petrified, he tugged Lyndon by the hand to suggest that they should run. She didn't move.

'Lyndon, what's happened to your face?' said the larger of the three males with the bushiest of beards, stepping closer.

'Hello there Fulton,' said Lyndon calmly. 'Oh, I misjudged my footing. I fell from the rubble behind the station onto a washing machine!' Lyndon said with a small, nervous and awkward laugh.

'And who is this?' said Fulton as he arched to the side to get a proper look of Everley, who was silently quaking behind Lyndon and pleadingly pulling at her hand.

'He's new,' she said and then changed the subject. 'Will you all help me to find Little Lyndon? He was playing earlier and now I can't find him.'

'New? What happened?' Fulton quizzed, eyeballing Everley.

'What was it? Eh? Get ill, did you? What's wrong with you? I don't want to catch it!' chirped another of the InOps standing behind Fulton. He was the untidiest, wearing a hard shiny box with arm holes cut into it and naked from the thighs down.

Lyndon moved her body so that she was directly in front of Everley to shield him and said, 'He's helping me find Little Lyndon. If you don't want to help, then—'

'Or decide you didn't want to operate anymore, did you? So you've *chosen* this life then? Surely not. Must be mad,' the untidy one carried on.

'New? We haven't had a new one in over a year. I thought they stopped banishing defective Ops to *this* InOp area. Where's he from? Let me talk to him,' said Fulton, attempting to reach around Lyndon and drag Everley forward.

'He's from another InOp area,' Lyndon spluttered, searching for a lie. 'I meant he's new *here*. Anyway, about Little Lyndon—'

'What's going on, Lyndon? He doesn't look like one of us,' puffed Fulton.

'Too clean to be one of us,' another InOp shouted from further back.

'He's not one of us,' a fourth InOp stated brutally.

'Where did you get those trousers?' asked the untidy one.

Fulton used all of his weight to scramble past Lyndon, grab Everley and wrench him forwards so that the two were nose-to-nose. With the power of the movement, Lyndon was thrown to the ground. The other InOps gathered quickly around Everley, who trembled on his tip-toes while Fulton held him by the throat. Heaving from their shared aggravation, their hot breaths caused a bitter, stinking mist to surround them all.

'Lump him one, Fulton! Then he'll talk!' shouted the untidy one.

'Shh!' Fulton hissed at his comrade. Turning back to Everley, he squeezed a little tighter at his neck and declared, 'You heard him though. I might, you know! I will if you don't talk! You better tell us who you are or you're going to get it!'

'Please Fulton, we don't want any trouble. We just want to find the little one,' begged Lyndon, lying on the ground. 'Don't hurt,' she hesitated, realising she didn't even know Everley's name, 'him.'

Everley did nothing but shake. He could say or do not a thing because in that moment he thought exclusively of the fact he was going to die. He had only seen death when he was causing it, but never before had he considered a scenario where he would die. At once, there was no doubt in his mind that this strong InOp could mash his neck in his big hand like the last wet remnant of a strip of soap.

'Who are you? Speak! Tell us if you are one of us or an Operative?' Fulton screeched into Everley's face, splattering him with saliva on every 's', 'p' and 't'.

Everley's brain had silenced the scene and he could hear only the voice inside. Fear was a feeling, and he was paying attention to it. The voice asked him, *'Why are you scared?'* and *'What is your life for, anyway?'* His life was for Brito, he reminded himself as he chanted inwardly, *'Get to work. Work for Brito. Hate the InOps.'*

Everley's mind raced. If he should die, it would simply mean that there was one less Operative to work for Brito. But the voice was right; if that be the case then he shouldn't be feeling fear.

Perhaps he was petrified because, for the first time, he wondered whether his life may be worth more.

With almighty force, Fulton punched Everley in the abdomen. Everley folded into two, clutching his stomach, wheezing and helplessly winded. He choked and heaved and began coughing uncontrollably. As he coughed, he showered spit over the others, and as the cough subsided he began to dribble, stagger and then drop into the stack of waste behind him.

'He *is* ill! See! Argh! I need to wipe this off!' said the untidy one, looking disgusted while backing away. The other InOps quickly followed.

'Forget him, Fulton, we need to clean ourselves. I don't want to catch anything,' said the last, who then turned and was gone.

Realising he was now alone, Fulton took a couple of steps back.

'I'm going now, okay, but this isn't the end of it. I'm coming back and, when I do, I want to know what is going on! Lyndon, *you* are one of us and we need an explanation.' Holding his hands outward as if they were coated in contaminant, he too recoiled into the night.

Lyndon sprang to her feet and over to Everley.

'Get up! Get up! We have to leave NOW!' She shook Everley frantically until his eyes fully opened and focussed.

'They didn't kill me... Why didn't they kill me?' he said, a little dazed.

'Kill you? Kill you! We don't just kill people!... I suppose InOps aren't like Operatives after all. *We* are human.'

She hauled him to his feet as quickly but as carefully as possible and, once sure he was able, she took his hand and led him into the depths of the InOp area.

They reached the very edge of the area approximately an hour of jogging later. All the way, they had shouted for Little Lyndon but hadn't found him. It was late, dark and very cold for a community with limited clothing, so thankfully the land was quiet, the InOps were in their shacks and there had been no other run-ins with the locals.

'There is a place I used to call home near here, before I was moved into the main InOp area. I'm hoping the little one sought shelter there, where it will be safe,' said Lyndon.

'When I lived at school, I sent myself to sleep each night by thinking I was walking to Mother's quarters. I knew every turn and every step. And when I arrived – in my imagination – I pictured getting into bed. As soon as my head hit that imaginary pillow, I was asleep. I'm sure Little Lyndon remembers the way home, too.'

Lyndon smiled at Everley, seeing some human in him.

The two arrived at the place Lyndon once lived, but all had changed.

'The tree has gone!' she said, looking up to the sky and down at the ground. 'This is the place though, I know it is! The trees have moved further back and the rubbish piles have grown... But it definitely was here.'

Under the light of the moon and a sky full of stars, a huge mountain of litter towered before them. So tall and wide and grimy as the vast scrapyard around it, this colossal peak looked as though it had erupted from the wasteland itself like a pus-filled spot. Everley was wide open-mouthed as he stepped closer to study the myriad of paper, materials and colourful things that held it together. The debris of a previous age.

'What's this?' he said, pulling a square crinkly and crackly packet with a bright red outer and a silver inner slowly from the stack. He handed it to Lyndon.

'I don't know,' she said, flattening it over her knee, rubbing the brown dirt off it and holding it close to her eyes. She shrugged, holding it up to Everley and pointing at red text on the front, 'What's this word?'

'I've never seen it before. S-s-' he paused before attempting to read the foreign word, then tried again, 'It's *sp-ahy-see*, I think.'

'Spicy. What does "spicy" mean?'

'I don't know. Here's another.' Everley plucked a second item from the pile. It was yellow. 'This one says *t-ting-glee pr-aw-n*.'

'What does that mean?'

'I have no idea. Up here it says "great new taste", see?' he pointed at the corner of the wrapper, 'so it must be a packet for something you put in your mouth. Maybe it was a bag of nutrition tablets,' Everley deduced. 'They do taste a bit strange sometimes.'

'How curious that they were in such colourful bags... Come on, let's find the little one.'

'Of course,' said Everley, who was midway through gingerly sliding another item from the mound so as to not cause an avalanche. It resembled an extraordinarily thin book of maybe thirty large sheets of paper that were not bound, but rather folded together. The title read *The Daily British Bulletin* in large letters, and underneath was an image of what appeared to be a circle of white lines against a black background. A slightly smaller title read *'Films, fashion, and now fireworks banned in Britain'* followed by lots of words split into four columns. Everley folded it into three vertically and pushed it into the top of his trousers so that he could read it later.

'Little Lyndon!' they called harmoniously while circling the mountain of junk.

'Look!' said Everley, rushing towards an edge that had fallen in on itself creating a deep, waste-filled hole. 'What if he fell in?!'

They both lunged forward and onto their knees. With fretful haste, they reached into the hole and scraped out the rubbish within it.

'Little one!' Lyndon wailed as they reached what felt like a solid bottom.

'Maaa!' came a child's cry from not too far away.

'Thank Brito!' said Everley as the two looked at each other in relief that he was not lost in the rubble. 'There he is!'

Behind Lyndon, from between the open doors of a brown cupboard, smiled and waved a small boy.

Lyndon raced across the wasteland and fetched him up with both hands. She squeezed his little body and kissed him all over. Everley hadn't moved, but watched from where he stood. It had been a long time since his own mother (or any other person) had held him with such tenderness, but simply viewing this embrace had brought him some warmth. He brushed himself down and wondered whether he should head back to his quarters. His work was complete; he had kept his word and helped Lyndon. His questions about Brito, InOps, Ops and the PRORA could wait until another time because she was happy now, he thought.

'Is he well?' called Everley loudly.

'Perfectly well!' she replied, her joy evident in the song of her voice.

'I will go and get you the medical supplies.'

'No, don't go!' Lyndon replied.

Everley watched as she bent to say something to the child, waggled her finger, cuddled the boy one more time and then raced back towards him.

'I told you I would help you. I can help by getting medicine. I want to show you that I am different,' Everley said as soon as she was close enough to hear.

'You have helped,' smiled Lyndon, 'And I have seen that you are different. Whatever you have done to break away from the bondage of Brito's control, you must keep doing it!'

'I am feeling,' Everley beamed. 'Capital Selby told me to take notice of my feelings. I feel happy for you now, Lyndon.'

'You *are* human.'

Everley's face filled with gladness.

'I don't need medical supplies tonight. Stay a little later and go back to the station at dawn. The InOps will still be asleep then,' she said while taking one of his hands and clasping it between both of her own.

'Oh... Okay.'

'Little Lyndon has found a bit of our old home – the cupboard. Let's sit there.'

'That was your home?!' Everley couldn't hide his surprise. He reminded himself that he was an Operative, with the safety of sanitary and heated quarters.

'A bit of it, yes.' As though she had read his mind, she added, 'I know it's not much, but it used to be somewhere safe to stay. I do miss being housed by Brito. You're warm, you're clean, you're comfortable. *You're* lucky.'

Everley wanted to ask her more about that, but she had already started walking back to the boy. Upon seeing Everley, the child shot into the cupboard and shut the door in fright.

Knock. Knock.

Lyndon grinned at Everley as she knocked on the cupboard door as though it was that of a house.

'Who's there?' came a muffled voice from within.

'It's Ma and I've got a kind visitor with me.'

'Who is he?'

'His name is... is...' She turned and whispered to Everley, 'I don't even know your name!'

'My name is Operative Everley,' he said, and then saluted like a robot that had just been switched on.

Unsurprisingly, there was a stunned silence from inside the cupboard.

Lyndon held her hand to her face and shook her head. 'Operatives!' she said to the sky, then turned to Everley to say softly, 'You are not only an Operative. You are a human too, remember? Try again.'

Everley cleared his throat and put his hand to the door.

Knock. Knock.

'Who's there?'

'My name is Everley. Everley the human. I will not hurt you or your mother.'

'Better,' smiled Lyndon, 'I think!'

The door of the cupboard carefully opened and a little face appeared from the darkness.

'Don't hurt Ma!' the boy said as though to give an order.

'I won't,' said Everley, reaching out to the child's shoulder and patting it three times, just as Selby had done to him.

'Everley is learning how to be a good person and we are going to help him because he helped me tonight. Now, let's get you tucked up tightly so that you can get some rest.' She lay Little Lyndon in the cupboard, grabbed a stack of papers, unfolded them and packed them around him layer after layer. 'There, nice and warm. Good night little one,' she said sweetly as she gave him a final kiss on the forehead and shut the creaky door.

With the child found and soundly asleep, Everley and Lyndon took a position close by and sat as comfortably as capable on the sediment of a lost civilisation. At first, neither said very much, both too conscious of the social chasm between them. Slowly but surely they spoke a little more easily but of generic topics, like how beautifully clean Brito was in the Operative areas, and how efficient, and how awful old Britain must have been by comparison, and how fortunate they both were to be born to Brito.

Everley gushed over the perfection of Brito and its systems and said how strong it would continue to grow without the influence of outsiders. After all, there were only Operatives and InOps in Brito.

And there were no enemies, except for the InOps themselves. InOps were the disease that would one day be gone, leaving no enemies to Brito at all. As he reached the point he was making, he stopped and looked at Lyndon.

'But you *were* an Operative too. Why are you an enemy now?'

'I'm not an enemy, Everley,' she replied.

'Why don't you come back? You can be an Operative again!' he said with the innocence of a child.

'I can't come back. It's not that simple. I have Little Lyndon.'

'He can go and live in school, and then he will be an Operative once he completes his years there. He might even grow up to be a Capital! Or a Command! If he managed to find his way here, then he's sensible enough to—'

'Little Lyndon is an InOp,' she interrupted. 'He was born an InOp. He has only InOp blood. He will not be accepted into a Brito school because it dilutes the Operative bloodline, you know that.'

Everley leaned back and shook his head in disbelief. 'He will be destroyed. But you... you said... but you said that you were an Operative! And he has your name! I don't understand!'

Lyndon stood up and carefully trudged down the slope to a rectangular area where the rubbish was at its flattest. Standing there below Everley, who remained seated on the synthetic hillock above her, she had the stage to tell her story.

Lyndon had indeed been an Operative by birth. Her mother, also named Lyndon, had been an Operative but had gone to The Other Place when Lyndon was just nine years old and after an accident pressing sheets in a Necessaries Workhouse left her unable to walk. Lyndon had been living at school at the time so had limited memories of her mother, except for a vague recollection of her facial features. She had always strained to retain the image of that face, knowing it would help to find her in The Other Place. But the memory didn't matter anymore. Now that she was an InOp, Lyndon knew that she would never get to go there.

As soon as she had completed school, Lyndon had been assigned to a sector and took the train from Point A to Point G for the ten-to-ten shift as a Nutrition Workhouse Operative. She had enjoyed the hypnotic efficiency of watching powder pouring into big drums, heavy and strong machines pressing it into billions of identical tablets that lay on conveyor belts in long lines with perfect regularity before cascading, one hundred at a time, into small cylindrical cans that had been salvaged from old Britain. Lyndon's job had been to "top the tins" by scrunching up pieces of paper (again, recycled from times past), and shoving them into the open tops of the tins so that they could be delivered Brito-wide without their contents falling out. There had been many times when Lyndon had scraped her knuckles on the sharp metal edges of those tin cans. She rubbed her hand as she recollected it.

Despite the stiffening strain to her wrists from the repetitive movements, the pangs of pain down both legs from the hours of standing and the brain-benumbing boredom from the task itself, Lyndon had been dedicated to Brito and satisfied with her life. Like all other Operatives, she had delighted in the verifiable truth that she had a purpose. She swore the oath and worked tirelessly to be a cog in the Brito machine: functional when part of the whole, but of limited significance alone. That was a beauty in it, Lyndon and Everley agreed. With the routine came security. With affiliation to the One came invulnerability, and she had never, ever wanted it to end.

But it had ended, and it had all started with the PRORA.

Lyndon recalled how in the early days of a year, some years ago now, she had been to the PRORA. She had worked for ten days and, on the morning of the eleventh, all of the female Operatives from her building had been called to the Health Centre. When she had arrived, she was instructed to queue in a long line down a corridor. A Health Centre Operative had given each one waiting a cup of water. The old woman she remembered for having a large 'W' engraved into the centre of her forehead (seemingly from seventy years of frowning), had told to drink it quickly, right away, and then keep hold of the cup.

At the front of the line was a toilet with no door. Lyndon had been instructed to 'Urinate into the cup!' as the old woman and the queuing Operatives stood and watched Lyndon collect her own wee. There had been no reason to question it at the time. You don't question things in Brito.

Once finished, Lyndon had been directed to another queue where a different (but equally old) Health Centre worker was placing long, thin sticks of paper into the pee as the Operatives held up their cups. She remembered looking at the funny colour of it and wondering whether Brito had found some sort of special or recyclable use for it.

After a couple of minutes, Lyndon had been guided into a room as many of her fellow Ops were directed to leave immediately and go to the PRORA. She realised she would miss her reward, but she didn't know if it was because of something good or something bad.

'The Health Centre gave me an injection and told me that from that moment on I was carrying a child of Brito.'

'So children come from...' Everley gasped, 'the Health Centre!'

'Yes. They give you the injection and you grow one in your belly. It is called a *pregnancy*.' She rubbed her stomach.

'What an honour!'

'I know! Just like our mothers, Everley, they were given the honour too. But something happened to the child of Brito I was carrying inside me.'

Lyndon didn't go into great detail, but she did tell Everley of how her stomach had started to grow, she had been given light duties at the Workhouse and rest days instead of the PRORA, and her feet had swollen so large that she couldn't tie the laces on her boots. When she slept, she had long and vivid dreams about holding a tiny baby in her arms. Each night the baby had grown a little bigger than the night before, but one night she had dreamt that she couldn't find the baby. In her dream, she had searched the InOp wasteland until finally finding it on the top of a pile of waste with skin the colour of the sky on a cloudy day. She could still remember the terrifying scene of her dream. That night, she had awoken in the early hours and found blood all in the bed.

'I ran to the Health Centre but there was no-one there. I sat on the step outside until dawn, when the first worker arrived. They said I had not protected my pregnancy,' she stared up at Everley and said, 'but I did! I swear to Brito that I did!'

Lyndon dropped to the flat land beneath her and cried. Everley slid down the mound, almost tripping over himself and the displaced rubbish as he skidded and leaped towards her. He held Lyndon until her sobs slowed, and then sat back silently to let her finish her story.

Lyndon recalled how she had thought she would be banished to the InOp area after the child died inside her, but the Health Centre had told her to just get back to her duties. A very short time later, and just before she had got to go to the PRORA again (which was unfortunate, as she was so looking forward to it), something happened that meant she had to leave the One, and not be an Operative anymore.

Lyndon had been standing on the edge of the platform at Point A while waiting for the Speed Line. She had noticed a kerfuffle developing into a riotous brawl beside her, but refused to engage. A group of Operatives were wrestling with an InOp and Lyndon had not wanted to involve herself for fear of losing her place in the line. Nonetheless, she had observed from where she was standing and cheered with every blow that landed successfully on the InOp's face.

One especially strong Operative had thrown a punch so powerful that Lyndon was sure the InOp's feet had left the ground on receiving it. His body had landed near to Lyndon and she remembered his white, bulging eyes that had stared blankly in one direction while his twisted body had faced another. He had been unquestionably dead as soon as he hit the concrete. Good riddance, she had thought at the time, of course.

It was only then that Lyndon had seen the female InOp who was dressed in a hundred scraps of paper that had been creatively ripped, folded and weaved together. She had thrown herself over the body, screaming and crying and shaking the male as though to awaken him from sleep while he dreamed of an afterlife. But all could see that there would be no waking him.

A group of Operatives had wrenched the female InOp away from the dead male, revealing a bundle of cloth in her arms. From inside the blanket, a baby began to wail at such high-pitched and piercing a tone that it had echoed around the station and had most of the Operatives plugging their ears with their fingers. Lyndon recalled letting the noise in. The sound had seemed to both comfort and sadden her; she wished for the feeling that Brito's next being was still inside her, instead of the empty void.

The maddened crowd had not been softened by the scene, however, and had circled in on the woman and baby with all the intent destroy these two, too. Lyndon had moved to the edge of the platform as a gaggle of Operatives less-than-delicately lowered the InOp and baby onto the track while chanting, 'Here comes the Speed Line!' tauntingly. The Speed Line was on its approach and Lyndon had felt it.

The female InOp had continued to clutch her child tightly as she looked up at the Operatives that stood high on the platform above. Distraught, she had shouted for mercy for the baby, but the Operatives had only spat and sneered. Her desperately darting eyes had fixed on Lyndon, who was as close to the edge as possible without falling from it herself. Lyndon had felt a sharp pain throughout her whole body as they both focussed on each other, and she understood what she had to do. With no words, a message had been sent with only a look and the mother lifted the baby upwards to Lyndon without hesitation.

The train's screeching brakes could be heard loudly as it tore into Point A. Lyndon had snatched the child up just as the Speed Line hurtled into the station and obliterated any sign of the mother's previous existence.

Lyndon had stared motionlessly at the part of the train that replaced the woman, but was soon jolted from this paralytic shock by the fellow Operatives that were then surrounding her.

141

'Kill it!' they had howled. 'Get rid! Get rid!'

The horde had disorientated Lyndon as she span around to shield the wailing baby from grabs, pokes and pinching hands. She had backed away until she felt the wall of the station and could escape no further. The fear of losing another child, she explained, had created a desperation within her that filled her with an inexplicable fight.

A Capital had barged his way to the front of the mob while calling something like, 'Give it to me!' and Lyndon had known with absolute certainty that to handover the baby would have meant death to the child. She wouldn't let that happen, so determined was the *feeling* – not the choice – to defend it.

She remembered making a step towards the Capital to suggest that she was going to comply, but fooled him. She had dashed past and into the gap he had left in the crowd, then under the large poster and into the InOp area.

Right then, Lyndon knew that to leave meant never to return.

'That baby was Little Lyndon,' she said with a glance up to the cupboard.

'And that's why you protect him,' Everley replied. He understood perfectly.

X

Films, fashion, and now fireworks banned in Britain!

2031 brings with it a new national crisis as New Year celebrations compromise the uneasy peace that exists between working class and high society. This time the threat is that of the firework.

The last two years have seen the grotesque hands of Joint Government Britain wrap its fingers around the throat of individuality, with everything from the clothes we wear to the food we eat being stripped of brand or colour to limit the power of personal choice. At first we asked, 'How can we choose one black t-shirt from another black t-shirt?!' but as time passed with fewer decisions to make about individual style, our tastes changed and we wondered why we need choose at all.

In Channel Two's last ever broadcast on 31st December, their "Yearly Round Up" declared "Simplification" as the winning ingredient in the recipe for a unified Britain. The segment announced that the removal of choice levelled the playing field between rich and poor so that more money no longer bought more extravagance.

I see this clearly on my busy tube commute. Those that work hard for little money and those that work little for lots are distinguishable only by the fatigue on their faces. No more can we use brand names stamped onto bags as weapons to beat our fellow Brits, and the rich now need to think of other follies for wasting their wealth.

So, it is no surprise that Joint Gov. have decided that the firework is another one of those unnecessary things that disrupts our growth towards social unity.

Yesterday, the Office of Complaint reported a record number of emails from individuals about neighbours setting-off loud banging and flashing fireworks in streets to mark the coming of the New Year. Unlike the eve of 2030, however, these complaints were not about noise, disturbance or the death by fear of a family pet. No. This year the OoC recorded 96% of complaints under the category "Advertising Affluence".

We will have to await the public response to the formal announcement of the firework ban by PM Frankie Smith-Bennett expected on the television at 7pm tonight, but it is anticipated to be positive.

Thanks to Simplification, we are now a more unified, calmer and contented a society than ever before, and I'm sure I can speak for us all when I say we don't want another spate of class rioting. Together we become stronger, and, as Embarkation looms closer with each passing year, we look forward to ruling ourselves at the fall of Joint Government Britain… and the firework.

- The Daily British Bulletin, 2nd January 2031

As he read the last line, Everley looked up and over the vast landscape in front of him that sparkled in the moonlight from the various materials that made it. A deep whine of night-time air broke through the silence at that moment. Everley imagined it to be the echoed voice of the writer of the article as it disappeared into the wasteland along with all of the past things it spoke of.

Everley turned a couple of pages, exciting himself at the stories he would save to read another time. There were sections that seemed sensible, like *'National exercise regimens proven to reduce heart disease and increase body confidence'* as well as peculiar headlines where the words themselves had no meaning to Everley, but rhymed like a song when he read them; *'Christmas a vegan treat! There's no more meat!'*

There was a huge brown splodge over the next page that had bled into all of the pages after it. The words were distorted but Everley would take some time to try to decipher them when he was back in his quarters. That reminded him; he really should get back there right away. He had never been out so late and he wasn't sure whether it would lead to some kind of reprimand from the Night Watcher or notice to a Higher Operative. The thought frightened him dreadfully, so he quickly folded the paper ready to put in his pocket only to realise he didn't have a pocket because he was still wearing InOp clothing.

Lyndon, who had fallen asleep comfortably on his shoulder, fell immediately backwards as Everley stood up in a panic.

'Sorry!' he said as he reached forward to pull her upright. 'I have to go! I can't go in your clothes. We have to switch back!'

'Okay,' Lyndon replied sleepily while stretching out and rubbing the back of her neck. 'I suppose the InOps will still be asleep so you'll be safe. You will have to be careful though,' she said while starting to remove his cosy coat from her suddenly shivering body.

'I would let you keep it, but I'd be in trouble. I might be in trouble anyway for being out late. I don't know what will happen,' Everley said as he turned away just before her nakedness would have been revealed. He stripped himself of the InOp cloth that had done well to warm him and handed it backwards.

'It's alright. I'm used to my clothes,' she said, stood and tapped him on the back.

He turned around tentatively and looked into her eyes. He felt immediately sad to be leaving her and made a mental note of his longing to stay.

'I will get you some medical supplies,' Everley said as he brushed a section of her hair away from the injury on her face and let the tips of his fingers linger on her skin. 'I could save you my nutrition tablet, too. Well, maybe we could share it, half and half? I tried not taking it once and I was ill.'

Lyndon smiled at him and reached up with one hand to take his from her cheek. He flinched to pull his hand away, thinking she had been offended by the touch, but instead she kept hold of it, lifted it back towards her face and kissed his knuckles.

'I hope I see you again, Everley.'

'You will... With medical supplies and half of my nutrition tablet!'

'I think I'll be okay without the supplies. It will heal naturally in the air. Plus, I don't want you to compromise yourself by asking for anything at the Health Centre. And I don't need your nutrition tablet because we get our own supply in the InOp area each morning.'

'What?' Everley said, as he pulled his hand away fully, took his coat from her, put it on, buttoned it up and put the folded paper into the pocket. '*Who* gives *you* supplies?!'

'Brito,' she said calmly. 'A Capital Operative gives them to us.'

'I don't believe you!' said Everley, disgusted at the very thought. 'You are the waste... Why would Brito feed you?'

'Brito doesn't want us to die of hunger, Everley.'

'Brito doesn't want you at all,' Everley replied without emotion, then grabbed his head and shook it. There were two Everleys in there: one robot and one human. 'Now I'm confused again. We do need to talk more, but you can only tell me the truth because... I just can't ask you all of my questions if I can't believe your answers!'

Lyndon grabbed him firmly by the shoulder and moved closer so that her eyes stared solidly at his. He could feel her breath on his own lips as she spoke.

'Trust me, Everley,' she whispered, 'I have seen and I have lived both sides of our Brito. I will tell you everything I know and answer every question honestly when you ask. In return, I want you to believe the things I say. I will die before you, Everley, from disease or murder by one of *your* Operatives, and I will have left no legacy except the life of Little Lyndon. Maybe my legacy can also be to tell you the truth, and for you to use that truth to change Brito from within. Brito can be better, and you can make it so.'

With that, she flung both arms around him and squeezed. Everley squeezed back. There was such joy yet such sadness in the strong way in which they held each other. Everley could feel her heart beating against his as their chests heaved together. An emotion seemed to rise up inside him and he let out a whining exhale with eyes screwed shut but tears breaking through, bleeding out and running down his cheeks into her hair.

'You will find me often at Point A. Shout my name like you have done before... only when it is safe. We will speak again and I will answer your questions.' Lyndon rubbed his back comfortingly as she too began to sniff and shake. 'You need to go now, before the sun comes up.'

Everley released her and stepped backwards, rubbing both eyes with both palms. He took one last look at her and nodded, then stumbled as he leapt down the rubbish pile.

'Oh, Everley!' Lyndon called out, forgetting to mention something, 'Make sure we meet before your next PRORA! Remember, *before* the next!'

Everley stopped and waved a hand to signal he had heard, then raced through the rubble back towards the station, hoping he would remember the way.

Everley went unnoticed as he quietly entered his lodging block by the unlocked front entrance and headed towards the stairs rather than risking any Operative being awoken by the loud scrape and chirr of the lift.

He glanced over to the front desk, where the elderly Night Watcher was loudly snoring from a slouched position, with chin resting on chest. It looked as though his body was shifting a little closer to the edge of the stool on which he was perched with each nasally snort. At any minute, he would probably fall. Everley sniffed a little laugh to himself as he passed into the stairwell. He was extraordinarily tired too, so used the handrail to heave himself up every one of the concrete steps to the twelfth floor.

Finally on his own floor and breathless, Everley stealthily crept towards his room. He pushed the door open with care, stepped into the pitch-black space and felt his way to delicately close the door behind him. Every creak of the hinges made him flinch until the final click of the latch signalled safety. He rested his head against the door and breathed out a sigh. Home.

'Welcome back,' came a voice out of the darkness, causing Everley to yelp in horror, spin around and hold both hands to his own mouth to suppress a scream.

Looking into the dark depths of his room, he couldn't see a single thing and wondered whether he had imagined it. Perhaps it was the voice inside playing tricks, he thought. He was fixed to the spot, breathing heavily and hearing only his own heartbeat in his ears.

'Come on in, Everley,' came the voice again.

There *was* somebody here. Here, in his room was someone waiting for him to come home. There was a fumbling sound at the window, some muttering and grumbling and then the blind began to lift upwards. As the moonlight gradually filtered into the room, a hand of a man could be seen, then the body and then the face of a man: an Operative, and not just any Operative. It was a Command with a silver pin. A Command was sitting on Everley's bed and looking rather comfy with their back against the wall and backside on his pillow.

148

'Step forward, Everley.'

Everley complied and took three steps forward slowly, shaking and with his hands still around his mouth.

'Do you know what this is, Everley?' the Command asked in a gruff voice.

Everley squinted. The Command had something resting between two fingers. It was a long, thin thing that he did not recognise.

The Command put the small white stick up to his lips and made a sucking noise, followed by a long blow of air out of his mouth.

'This,' the Command said, holding the stick into the ray of moonlight, 'is a cigarette. A ciggy. I used to smoke these when I was your age. Do you know why? No reason. No reason at all. It was fun, I suppose. It made you look "cool". Hard. Tough. It calmed you down if you were stressing out. Oh,' he spoke with a groan, 'oh what I wouldn't give to light this now and smoke it. To drag in all of that bad, toxic and *unnecessary* air into my lungs and breath out a big smoggy cloud of it into this perfectly healthy room!' He sucked on the thing again and blew out, continuing, 'I can't even light it. All I need is a flame. Where can I find *that* in Brito? The boiler room of the building maybe? I could have a look down there actually...' he tailed off.

Everley was still standing opposite the bed not more than four feet away. He was thoroughly confused, but knew that having a Command Operative in his quarters at what the clock outside was now showing as seventeen minutes to three in the morning surely meant he was in trouble. He lowered his hands from his mouth and positioned them to salute, then cleared his throat.

'Ah yes,' the Command said, roused from his wonderings of whether it would indeed be possible to venture down to the basement and light the ciggy from the gas boiler's pilot light. 'Do you know where I found this glorious souvenir of the past, Everley? I found this when I was walking in the InOp area. And do you know why I was in the InOp area? Hmm?'

Everley didn't know the answers to any of these seemingly bizarre questions, so he kept his position and shook his head.

'Well, I'll tell you. I was in the InOp area because...' he took a long pause, thinking it incredibly amusing to him to keep Everley poised to salute. 'Because I was looking for you, Operative Everley. I know that's where you've been tonight.'

Everley had no justification at all for being in the InOp area after dark. He could think of no excuse either. He licked and bit his lips, but said no word. He was still saluting.

'Yes, yes, *'Best Evening Briton'* and all that! You can stop saluting now! Sit here,' the Command said while bending his knees and moving his legs upwards to leave some space at the end of the bed for Everley to sit.

'Command, I... well, I'm afraid I don't know what to say,' said Everley with a remorseful tone as he dropped his head to look at his feet.

'No need to say a word, son. I *know* what you've been doing,' he said slyly, 'and I have to say... I am impressed.'

Everley looked up at him in surprise, then sank onto the bed and sat there at the Command's feet.

'There just aren't enough taking the initiative like you, dear boy!' the Command continued.

'Sorry, sir?'

'Oh, come on now, don't be coy with me! I think it's bloody brilliant!'

'Sir?'

'By *bloody* brilliant, I mean... commendable. I didn't think you young Ops had it in you, to be honest. Despite all the work *we* do to make it so, you Ops are all still so... so... measured. But not you, Everley, not you. You've got a bit of fire in your belly! The kind of fire I need to light this!' He puffed again on the cigarette and then muttered something to himself when it became absolutely clear that it was not only unlit, but also falling apart. Brown fuzzy strands

150

were dropping out of the end of it and onto the sheets. The Command placed it into his pocket and, at the same time, took out a notebook.

'I'm sure I don't know what you mean, sir,' said Everley.

'I'm sure you do,' replied the Command, while flicking the pages of his book.

'Am I in trouble, sir?'

'Well no, I don't think so. We just need to decide what to do with you,' he said, still distracted by the book. 'Ah ha! Here it is!' the Command bent the notebook in half backwards and thrust a page into Everley's face.

'Everley, male, absent day one...' Everley read the untidy and non-Brito-like handwriting aloud. 'But, sir, an InOp spat in my face! I was excused for one day. I came back here and slept. The Health Centre will tell you!'

'Yes, yes, I'm not worried about that. Read on,' the Command insisted, waggling a finger at Everley.

Everley shuffled on the bed and then held the book upwards towards the window so that the light of the night outside would illuminate the words on the page, which were much fainter and written in pencil.

Observed via drone:

Op in S3 ignored direct order to detain InOp intruder at windmill 7.

Op attacked – repeated blows till exterminated. Disposed waste into sea. Returned to windmill tasks as normal.

No report made by Op into Watch Tower. Why?

Op attended last PRORA. BUT these actions not taught.

Test further.

Everley passed the book back slowly and solemnly said, 'I am in trouble, then.'

'Well, of course I was pretty pissed off– disappointed to have been disobeyed. I am *your* Command, remember! But then I thought about it, and I thought *"Fucking hell this kid is beating the shit out of that InOp!"*... I mean... *"For Brito, this Operative has some anger in him, and he's channelling it into violence against the waste of our society."* Brilliant! What made you so angry, Everley? Did getting spat at in the face by an InOp make you wild with rage? Was that it?'

The Command rocked his body forward onto his knees, bringing his face much closer to Everley's. He was blood thirsty and panting in desperation for an answer to the question.

'I'm sorry I didn't alert the Watch Tower. I believe the event left my mind for the rest of the day.' Everley shrugged and looked away, breaking the intense eye contact of the Command.

A hand shot forward and grabbed Everley by the chin. The fingers of a strong but old man's hand pressed into his cheeks so hard that his gums grated on his teeth.

'What made you do it?!' the Command bawled into his face. 'You'll answer me because I *command* you to do so!'

Everley closed his eyes and convulsed in fear. This had to be a dream, he thought. He begged it inside his mind. Twice in one night had he been confronted by his own death. The InOp didn't kill him, but maybe the Command would, he feared with all the knowledge that Operatives kill without thinking.

There was a groaning sound and then some bumping about from the neighbouring quarters followed by two thumps on the wall. A muffled voice asked what was going on and why Everley wasn't asleep.

The Command loosened his grasp on Everley's cheek and nodded at him to reply.

'S-Sorry Briton, I... fell from my bed!'

The two sat motionlessly and waited for the neighbour's bed to creak with him back in it.

'Right son,' whispered the Command, 'you are not in trouble, okay? But you need to talk to me.'

Everley nodded, rubbing his cheeks. 'I don't really know why I did it, sir. I just hate the InOps!' He was confident that this would be justification enough, and he had to make sure that none other than Selby knew about his developing feelings for Lyndon.

'Is that why you went into the InOp area tonight – to get rid of some more?'

'I didn't...'

'Don't deny it, Everley, I know you were there. Where else would you have been? I looked for you in the Service Room and in the Entertainment Centre. I even went to the Health Centre, but that closed much earlier and you were out – out at night – until... now!'

'I didn't kill anymore InOps tonight.'

'Have you ever heard of Batman, Everley?'

Everley shook his head.

'No, obviously you haven't. Okay, well let me tell you a story of a character... No... a *history of a person* who existed before Brito. The Batman was... my friend. And he, like me, was very unhappy with the state of old-Britain. Before there were Ops and InOps there were just *people*. And all of the people lived together. Not 'lived together' in the same building, you understand, but lived amongst each other. Some people worked and some didn't work. Some were healthy and some were ill. The healthy ones tried to help the ill ones... and you couldn't just walk around killing people like nowadays! Back then, killing people would land you in prison. A prison is like this very room, I suppose, only you can't leave. You can't open the door because it's locked. You're locked inside and you can't go out for years and years and years. Okay?'

Everley looked bemused.

'But although it would land you in prison, some people were bad and *did* hurt and kill other people – good people. Or maybe the bad people stole things belonging to the good people. Like, say, if

153

someone came in here right now and stole your...' he looked around the room searching for a possession, 'soap'.

'That would be awful!'

'Indeed. But over time, there became more bad people than good people in old Britain. The bad people would do all kinds of nasty things that I can't describe to you because you wouldn't understand them. Thank Brito!'

'Thank Brito!'

'Well, the Batman wanted old Britain to become great again, but he knew there was nobody and no government that would help him to clean it up.'

'Government!' thought Everley, *'Government used to be the Command.'* He casually rubbed his ribcage from the outside of his coat to make sure the paper was still safely in his pocket and not poking out, ready to be found by the Command who was still talking about a bag man.

'He would go out in the night and purify all the horrid places by getting rid of the wickedness. He would scrape the waste off the streets, capture the bad people and take them to the prisons. Batman showed us all that the power is in our own hands if we rise up and take it. He was just a man like me and like you. Really like you, Everley!'

'But I...' Apart from the one tiny moment where he did kill the InOp intruder quite angrily because of his feelings for Lyndon, Everley couldn't draw any similarities.

'And Batman would wear clothes to disguise himself because he didn't do all of the clearing up just for the glory of it. No! He did it because it was the right thing to do. *That's* why you didn't contact the Watch Tower to report what you had done, and that's why you told me you haven't been out all night killing InOps! When I went out to look for you and ended up in the InOp area I found two very interesting things. This cigarette,' he said, tapping his top pocket, ' and one dead InOp. Oh, he was mighty, Everley! What a fantastic job!'

154

'Mighty?'

'You don't even remember do you? I bet you can't remember how many InOp lives you've taken tonight! Did you hunt them? This one was fat! A real large one! Slumped on the floor with vomit all out of his mouth and into a big bushy beard!'

'Fulton!' Everley knew who the InOp was by the description. He wondered who had managed to kill such a big man.

'You found out his name before you killed him! Very savage, Everley! I think we are going to get on well! Look, the long and short of it is, I didn't think there was anyone in Brito who was doing anything other than what they have been program– uh, *taught* to do. So that tells me you've got something: a strength of mind. Your vigilante behaviour... I mean... the way you guard the Ops and hate the InOps shows that you're really in it for Brito and I'd like to get to know you more. Would that be okay?' he ended on a softer tone, knowing he had frightened the fellow by skulking around in the dark and then shouting at him.

'Certainly, Command. I am terribly sorry that I disobeyed your orders. Thank you very much for coming to visit me. I would be happy to know you more, too.'

Everley was chuffed: first Capital Selby and now this Command Op! Although there had been more fear in him in the last few days than he had ever known, he assumed that he must be doing something right.

'Excellent. I am leaving now so that we can both get some sleep. We will be very tired tomorrow. I know where to find you,' the Command said as he eased himself up from the bed and then rubbed his legs vigorously while saying 'Bastard cramp!' and some other words that Everley didn't recognise.

'Before you go, Command, may I ask your name?' Everley stood and saluted, as was proper conduct.

'Raines,' he said and reached for the door handle.

'Uh... Command Raines? What happened to the Bin Man?' Everley asked, wondering whether he was still helping out in Brito.

'What? Oh, Batman! After a while there came to be more bad people than good, and he couldn't keep up. One man can't do it all, Everley. He wasn't Father Christmas!'

'Who?'

'Never mind. There were not enough prisons to put the bad people in, so all the people Batman caught had to be set free. And once they were free and living amongst all of the other people, they did more bad things. The bad people ruined old Britain, wicked act by wicked act, until every part of it was gloomy, cold and dangerous. Even on the sunniest day of summer. That's why old Britain died. The end.'

'Oh... thank you Command Raines. Best Night!'

'Best Night,' replied Raines quietly as he opened the door and closed it behind him, heading down to the boiler room with a mischievous grin on his face.

XI

OFFICIAL

Head Cardinal Quarters, Office of the Chief Operative

Transcript of Telephone Conversation

From: Command Raines (R)

To: Cardinal Abney & Board (CA)

On: Day 90, Year 26 AE, at: 0647

R: Verbal update of report in draft re: Operative behaviour following mental programming at reopened PRORA. All as expected: Ops work systematically through their functional routines. Efficiency and productivity monitors recording highest levels in Brito history. New suggestion techniques to increase Social Contribution in addition to standard Operative working hours a great success, with 89% of daytime windmill Ops arriving at Point A recycling plant in evening hours to offer voluntary work - without official request from Higher Operative.

CA: Board concerned that overwork may deplete energy levels for day work. Order: At next PRORA, to programme three hours' voluntary work on days one, three and ongoing odd numbers for Group A, and one hours' voluntary work on days two, four and ongoing even numbers for Group B. Order: To report on efficiency and productivity levels of both groups, draw conclusions and make recommendation to the board. Order: To track 11% not complying and analyse.

R: Wilco. Request this is delegated. Request immediate return to home quarters.

CA: Denied. Order: Follow all orders as priority.

R: Have identified Operative subject of interest. Example of successful PRORA programming. It may please Cardinals to test this individual at Headquarters. Request to be present for all testing. Request immediate return to home quarters.

CA: Order: Provide name and details of subject of interest.

R: Denied. Request immediate return to home quarters.

CA: Denied. Warning given for foul language. Order: Follow all orders as priority. Monitor subject of interest throughout next PRORA round and bring to home quarters on return - once all other orders are completed.

R: Request to be considered for Higher position.

CA: Order: Confirm all orders will be complied with.

R: Will not comply unless request for Higher position is considered.

CA: Second warning issued for foul language. Official reprimand will follow if orders not completed.

R: Request retirement release to The Other Place.

CA: Third and final warning issued for foul language. Order: Follow all orders as priority. Application for retirement will be considered on return to home quarters once all other orders completed and if Operative subject is impressive.

R: Would like to remind Cardinals of personal creation of the PRORA and devoted contribution to the Hard Line and building of Brito.

CA: Acknowledged. Order: Confirm all orders will be complied with.

R: Wilco, then will press for promotion or retirement.

Call ended by CA.

Raines had been lying on the carpeted floor of his office for over an hour. At first he found himself there by accident, having tripped over the wire from the phone that was stretched across the carpet after he threw it from his desk in rage. Thankfully, nobody was around to watch the somewhat athletic fall and forward roll that landed him flat on his back, sobbing and staring up at the square boards of the ceiling. After lying there a while, his mind day-dreamed and wandered away, leaving only his body in the room.

One of the ceiling panels was hanging loosely with a corner flexed downwards. Raines wondered what was beyond the board, and whether – if he stood on his desk and pealed the panel away – he could climb into the hidden parts of the building and escape. When he had been in prison (post-teenage years but pre-Brito) he used to stare at the plastered walls, cracked ceiling, solid door and window bars and concoct impossible but entertaining methods of escape. It passed the time.

This felt the same; Brito was his prison, and the walls were closing in.

Prison was better than Brito, Raines thought. You had your mates, your fun times, your moments of power and moments of weakness, your flagrant disregard for the Screws and the time to plan your best schemes for life on the outside. And, unlike today, there was an outside. Release (or imagined escape) back then meant bunking the bus into town, being a little light-fingered in the supermarket and again in the local off-licence, a prompt phone call to Dippy, a quick visit to gather gear from the flat and a whistle-stop tour of the bad and worst of places to deal downers to those bums and slackers so desperate for something to numb them that they'd snap up the stock in quick time. Finally, a financial transaction with a bad lad on the low road to solicit superior stimulants and depressants for personal use, before returning home to put Columbo on TV, mainline brown and nod in the blissful median between sleep and consciousness.

But what would there be for Raines if he climbed into the ceiling and escaped from Brito? There would be nothing to steal, no money to make and nothing to trade. There would be nowhere to go, no friends to see and nothing to do. And there would be no joy to experience - artificially simulated or otherwise. If he left his Command position now, there would be no reward for his years served. Escape wouldn't free him from this miserable loneliness, this wretched boredom or this unhappiness. It would only add hunger and homelessness to the list. No, without a commendation and VIP-pass to The Other Place, escape or dishonourable dismissal would mean the life of an InOp: as low as a rat, but with less opportunities.

'I've got to get out, and I've got to get out soon,' he huffed, 'else I shall go mad, fuck it all up and get myself banished!'

Raines closed his eyes and banged his head against the floor, reciting *'Fifteen more days, fifteen more days, maybe fifteen, maybe more days,'* in his head until the thought of something made him stop; Everley could be the key. Once the next PRORA round was done, he would take Everley back to base and flaunt him. The Cardinals would be so impressed with the indisputable strength of the fresh, Brito-born and PRORA-programmed generation that Raines' own age and weaknesses would glare blindingly at them like a blinking bulb, causing them to retire him at once. A brilliant plan!

Although it had always been his wish, Raines knew that the promise of a promotion was now a lost cause. There would always be another report to write and another situation to manage. Even if they did promote him, he wasn't sure he would be able to muster the energy anymore. Life was too tiring these days and he simply *deserved* a restful retirement in a beautiful forest in a nice warm house with a family of friends to entertain him.

There was a very tentative knock at the door to Raines' office, followed by the appearance of a face pressed against its mottled glass.

'Command! Are you alright?' questioned the Capital as she snatched the door open and raced into the room.

Raines didn't move, but left himself lying on the floor. He wasn't sure whether his old body could twist, turn and get himself to his feet anyway, but he was certain he couldn't do it quickly. And he was quite comfortable.

'Did you fall? Let me help you up, Command!' she said, with bended knees, an outstretched arm and open hand.

'Did I say you could come into my office?' Raines asked calmly and without any movement from the floor.

'But, but, Command! I looked through the glass and saw you here on the floor. What has happened? Please let me help you up!' She lowered herself closer to Raines.

'Get... out... of... my... office,' he puffed through gritted teeth with eyes closed.

'I, I, but...' she paused as Raines took a deep intake of breath ready to shout something, 'of course, Command. I will be right outside should you need anything.'

As the Capital backed away hurriedly and shut the door behind her, Raines let out the breath he was holding. Opening one eye, he could see the Capital taking another look through the glass in bafflement.

He giggled to himself from his fixed position on the floor.

Since the evening of Lyndon in the InOp area – and Command Raines in his lodgings – Everley had felt tired. Although he hadn't managed a proper sleep for the three nights following, the fatigue was deeper than that caused by restlessness in bed. The tiredness was in every part of his body. It felt as though an insect had crawled up his nose and into his brain and started tugging on the nearest vein, winding it up like a ball of string and tightening everything attached to it. Every movement felt like a struggle to stretch out. His limbs ached when he paced to the station and his knees creaked like the rusted hinges of an old door with every leg lift, bend and extension. His body complained, and in the silence of Brito's walkways Everley could hear his bones gripe and groan and his tummy moan at him loudly, but not from hunger. This taut tiredness had caused his shoulders to roll forwards and his back to curve. There was a heavy load to carry and he didn't have the knowledge or experience to do so.

And then there was the voice inside. Oh, how it gibbered on and on with each of its many personas fervidly narrating any one of a jumble of thoughts. There was Selby and the Special Project, Lyndon and the questions, Raines and the killings, and himself and the feelings. Occasionally Everley was convinced that the voice had stopped, only to realise that the babble had become a monotone murmur that would rise again if he studied it for more than a moment.

Everley didn't feel *right*. That feeling of comfortable normality had left him as soon as these new Capitals, Commands and Lyndon had entered his life and, although he was intrigued by it all, he did crave the past pace of previous days when he went to work, worked for Brito and hated the InOps without complication or thought. Perhaps he would seek out the answers, be part of a Special Project, become a Capital and kiss Lyndon, but for now his body and mind were weak and he had to stop himself from breaking altogether.

For three days, Everley left his lodgings at the same time as most other Operatives on his shift and marched together with them to Point A via the shortest route to prevent running into Selby. For three days, Everley waited for the Speed Line at the far side of the station and at a distance from the low-hanging poster that was the portal to the InOp wasteland and the home of Lyndon. He did not stand alone on the platform and he did not call her name. For three days, Everley worked diligently, but did not kill any InOps. He did not want Raines to think he was a secret bin man.

Everley was not so much avoiding these encounters, but rather was not feeling right or ready to seek them out. He was certain it was only a matter of time before they would find him, though.

On the fourth day, Everley woke a bit before the buzzes and beeps to the sound of a shuffle at his door. Two pieces of paper were pushed through the gap underneath and slid into the room. He clambered out of bed as quickly as he could, hopped across the room and ripped the door open. Standing naked in the hallway, he turned from one side to the other but saw and heard no one.

The lift clunked and rumbled down the shaft as its antiquated pulley system lugged it to the ground floor. Everley raced back into his room, shut the door, leapt onto his bed, flung the blind upwards and pressed his head against the glass so that he could see the main doorway below. He waited for what felt like a long time while holding his breath to stop the glass from steaming up. He didn't blink or look away, not wanting to miss the next person to leave.

A person emerged wearing a long black coat and walking very quickly through the alley between the two buildings. Everley knew it was Selby from the powerful posture, a walk that meant business, and thick black hair that was visible even from the height of the window. In an instance, he was away and out of view.

Moving back to stand over the pieces of paper on the floor, Everley felt a worry bubbling up in his stomach. One was the size of a standard written request delivered by BritPost, and the other was a tiny strip of paper that had been wound into a ball so tightly that it was starting to unroll of its own accord. He picked both items from the floor and returned to sit upright on the bed. He pressed the small roll into the crease of his palm and squeezed it safely there while he read the official post.

TELEGRAM

TO: OP. EVERLEY

FROM: BRITO

YOU ARE WELCOMED TO REMEMBER SOCIAL CONTRIBUTION IN REPLACE OF YOUR PRORA DAYS STOP SPECIAL POINT: MEET AT RECYCLING PLANT 0800 STOP PROJECT NUMBER A-06250001 STOP P. S. GOOD MORNING BRITON STOP

Everley knew he had to sacrifice his PRORA round following his day in bed, but he hadn't expected Selby to be hand-delivering such a standard request. He unrolled the petite strip of paper and smoothed it over his knee. In miniature numbers that had been written by hand, it simply read, *'5 11 15 23 17 18 26 18 16 25 1 2 25 30 32 29'*. Everley stared at the telegram, the numbers, then back at the telegram. Selby must be trying to tell him something secretly, he thought.

He looked again at the telegram and read each word slowly, tracing the sentences with his finger. When he reached the word 'special' he stopped. He smiled as he felt the deep dread that had been sitting ominously in his stomach transform instantly into excitement. His finger shook and he took a big breath inwards as he searched the remaining words to find the word 'project'. Indeed, it was there!

'This is a secret letter from Selby about the Special Project!' he yelped to himself as he hastily snatched both papers from his knees and put them side by side on the windowsill. Keeping his hand on the flattened strip to stop it re-rolling, he shuffled himself into a kneeling position so that he could examine them closely – his nose so close that the papers shivered with each sniff.

Everley beamed as he counted the number of words that had come before 'special' and found that word to be number 15. He did the same with 'project', finding it to be number 23, and referenced the little strip only to find 15 and 23 next to each other. Everley grinned proudly, realising he had worked out the secret.

Remember your Special Project.

Meet at 0625 at Point A.

You are a good Briton.

S.

It was the day before the PRORA – or the Special Project as was the case – and Everley was struggling to contain his excitement. With a growing self-awareness, he realised that this secret knowing of being selected for something very exclusive and important had somehow changed his relationship with his fellow Operatives. He had been sitting away from those watching the television and jeering at the screen for the last couple of evenings. From a corner of the room, he had observed his peers with a raised nose, lowered eyes and conceited smile that said, *'I know something you don't!'* He caught himself in this superior pose a number of times and on the last night, feeling unusually guilty, he took himself to his quarters early so that he could be alone.

Now that Everley had only one more work day to go, he could hardly control his hyperactivity. Unintentionally, he had woken up so early and stormed to the station at such speed that he arrived there as the *BUZZ BUZZ BEEP BEEP BEEP* alarm sounded from his own building. He knew it was loud enough to raise the dead, but he had never thought that it might be heard from as far away as Point A. That sound also meant that he was absurdly ahead of time to wait for the train.

Everley glanced over both shoulders then stood still with a tilted head, ear in the air and wide eyes. When he was positive that there were no people present and that the only sound was the soft whisper of the morning breeze, he crept towards the large poster that was hanging there in the corner and lifted it slowly upwards from one side with a single finger. Taking another look behind him, he sneaked underneath and into the InOp area.

'Lynd—' Everley began to shout, but stopped in fright as a hand grabbed him by the leg and yanked, sending him skidding down the hill of waste. Slipping sideways and ultimately coming to rest on his bottom, he looked backwards to find the owner of the hand.

'Shh! Shh!' It was Lyndon. She was expertly hopping down the hillock, jumping from bottles to bags and from one teetering mound to another. She landed right above Everley and immediately dropped to her knees to squeeze him warmly with both arms.

165

'Lynd—' Everley started again at normal speaking volume.

'Shh!' Lyndon smiled as she held four fingers over Everley's mouth. 'We have to speak quietly.' She scanned her eyes around the area and then continued, 'Let's go somewhere safe so we can talk.'

Lyndon took Everley by both hands and pulled him to his feet. She led him to what appeared to be just another waste pile, but was actually a rather neatly disguised shelter that only revealed itself at a foot away. Lyndon rolled away a cylindrical bale of clear material that had bubbles in it and had been coiled into what looked like a fallen cloud. Behind the barrel was an opening.

'Here!' whispered Lyndon as she crawled inside and signalled for Everley to follow. 'I'm so glad to see you today Everley! It's the PRORA tomorrow, and–'

'No. I don't have to go. I have been asked to do Social Contribution instead.'

'Really? Thank Brito! I was so worried because I thought you were going tomorrow and I wouldn't be able to see you beforehand and I couldn't warn you, and then you would forget me.' Lyndon slapped her cheeks lightly while blowing through pursed lips to calm her panic. 'Thank Brito.' she said again, but more to herself.

'I won't forget you, Lyndon. I couldn't. I remembered you before, didn't I?' Everley said.

'You remembered *some* of me. You forgot other things. You will forget if you drink the blue liquid. I'm sure it's the drink that does it. It must be.'

'A drink that makes you forget things?'

'Think about it. In all of your PRORAs, how many do you remember?'

'I remember... I remember it was the best type of place. It was beside the sea,' he started slowly, noticing he was searching for the memory in the farthest part of his brain and grasping at dissolving images to try to pull them into focus.

'And what else?'

'And the gates were golden. There was a large black floor... and a Command Operative gave a speech. Hey,' Everley smiled, 'I know that Command now!'

'But what did you do there? What else do you remember from the *two whole days* you were at the PRORA?' Lyndon probed.

'I remember...' Everley sat there quietly with eyes raised, then eyes closed while chewing his lips. 'I really don't remember anything else,' he said in conclusion.

'Exactly! The only PRORA I remember is the one where I was already feeling a bit sick before I even got there, and I felt worse as soon as I arrived. I felt even funnier after the drink but then I don't know what happened. Later, I found myself in another Operative's room. A male Op. He was asleep and I was over the toilet being sick.'

'Yuck!'

'All this bright blue liquid was coming out of my mouth, it was horrible. But as soon as it all came out, I felt better somehow. I felt awake. I don't know how to describe it. I remember what we did the next day of that PRORA, and I have remembered every day since then because I never went back. That was my last PRORA before Little Lyndon came to me.'

'I will always remember you, Lyndon.'

'You will if you don't drink the blue liquid! I'm so glad I could tell you all of this today, even though you aren't going tomorrow. I have been so worried that I wouldn't be able to tell you. If anything happens to me, or if we don't get to speak before your next PRORA, you *must* remember *not* to drink it. Alright?'

Everley nodded but was silenced by the sombre thought of anything happening to Lyndon. The very idea of it hurt him.

'Say you won't, Everley, please,' she begged.

'You won't Everley,' he smiled.

'You made a joke! You're becoming more human every day!' she grabbed him again and nestled her head into his chest, cushioned by the black coat he was wearing.

Everley's whole body sizzled with sensations so glorious that the joy instantaneously overwhelmed him and was completely converted into sadness. It was as though he was helpless to a yearning inside him that could not and would never be fulfilled. For the first time, he wanted something for himself – not for Brito. Just for himself. He wanted to stay with Lyndon, but the known impossibility of it was killing these newly found feelings inside.

'I'll have to go soon for the Speed Line,' he said, pulling away from the embrace and unable to take the beautiful torture of it any longer.

'Of course. I hope I see you again, Everley,' she said as she loosened her tender hold.

'Me too, Lyndon,' he said in such a way that made them both doubt whether they would.

'What about your questions? The truth to change Brito for the better?'

'Yes, you're right. We will speak again, Lyndon. After my Special– Social Contribution.' Everley crept out of the shelter and took a few steps forward without looking back.

'Everley!' came a hushed whisper.

'Yes,' he said over his shoulder, but still unable to face Lyndon for fear he would run back to her and never, ever leave.

There was a long pause. Lyndon waited to see if he would turn to face her, but realised that there was something stopping him doing so.

'Be careful,' she whispered.

Without turning, he waved with the back of his hand and continued up the waste pile to the station. The echo of her voice was with him all the way.

Lyndon wriggled out of the hut shortly afterwards, lifted herself onto all fours and then to her feet. With face forlorn and head low, she hiked up the mighty mass of refuse. Without Everley expressing it, she understood the problem because she felt it too. They were connected, but, with his life and hers so distinct, to come together any closer would be to compromise them both.

Arriving at the poster that hung between the two worlds, she sat behind it, cross-legged and peering around from one side. From a distance and without another word, Lyndon watched Everley. He was standing stiffly, alone at the top of the platform with his feet at the very edge, hands held behind his back and eyes gazing out beyond the tracks. He was so fixed in the formal stance that he looked more painted or sculpted than breathing and real. Lyndon simply stared at him.

Some time had passed before Lyndon – but not Everley – became aware of another person at the station. Lyndon observed the stranger, who, rather than joining Everley on the platform, was leaning against the brick wall and obscured by the shadows of the roof and a protruding ledge from an old window. What really concerned Lyndon was that the figure was intently watching Everley.

As other Operatives entered the station and joined Everley on the platform in neat lines to wait for the Speed Line, the strange figure still watched without moving.

Lyndon waited as the train arrived, released the Night Shifters and took aboard the Day Operatives (including Everley, who was first in the queue). Only then did the figure move. Lyndon was still watching as a man emerged from the hiding place and ran forward, banged a hand on one of the silver sliding doors and shouted until it opened to let him board. The Speed Line then departed, leaving the platform in silence.

'I have to tell Everley he's being followed,' Lyndon said to herself, with both hands on both cheeks in worry.

XII

Test ID: 002 Baseline

Duration: 1-2 hours

Objective: To record subject's natural reactions.

Preparation: Prepare simulation with sound bites and stock photographs.

Playlist: Load simulation. Monitor initial actions. Play 'Resisting Neighbour' scenario with pre-loaded questions. Aim to disorientate. Monitor reactions.

Expectations:

(1) Subject will accept surroundings passively.

(2) A Brito-programmed Operative will support the banishment or capital punishment of a resisting fellow Operative without question, as governed by the oath, PRORA practices, subliminal techniques and constant propaganda.

Flags: Pay particular interest (and test further) if subject exhibits investigative and/or analytical behaviour of any kind.

Case Manager to be present and note any known dishonesty or willing deception in responses given during scenario questions.

Risks: Adverse reactions to this scenario are common to all others (please see the testing handbook), but are most likely to include shock, nervous breakdown, self-harm and psychosis.

> *- Testing guidance sheet from a filing cabinet in The Hidden headquarters*

The following morning, Everley was sitting in bed and staring at the clothing pole that was fixed on the opposite wall. He hadn't allowed himself to lay down all night because he refused to fall into a deep slumber, to wake only by the building alarm and therefore to be late for his twenty-five minutes past six meeting with Selby at Point A. Instead, he spent the night uncomfortably in and out of sleep whilst propped upright by the cold wall behind. He was now rubbing his neck – which was sore from the nodding – and assessing the clothes were hanging on the rail.

There were work clothes: one black fleeced coat, two pairs of black trousers, two black shirts with crisp collars and one pair of rather scruffy black work boots. There were indoor clothes: two grey t-shirts and two pairs of grey baggy bottoms (and no shoes). And there were PRORA clothes that were also permitted for rare occasions in the Entertainment Centre, for such events as a live InOp fight to the death: one pair of bright blue trousers with a stretchy waistband, a red vest without sleeves that fit Everley loosely over his slight frame, and one pair of white shoes that he had recently painstakingly cleaned of soil using his own toothbrush. They squeaked when he walked.

'I don't have Special Project clothes!' he thought, truly confused as to what was the most acceptable clothing. Never in his entire life had he needed to make such a decision. Operatives simply knew what to wear because it was predetermined and issued by Brito for a specific purpose. After deliberating, he settled on pairing his windmill workwear with his PRORA shoes, which looked tidier and were less tight-fitting than the bulky boots. Hopefully this would please Selby; Everley didn't want to make a mistake or disappoint him right at the beginning.

He looked out of the window at the clock opposite. Five o'clock, it read. Not long now.

As Everley approached the entrance of Point A he could see Capital Selby, who was already waiting and pacing from left to right.

'Best Morning!' Everley said from a little way away. He saluted as he continued to march forward with a wide smile on his face. 'I am not late am I, Capital?'

'Best Morning, son!' Selby looked up and smiled back. 'No, not at all. Right on time in fact! I was here early. You got my message and understood it then?!'

'Oh yes, it was very good, sir!' Everley said as he reached Selby and lowered his saluting hand.

'Well done! Excellent work!' Selby responded, tapping Everley on the shoulder. 'We will go right away. We need to be quiet now, Everley. Follow me,' he said as he began walking away from the station and towards the edge of the road where there was a low fence. He glanced back to Everley, who was eagerly trailing behind, and said, 'Are you ready for this?'

'I believe so. I will do my best, Capital. Thank you for selecting me for this special—' He stopped mid-sentence as Selby disappeared in front of him. Everley peered over the edge of the road.

Selby had jumped over the fence and was balancing unsteadily on a rough bank beside a river below. 'Come on!' he said, grinning, as he held his hand back up to where Everley was still standing on the road and looking dumbfounded.

Everley awkwardly hobbled over the low fence and onto the bank, then – with Selby's support – down to a walkway.

'That's the hard bit over!' Selby chuckled. 'We are going a short way down here. Keep your body tight to this wall.' He motioned Everley to the left with his hand while he led the way.

With each step, Everley took in new sights from all angles: a flowing river, a brick bridge and a metal basket with wheels that was upside down. He had never seen these things before. He realised that he had only ever known the same routes through Point A and had never seen (or considered) anything beyond.

'How have you been *feeling*, son,' Selby hovered over that word, 'after our talk.'

'Alright, sir. I must thank you for your note. I mean, for saying I am a good Briton.'

'We were meant to meet the following day, but we didn't. Have you been avoiding me?' Selby asked directly.

'No, sir. I haven't been avoiding you... but I suppose I haven't made certain to see you either. I have been trying to give myself the time to understand my feelings. Just like you said.'

Selby uttered a 'Hmm,' finding the response to be plausible. 'So? Have you been letting in those natural *human* emotions?'

'I am human, Capital! I have realised that there are two big feelings,' Everley started.

'Two?!'

'Yes, two. There is the feeling we all have against the InOps: InOps we *hate*!'

'And the other?' Selby asked curiously.

'There is the opposite to hate. It feels as strong, but it's the opposite.'

'How so?'

'Well...' Everley groaned wondering how to articulate it effectively, 'if hate is the night-time, then there is an opposite feeling that is the daytime. Hate is bad. The other one is good. I think it's good,' Everley said as he stumbled on the rugged ground and tried to keep up with Selby. 'It can make you feel bad, too. It can make you feel sad.'

'Alright, son, I think you might be getting there slowly!' Selby laughed as reached back to take hold of Everley's arm and pull him around a large metal post. 'We're here.'

Everley found himself facing an old wooden door with a '0' pinned to it.

'I feel fear now, Capital,' he said, suddenly confronted by the deep unknown of the Special Project.

'Everley,' Selby began as he held him closely by one arm and squeezed his shoulder with the other hand, 'remember what I have said: you are special. You have nothing to fear because you are with me. The Special Project starts with some tests. All you need to do to pass the tests is to be yourself.'

'What if I fail?'

'You can't fail. You don't need to do anything other than be *you*. Alright?'

'What if I get something wrong? I will disappoint you,' Everley looked at his feet, sighed and added, 'like I have with my wrong shoes.'

'Your shoes?!' Selby looked down and noticed Everley was in his white PRORA shoes that were now dotted with brown dirt and scuffed on the side. He sniffed a soft and sympathetic giggle, then reassuringly said, 'Oh, son, your shoes don't matter! Listen, there is no wrong and no right. There is only you. It is impossible for you to disappoint me.'

Everley felt calmed. He truly admired Selby and felt contented in his company. Now he was ready for the Special Project.

Leaving Everley to change into a different set of clothes in the waiting area, Selby entered Control Room Seven. Three Hidden Servants occupied the brightly lit room that was full of computer equipment and television screens. Two were playing a game of cards over a table and the other was tinkering with a cable, trying to force its wide metal end into the back of a tape recorder. A few groans, a wiggle of the wire and a smack of the screen later and the telly fizzed from white noise to a picture. The image was of an empty room.

'Snap!' said Selby as he approached the table, snatched one card from the Servant's hand and threw it on the pile. Both smiled up at Selby but continued to play. Neither panicked at his presence. Neither saluted.

'All ready,' said the one who had fixed the machine. She was wearing a white coat with a square badge pinned to a pocket that read "Servant BN43" and asked Selby, 'Which test are we starting with?'

'Scenario Two will be fine. We'll use that as a baseline and go from there.'

'No problem. Go and fetch the Op!' demanded BN43 as she stepped over to the others, plucked the playing cards from each of their hands and gathered up the rest from the tabletop. 'Games are a useless distraction! You might have been freed from Operative life, but you'd have thought some of it would have stayed with you!' she tutted.

There was a chorus of *'Aww'* from the other, younger two as they plodded slowly out of the room.

A few minutes later they strolled back into the room and resumed relaxed seated positions on stools in the corner.

Selby took a pair of headphones and squeezed them over his head. The foam was old, crunched as he pushed them into place and made his ears itch immediately. He sat down on a chair that had wheels and shuffled it forwards to give himself a closer view of the television screen. He signalled over to the others with a thumbs up.

Taking this signal, BN43 lifted a protective clear cover on a panel and pushed her finger into the button beneath. A high beeping sound rang in the Control Room and a green light illuminated on the wall. The room that was showing on the television screen filled with light as a door simultaneously opened and there was an outline of a person in the doorway. It was Everley.

Everley did not move.

'Walk forwards into the room, Operative Everley,' commanded BN43 in an official tone through a microphone.

As soon as Everley had taken a couple of cautious steps, BN43 pressed her thumb back into the same button as before. There was another beeping sound, the light in the Control Room went red and the door behind Everley slammed shut. The television screen went completely black.

The camera in the room automatically clicked into a different mode so that the viewers in the Control Room could see Everley. Although, with this night-vision, everything on screen was bright green.

Selby watched as Everley staggered about, clearly confused and blinded by the darkness. He was rubbing his eyes and spinning his body from side to side to try to make out the contents of the room. He also seemed to be shouting something.

'Turn up the volume!' ordered Selby.

'Yes,' replied BN43 as she fooled with a dial and twisted it to the right, to the left and back to the right again. 'Ohh! Blame it! It's not working!'

Selby's face creased with annoyance. He glared over at her and signalled his impatience with opened palms raised to the ceiling.

From the back of the room, one of the youngers sauntered over to the desk and, with a single flick of the finger, calmly flipped a toggle switch to the "on" position. The wall speakers blasted a deep growl into the room, followed by Everley's mighty 'HELLO?!' which made everyone jump up and grab their ears.

BN43 scrabbled for the volume dial and turned it down.

'Hello? Capital Selby? Sir? Hello?' continued Everley from within the dark room in an increasingly panicked tone.

Sick of the Servants' lack of professionalism and concerned that they would befuddle Everley and bungle the tests, Selby snatched the microphone from BN43 (while tutting).

'Everley, it's me, Selby. If you can hear me alright, raise your right hand.'

Everley raised his right hand slowly.

'That's good,' said Selby softly. 'The tests will start shortly, but in the meantime I would like you to make yourself very comfortable in your surroundings. Relax,' he continued in a low voice, 'and take some deep breaths. Just relax, Everley, relax.'

Selby watched as Everley tottered forwards with arms outstretched until his hands touched a wall. He then turned and sank to sit on the floor with crossed legs.

Everley blinked his eyelids open and shut with such a squeeze that the centre of his head began to throb. His sight adjusted to the blackness gradually until he managed to make out a bed in the corner much like his own in his quarters. As far as he could tell, there was nothing else in the room.

Feeling a touch terrified by finding himself in a locked, dark room, Everley tried not to panic. He rubbed his forehead, which was wet with the sweat that the confusion had caused him, then brushed the back of his hand under both armpits. Wiping the wetness away on the knees of the long, loose and thin-fabric trousers that he was told to change into in the waiting area, Everley wondered how long it would be before the tests started. He was so eager that he could sense the nerves in his body skipping about in excitement. His fingers were tapping on the few hairs of his bare chest and even his toes were twitching.

Everley sensed a whole hour pass by; he had always been in tune with time. Just as he had programmed himself to awaken each day before the building alarm, so too had he a clock inside his body that let him know the definite hour, probable quarter-hour, likely minute and estimated second of any given moment. Waiting for the tests to start, Everley's beating ticker broke this solitary silence with an inner 'tick, thump, tock'.

Everley's spirits – first excited and then impatient – were dampened. His enthusiasm was curbed and his bum was numb from sitting on the cold concrete floor. He eased himself onto his feet and scanned the room with now well-adjusted eyes in case he had missed some object or other item in the haze of the darkness. Nothing. There was nothing except the bed. Disheartened, he moved towards it, sat on the edge and then lay down with arms crossed behind his head. If he had to wait for the tests, he may as well be comfortable, he decided.

Everley let his eyes naturally close, but sensed a change in the room as soon as he did so. It was a kind of light. Rolling his head ever-so slowly to the left, he could make out a faint outline of something on the opposite wall. He didn't move to investigate, but rather waited as the thing gradually lightened, brightened and filled with colour and detail.

As the blurry image crisped into focus, Everley knew exactly what it was, for he had seen it every day of his life. The thing on the wall was *his*. It was his only possession that was neither a toothbrush, clothing nor soap. It was his little picture of The Other Place that hung on the wall of his very own bedroom. It was not merely a copy of his picture, but rather it was the picture itself. Everley had stared at it morning and night in his bedroom as a reminder of his future reward for a lifetime dedicated to Brito, so he knew every piece of it. The raggedy edges where it had been torn from an old school book were one and the same. It was even the same distance from the bed. *His bed.* Everley sat up, disorientated and wondering whether he had fallen asleep and Selby had taken him back home.

'Selby? Capital Selby?!' Everley shouted out in fright and shot back to his feet.

There was a groaning sound and then some bumping about from next door, followed by two loud and heavy thumps on the partition between the two rooms. A muffled voice he recognised to be his neighbour asked what was going on and why Everley wasn't asleep.

'Sorry Briton, I had a bad dream,' Everley called out.

Everley returned to sit on the bed. If it were so – that he was in his own bedroom – then the window would be directly behind him. The rickety blind would be hanging there, either up and open or down and closed. The huge clock would be on the wall of the building opposite. And he would be able to look down and see the ground, twelve floors below.

Not certain whether he would find these things truly there, Everley warily swivelled and turned to face the wall behind him. The window *was* there! Everley reached out to touch the sill, to know whether it was the same sill on which he had regularly rested his elbows to watch the sunrise. With fingers extended ready to feel the smoothness of its top and the curvature of its side to confirm he was indeed "home", Everley stopped short of touching it.

The window *wasn't* there.

Everley wiggled his outstretched fingers. The colours, angle and corners of the sill seemed to bend a lighted image across the back of his hand. Inquisitively, he raised his palm further upwards until the image of the clock face from the building opposite jumped onto the back of his hand. The big and little hands pointed horizontally up his middle finger to where the number twelve was resting on the smallest knuckle below his nail. Everley waved to and fro, playfully causing the numbers to ripple across his fingers, then pushed his hand onto the cold wall behind and stared happily as it completed the picture: a *picture* of his window.

Thwack!

A loud bang from above called Everley away from his exploration of the realness of the view, the window and its sill.

There was another hefty smack from directly above that made a cracking sound on the ceiling. This time it came with such force that Everley felt the wall he was touching sway inwards with the vibration. A third colossal crash caused him to jump from the bed and stand in the centre of the room.

There was a clamorous babble of voices coming from overhead followed by a very clear chanting of 'Traitor! Traitor!' then a few more booming bangs and a thundering slamming of something – or someone – to the floor.

'What's happening?!' Everley called out with his neck bent towards the ceiling. If he really was in his own bedroom (though he was sure he was not), then the Operative on the higher floor was in trouble. He put his palm to his face and clawed at his forehead trying to hastily recall that neighbour's name. He couldn't, so called again, 'Briton! What's happening?'

'Traitor! Traitor! Traitor!'

Everley lurched to where his bedroom door should have been... but it wasn't. He banged with both fists against the wall faster and faster as he felt a fearful frenzy rise within him.

'Where am I?!' Everley howled helplessly as he moved back into the centre of the room.

There was a stampede of sounds coming from above so loudly that he was certain the ceiling would crumble on top of him. The only lighted things in the room seemed to start moving and circling around him. The window on one wall and the picture of The Other Place were rotating clockwise along the walls, just as the second-hand of clock does, only this was quickening. The two opposite images gathered momentum and revolved around Everley with such mounting speed that his eyes flicked and head shook as he tried to process the terror. The swooshing lights, stomps and chants made Everley so dizzy that he dropped to his knees and curled himself into a tight ball with both arms.

Then all was silent.

Hesitantly, Everley lifted his head so that his eyes could peer out above his trembling forearms. The picture of The Other Place was back where it would be in his own room, and it had stopped spinning. The window was there, too, and was still.

'A traitor to the oath is not one of us!' blared an accusatory cry. It made Everley shudder; he had heard the same call from the same voice once before.

There was a clanging from the room above, then the sound of something being dragged. Everley could hear the indistinguishable murmur of too many people talking at the same time, then the distinct clatter of a bedroom blind being lifted and a window being opened.

There was a moment's calm.

From his curled position, Everley continued to stare over his forearms and solidly at the window in dread and frightful anticipation.

Accompanied by a sudden shrill scream that pierced his ears, Everley watched the window in horror as an outline of a person plummeted into view, and very quickly out of it again; an Operative had been thrown from the window of the room above. Everley felt paralysed. His lips were squished together and his nose was puffing in and out loud blasts of air as his chest expanded and contracted strenuously with his heart beating hard within it.

Knock. Knock. Knock.

Somebody was rapping their knuckles on the door. *His* door. These were the kind of knocks that sounded official. They weren't the jolly knocks of the Night Watch Operative, visiting to advise on weather conditions for work in the morning. They weren't the listless knocks of the Necessaries Operative, coming to deliver a fresh ten-day stock of underwear. Nor were they the thirsty knocks of a Health Centre Operative, calling to request a donation of blood for Brito (and test for infections). No. This was the precise knocking of a Higher Operative.

Holding his breath, Everley slowly lifted himself to his feet.

Knock. Knock. Knock.

'Y-Yes. I'm coming,' said Everley, taking one step towards where he hoped would be the door but where it wasn't before.

With a clinking sound and creak of the hinge, the door appeared to open.

Everley froze.

A rectangular shape illuminated that corner of the room. In front of this intense glow stood the black silhouette of a person. Everley could see no definition in the person's face or clothes, and behind the person was not the hallway he expected to see, but rather a white light. On this shadowed figure, Everley saw a glint of something shining. Bronze or silver, he could not be sure with it flickering brightly like a twinkling star, but it was the pin of a Higher.

Everley saluted firmly and properly, and waited to be addressed.

'Your neighbour above has announced that they no longer wish to operate. As a result, they have been,' the voice paused for a breath, 'let go.'

Everley let out an almighty wheeze of relief. He nodded and calmed himself immediately, saying, 'Very good, very good indeed,' in admiration of his Higher.

'Have you been aware of any resistance in your building, Operative?' asked the voice of the silhouette.

'Not at all,' Everley replied as he lowered his saluting hand, wiping the worry from his brow on the way past.

'You've seen no defiance here to the duty and responsibility of giving ourselves to Brito?'

'No,' Everley stated calmly.

'And you've witnessed no chosen inefficiency or lack of productivity in your neighbours?'

'Definitely not,' he insisted, adding, 'and if I had, I would have reported it... or resolved it myself!'

'How do you feel about your neighbour's death? An Operative's death?'

Everley took a second to consider the question, then shrugged. 'I feel nothing at all, for they were no longer an Operative,' he replied, smiled and nodded one determined nod. 'It is right and good that an Operative who refuses to operate is removed from the safety of Brito.'

'Are you aware of any other oath-breaking in your building?'

Everley gritted his teeth and rolled his tongue along the back of his lower molars. His growing connection to InOperative Lyndon, of course, was breaking the oath. But he knew he had to answer dishonestly.

'No.'

'Very good, Briton,' came a final reply from the silhouette, but now the voice was familiar.

'Selby?' Everley said hopefully while rushing towards the doorway.

There was a clunk and all went black.

Everley was dazed. His eyes flashed with the visual echo of the bright doorway around the shadowy figure. Everywhere he looked the image echoed until, with enough blinks and rubbing of his eyes, it was gone. He rushed to where the door was – and where, in his own home, the door should be – but there was no door at all. It was a wall.

Everley felt disorientated. He looked over at the window and at once noticed the problem with the view: the time on the clock opposite read exactly midnight. He deduced that as the hands hadn't moved in all of those five-or-so minutes, then it must be a picture. A projection, perhaps, just like the television.

'This must be a test,' thought Everley as he eased himself back onto the bed. *'I hope I passed.'*

XIII

The fourth order of Brito is to maintain control and conformity through coercion.

This practice includes, but is not limited to, threat of banishment.

- The Cardinals

BUZZ BUZZ BEEP BEEP BEEP

Everley shook violently from the very vivid dream he was having about being thrown from his bedroom window for being a traitor. For Brito, he would never resist this purposeful life. He was an Operative, and operating was his only reason for existing, he chanted inwardly as he looked around the room.

His surroundings seemed to be brighter than the blackness of before, and, glancing up at the wall above the bed, Everley noticed that the projected picture of the window at midnight had now changed. It was still *an image* of his view alright, but the time of day had changed. The long straight arm on the clock face was pointing vertically to twelve; the smaller hand was hanging straight down to the six. Beyond the buildings, a rising sun created an orange crescent that sliced the night sky above it with a fan of far-reaching rays. Three or four stars were visible above the few clouds whose bottoms were glowing from the morning sunshine below, but the moon had faded away.

It was a pretty picture, but Everley knew it was not real. He was not home; even the buzzing of the building alarm could not convince

184

him of that. He reminded himself that he was still in a secret place, having serious tests for the Special Project. Plus, his body clock told him it was more like half-past two in the afternoon.

Remembering that Selby said to just be himself, Everley rose, let out a forced yawn, settled his feet on the cold floor below and stood up. He went to make the bed by pulling the sheet back, only to realise there was none. He patted the bare mattress with his palms as though to tidy it, plumped the clumpy pillow and then turned his back on the bed. He let out a contrived sigh of contentment whilst standing to attention with both hands clasped behind his back as he let his eyes adjust.

Everley's morning routine would naturally be to go straight to the toilet, then to the shower, then back to his room to dress. There was a door, thankfully, but if this was really to be his bedroom then the door was on the wrong side, that was for sure. He was also confident that the door would not open onto to the dusty grey corridor of his building, but rather into part of this hidden place; a hallway of white walls so intensely illuminated by long bands of bedazzling overhead lights that it was almost foggy.

Everley walked towards where *his* door would have been in his own room. As he approached the wall ahead, he reached across with his left hand to take his soap and toothbrush from his little shelf. Neither the soap nor the toothbrush (or the shelf itself) were there, but Everley continued the facade and clasped an empty hand around the clear air. The fingers of his other hand curled around an imaginary door handle and turned it clockwise. He stopped. Standing there, not more than a centimetre from the wall, he tried to decide what to do next.

Everley was as still and quiet as a paused moment in time (but for his breathing) waiting for the next part of Selby's test. With no outside intervention – and no thoughts in his own mind to help him – Everley was at a loss. He released the non-existent door handle from his right hand, threw the theoretical soap to the ground and dropped both hands to his sides.

With eyes low, Everley noticed something there on the floor: A note! He seized it hurriedly, then cradled the paper carefully in his hand, knowing it would be something of great importance. In wonder, Everley delicately pinched the corner and unfolded it to reveal another telegram. He read the words aloud.

TELEGRAM

TO: OP. EVERLEY

FROM: SPECIAL PROJECT

YOU HAVE BEEN IDENTIFIED AS A TRAITOR STOP

YOU HAVE COMPROMISED THE SECURITY OF BRITO STOP

YOU WILL LEAVE IMMEDIATELY STOP

YOU ARE BANISHED TO THE INOP AREA STOP

Everley felt a panic shoot through his body. Instantaneously, he was too hot. Every single one of his hair follicles wept a driblet of sweat. He felt a drip slip down the back of his neck, moisture slide into his ears and a river of it running down his forehead and into the bush of his eyebrows. And then there was the hard thing that had materialised in the back of his throat. It felt like a solid mass that he couldn't swallow down. It was a wad of emotion. A lump of pressure. A knot of terror. *Banishment!*

Banishment meant Everley would no longer be a Briton. He would be cast out and pushed to the other side: the outside. As a piece of Brito's disregarded rubbish, his life would have the same meaning as that of an old, broken-down and scrapped machine: nothing. He would become without use, without place and without purpose.

A string of thoughts spun wildly from Everley's brain and strangled him. He couldn't breathe. His legs buckled and he dropped to his knees with the telegram crushed against his chest. He croaked as he dragged air into his lungs, and with the exhale he wailed a

186

noise without words. He hurled himself forwards and bent his body over so that his forehead touched the floor. A torrential downpour of tears soaked his eyelashes and pooled on the concrete beneath him.

'No! No! No! No!' he called out in distress. 'No' was the only word he could articulate. This terrible turmoil was misting up his mind so that he could not see, speak or think clearly. With one deep breath, he screamed Selby's name and then returned to his woebegone weeping.

Everley had been moaning so despairingly and gnawing his teeth together so noisily that he hadn't noticed a person enter the room. That was until he saw a shiny, Brito-issued shoe to his side, right next to his forehead. With a huge gasp, Everley uncoiled and sat upright on his knees. He squinted his eyes so that he could identify the person standing there.

'S-Selby?' he snuffled.

'You are banished, Everley,' came the voice Everley recognised, and the voice that had given him so much comfort until this moment. But Selby sounded much more direct that usual. The tone shocked Everley and he was petrified.

'What have I done? Tell me what I have done! Did I fail you?' Everley cried while looking up at Selby, who he could see clearer now. He reached up and grabbed his leg while pleading, 'Please, Selby!'

'It's *Capital* Selby to you,' Selby said bitterly and brushed Everley's hands away with the back of his hand, which he then wiped on his trousers whilst uttering to himself (but deliberately loud enough for Everley to hear), *'Filthy InOp.'*

'No! Please Capital Selby, tell me what I have done!'

'You are a disgrace,' Selby said without emotion.

'I am an Operative! I work for Brito! I give myself entirely to Brito and I would never abandon it, I...' As he spoke, Everley could hear his own grovelling tone. He was speaking in earnest, but with all the breathy degradation of a humiliated and less-than-worthless InOp.

'You are banished. This is the end of your Operative life now,' Selby stated.

'I... I...' Everley had hardly heard him. He hung his head and, with both arms wrapped around his own torso, he began to recite the oath. 'I do solemnly and truly declare that I faithfully give unconditional and absolute allegiance to Brito, the safe land that gives us life. I, by willing choice, duty and responsibility, give myself efficiently...'

Selby scoffed disgustedly, vulgarly sucked saliva into the back of his throat and spewed out a large spittle that landed on the floor next to Everley.

'...And productively, for the good of all Britons and in defence of our Brito against any individual InOperative. To this purpose we pledge our lives and give ourselves entirely for our One. For Brito, for Brito, for Brito, for Brito, for Brito, for Brito...' Everley recited the final words over and over and over.

'Stop it, Everley!'

'For Brito, for Brito, for Brito...' Everley continued, his voice now a mantric whisper. With eyes closed, he took his mind away and fantasised that he was at work, at the very top of a windmill on a bright but windy day. With each recited *'for Brito'* he imagined one rotation of a windmill blade; a soft and rhythmic salute to Brito from the highest part of the sky. It soothed him.

'Everley!' Selby grabbed his arms and shook him forcibly. 'Stop this! You need to accept your fate!'

Everley silenced his chanting, stopped his imaginings, lifted his head and opened his eyes. He looked only at Selby, noticing his eyebrows were raised in such a way that showed pity rather than contempt. He sniffed and gazed up at him weakly. He watched as Selby's brows lowered and creased his forehead, his eyes hardened and his nose twitched on one side lifting his top lip to reveal gritted

188

teeth. Everley began to weep again, feeling lost at seeing the striking change in his... friend.

'Sel– Capital Selby, you said you would help me,' he snivelled.

'That's quite enough! Look around you! Look where you have found yourself, you *InOp!*'

Everley moved his head from side to side, blinking and absorbing the suddenly new view. It was the InOp area. He didn't recognise which part of the InOp area it was, although most parts of it look the same anyway with one grubby pile of litter after the next. The ground was covered by a flat blanket of paper pieces from the olden times. A carpet of long-forgotten literature had been laid and disorderly displayed a disarray of pictured pages with printed words that dotted straight lines along the grey earth.

Everley touched the floor and scratched at it in an attempt to lift a sheet beneath him that read, *'The end IS nigh!'*, but it didn't move. He could not physically grab it off the floor. It *was* the floor. It was one solid mass of bewildering chaos that extended as far as he could see.

'Where are you, InOp?' Selby's frank tone demanded an answer.

'This is the InOp area!' Everley's hand shook as he raised it to his mouth, which had fallen open in shock.

'This is where you belong! I'm leaving you here,' Selby said as he reached into a bag he was carrying. He pulled out a cup and pealed from it a seal that was keeping the contents from leaking out. 'Here,' he said, as he held it down to Everley, 'drink this water.'

Everley licked his lips and realised how dry they were. He suddenly felt as though he hadn't had a drink for days and so grasped the cup and slurped without savouring a drop.

'Greedy InOp!' Selby scorned, adding, 'That will be your last gift from Brito!' before turning to walk away.

'Please don't leave me! Please! I beg you!' Everley screamed from the ground, still on his knees. He held both hands in the air just as a young child pleads to be picked up.

Selby turned back towards him, reached into his bag once more and pulled out an Operative belt. It was Everley's own belt and was full of tools for working on the windmills. Selby removed an item from one of the many loops in the fabric. It was Everley's metal hammer.

'InOperatives are nothing and if they die by their own hands then so be it! Isn't that right?' Selby said with a menacing grin that reminded Everley the words were once his own. He handed Everley the hammer and said, 'One smack to the head with this will do the same as those many blows and punches you threw when you killed that InOp. Do Brito a favour and rid it of you!'

As Everley took the hammer, the heaviness of it drew his hands and his attention to his thighs. He sat there, looking pensively at the tool and mentally agreeing that it could indeed be used for such a fatal purpose. The satiny sheen of the metal top caught a glint of light and glistened in his hand, which held his attention spellbindingly.

Everley's focus began to fade in and out. Perhaps it was the shock of this sorrowful situation. It may have been the tool in his hand, which had captivated him hypnotically with its power to destroy life. He decided that the light-headedness was actually caused by the damage of the last words that Selby spoke. Those words had cut into Everley with such a hateful bite that it had snatched away any and all belief he had in himself.

Selby was right: *InOps we hate.* Everley knew he had to do the right thing by Brito and unburden it of one more InOp. He *had* to end his own life. But, confronted with this brutal reality, he found that death did not scare him any longer. He would die for Brito, and gladly so. Instead, the inner fear – no, terror – was that of never seeing Lyndon again. His heart ached at the very thought of it. And of never being around her. And of never feeling the comfort of her presence. And of the pain she might feel because he never said goodbye.

'Lyndon,' Everley said aloud as he dropped the hammer to the floor.

'Lyndon's dead!' Selby snapped.

'What? No!' Everley cried as he grabbed his short hair with his hands and pulled at it in disbelief. 'When? How?'

'I did it,' said Selby without feeling.

Everley thrashed at the air in an attempt to attack him, but Selby stepped back and out of reach. Everley's arms lashed about ever slower as a feeling of extreme disorientation and drowsiness fell upon him.

'Do it!' hounded Selby as he lifted the hammer from the ground, thrust it into Everley's hands and walked away.

Everley's vision wobbled and he could no longer keep his surroundings or the hammer in focus. Even the InOp area around him seemed to be vibrating. The dizziness was sickening, and he squashed his eyelids closed in the hope that the darkness would make the shaking stop.

Hearing Selby's steps moving away, Everley feelings of connection and fondness seemed to trail behind and leave with him. Everley had trusted him, but he had wiped that friendship out and taken Lyndon with it. More than ever, Everley was all alone. But the empty void within him felt even lonelier than the desertion without. With such a gaping hole in his heart, he had nothing to live for anymore.

With eyes still closed, Everley tightened his grip around the handle of the hammer. He felt the top of it with the other hand to identify which would be the most destructive part of the weighted head. Slowly holding it up to the side of his face, he angled it until the cool metal touched his temple. Everley took three very deep breaths in, and then drew his hand backwards so that it was outstretched and ready to swing with a strike so powerful that it could only end in death.

Raines was pacing to and fro in his office while rehearsing the very same speech he had given to the Operatives at the start of every PRORA round for so many years. He still couldn't remember it.

'Britons, in your number and strength, I admire you all. You have taken my words from my lips. Your dedication and purposefulness is for all and for Brito to applaud,' he reeled off quickly and without inflection. 'Then they all go *"For Brito!"*, yeah, yeah, yeah. Right, I've got that bit.'

He huffed as he lifted the piece of paper he was holding to his eyes.

'Yes, okay, right. So then I go...' he dropped the paper on the desk as his pacing passed it, and continued to test himself. 'Then I go... *You are welcome to this...* No. *Dear Britons, you are welcomed here to this Purposefulness Rewarded: Operative Reparation Area.* Then it's the bit about efficient service for each other, future of Brito et cetera, et cetera. Then something about praise and reward.'

He paused again and tapped his forehead with a knuckle. Cheating only himself, he peered over the desk so that he could just about read the words on the note (by squinting).

He spun on his heel and started again confidently in an official tone, *'Today and tomorrow you will all be commended for giving yourselves to Brito every day. For your pleasure...* oh what is it next? Productivity scores? Possibly. Okay... *Through your productivity scores, you have each chosen a programme to serve you best. These include...* blah, blah, blah. Mention exceptional rewards, definitely mention "open minds" ... then close with... close with... with...?'

There was a knock at his office door and it swung open before he had chance to respond.

'FUCK OFF!'

The nervous Capital Operative assigned to assist Raines stopped in his tracks. His eyes were wide and bottom lip quivered while Raines snarled at the young man who had dared to interrupt his practice.

'C-C-Command–'

'You might not understand the word, but you know I'm telling you to get out of my FUCKING OFFICE!' he yelled the final two words so wildly that a few frothy spots of saliva sprayed from his mouth and dissipated in the air quite close to the Capital.

Taking a step back out of the office and to the safer side of the doorway, the Capital jittered as he said, 'You asked m-me to notify you of the arrival of the S-Speed Line.'

'And?'

'It has arrived, Command.'

'Yes, of course it's fucking arrived! Have you ever known it not to?!'

'No, Comm–'

'I told you to notify me of Operative Everley's arrival!'

'We haven't yet identified–'

'Bloody hell!' Raines shouted to the ceiling with a frustrated growl. He stomped over to the window and watched as four hundred Operatives descended down the hill and into the piazza. All had identical clothing with identical haircuts, and all had a walking march so well-conditioned that any individuality was invisible.

Raines turned to the Capital and beckoned him to join him by the window.

The Capital warily lifted his foot over the silver edging plate, back through the doorway and onto the carpet of the office floor. As he timidly advanced, Raines nabbed him by the arm and pulled him to the window. Taking a rough grip of the back of the Capital's neck, Raines crushed his head against the pane.

'Find Operative Everley,' commanded Raines as he pointed at the crowd. 'Got it?!' he said as he gave the Capital's forehead a last bash against the window before releasing his hold.

The Capital nodded while stroking his head, which was red from the painful pressure and would probably bruise. He backed away quickly and ran down the corridor without closing the door. This was a further point of annoyance for Raines, who pounded towards it and threw it shut with a belligerent slam. He winced as he watched the mottled glass rattle in the frame. Incredibly, it did not fall out.

Raines stood in the middle of the office with his arms crossed.

'Right. *With open minds...* No. *Open your eyes and minds. Receive all that is given. This is your gift.* That's it. They won't bloody remember it anyway. Now, one more time, from the top. *Welcome...* No. Oh for fuck sake! *YOU are welcome...* or is it welcomed?'

Raines rescued the paper on which his speech was written in erratic, scrawling handwriting from the desk and folded it into his pocket, under no illusion that he would be relying on reading it at the podium shortly.

The expectant Operative body gazed so respectfully at Raines that he felt intimidated. It was always the same. He had learned to not look at the masses directly until he was absolutely ready to speak, otherwise his shakes would start.

While Guide Operatives distributed the blue liquid for toasting and drinking as though to guests at a wedding, still the congregation were attentive only to Raines. The quiet was eerie. In those few hundred souls, not one remarked to another about the events ahead, the sea beside them or the great Brito weather. So well had Raines trained them that silent compliance was a customary habit. He let that thought sit with him for a moment as a metaphorical pat on the back.

Tapping lightly on the microphone attached to his collar, a deafening double-boom sounded through the speakers. Raines waved to a Tech Operative, pointed to the microphone and signalled for it to be turned down by motioning with a rotating hand in the air. He then noticed his assistant hopping up and down on tip-toes at the edge of the stage. As Raines walked over to the Capital, he could feel each one of the eight hundred eyeballs follow him, and was aware of the Mexican-wave of turning heads in the periphery of his vision.

'Everley?' whispered Raines with a hand held over the microphone.

'No sign of him, sir.'

'What?! Check again!'

'Three counts were made, Command. He is not here,' the Capital said in a factual tone. 'Only three hundred and ninety-nine Operatives arrived.'

Raines paused to admire the now-purple bruise on the Capital's forehead. ' I want you to investigate this urgently. Contact the Watch Op for his lodgings. Contact the windmills Capital Op. Contact the Health Centre. I want you to do this at once!'

'Shall I—'

'At once!' Raines had lowered his hand and forgotten about the microphone. The words rang out across the piazza and echoed through every corner of the PRORA.

He paced slowly back to the podium attempting to ignore the fixed attention of the mighty mass. Not one step away, his written speech fell from his hand after the daunting presence of the crowd caused him to clumsily remove it from his pocket. As he bent to collect it from the stage floor, the eyes were still unwaveringly watching, just as a cat does a fly. And Raines was that fly. He felt as though they would one day realise he was merely a faulted human being and rise up to destroy him.

Back at the podium and ready to begin, he tried to calm the emerging nerves.

'Dear Britons!' he began. Making no effort to recite from memory, he read directly from the paper. As he did so, and from his elevated position on the piazza stage, Raines scoured the crowd for his ticket to freedom: Everley.

His eyes jumped from face to face, examining the features of the front row – for he knew Everley would always be at the front – but it was clear that he really was not there. He rushed the speech. It wouldn't be long before these unknowing Ops would down the drinks, the music would play and the simulated "Summer of Love" would start. Then Raines could investigate.

As he led the recounting of the oath, Raines felt an emotion. He wasn't sure whether it was power or pride, but it was most definitely the further inflation of his ego. He always felt like a rock star whose fans were singing his own song lyrics back to him at a gig. Something genius. Something brilliant. Something captivating, like the *nah nah nahs* of "Hey Jude", or the *ay-ohs* of Freddie Mercury, and the power of influence one could have on so many. In Brito, Raines was the celebrity.

As the oath came to a close and the glasses were emptied, that powerful feeling turned to fear. He didn't know what would happen to him if he couldn't find Everley. It could be years before the Cardinals released him and he wasn't capable of containing the growing rage of Bunky Baines inside him for that long without doing something stupid. He had recently considered setting fire to the PRORA with all the Ops inside it. But then he'd have to find another way to get to The Other Place. Under an assumed identity possibly? Or he might just let himself go up in flames too. It was a moot point without a match to light it with, he thought. No, he had to stick to the plan; he had to find Everley.

As the intentionally meditative binaural beats flowed from the speakers and sent the congregation into a hypnotic trance and a slow, dreamlike dance (aided by the ingredients of the blue liquid), Raines left the piazza and returned to his office.

Raines watched the developing comedy of intoxicated Operatives falling about each other. It wouldn't be too much longer before the contents of the drink would override the sexual suppressants within their daily nutrition tablets and encourage their carnal desires to be unleashed. The so-called music was also an influencing factor in softening the souls and whetting the appetite for sex, and Raines was jealous for not thinking of such a combination himself. At least he could take solace in the knowledge that the blue liquid's recipe was almost completely (if not, fifty percent) his own. In any case, the mixture of psychoactive drugs and music was consistently successful in heightening the power of suggestion.

Raines remembered the first time he and Dippy had created the precursor to this very substance in their dingy flat, now thirty years ago.

'Come on, Bunky, let's give it a go!' Dippy said excitedly, dropping two large grey tablets into two tall glasses of neat vodka and watching the cocktails fizz. He giggled naughtily as he handed a glass to Raines and teased, 'Too chicken, are you? Well I'm doing it, you fuckin' chicken! I'm going to start calling you... erm... Chickie Bunky from now on!'

'Chickie Bunky?! That doesn't even rhyme,' said Raines with a patronising eye roll. 'It's better than you calling me Junkie Bunky though, I suppose... Or Skunky Bunky!' He laughed, adding, 'All those drugs are making you lose your rhyming and rapping skills, man!'

'Oh, whatever! Are you going to try it or not?' Dippy said, swirling the contents by shaking his wrists. After a pause he added, 'You fuckin' gutless chicken!'

'Alright, fine!' Raines snatched a glass and moved to the door of his flat. 'But I'm locking us in, okay, 'cause who the hell knows what'll bloody happen when we drink this shit.' He locked the door and placed the key on top of the fridge, then nudged it so that it jumped backwards and out of easy reach.

With a retro cassette of Pink Floyd playing (on a vintage Hi-Fi he had nimbly unplugged and pilfered from a little old man who had left the back door of his bungalow open whilst asleep in an armchair), and the curtains drawn, Raines and Dippy downed the drinks.

When they regained a sober awareness of their surroundings, three days had passed. The kitchenette area looked at first as though it had been the scene of a violent crime, but upon closer inspection had merely been the spot where a bit of home baking had been attempted. Baking with flour, sugar, frozen peas, blueberry jam, a tin of sardines, citrus shower gel, a wooden spoon and a worn sock, that is. The posters on the walls had been torn down and shaped into a rather impressive collage on the floor in the shape of a penis. Both of them were naked and neither of them could remember any detail of their time under the influence. Admittedly, they had got the mixture a little strong.

Dippy did well in Brito to begin with and was a Capital Operative long before Raines with a variety of mind-bending blends that got him noticed by the Highers. But after many a year of inhaling, drinking, snorting and injecting one stimulating, suppressing and/or hallucinatory narcotic after another, Dippy lost his head. When asked, he would tell you that he put it in a bottle and sent it out to sea.

Raines had given the order to expunge him. He knew he should have been sad about that. He wasn't.

Still in his office at the PRORA, Raines continued to watch the crowd from the window in his office. The Operatives had gone from their spaced-out dancing to coupling up. Some headed excitedly to the dormitories, hand-in-hand like free and easy University Freshers on the first night of term. Others touched and kissed and started screwing right then and there. Raines observed his Guide Operatives coax them towards the spare rooms near the piazza that were designed for those desperately entwined and unable to stop.

In every one of Raines and Dippy's early tests on PRORA cohorts, they found that the concoction simply aroused some

Operatives more quickly (or more excitedly) than others. It was impossible to predict the results since Brito had forcibly sterilised the nation and removed promiscuous liberty from old Britain.

As the piazza emptied out, Raines turned away and was instantly bored. He sat in the chair at his desk and pressed a button on his phone. His assistant answered immediately.

'Where's that update, Capital?' Raines asked.

'Just typing it now, sir. I will bring it in right away.'

Raines did not respond. He arched back, lifting the front two chair legs from the floor as he leaned. He was still day-dreaming of Dippy.

When the Capital knocked on the door two minutes later, Raines flinched and was forced to grab the table in front to stop him from falling.

'Yes, come in!' he called out.

'Sir,' said the Capital as he slowly approached the desk with a single piece of paper that was folded in half.

Raines commanded him to wait while he read.

FAO: Command Raines

RE: CONFIRMATION OF DIRECT ORDER FROM BRITO

FINDINGS: Point A Health Centre was authorised to order Op. Everley to two days' Social Contribution (Recycling) in place of PRORA following an altercation with an InOp that caused Everley to miss one working day. The order was given by Brito to the Health Centre doctor by phone.

'And you couldn't have just told me this rather than type it up, no?!'

'I... I...' the Capital was lost for useful words.

'This tells me nothing! *Who* authorised it? *Who* telephoned the Health Centre to make this order? Did you even ask?'

'Yes, Command. They said the order had come from Brito.'

'They weren't given a name? Only a Command or Cardinal can give such an order!' Raines stood.

'No, sir. The doctor dealing with Everley recalled receiving a phone call and being told that, on the direct order of Brito, Everley was to attend Social Contribution. They had no further information.'

'What about a direct order reference number?'

'They did not have it on record, sir.'

'Get out!' he huffed. 'I'll sort this,' he said, but this time to himself as the Capital exited sharply, leaving Raines alone.

Raines pressed the '0' on the telephone.

'Brito Head Quarters, Office of Operations. Please state your name and request so that I may forward your call to the correct Operative,' came the monotone voice of a worker on the switchboard.

'Raines, Command Raines. Request to discuss a direct order.'

'Direct Orders Department. Putting you through now.'

A single note played ad nauseam in replace of hold music. Raines rapped what was left of his bitten fingernails on the desk.

'Direct Orders Department. May I take your order reference number?'

'I don't have an order reference number,' began Raines.

There was silence on the end of the line.

'Direct Orders Department. May I take your order reference number?' The robotic call handler was clearly unable to compute any change to the usual script.

'I said I don't have an order reference number! Look, I am Command Raines, and I need to identify the source of a direct order.'

'May I take the order reference number?'

'Listen to me,' Raines said through gritted teeth, trying very hard to not lose his temper. He was on a final warning for his language as it was. 'I want you to search for an order given by Point A Health Centre. Can you do that?'

There was another pause, followed by a hum of understanding and compliance.

'When was the order given?'

'Eleven days ago.' He rubbed the wrinkles in his forehead to calm himself.

'One moment please,' said the voice, accompanied by the sound of ferocious tapping on a computer keyboard.

'Well?!' Raines couldn't wait much longer. The only image in his head was that of an old fashioned gas hob kettle: the water was boiling and the steam was about to scream.

'One moment please.' Finally the call handler answered, 'There is no record of a direct order, sir.'

Raines was stunned. 'Please confirm? There is no direct order on record from the Health Centre eleven days ago? Could it have been recorded against a different day?'

'I can confirm, Command. The last direct order given by Point A HC was one hundred and thirty two days ago. Shall I create an Incident Report, sir?'

'Err... No, no. I must have incorrectly recorded this information. Thank you for your assistance,' Raines said hurriedly.

'Thank you for contacting the Direct Orders Department. Have a utile day!'

The connection clicked off and the line went dead.

It seemed certain that Everley was colluding with others. How else could he have manoeuvred himself out of a PRORA, Raines wondered. Most concerning, however, was the notion that one or more Operatives had been able to free themselves from the mental chains that Raines had created.

He had to get to the bottom of this.

XIV

The twenty-sixth order of Brito is to
exploit a human life for as long as it can be made use of,
regardless of age.

- The Cardinals

The streets were empty. Operatives were either on a working shift, carrying out Social Contribution or at the PRORA. So self-organising were the rotations that there was never any ambiguity as to where a particular Operative was at any given time. Nor was there any freedom – or escape – from the hours and tasks assigned to you.

Lyndon was leaning against a stack of concrete topped by a narrow white pole holding a small and red triangular flag that denoted the border between InOp and Operative areas. She shuddered. The scant InOp frock she was wearing provided no protection against the cool evening air, but the shudder was that of adrenaline. Although the Ops were all occupied, Surveillance Operatives patrolled the area and ahead of her was a perilous obstacle course towards the Operative lodgings.

There had also been a rumour of a renegade InOp hunter on the loose.

It had gone seven thirty in the evening, and by Lyndon's calculations she had under half an hour to get to Everley before the group from his building arrived back from the PRORA. She concluded that Everley must be home and in his quarters by now because Social Contribution finished at six o'clock. She wanted to see him desperately and to know he was alright, but the challenge would be to pass through the Operative zone to his building and get inside undetected.

One... Two... Two... Lyndon reluctantly counted herself in while staring at the open and unsheltered road she needed to cross. Without cover, she could easily be seen. If she were to be seen, she would be caught. Caught and then killed, without a doubt. Courageously, she took a step forward.

Two... Thr–

A doddery BritPost Operative emerged from between the two tall buildings, causing Lyndon to jump back into hiding. Holding her mouth so that her deep gasps could not be heard, she peered around the concrete post to watch which way he went. The very old (but wondrously still working) man walked with a stick and a limp. He had with him a black satchel with papers in rolls poking upwards and out of the top. The elderly Operative was clearly unable to lift and carry it, so was dragging it by the strap across the gravelled land as he lumbered forward. He began to whistle.

The tune he made with his lips bewitched Lyndon for a moment. In Brito, you would only hear such a sweet sound from the birds. And it had been many years since she had heard them sing. The birds left after the trees were bulldozed.

From the pleasing whistling sound, Lyndon understood that the old man was content with his limited lot in life. He had a purpose, at least, and Brito certainly expected him to fulfil it to the last.

As he turned right and set off up the road, bag in tow and oblivious to being watched, Lyndon knew this to be her chance. She stood straight, poised her bare feet for running and counted again. This time on 'Three!' she scampered into the danger of the open road, just like one of the many rats she had chased out of her home (the shack she called her own).

If she could make it all the way across, she would get to the corner of the building where there was a giant dustbin on wheels beside the back door. If she could reach that, she would hide behind it to catch her breath and plan her next move. As she sprinted across the exposed road, she focussed her vision solely on the dustbin.

Bang!

Not even halfway to safety there was a terrifying crashing noise that echoed down the road. Lyndon threw herself down and into the sharp gravel, tucked her legs underneath and wrapped her arms around her head to protect it, expecting a beating from a group of Operatives. Again.

She couldn't hear the all-too-familiar sound of Brito boots scuffling towards her, the tormenting cries of *'Filthy InOp!'*, *'You're dead, InOp!'* or the clap of metal bars or wooden clubs against palms, ready to hit her with. There were no noises so perhaps she was safe.

Lyndon lifted her head bit by bit until her eyes could see past her elbows. The old BritPost worker – thirty meters down the road and thankfully facing the other way – had dropped his walking stick. With one hand still on the strap of his satchel which was sat on the ground, he was reaching to grasp the stick. Arching forward ever-more precariously, Lyndon watched as he leaned too far, wilted and fell. A plume of dust leapt into the air as he landed.

This was her chance, she thought. She had to move, and right now!

Pushing her body to its feet, splinters of shale sliced into her palms, slashed her knees and serrated her bare feet. Unfazed, Lyndon rubbed her hands down her clothing, leaving two bloody smudges. Running for cover, she glanced over to the old man, and stopped. He had shuffled himself onto his side and was now facing her. Both froze for a moment as both looked at each other.

Taking a cautionary look in both directions to confirm the coast was clear, Lyndon hurried towards him. This was a risk. He might shout out to other Operatives. He might hit her with his stick. She might be seen. These were all risks she considered and immediately ignored with every step toward him, because she simply couldn't fight her instinct to help him. She felt compelled, Op or not.

'Let me help you up,' Lyndon said as she swiftly tucked her hands beneath his shoulder blades and pulled him to a seated position. He was so frail that he was almost weightless.

Both quizzically and gratefully, he looked into her eyes without looking away.

'One... Two... Three...' Lyndon said as she took him by his tiny waist and lifted him to his feet, careful not to crack him by squeezing his old bones too tightly.

Still he stared at her. His mouth opened as though to say something, but no sound came out.

'And here's your stick,' Lyndon said with a small smile as she handed him the wooden cane and began to back away, conscious that she had been too long on the open road and had to keep moving. There was also the chance he would now use the stick to beat her with.

But he didn't even flinch. Staring as though he had been reminded of a past memory of a forgotten time, his eyes glazed and twinkled with the wateriness of near tears. Lyndon continued to back away, then turned and ran faster than before. She turned into the gap between the two buildings, darted behind the large dustbin and crouched down, panting.

Once she caught her breath, Lyndon stood up slowly and, with her back to the wall, side-stepped along the length of the building until she reached the back door. To her surprise, the wide glass doors opened automatically upon sensing a person to be there. Knowing the swishing sound of them opening would alert the building's Day Watch Operative (and not having a plan to overcome such a confrontation), Lyndon wasted no time. She flung her body forward and through the entrance, slipping across a glossy tiled floor which was wet from being recently cleaned and scurrying into the nearest alcove.

'Did ya forget somethin'?' called the Day Watcher to presumably the BritPost man from the main desk that was around the corner but not far away.

Lyndon chewed on her lips not knowing what to do next. She could hear the scuttle of the Watcher leaving her post and heading towards the door, so she definitely had to move, but didn't know where. Opposite was a stairwell, so she leapt across the floor and sprung up the steps two at a time. As the stairs bent around the corner, Lyndon stopped and listened out.

The sound of the Watcher hauling her own heels as she walked came closer. With each slide and pat came a huffing sound. Another aged Op, thought Lyndon, although she couldn't be complacent. The old woman would still be capable of raising the alarm.

'Where are ya then?' called the Watcher to nobody, as she reached the area at the bottom of the stairs. She paused to wait for a reply.

Lyndon held her breath.

'Well, I dunno. Movin' me off me post. Must-a been the wind. Yeah, must-a been, yeah,' Lyndon heard the old woman mutter.

Her shoes slid away as idly as they arrived with a dragging sound that became fainter the further she slithered away. After a distant groan there was a squeak of a chair, signalling that the Watcher must have reclaimed her restful position at the main desk.

Lyndon stretched her neck around the corner slowly to see that the danger had gone. For now, all was clear. But as she crept back down the stairs, her own mucky footprints glared up at her like gigantic warning signs. As quietly as she could, Lyndon lifted up her frock and bit into it with the teeth at the side of her jaw. She managed to fray a section of fabric and then tore it a tiny amount at a time while wincing and worrying at every louder-than-expected ripping sound. Finally, a segment was free. Lyndon spat into it, speedily sponged the sole of one foot, then the other, and then wiped the footprints from the hard, glossy steps.

Putting the experiences of her previous life as an Operative to good use, Lyndon knew she had to get to the lift area. Beside the ground floor lift would be an information board with a long list of all the residents, their floor and room numbers. Getting to the lift would mean swerving past the Day Watcher, but Lyndon knew she was fast running out of time. In probably fifteen minutes, four hundred Operatives would be marching into the building, and from them there would be no hiding.

Resolved to find Everley at whatever cost, Lyndon checked her feet one last time, stooped low and tip-toed across the tiled floor, around the corner and down to the lifts. From a distance she could see the old woman whose forehead was resting on the top of the desk as though dead (but more likely dozing). Lucky.

Lyndon's eyes searched the list for Everley's name. At first, she just couldn't see it. The time bound and panic-inducing situation made all the names blur into each other. She blinked once, hard, then fixed her eyes at the list. Immediately, and in focus, she saw it there: EVERLEY B12.13.

'Floor 12?!'

Using the lift was an impossibility. Its noisy clunking and loud ding would surely alert the Watcher. Plus, if caught in the lift by an Operative, Lyndon would be cornered with nowhere to run. No, it had to be the stairs. All twelve flights.

Lyndon was huddled in Everley's room, in the space where his clothes were hanging. It was not a wardrobe as such, but rather a single rail and shelf. A pair of pressed trousers hung to her side and provided enough cover should someone unexpected enter the room.

Lyndon had been there for an hour and seven minutes, watching the time pass on the clock she could see from the window. Her eyes wanted to close from both sleepiness and the luxury of being in a building rather than out in the elements of the wasteland, but she didn't want to sleep. She wanted Everley, and the pain of each moment that passed without him caused a cluster of thoughts of worry to whirl around her mind.

Without warning, there was a clunk-click of the handle being turned and the door gradually opening. Lyndon held her knees tightly so that her legs were out of view. The beating of her heart was clapping loudly in her ears as she waited to see who was there and begged for it to be Everley.

Someone entered the room slowly and closed the door before painfully pacing across the room whilst sombrely sniffing. The figure eased himself onto the bed and then sat still, staring at the floor.

'Everley!' Lyndon called not-too loudly as she hopped out of the spot and grabbed hold of Everley.

Everley pulled back and looked at her in surprise.

'It's me, Everley! It's Lyndon!'

Tears began to spill from Everley's eyes and his nose ran into the bow of his lips. He dared not to blink, for fear that the image of her sitting in front of him was only in his imagination. He snorted a huge sniff and started spluttering breathlessly.

'Do you remember me?' she said with hope in her eyes.

His mouth coughing and his mind and body erupting with emotion, Everley patted at his chest. He blinked once then lightly pinched her arm, and then his own. She was real! Wordlessly, Everley gathered Lyndon up into his arms and burrowed his head into her neck while continuing to cry.

'Everley!' Lyndon joyfully hushed while squeezing him with one hand and rubbing his back with the other.

'I- I- I- I- I-' Everley started, but just couldn't get his words out, so he pressed his nose even closer into the space underneath her chin.

'It's alright. I'm here with you,' Lyndon said as she kissed the side of his head.

Gradually, Everley regained control. The tears had run dry, his breathing regulated and his hold loosened. He softly straightened his back and lifted his head so that they were facing each other.

'You're alive!' was all that Everley could say at first, but he did so with a beaming smile.

'Yes, of course!' Lyndon grinned. 'Where have you been? What happened these last two days? You didn't go to the PRORA, did you? You do remember me, don't you? All of me?'

Everley wasn't sure which question to answer first.

'I came here to warn you. There is someone following you,' she continued without waiting for his reply. Everything she had wanted to ask and say was coming out all in one go. 'I also came here to see you, Everley. I wanted to see you and speak to you, and... You do remember me, don't you?'

Just as Everley opened his mouth to speak, there was an official-sounding knock at the door. They both started at each other in fright, knowing the ramifications of an InOp being found in Operative quarters.

Everley stood and looked desperately around the room for somewhere for her to hide. Lyndon darted back behind the hanging trousers, but Everley frowned and shook his head because she was far too obviously in view.

There was another knocking at the door, this time a little louder.

Everley's mouth contorted with a lack of ideas, but Lyndon had spotted a space underneath the bed. She flew to the ground and shuffled as far back as possible.

'One moment, please!' Everley called out as calmly as he could muster. 'I am dressing myself,' he added, whilst tearing off his coat and work shirt, hanging them and hastily pulling his grey, indoor t-shirt over his head. He bent down to take a last look at Lyndon under the bed, then stood straight and tugged the sheet so that it draped over the side of the mattress to conceal her more completely.

He took a breath, walked over to the door and opened it.

'May I come in, Everley,' said Selby.

Everley didn't move either back or to the side to allow Selby in, but rather looked at him warily.

'Everley,' Selby said with a smile as he stretched an open palm forwards and patted it on his shoulder, 'we need to talk about the tests.'

Inexplicably, Everley felt full again. He felt whole. His heart was repaired and his friend had returned. It was a kind of warming feeling in his belly, and, not knowing why, he reached forward and hugged him.

'Everley!' Selby said with a little laugh as he gave him one squeeze and released himself from Everley's grip. 'Are you going to let me into your room so that we can talk?'

'Certainly, Capital Selby!' Everley said eagerly, and signalled him into the room with a waving arm, momentarily forgetting about Lyndon.

'You can call me Selby now! I am sorry about all that, Everley, that's why I have come to see you.'

Selby hovered in the middle of the room. Noticing there was not even a chair, he perched on the edge of the bed. As the mattress bent downwards with his weight, it creaked. Everley swallowed deeply, hoping Lyndon wouldn't be crushed – or found. Knowing the bed would really sink under the weight of him too, Everley sat on the floor and crossed his legs. He gazed up at Selby, as a child does a teacher about to read a story to the class.

'How much do you remember about the last two days?' Selby asked.

'Everything. Except for how I got here, I remember it all. I found myself downstairs in the Service Room. But I remember I failed the tests. I do not know how or why I failed, and I apologise for letting you down, Selby.'

'So you remember that they were only *tests*, Everley, and not real life?'

'Yes. I thought they were real at the time, but I now know that they were only tests,' Everley said with a nod.

'How do you know,' Selby said with a side-smile.

'I know because...' Everley paused, realising that he couldn't end the sentence with *'Lyndon is alive'*. Instead he said, 'because you are here! You are different. You are the Selby I used to know. And also I know because *this*,' he swirled his finger in the air, 'is *my* room. I appeared to be in my room for the last two days, but it wasn't real. Over and over, I kept reminding myself that I was at the Special Project, and not in my room. I managed to remember. Also... the door was on the wrong side!'

Selby laughed. 'Nothing gets past you, hey! That's very well done, Everley. I am really impressed.'

'Then why did I fail the tests? I failed you,' Everley said as he looked at his feet in disappointment.

'You didn't.'

'But you said...'

'Everything in the last two days was a test. Well, a sort of series of tests. Okay?' He leaned down and patted Everley again on the shoulder. 'I must tell you, Lyndon is not dead. I have not killed her. I have not even seen her.'

Despite smiling broadly, Everley felt himself tear-up again as though he had heard the news for the first time. He swept his eyes with the back of his hand and sniffed.

'Every single thing that I said during the tests was not true. You are a good Briton, Everley, a really good Briton. I've always said that, haven't I?'

Everley couldn't control his widening smile, and was now showing all of his teeth.

'I know that things may have seemed extremely confusing at the time. So I wanted to let you know personally, and now that you're back home, that you are special. You're one in four hundred, Everley... and you passed the tests!'

'I passed?' he sat up on his knees so that his face was much closer to Selby's.

'You passed! There will be some more tests though, if you think you're up to it?'

'For Brito!' Everley bobbed up and down. 'Of course! What do I need to do and when?' he asked eagerly.

'I will meet you at the same place and at the same time when the next PRORA is due. I will make sure you are excused from attending again, alright?'

'I will be there. I will be there!' Everley stood, wanting Selby to now leave for fear Lyndon would be noticed and his opportunity would be ruined.

'First, you do have ten days of work ahead of you. Continue to work hard, but don't forget to keep paying attention to those feelings, there,' he said, standing and poking Everley gently in the chest, 'and there,' he added, poking him in the stomach. 'Right, I'll leave you now and let you sleep.'

As the pair reached the door and Everley held it open, Selby looked back.

'What time is it?' he said, looking at the clock outside but seeming to be distracted by something else. 'It's... It's...' he looked at Everley, then into the room, then back at Everley and smiled. 'Well, it's nearly ten in the evening! We must all be going to bed now, mustn't we! *All of us.*'

'Best evening, Selby,' Everley said slowly, his eyes squinting ponderously as he asked himself whether there was any added meaning in his final statement – and whether they had been rumbled.

'Best evening, friend.'

Pivoting on one foot, Selby turned and walked out of the room.

From the doorway, Everley watched Selby march masterfully down the corridor with wide, even strides. Seeing him press the call button for the lift, Everley had an urge to run after him. Before he knew it, he was following the feeling and bounding down the hallway towards Selby, who merely watched him with a baffled stare.

'What is it?' Selby said, grinning.

There was a chime as the lift arrived. Selby stepped in partially and then leaned against the metal so that the doors could not close.

'Friends?' Everley gasped as he reached him. 'You are my friend?'

Everley understood the concept of friendship, but only within strict terms: *Exhibit friendliness to your fellow Operatives; We are all friends of Brito; The InOps are not your friends* and so on. But there was a kind of connection he had felt with Selby for some time now that was more friendly than those previous ideas. For Everley, the bond began when they discussed the killing of the InOp, and Selby helped him to listen to his feelings. It was a bond that Everley now understood more than ever because, thanks to the tests, he knew what it would feel like to lose that relationship. The things Selby said when he left him with the hammer had injured him more than any cut could, but seeing him again – the real Selby – had repaired the wound. Everley was so comforted that he felt as though he was wearing both of his warm coats at once.

'Friends.' Selby smiled warmly. He meant it. Selby understood their budding connection to be a kind of friendship, or a paternal guardianship, despite them being of a similar age. He himself was wise to the ways of Brito, but young Everley was naive to it all, so Selby had made it his job – no, duty – to teach him. He also knew that he wouldn't have been able to sleep tonight with the thought of Everley upset after the tests. Selby was surprised by how happy this meeting had made him. He was so touched by the moment that he felt as though he was lying under the warmth of a summer's sun.

There was a grinding sound from the metal doors which were pushing against Selby's body, so he stepped back. With another chime, they began to shut. As the window through which they could see each other gradually closed, the two grinned speechlessly.

Alone now, Everley stood there a little longer while smiling at his own reflection in the shiny metal. He tore himself away as soon as the thought of Lyndon interrupted his daydreaming, and headed quickly to his room.

'It's safe,' whispered Everley to Lyndon as he held the hanging sheet up with one hand and offered her the other.

Lyndon took his hand, shuffled forward and rolled out from underneath the bed.

'We are safe,' she said as she stood. 'I have seen that Capital before. He is good to some of the InOps.'

Everley was going to ask her something, but his brain was not functioning. All he could see was her beauty. Her eyes. Her body. Her lips. She licked them. Those full lips, so usually pale, were a pink shade of red and glimmered with wetness. He was overcome with desire and *had* to kiss her. He bent forward and, without hesitating, pressed his mouth to hers. Lyndon's lips pouted out and she thrust both of her hands up the back of his neck and into his hairline, making him shudder. Everley felt a surge of desirous urges shoot down his body, stimulate every centimetre of skin and scare his hairs until they stood straight upwards, tingling.

With the confidence of a Command and the desperation of an InOp, Everley seized her slight body in both of his arms and squeezed. Their chests pressed against each other and heaved. Their kisses quickened and tongues teased. Hands searched and fingers weaved through hair and clothes until there was nothing between them but the hot air they breathed.

Everley was sure he had not done this before, but there was an inner knowledge of what to do, and how to do it. With eyes closed, his mind flashed with images of quick and hurried sex, though he couldn't identify the women in those scenes. He did not want this all to be over too quickly. He felt connected to Lyndon and he wanted to explore that. He wanted to explore her. So, he opened his eyes and pulled their lips apart slowly. Taking her softly by the hand, Everley took a step back and looked at her.

'You are beautiful. You are the sunrise, the sunset and the sunshine.'

'Everley, I... I... I don't know the right words!' Lyndon said as she tickled his tummy hairs. 'Kiss me again.'

And he did. Every part. Carefully at first, he kissed her lips, neck and shoulder blades. Then her breasts, belly and everything below. He was sensitive still when they lay on the bed. Before long, the deep thrusts of passion intensified. They moved together faster, harder and stronger until they found their sweaty selves holding hands over mouths to silence the sounds of their climactic coming together.

XV

Everley awoke from the most serene and satisfying slumber of his life. Part of him wished he hadn't slept at all so that he could have savoured every passing second in this peaceful position. Lyndon was sleeping with her ear on his shoulder, her face on his upper chest, her naked body draped across him and her feet tucked under his legs. Everley smoothed her hair with the nearest hand, and stroked her arm with the other. He estimated there to be under thirty minutes before the building alarm would ring, but was reluctant to move and check the clock for fear of stirring the beauty.

It was only a shortening matter of time before this bliss would end. He had to wake her soon, he thought, because four hundred Operatives would soon be up and about and violently intolerant of an InOp in their own home. But, while smoothing Lyndon's long and tangled hair, Everley had been concocting a plan to get her to safety.

'Lyndon,' he hushed, shaking her arm, 'we must get up.'

'Little Lyndon!' she said, waking suddenly and jerking forward. She looked around the room in confusion.

'It's alright, you're with me,' said Everley. He rubbed her cheek, tenderly took hold of her jaw and softly turned her face to his.

'Everley!' Lyndon cooed as she cuddled back into him and rubbed the curled and wiry hairs on his tummy.

'Where is Little Lyndon?' Everley asked, her waking statement having reminded him of the child.

'He is with an InOp couple. The woman recently created a baby – it must have been in some medical supplies they stole from the Health Centre. They have a sturdy shelter, so I knew the little one would be safe with them for a while... I didn't think I would be with you all night though!' she giggled into his chest.

'Good,' said Everley. 'I don't want you to go. I want us to stay here all day, but we need to get you out of here and out of danger. Then I have to go to work.'

'You're right,' Lyndon replied, kissing his chest three times and then sitting upright. 'I'll have to creep out the same way I crept in.'

'No! That's too dangerous... but I do have a plan.'

Lyndon watched him as he slipped out from the bed sheet and stood in front of her naked, lean and with skin so shiny, glowing and clean that it reflected the morning sunlight. She looked down at her own body. There were grey marks and brown marks and mottled areas of deep darks. It was impossible to tell a blue bruise from a soil stain, or a spot of dirt from an area of pain. And Lyndon felt immediately ashamed. She gathered up the sheet and hid her body within it until only her head was showing.

Everley hadn't noticed her self-consciousness. He walked over to the hanging clothes and pointed at them.

'I have two sets of clothes here, see? I have two pairs of trousers, so you can wear one. We can roll up the bottoms so that

218

they don't drag on the ground. I've got two shirts, too. I've only got one coat, but I don't think that will matter if we leave quickly. And I've had an idea about the shoes...' Everley started.

'I will be found out, Everley! I can't pass for an Op! Look at me!' Lyndon poked three fingers out from under the sheet and grabbed a clump of her long and unquestionably inappropriate hair.

'I've had an idea about that, too. We need to cut it off,' he said plainly.

'Everley! I know you Ops don't understand it, but my hair is part of my identity. It makes me feel like my own person... Not like you robots! Just let me slip out quietly. I can do it. I got in alright didn't I?!' Lyndon kept a tight hold of the sheet as she shifted to the edge of the bed and stretched a leg out. With her big toe, she hooked the strap of her InOp frock and slid it to within fetching distance, exclaiming, 'This will do fine!'

'It is more dangerous than last night,' Everley snatched the cloth from her foot and held it in the air. 'This will not do! The Night Watch Operative will swap shifts with the Day Watcher in...' he glanced out of the window, 'exactly seventeen minutes. That means the Night Watcher will be running around down there, checking everything is clean and proper after napping at the desk for most of the night. Also, the Clean Keeper will be on the first floor by now, having scrubbed the building from top to bottom through the early hours. They usually finish by sweeping the stairs, so you won't be able to leave that way... and you won't be able to use the lifts either because there is a camera in there. And you can't stay in my quarters because an Enforcement Operative inspects each room on the first day of work after the PRORA. *And,* when the buzzing and the beeps start, in...' he confirmed the time again, 'sixteen minutes, four hundred Operatives will be in the corridors, the showers, the toilets, the lifts, the stairs, the Service Room...'

'Okay, okay. I understand.' Lyndon looked solemn. Her waking joy had been rapidly replaced by the horror of her daily reality. If found, she would be killed and Everley would be banished.

'I... I have a feeling inside for you, Lyndon,' Everley said more sensitively as he reached around the sheet she was swaddled in and lifted her to her feet, 'and all I want to do is protect you.'

Lyndon nodded. 'Tell me your idea.'

Naked, Lyndon tore down the corridor so fast and with such wide strides that she was sure her feet had only touched the ground twice before reaching the toilets. Thankfully, there was no sign of a soul about. Above all of the facilities flickered a green light to indicate that they were vacant. Just in case, Lyndon cautiously poked the door of the shower room ajar before stepping inside, not wanting to be directly confronted with an angry Op, mid-wash.

Lyndon panted in relief once inside but didn't hesitate to waste any of the remaining safe minutes. She stood underneath the circular pattern of holes in the ceiling, which immediately sprayed her with slightly warm water on sensing her there. As soon as the water touched her sooty and long-unwashed skin, she felt beautifully soothed. The heavy force of the water was not unpleasant. It hit her body with pulsating pats, as though tapped by the fingers of one hundred helping hands, and she felt gripped by it. She stood beneath it with eyes closed and senses tuned to the rivers of water that clutched her body as they ran simultaneously down her spine and between her breasts.

Holding Everley's soap, Lyndon smeared it over her face and down her neck, chest, hips, thighs and lower legs. She opened her eyes to watch the soapy bubbles slide from her cleansed skin and collect in the creases between her toes. The muck that had previously soiled her skin had muddied the water and was now leaving through the holes in the floor. A few seconds before the shower stopped, the water ran clear.

With a click, the dryer cycle started. Lyndon remembered this part. She held her arms out straight, letting the full force of the air push the water and leftover suds from her skin. The air dryer provided a final warm kneading of her body and massaged her muscles. Spinning slowly on the spot, she enjoyed every one of those sixty seconds.

Lyndon stepped towards the mirror and confronted her reflection. It had been so long that she had forgotten what she looked like. With a finger, she traced the shape of her eyebrows, and then down the soft curve of her nose. She looked closer into the mirror and noticed a fan of little lines around the outer corner of her eyes. They were small scores, like the creases on a piece of paper. She didn't dislike them so much as was surprised to see them. Time had been slipping away, and she now knew that her youth was leaving with it.

Returning her attention to the limited time left, she held her finger below a device in the mirror and watched as a puny amount of toothpaste foamed out. She used her finger as a brush and speedily scrubbed up and down every tooth. Taking one last look at her own reflection in the mirror so as to be able to recall it in the future, Lyndon nudged the door open and peered out. With the corridor still empty, she hopped into the hallway and rushed towards Everley's room without looking back.

Gripping the handle of Room 12, Lyndon paused. She trembled as she took her hand away and stared at the door number. She couldn't remember whether it was twelve or thirteen.

'Was it room twelve on floor thirteen? Or room thirteen on floor twelve?' her mind quizzed in panic.

BUZZ BUZZ BEEP BEEP BEEP

Lyndon leaped back and lunged to the right. She took the handle of Room 13 and, without another thought, turned it quickly and darted inside. Even before she had chance to turn to close the door, an Operative followed into the room behind her. She fell to her knees, curled into a ball and cowered.

'It's me!' said Everley quietly as he closed the door, sprung towards her, threw his body over hers and cuddled her on the ground.

'Thank Brito it's you! I thought I had the wrong room!' Lyndon said as she slowly straightened her body and stood. She was still shaking.

'You look...' Everley was lost for words.

'Clean?'

'Yes, very clean!' Everley smiled as he stroked her shining shoulder and noticed the rosy hue that flushed her body all over. 'I've got them,' he added, brandishing a pair of scissors in his free hand.

'Okay. I suppose it is the only way.' Lyndon dragged both palms down the length of her hair and twisted the ends into curls for the last time.

'I'm sorry if it makes you sad. Do you want me to do it?'

'Please. Do it quickly, before I have chance to think about it,' she said as she sat on the end of the bed, gathered all of the dark brown strands and pulled them straight upright and vertical for easier cutting.

Everley sat behind her and pushed the open scissors he had stolen from the Service Room into her mass of hair. Taking a deep breath, he started cutting. Her hair was so thick that it crunched as the sharp blades broke through it. Lyndon grimaced with every chomping gnaw.

'That's most of it,' said Everley after some time spent tackling the thick clumps. 'I'll tidy it up now.'

Lyndon's fingers were still clutching at what had been the ends of her hair. She drew her arm down slowly and draped the long lengths across her thighs. She studied the bright and light bits which made the dark brown stripey, and noticed how its natural waves rippled all the way down to the calm curls at the bottom. After one last stroke, she rolled it into a ball around her fist and said, 'I will use this in a pillow for the little one.'

Everley used his fingers to comb the short strands that were left and took little snips to even up the ends. Accustomed to styling his own hair into an approved, Operative cut, Everley finished tidying it in no time. He pursed his lips and gently blew Lyndon's neck free from the tiny tufts of hair that had fallen onto it.

'Ooh!' Lyndon chuckled, reaching back and feeling the lack of hair that was there. 'It's been years since I felt the wind tickle my neck!'

Everley didn't reply in words, but rather kissed the area. As his lips touched the sensitive spot, Lyndon melted.

'Well that makes losing my hair worth it,' she said sweetly.

With another kiss and caring squeeze, Everley stood and took some clothes from the hanging area.

'We are running out of time to get you to safety. Here,' he said as he handed her his work shirt and trousers, 'get into these while I sort the shoes.'

Everley stretched into the back of the shelf for the small tin of black polish that was there. Twisting it open, he peeled a rag from inside the lid. It was sludgy from the many times he had used it to buff his work boots to Brito's required amount of shine. He took his white shoes, which were still a little dirty from the walking route to the Special Project, and purposefully ruined them by blotting them with black all over.

Fully dressed and now wearing the dyed footwear, Lyndon saluted at Everley mockingly.

'What a fine young Operative!' Everley said, saluting back for real before understanding the joke and then grunting at his own dullness of mind. 'Right, I must shower myself, and then we will leave together.'

'Won't it be more dangerous together. If I am found, you will be...' Lyndon started.

223

'We will leave together,' he said as he kissed her again – this time on the lips – and headed back out of the room.

Lyndon smiled still, even after he had left. Her body was warm not only from the splendid shower and comforting clothes, but from the feeling of being with Everley.

She wiggled her toes inside the shoes (four sizes too big), and knew she had to leave this instance. It was the only way to protect Everley if her costume was not enough to convince the Operative crowds. She fetched her old and filthy frock, tucked it into the waistband of the trousers and slipped into the corridor amongst the other Operatives.

Raines had intended to get the train back to Point A with the returning Operatives as soon as the PRORA was over to try to find Everley, but those confounded Cardinals had demanded an immediate update. After a telephone conversation during which he found himself biting his lips to stop an illegal word from falling foully from his mouth no less than eight times, he spent the evening writing his report. He elaborately played-up the progress of his selected protégé, growing ever more furious with Everley with every word he typed. He could not fathom how this fine example of the next generation had excused himself from the PRORA, and the Cardinals definitely could not find out about it. Or else.

After submitting a largely-fictional report to the Office of the Chief Operative, where it would no doubt sit for days before being skim-read and then shredded, Raines had been unable to rest. He remained in his office all night without a wink of sleep. One minute he was launching items across the room in rage, and the next he was whimpering tears into his sleeves in self-pity. He imagined himself on a crazed rampage, battering Britons, using their bodies to construct a raft and sailing into the sea in the hopes of living out his days on Crusoe's Island or any other secluded sanctuary he could colonise. But, by morning, he had resolved to simply stick to the plan and find Everley.

If he found that Everley had indeed been at Social Contribution, not a separatist but rather the victim of some silly administrative error, then Raines could still sell him to the Cardinals in return for his own retirement. If, however, he found Everley to be one of a group of mutineers rebelling against the Operative lifestyle, then Raines would track down, capture and expunge them all. He would be hailed as a hero by the Cardinals and rewarded with retirement. As far as he could see it, it was win-win.

At six in the morning, Raines had cycled along the seaside to the station just one stop short of Point F. There, he joined the cohort of Operatives who had worked all night on the waterside windmills and were waiting for the train to take them home. Just before seven, he had boarded the Speed Line with the Night Shifters and was on the approach to Point A.

Struggling to keep his eyes open, the rhythmic rumble of the railway rocked him almost to sleep on his feet. His daze took his mind to past places, pre-Brito: a time of free will, choice and liberty, when you'd take the train to work, get your ticket hole-punched, buy an overpriced sandwich for lunch and sip tea from a polystyrene cup whilst wishing the kids opposite would shut up. You'd listen to music on headphones, read the newspaper and tut about the delays. God forbid there might be leaves on the line.

With a shrill screech, the Speed Line came to a halt. As the Night Shifters marched from the train one by one as though partaking in the most mundane conga line, they received their customary calls of congratulation and thanks from the Day Operatives waiting to board. The cries of 'For Brito!' irritated Raines to such an extent that he cringed every time he heard it.

He hung back so as to give himself an opportunity to identify Everley in the waiting crowd, but with every Op so boringly similar he soon realised he had little chance.

'Speed Driver!' Raines called into the cabin at the front of the train where there sat an old man staring aimlessly at the tracks ahead through thick glasses that hovered from the tip of his nose.

'Sir!' the man exclaimed, not used to seeing a person at his window.

'Command Raines,' he said, pointing at his silver pin. 'Don't open the doors until I return.'

The driver pushed his glasses up his nose and against his face so forcefully that the lenses caused his lashes to bend and his eyes to appear goggled. He straightened his back and saluted.

Raines frowned at him, disappeared from the window but quickly returned to add, 'I'll be back in one minute!'

Using the thick red line painted one foot from the platform's edge as a guide, Raines stomped the length of the ten carriages. At each queue opposite a silver set of doors, he stopped to examine the face of the first in line. Reaching the end, he had not found Everley.

Raines walked halfway back to the front of the train, then waved up towards the driver and gestured for the doors to be opened. Glancing at the queuing Operatives beside him, he noticed that they were all saluting. That was pleasing. At least the power of authority could momentarily make him happy, he thought.

But still the doors didn't open. With arms waving, he gesticulated in the direction of the driver, but soon gave up and crossly clomped to the cabin.

'Open them, then! Blame you!'

The old man was shocked almost off his seat, and was all fingers and thumbs trying to locate and press the door button. When he finally managed it, Raines darted back to watch the first (and Everley's usual) queue. The boarding was a wash of Brito bodies, too quick and too identical to find him in all the movement.

It was futile.

Raines approached the front desk of Everley's building.

'Where is your Enforcement Operative?' he said to the Day Watch Operative on duty.

'Well Best Mornin' to you too! Young Operatives should 'av better manners than all that!' she said without looking up from the stack of BritPost mail she was opening at the counter.

'You dare to speak to me like that!' Raines roared as he kicked the front panel of the desk.

The Day Watcher looked up at him and squinted. 'Oh! A Command Op, are we? Still, the Commands are meant ta be more proper! I ain't sat 'ere on this 'ere desk for these many years so you can talk to me bad, 'av I?'

'I have requested that you tell me where your Enforcement Operative is. You will do as I say and without question,' Raines said as calmly but officially as he could, while holding his fury in a ball in his hand.

'Yes, this is Brito, but you should know as well as I that a bit of kindness don't do no harm. We're all operating, aren't we? I has got an important role! I has still got a purpose, you know—'

'But you're coming to very end of your usefulness, aren't you?' Raines said, pinning her weathered hand against the desk with his own, stronger palm as he eyeballed her angrily. 'So I'd watch what you say to a Higher, if I were you...' he looked down to a chalk board that hung from the side of the desk, 'Operative Boone.'

'He's just arrived, so he'll be on floor twenty... sir,' she said, reluctantly.

That was good, thought Raines, as he wanted to hurry straight to Everley's room on Floor 12 (and didn't have the patience to converse with any other Operatives this morning). Raines patted her on the hand and sarcastically said, 'There, wasn't that difficult now, was it?!' as he turned towards the lifts.

'He's nearly same age as me! Should remember old Britain. Us older ones are meant t'av a bit of respect for each other,' her mumbles quietened as she spoke a monologue to herself.

'You lot need the PRORA, too!' Raines said as he disappeared into the lift. But the PRORA was wasted on the older ones, he considered as the doors closed and the lift travelled upwards. Those from old Briton knew that they *had* to do their duty, for there was nothing else. Plus, there was no need to worry about an uprising from the old generation, who were too exhausted to envisage an alternative to Brito (with no governing body to petition, even if they did have the energy to fight for it).

Arriving on Floor 12, Raines sauntered towards Everley's quarters. As he approached, he could clearly see that the door was partially open.

'Everley?' he called as he pushed at it.

Inside was standing an Operative that Raines did not recognise – and was not Everley. The individual turned to face him, dropping a pair of scissors to the floor in his surprise. He then stood to attention and saluted.

'Identify yourself!' Raines demanded coldly as he moved closer to the imposter.

'Selby, sir. Capital Selby.'

With forehead furrowed, Raines scrutinised the man from top to bottom.

Selby held his solid salute.

'I don't know you, Capital,' Raines finally stated as he stepped uncomfortably close to Selby and took hold of his bronze pin between his thick thumb and forefinger. He spun it around slowly and sinisterly said, 'That's puzzling, isn't it?'

Selby brushed Raines away from his pin with the back of his hand. He did so in a way that could have been mistaken for an accident while lowering his salute, but both parties knew it was intentional. Selby then stood at ease, despite no permission to do so.

This action was more insulting to Raines than if he had been spat at, sworn at or smacked, and Raines was getting redder with rage by the second.

'No, I don't believe so, Command,' said Selby with a nonchalant tone.

'Is it not?' Raines asked brashly. 'I have personally recruited all of the Capitals in my area of responsibility, and...'

'Aren't the PRORAs your area of responsibility, sir, not Point A?' Selby smiled arrogantly as he delivered the sentence. Unbeknown to Raines, Selby had heard of him before. Tales of Raines – who was 'getting on a bit', 'due his comeuppance', had 'a shout that could make concrete crumble' and 'a temper that scared old Britain into the history books' – had been circulating The Hidden for some time now. While Raines was often the pun of a mocking joke, now that Selby was actually facing this figure he thought better of goading him further, just in case the worst stories were true. He sucked in his cheeks to straighten his smirk.

'Woe betide the Capital who questions me!' Raines snapped as he lifted his foot and slammed his work boot to the floor. Annoyed upon noticing that Selby did not even flinch, Raines continued, 'I will have you demoted before the hour is up!' as he yanked the notebook from his top pocket and patted at his trousers for a pen.

'Calm yourself, sir,' Selby smiled as he patted Raines on the shoulder. Selby maintained his calm. In fact, he was well practised at wriggling free from confrontation. As a member of The Hidden, Selby's own mind was open. But over the years he had found that all Operatives, whatever the grade, were so accustomed to the same efficiency-focussed exchanges that they were easily eluded by a little confident conversation.

'You...' Raines was flummoxed. He felt both furious and speechless at the same time. And being lost for words was not a feeling that Raines was familiar with. Capitals were always so jittery and shy around him that the spirit of this one was throwing him off his usual staggeringly-abrasive style.

'As you know,' Selby said patronisingly, 'I operate for Point A Enforcement.'

'Well...' Raines looked suspicious still.

'I am inspecting the rooms, *obviously*,' Selby said with a shrug of the shoulders as he tugged the bed sheet, pulled it tight and re-tucked it underneath the mattress, then walked around the small and bare room, nodded and said, 'Very good indeed. Room approved,' aloud but as though to himself. He then stepped around Raines and made a move for the door.

Raines grabbed his arm.

'Look, sir, I must be on my way,' Selby said.

'Why... are you... here?' Raines said with difficulty. It was as though language had temporarily left him and sound needed to be persuaded back into his voice box.

'Why else would I be here?'

'You dare to question me *twice*?!' Raines' fury raised its head so fiercely that the words shot loudly from his mouth. He coughed gutturally, involuntarily releasing Selby's arm so as to catch his own spraying slobber.

Selby used this as an opportunity to promptly leave.

'I must go, sir. Have a utile day!' he called over his shoulder as he slipped out of the door without a salute.

Raines was left standing in the centre of the room, bashing at his own chest to ease air back into his lungs. With one huge intake of breath, he growled towards the ceiling. With eyes closed and fists pummelling his own thighs, Raines could only reflect on how the young Capital had maddened him more than the many other bothersome things that blew his top on a daily basis. He had entirely lost control of this situation and could only condemn himself.

Once he had regained some self-control, Raines moved to the door. He knew Selby had lied to him and that, without a shadow of a doubt, the so-called Capital would not be continuing his inspection in the neighbour's quarters. Nevertheless, Raines needed to check.

He stuck his head out into the corridor, looked up and down and listened out for any noise at all. Of course, there was no sign or sound. Selby had disappeared.

For Raines, this was confirmation of a rebellion. He had evidence that Everley was killing InOps, as well as missing the PRORA. While Raines didn't know which side Everley was fighting for, he certainly knew that Everley was not fighting alone. If Selby was helping him, there might be more besides, and Raines wanted to be the one to bring down the whole lot of them. It would mean more work when all he really wanted to do was retire, but the opportunity for more notoriety excited him. It could be the pinnacle of his career. Still, the very thought of all of the time and effort required for this crusade sent him spinning into another frenzy.

Slamming the door, Raines tore around the room displacing the few belongings from their original positions and causing chaos. With the bed dishevelled, clothing hangers flung across the floor and little else left to make messy, Raines stared out of the window and wondered whether throwing himself from it would provide the settled release he so desperately needed.

If only the window could be opened.

XVI

The eleventh order of Brito is to

increase the Operative population by any means necessary.

Addendum six to the eleventh order is to

harvest young lives for early indoctrination.

This practice includes, but is not limited to,

acquiring the offspring of the InOperative side of society.

- The Cardinals

Everley had been far more efficient in his working day than he had expected to be, considering he was so worn out after what he knew to be the most energetic night of his life. Not only was his body drained, but his mind was elsewhere. He had thought of nothing but Lyndon, replaying all he could remember of the night so as to keep the memories vivid and remind himself that something so dreamlike was really real.

He had spent his midday rest minutes sitting atop the windmill and dreamily staring out to sea, but was abruptly awoken when his harness caught itself on one of the propellers and began dragging him towards the very edge. Thankfully, he had his knife to hand and was able to free himself from being tethered just in time to watch his tools tumble one hundred and thirty-three metres to the ground. He climbed down to collect them immediately afterwards.

Everley had been smiling all day, despite thinking endlessly of the moment that had been snatched away: a tender goodbye. With Lyndon leaving while he was in the shower, Everley had eagerly returned to his room to find only a lock of hair to mark she was ever there. His mouth tingled all day with the last kiss that he hadn't been able to give her. He had touched his lips with his soft fingertips so many times, as though to keep the feeling lingering there. Now that he was on the Speed Line and almost back at Point A, he was so full of anticipation at the thought of seeing her and give this long-awaited kiss that every part of him fidgeted on the spot.

He peered out of the train window as it charged into the station in the hopes of seeing her (but couldn't). He waited for the silver doors to open with his nose almost touching the rubber seal for what felt like a month of minutes. Everley knew that with her hair cut short and wearing his clothes, Lyndon would be able to pass through the Operative area with less risk, and he was certain that she would be waiting at the station for him. Almost certain. Well, he had certainly hoped for it all day.

Everley skipped out of the carriage, hurtled down the exit way, came back through the station entrance and then paced behind the Night Operatives who were boarding the train for their shift. As the platform emptied out and the Speed Line thundered away again, there was no sign of Lyndon. His face fell to a frown for the first time since morning.

After treading the area for less than half a minute, Everley couldn't hold onto his patience any longer. He removed his coat, turned it inside out, put it back on and climbed under the large hanging poster into the InOp area. It was only as he twisted to straighten the poster back down that he noticed a figure watching him from the corner of the station. He would worry about that later, Everley thought, for now all his thoughts were with Lyndon.

Everley retraced what he remembered to be the steps to Little Lyndon's cupboard shelter, but, with a ground of undulating, multi-coloured mounds, it was extremely difficult to discern a right turn from a wrong one. One area of disregarded objects and purposeless items looked like any other, and he was very quickly lost.

Everley stood facing a high bank of stacked scrap and decided to climb to the peak in the hope that he could identify the route – or Lyndon herself – from the elevated viewpoint. For a short moment, he considered which solid things would make the most secure footholds and which protruding bits would be the best handholds, then daringly vaulted upwards. No sooner had he set off did his clean, Operative palm grip the cracked edge of a huge sheet of what looked like clear glass or plastic. With a pained whine that rang throughout the InOp area, Everley clasped his hands together and tumbled the few steps down to where he had started.

Landing on his side, he stayed there and stared at his clamped hands. Everley blew at them to fan the injury away, but the tingle was now a sting that moved a burning sensation up his arm. As soon as he released his squeeze, blood leaked out from between his fingers and down his wrists. He could barely look at the horrible mess the slice had caused, and felt sick at the sight of the severed skin.

Thanks to Brito, his Operative training had included minor injuries, so he squeezed his hands back together, took a few calming breaths and scoured the immediate area for something to stop the bleeding and dress the wound. The InOps had taken most of the flexible material to fashion into garments. Instead, the waste piles were full of hard objects for which Everley had no idea of the use. There was a pink thing in the form of a muscly man with only underpants on, but it had lost its head. There was a spherical shiny blue thing with green shapes and lots of names or words written in a barely readable size, but it had been crushed and had a hole in the side. Everley recognised the word 'Ocean', but had no knowledge of the words that were around it.

After a little more looking, Everley saw a black thing that appeared to be smooth and palm sized. The blood spilt free as soon as he released his grip of himself and grasped the object with his unharmed hand. The thing seemed to be attached to the hoard of rubbish by a long black string that was coming out of its bottom. Everley tugged at it and then, more desperately, yanked at it until it was free. There was about a metre of this strange wire, and Everley questioned for only a moment what it may have originally been connected to. He quickly examined the shiny surface of the object, both sides of which could be depressed and made a clicking sound as he did so. There was also a small rotating wheel in the centre which did nothing when he spun it to and fro with his thumb. He placed the sleek part of the object in his palm and wound its wire round and round his hand until everything was tightly secured into place.

By this point, Everley's hands, arms and feet were splattered with the red of his own pure-Briton blood and he felt dizzy. He perched on a large white box of some sort that had white shelves inside and was missing a door, and wondered whether he could visit the Health Centre before it closed and make pretend about being hurt at work.

'Everley!' Lyndon shouted from the next mountain of litter as she approached him hurriedly. Her tone sounded angry.

'Sorry. Should I have not come?' Everley said as he rose to his feet.

Lyndon continued to bound towards him. Her face was all screwed up, her forehead was creased and eyebrows were lowered to almost meet in the middle. She said nothing but held her lips together.

'I wanted to see you. I couldn't wait...'

Lyndon stopped a foot in front of him, withdrew her arm and slapped her hand right across his face.

Everley held his cheek with his unhurt hand and silently looked into her eyes.

Lyndon smacked him again, then pushed and thumped at his chest as she cried. She threw her fists into his front and walloped him with all the weight of her fragile frame. Everley didn't move. He stood straight, allowing her to attack him with all of her might. His strong body barely felt each bash. His flexed muscles protected everything inside him except the feelings of his heart. In the greatest emotional pain, he too began to cry.

'Why are you doing this, Lyndon?' he said as he took a hold of one of her arms to stop it from hitting him again.

'Why did you do it, Everley? Why?!' she screamed. 'I don't understand how you could do such a thing! Are you so damaged by Brito that you hate yourself for what we did and had to take it out on an InOp? Why did you do it?'

Everley looked entirely confused.

'Answer me!'

'What did I do?' Everley said holding his arms out with palms facing upwards.

'Did that happen whilst you were attacking her? Did it?!' Lyndon pointed to the dripping wound he had just bandaged.

'Attack? I don't know what you mean.'

'You've killed her! You killed her when she was searching for her baby.'

'Baby? I don't know what you...'

'The Child Catcher took the baby!'

'Child Catcher?' Everley had never previously considered why there were very few InOp children. In fact, except for Little Lyndon's daily disturbance of the queue at Point A, he had never seen another young one.

'The Child Catcher! He comes at night. He came last night while you and I were...' she looked away in disgust and swallowed, '...together. Little Lyndon ran–'

'Is Little Lyndon alright?' Everley asked with genuine concern that a catcher of children had snatched him as well.

'Don't act like you care! The Child Catcher took the baby and she was out trying to find it, and you... you killed her! Why did you kill her?!' Lyndon said with a voice that was choking with both anger and sadness.

236

'I haven't killed anyone! I have been working all day. I came here because...'

'You murderer!' Lyndon said as she took one last look at his harmed hand and backed away.

'I cut this on there,' he said, turning his head towards the transparent sheet that was sticking out of the mound and now tainted with a dripping dark-red liquid.

Lyndon continued to back away, stumbling every third step on the uneven land. She wiped the tears from her eyes with the back of her hand and sniffed.

'Please don't go! I came here because I had to see you. I have been thinking only of you all day.'

Lyndon turned away from him.

'Please believe me! I didn't kill anyone!' Everley shouted out to her with only anguish in his voice.

Lyndon turned only the side of her head back to face him and said in a flat and exhausted tone, 'You used the scissors. The same scissors you used to cut my hair. So I know it was you. I don't want to ever see you again.' She then turned and continued to walk away.

Everley's mouth was open. His chin fell. Tears dripped from the bottom of his jaw. His shoulders lowered and hands dropped to his sides. All he felt was a hole where his heart had been. He couldn't hear it beating anymore. All that seemed to matter was lost and even the brilliance of Brito wasn't enough to bring the breath back.

After visiting the Health Centre to lie about the cause of his hand wound and have it bandaged, Everley traipsed up the stairs in his building. The lift would be regularly going up and down to carry his fellow Operatives between the solitude of their own quarters and the group entertainment of the single television in the Service Room, and Everley had no energy for evening conversation.

He puffed with every step upwards. He allowed his brain to think over the accusations hurled at him by Lyndon. He knew he hadn't committed *this* murder, that was a fact, but he had committed many more, that was for sure. He had killed more InOps than he could remember (not to mention the one at the windmills), and he had assisted in murders, too. He was one of the self-righteous Operative body with a shared belief in the immorality of waste, the morality of waste management, and the weight of the oath as back up. Many a-time had he been one of a pack that had pushed a pointless InOp from Point A's platform edge and watched with great satisfaction as another worthless life was stricken from existence. It was all to lower the burden on Brito, they were taught. And although Selby had reminded him that killing an InOp was not murder, it suddenly felt wrong. Reprehensible. Unfair. So, despite having not committed *this* crime, Lyndon's recriminations were nonetheless apt and Everley accepted that he justly deserved her disdain. He was an Operative, and Operatives were murderers.

The long slog up the twelve flights seemed a fitting additional punishment for all that was wrong. And the cut on his hand. And the loss of Lyndon. As well as the self-deprecating monologue that tormented him as he continued up the stairs, a concerning question lingered in his mind: *'Who took the scissors?'*

Everley had been in a rush that morning and, on returning from the shower to find that Lyndon had already left his room, he had hurried out on the off-chance he might catch a last glimpse of her before work. In his haste, he hadn't paid attention to whether the scissors were or weren't on his bed. He had forgotten all about them.

On reflection, forgetting about the scissors was a thoughtless and incredibly risky thing to do. Everley knew that an Enforcement Operative would have inspected his room, just as they do with all quarters on the first day after a PRORA. If they had found a pair of scissors, Everley would be in real trouble. He had no plausible excuse for removing them from the Service Room and none he could invent either.

Perhaps the scissors hadn't been found. Perhaps it was a different pair that was used in the killing in the InOp area. Perhaps the truth would reveal itself in time. For now, he could think only of climbing onto his bed and sleeping this day away. Perhaps everything would be okay tomorrow.

As Everley approached the door to his room, he could see a yellow ticket hanging from the handle. His heart boomed throughout his body as the panic set in. At least it wasn't a red ticket. Reds were the worst.

He slowly slid the string from the handle and lifted the ticket to read it.

ENFORCEMENT NOTICE

ISSUED BY: BRITO

DATE OF ISSUE: *Day 99, Year 26 AE*

1. THIS NOTICE HAS BEEN ISSUED BY THE ENFORCEMENT OPERATIVE BECAUSE THERE HAS BEEN A BREACH OF:

[Write Section number, as applicable]

Section 7(1)(a): 'Protection of items provided by Brito'

2. THE LEVEL OF THIS BREACH IS: [Mark as appropriate]

~~(i) MINOR INFRINGEMENT~~

(ii) VIOLATION

3. REMEDIAL MEASURES: [Mark as appropriate]

(i) Refresher training must be completed as below:

Refer to Section 7(1)(a) in the Brito manual.

(ii) Corrective action:

Room B12.13 must be presented to Brito standards.

Bed must be repositioned and made ready for sleeping.

~~(iii) Disciplinary action:~~

~~Report to your Higher Operative immediately.~~

4. COMPLAINCE OF THIS NOTICE WILL BE CONFIRMED ON:

Day 100, Year 26 AE

5. THE ENFORCEMENT OPERATIVE HEREBY ISSUES THIS YELLOW NOTICE AS A WARNING. FAILURE TO COMPLY WILL RESULT IN A RED NOTICE, FOR WHICH YOUR HIGHERS WILL BE IMMEDIATELY NOTIFIED.

HAVE A UTILE DAY!

'The bed?!' Everley said out loud. The side of his nose lifted as he considered why the bed – and not the scissors or missing clothes and shoes – was cause for a yellow notice.

As he opened the door, the chaos within his quarters revealed itself inch by inch. The wire-framed bed had been dragged into almost the centre of the room. The single sheet had been pulled backwards. Hanging diagonally from the bottom corner of the bed, the remaining three-quarters were rumpled on the floor. The few clothes that had been left there that morning had been torn from their hangers and were strewn across the bed. His soap was still in its rightful place on the little shelf, but his picture... No! His picture of The Other Place had been ripped through the middle (but remained hanging from the wall by its four corners). The beautiful image was ruined.

Everley stood looking at the mess not knowing what to make of it. It was as though the most ferocious wind had whirled in through the window and collected up all of the items inside, swirling them around wildly before releasing them to rest wherever they landed. It could not have been the wind though, for the window could not be opened. It must have been a person, and an angry one at that. That same person must have taken the scissors to kill the InOp with.

Everley had no energy to question the whys and hows of the situation; his heart longed for Lyndon and his hand ached beneath the bandage. With the path to Lyndon dissolving, Everley knew he had to get back to his dedicated Operative ways and be a better

Briton. His recent actions had deceived Brito, and whatever had occurred in his room did not make amends for his breaking of the oath by cavorting with an InOp.

Obediently, he began to tidy the place. He was filled with the impending doom that he would be found out soon in any case.

Another day and another day's work at the waterside windmills.

Everley moped through his designated tasks. He knew them so habitually that his body continued moving through the motions even if his mind was elsewhere. But today his mind was nowhere. It was neither day-dreaming of The Other Place nor questioning the meaning of life (and it was certainly not thinking excitedly about Lyndon, as it had been the day before). His mind was too weary for any kind of thought at all after a sleepless, lonely and emotional night that had left his body sensitive and his eyes stinging.

Everley sealed windmill number five in his section by lifting the white metal handle upwards toward the sky. Although he had heard the door lock with a heavy clunk, he gave it an extra nudge with his shoulder just to make sure.

The buzzer for the small break that was permitted at midday had not yet sounded. Everley checked his internal clock. There was probably twenty more minutes until the rest break and no need to not use them productively, he thought. So, he collected his coat that was folded neatly on the ground, adjusted his tool belt to sit it more comfortably on his hips and plodded the short distance to windmill number six.

Everley was both wet with sweat and feeling chilly at the same time. The sun was beaming warmly from a sky without clouds but there was a light breeze coming from the sea. Between the two windmills was a small plot of green land surrounded by sand. Flicks of grass sprouted upwards in patches and there were two or three tiny trees with budding handfuls of fresh leaves. As he approached the edge of this pastoral oasis, Everley stopped. All around him was the rare sound of birdsong. He closed his eyes and listened to the *coo-kee coo-kee,* the *pip-pip* and the *ch-ch-chirp-chirp.* He wondered what they were saying to each other while going about their own work for Brito. Whatever work that was.

With a rush of air and a shocking impact, Everley's legs were taken out from under him and he fell forward to the ground. His face filled with grass and sand, and he inhaled gritty bits as he landed. Scraping his tongue with his fingers, spitting and then brushing his eyes, Everley flung himself over onto his back to identify the diving cause of the attack that had so forcefully flattened him. With the sun directly overhead, he was blinded. He shielded his eyes with the back of his hand but could only see two legs towering over him.

'Well? Salute to your Higher Operative!' came a demanding voice that Everley recognised to be the man in his room that night.

Everley saluted, still lying there and coughing sand.

'I want an explanation, boy! You had better tell me now, and I mean right bloody NOW, what you and your gang are up to!' Raines blasted at him.

'Gang... sir?'

'Your gang of rebels!' With Everley still silent, Raines tutted, muttered, 'Hmm... 'gang' in Op speak...' then continued loudly with 'A team. A troop. A group! For fuck sake! You know what I'm talking about! I want answers, son!'

'I operate with all those on the eight-to-eight shift for the waterside windmills. I am not in any *other* group sir.'

'Rubbish! I trusted you, Everley. I thought we had an understanding. We were going to get to know each other more.'

'Sir, I...' Everley wanted to explain sincerely that he still wanted to get to know Raines, only he had expected him to visit him in his room again and hadn't seen him since. He wanted to say how much he admired him as a Command and understand more about why he had singled out Everley in the first place, but he was silenced.

Raines had positioned his foot on Everley's chest and was pressing down hard. The indents in the boot's bottom bore into his skin.

'You better tell me the truth, son. I thought you were out killing InOps for the good of Brito, or just for the fun of it... but now I find you are conspiring with others!'

Everley stuttered without forming any tangible words. He needed to think. What did Raines know... and how? He must have seen him in the InOp area with Lyndon. For a flitting moment, Everley considered coming clean and letting this heartache be over by admitting his relationship with Lyndon. That would mean certain banishment, of course, and he would have no purpose without Brito. It was best to lie, he decided.

'There is only me, sir.'

'Liar!' Raines flew to the ground, bent his knees onto Everley's shoulders and grabbed his throat. 'I'm going to squeeze your neck so tight,' he said as his nails started digging in, 'that this will be your last breath! Use it to TELL ME THE TRUTH!'

Everley tried to push him away but his arms were pinned underneath Raines' shins. He gasped and choked on the lack of air.

'I don't know...' Everley struggled to whisper.

'Who is Selby?'

Selby? ' he said only to himself, thinking that all of this was about Lyndon.

Noting Everley's look of confusion immediately on saying the name, Raines released his grip. There was an innocence in Operatives that made it almost impossible to conceal the body's language telling a truth.

'Could it be that you really don't know what I'm talking about?' Raines said as he took Everley's head in both hands and lifted it. 'Breathe, Everley, breathe!'

Everley took a series of tiny breaths and then allowed a huge gulp of air into his lungs with such force that his chest raised and pushed Raines upwards.

'Come on, it's alright,' Raines said as he eased his knees from Everley's shoulders and resumed a standing position with a groan. 'I'm too old for this,' he added to himself.

Everley's pants slowed as his breathing returned to normal. He rolled onto his side, lifted himself by pressing an elbow into the sand and propped his head up with a fist. He lay there silently with eyes squinting suspiciously upwards at Raines.

'Oh, come now! You can't blame me for being angry!' Raines laughed. 'So, you're going to tell me you don't have a single idea why a man named Selby might have been in your room?'

'He was in my room?' Everley said to Raines but also to the air as his head fell back in thought. His voice showed his concern. If Selby had been in his room, then he must have been the one to muddle it. There seemed to be no reason why Selby would have created such chaos there. Could it truly have been him who wrenched the bed from the wall, the sheet from the bed... and the scissors from the sheet? He looked back at Raines and asked, '*When* was he in my room?'

'Yesterday it was. Yesterday morning,' Raines said so much calmer now that it was as though the contemptible Command had been replaced by a different human being altogether. He picked a few pieces of grass from his trousers and flicked them away. 'So you have no idea why he was there? No idea at all?'

'No, sir,' Everley said with all believability because he really did not know why Selby was in his quarters, trashing the contents and taking the scissors.

Everley's brain swirled between questions and possible answers. As it did so, his head turned from left to right, as though to find the answers in the air somewhere around him. He shifted onto his knees when a realisation found him: If Selby was tearing up his room, he must have found the scissors and taken them, for they were not there when Everley returned home that night. Those scissors were used by an Operative to kill an InOp. A female InOp. *'Selby must have thought it was Lyndon, and tried to kill her!'* Everley concluded and held his mouth in shock.

'What is it, boy?' Raines said, perceiving an inner turmoil developing within Everley. 'Do you know a Selby?'

'I do know a Selby, sir,' he said as he stood. He looked at Raines and continued slowly, 'He's a Higher Operative. A Capital.'

'And how do you know this Capital?'

'He... he...' Everley was conflicted. He assumed that Raines – a Command – would be aware of such things as Special Projects, but he couldn't be sure. Upon realising Selby could not be trusted, Everley wanted to be honest with Raines, but there may be more trouble to be had if he was anymore associated with Selby and his underground 'gang' than he was already.

'Yes?' snapped Raines, starting to lose his rag again. As it was, he was being more patient than usual.

'Command Raines,' Everley saluted as he said it, then lowered his hand again. 'I walk the longest route from my building to Point A. I do this because I like to make my body work a little harder in the morning before work so that I will be stronger and more efficient, you understand?'

'Yes, yes. Go on.'

'Well, this route takes me through the InOp area.'

'Yes?'

'A short time ago... although I can't remember when exactly... a Capital introduced himself to me. He talked to me about hating the InOps and other such oath-worthy things.'

'Yes, very good. And?'

'And I saw him a number of times there in the InOp area. He was friendly... But I think he was following me. Yes, it must have been Selby she meant!' Everley said the last sentence aside.

'She?'

'I was told by...' Everley stumbled, not wanting to bring Lyndon into this, 'an Operative in my building. She said she'd seen somebody following me. Anyway, he *has* been following me, sir.

And as you say, he was in my room! Maybe he is the secret bin man you thought I was. Do you think that's it, sir? Do you think he is killing the InOps and making people think it's me? Could that be it, sir?'

'Let's not get ahead of ourselves.' Raines paused. 'Why would a Capital do that though?' he added with real curiosity.

The pair didn't speak. Birdsong and the distant sea waves were the only sounds for some time as they each mulled over the question.

'In any case, there is the small matter of the PRORA,' Raines said as he took a strong step towards Everley that sent a puff of sand smoke into mid-air. 'You missed it, and missing a PRORA comes with *dire* consequences.'

Everley nodded.

'Where were you?'

'I received a telegram, sir, telling me to go to Social Contribution at the Recycling Centre,' Everley said, not lying.

'Right. I want to see this telegram.'

'Certainly. It is in my quarters. I will get it for you–'

'No need, no need.' Raines had tested Everley enough. He didn't need to see the telegram (nor the odd little note that was with it), because he had already taken it from Everley's room. Raines slid his hand into his pocket and fingered both pieces of paper. He considered asking Everley for the meaning of the series of numbers, but was determined to figure it out himself.

'You will be at the next PRORA, and that is a direct order!'

'Of course, sir! I very much look forward to the PRORA! The floor is all shiny and black and it is beside the sea!'

'Yes, that's right,' said Raines with a little suspicion that Everley may be able to recall too much. 'And what else do you like about it?'

'The golden gates! I can't remember much more than that, sir... but I know that afterwards I felt the most happy an Operative could feel!'

'That's it, Everley!' Raines patted him hard on the back and grinned. 'Well you are going to be my guest at the next PRORA, okay?'

'Guest?'

'You are going to be by my side. You can be the one to hand me my speech, okay? And you will stand on the edge of the stage as we recite the oath.'

'Sir!' To an Operative, this was a daydream come true.

'And maybe... if you follow everything I say... and do everything I tell you to...'

BEEP BEEP BEEP BEEP BEEP

The alarm for the midday rest minutes sounded loudly through tall speakers between the windmills and echoed throughout Everley's Section.

Raines dug his finger into his ear and waggled it while uttering a word that Everley had never heard before.

'Sir?'

'Yes?'

'I would always abide by your words, for you are my Command, but you were about to say what would happen if I follow everything you say and do...?'

'Oh yes! These fucking alarms scream so bloody loudly that it scares my thoughts right out of my ears!'

Everley looked quizzical.

'If you follow me, then there will be a promotion to Capital in it for you!' Raines said with an eyebrow raise. Seeing the look of joy on Everley's face, he couldn't help but hold his belly and let out a loud laugh. 'Come on, you and I have five minutes before you have to be back up that next windmill!'

Everley smiled as the two walked up a sandy knoll. Following closely behind Raines, Everley carefully matched his steps and placed his own feet into the deep dents of the Command's footprints.

'Capital Everley!' announced the voice inside.

XVII

'The dominant school of thought is that absolute uniformity is best for Brito.

To keep individual identities suppressed, the regime is based on deprivation.

With their minds muzzled, the bad and broken people in charge, and no positive personalities to influence them, the nation is contaminated from within.'

- Servant SV23 (alias "Capital Selby") addressing The Hidden management board

Raines had cycled back to the office building at the PRORA. As he rested the bike against the wall that partitioned the sandy shore and the concrete of the piazza floor, he looked out wistfully. The sea was so still and blue that it blurred indistinguishably into the sky. The sun lit his face and warmed his cheeks in such a way that he felt caressed and pulled towards its direction, high in the sky.

Raines stepped onto a ledge that had been cut into the wall. These had previously been used for seaside seating whilst eating an ice cream or fish supper, but that was all history now. He shifted his bottom onto the top of the wall and sat there restfully on its wide and curved concrete. His legs dangled to the side above the ledge as though he were a child. And as a child, there would have been boats on this strip of sea. Ferries and freight ships and the odd cruise liner. There used to be so much movement and noise, hustle and bustle everywhere, but now all was silent. Lifeless. Lost.

This was no time for nostalgia. The repeated thoughts of his past life were paining Raines. With each happy recollection he felt drawn deeper into a sunken sorrow. The sadness made him angry. He had to maintain a balance, and control of his senses. But not for much longer, he hoped.

Raines took the two pieces of paper from his pocket and held them out, side by side. The telegram looked official enough, but there was something in the language that seemed unusual.

'Hmm... "P.S. Good Morning Briton." Do we really sign off a telegram like that these days?' he thought as he read to the end.

It was possible. The Education Office would often issue refreshed guidelines on how words should be used and how sentences should be phrased when communicating with Operatives. Guidelines, that is, to mentally manipulate the maximum amount of effort out of an Operative. Raines hadn't read the updates since he lost his passion for it all. It could have been years.

He read the tiny, handwritten numbers from the small scrap of paper.

'5 11 15 23 17 18 26 18 16 25 1 2 25 30 32 29'

His head moved from side to side as he compared the numbers in his left hand to the telegram in his right. With mouth downturned and a crease between both bushy eyebrows, he raised his mystified eyes and looked out to sea.

'C-C-Command?'

'What the–?!' Raines swore as he was rudely shaken from his deep contemplation and almost fell from his perch into the water below. He scrunched his hands into his pockets, and the papers with them.

'Apologies C-Command. I have the report on Capital Selby you asked for.'

'Creeping up on me like that! Are you trying to...' Raines stopped himself and took a breath through gritted teeth. 'The report, yes. Thank you. Put it on my desk and I will be inside momentarily.'

'Wilco.' The nervous Capital began to leave, then hesitated and asked softly, 'Is everything alright, Command?'

'Yes! Why do you ask?' Raines had a fleeting thought that the Cardinals were having him spied upon. Perhaps they were. Perhaps he was just feeling self-conscious because he knew he was behaving secretively. He crunched the paper in the palm of his left hand but couldn't feel the telegram in his right.

'You're sitting on the wall, sir.'

'Yes?' Raines said hurriedly, wanting the Capital to disappear so that he could look for the telegram.

'For what purpose is that, Command?'

Raines smiled. He wasn't being spied upon. It was simply so incredible to an Operative that anyone would gaze at a view for the sheer joy of it. It didn't serve a purpose; it did not contribute to the whole and was therefore an inefficient use of time and energy.

'I am using the sun's rays to wipe these lines from my skin,' he said mischievously as he released his right hand from his pocket and pointed to the long wrinkles that spread across his forehead. He raised his eyebrows to make the creases so deep and pronounced that you could have clamped a separate sheet of paper in every single one.

'Really, sir? For Brito! Should I do the same?'

'Only when you are as old as I am,' Raines grinned. Maybe he had given the young Capital the gift of a few moment's relaxation in his later years (if his moulded mind still remembered this conversation by then). 'I'll take that report now actually,' he requested with an outstretched arm.

After the Capital provided him with a perfectly folded paper and then scurried off, Raines emptied his pockets. The numbered paper was there but not the telegram. He looked on the top of the wall and on the ground but there was nothing.

'Oh, fucking hell!' he said as he saw it bobbing along a mellow wave that was taking it out to sea.

With a long snarl, Raines shook his head. He unfolded the report that the Capital had provided, which simply read:

FAO: Com. Raines

RE: A CAPITAL OPERATIVE NAMED SELBY

Findings: Brito does not have a Capital Operative named Selby.

Raines had spent very little time in the InOp area. He preferred to avoid it at all costs, knowing a lone Command wondering through their area would be a prime candidate for an InOp attack. Plus, he had always worried about catching the virus or some other horrible disease from these wasteful reprobates. But needs must. He had to find out more about Selby, and the InOp area was the place to do it.

Raines rose to his feet from behind a large industrial oven that was upturned and standing on its hobs atop a heap of other large silver, black and white goods that had once been fitted in restaurants, takeaways or home kitchens. Over his Brito-issued clothes, Raines was wearing a huge tapestry of materials that had been woven together into a vast cape. He had acquired it in the middle of the night by snatching it from a sleeping InOp as he breezed past. It would definitely provide a disguise.

Raines yawned as morning dawned over the wasteland. With his amazing monochrome Dreamcoat dragging behind him, he shuffled down a flattened pathway to find a better surveillance spot. As soon as he approached the barren space in front of what he recognised to be the rear of Point A, he saw a small huddle assembling. He would need to get closer to hear what they were saying, but Raines wasn't feeling so self-assured now. One InOp he could handle, but he couldn't risk being identified by a bigger crowd.

Raines kept his back to a stack of what should have been recycled paper. Taking slow side-steps, he was camouflaged in the environment. Reaching the last part that felt safe, he bent his knees and sat on the ground. The cape engulfed him so completely that to see him would be only to see a molehill of material amongst a mountain range of rubbish.

It wasn't long before the reason for the InOp meeting was clear; they had a visitor. That visitor was dressed like an Operative. Raines squinted his eyes to try to recognise the figure. He couldn't be sure, but it did look like Selby. The figure had the same height, weight and skin colour, and walked with a certain swagger that said, "I'm confident and comfortable amongst you". That was highly unusual in itself, but it would certainly explain why Brito had no record of a Selby if he was, in fact, an InOp.

Raines continued to observe the meeting through strained eyes. The InOps queued around Selby, who had removed something from his pocket. The thing glinted as it reflected the glare of the morning sun and Raines recognised it immediately to be a metal tin can. It was just the type of can that would contain nutrition tablets. Raines watched as Selby reached into it and handed a single item to the patiently waiting InOps, one by one. As each received their allowance, they bowed gratefully and left quickly.

In no time, the queue was gone and Selby was left alone with one last customer. Whatever was left in the tin can was poured into the hands of this InOp, presumably to be distributed to the rest of the community. There was some communication between the two, they shook hands and then Selby departed out of view.

Raines freed a hand from deep within the cape and scratched his head. He would need a shower after this, he thought with a disgusted look on his face. His self-commanded reconnaissance mission was successful and he had gathered some information, so now it was time to leave.

It had been a strange time. For as long as he could vividly remember (which was only fifteen days or so), Everley had moved through a variety of emotions that he was sure he had never experienced before. From the elation of his selection for the Special Project and the joy of feeling friendship, he had been confronted by the hurt of feeling betrayed. From the electricity that sparked his every nerve at the sight of Lyndon, came the bottomless despair that missing her had brought him. From feeling proud about a possible promotion to Capital, to being reproached by his own conscience; Lyndon said he was part of a *change*, not part of the thing that divided them. Lastly, from feeling confused about the ways of Brito and determined to learn the 'truth', to losing the energy to question anything anymore.

Everley was busy working another shift at the windmills (and imagining his role with Command Raines at the next PRORA). It was nearly the end of his day and, as he wheeled his bicycle across a stretch of grass towards Point F station, he considered doing voluntary Social Contribution at the Recycling Plant that evening. He decided that such a use of his time would bring the greatest benefit to Brito and the One, and hoped he would forget how drained his body was as long as he could keep it moving.

'Whiskey Tango One, Whiskey Tango One, this is Sierra Two. Urgent. Repeat. Urgent. Come in. Over,' came a voice through the radio that was clipped to Everley's belt. Before there was a reply, the same voice said, 'Calling all Sections! Calling all Sections! Urgent! Over!'

Everley let go of his bike. It fell slowly, cushioned by the long grass. He reached for his radio, but it hissed as the Watch Tower responded to the call before he could unfasten it from his belt.

'Sierra Two, this is Whiskey Tango One. Go ahead. Over.'

'Urgent! Urgent! Code 6... Windmill eight spinning out of control!'

'Sierra Two, are you in a safe position? Over.'

'Yes. Dismounted. Over.'

Everley was stood on the very border between Section Three (his own) and Two. Without a thought, he heaved his bike upright and plonked himself onto it. He pedalled speedily, taking himself across the uneven land with one hand. In the other was on his radio.

'Sierra Three on way to assist,' Everley said with a finger on the button.

There had been no reply from the Watch Tower. An Operative there was likely looking through a manual to establish the best course of action.

As Everley continued to pedal, the sky in front of him was filling with huge plumes of thick grey smoke that pumped from the turbine generator of a close-by windmill.

'Urgent! Urgent! Code 7!... Windmill eight now on fire!' came the panicked voice of the Operative in Section Two.

'Sierra Three on way to assist,' Everley repeated as the speed of his legs span the wheels even faster.

'This is Whiskey Tango One. Emergency Office contacted... Fire Operatives... when available. Leave Section... report to Point F. Over.' The line was fading in and out.

'Say again?' called the panicked Operative waiting for guidance.

Everley arrived in the area and could see the Section Two Operative standing below the windmill and looking up at the bellowing flames. It was Harford, a dedicated Operative who had helped Everley recently when his bicycle chain broke.

'I'm here!' yelled Everley as he hopped off his bike and ran over.

'Take no action. Return to Point F. Repeat. Return to Point F. Do you copy?' spoke the Watch Tower in an unemotional tone that did not match the danger of the situation.

BOOM!

Everley stopped running. He watched as all three spinning blades detached themselves from the centre of the turbine with a flash of orange and an almighty bang that made the ground quake. They were shooting towards the ground.

'Harford, RUN!' screamed Everley as they both turned away from the windmill and ran in the opposite direction.

Everley didn't see which way Harford went but kept running as fast as his feet could carry him. With a loud swoosh, an enormous shard of shiny blade flew directly above his head and crashed destructively into a fence and row of brambly bushes ahead. Everley dropped to the ground and held his arms over his head. There was a cluster of other crashing sounds, but then the area fell silent.

'Do you copy? Over.'

Everley could hear the Watch Tower calling over the radio, but the sound was distant. He must have dropped it in all the commotion. He looked back at the windmill, which was no longer aflame but now just a pole in the ground. Blade parts and pieces were sticking upwards in the grass, but Harford was nowhere to be seen.

'Harford? Are you alright?' Everley called out. He darted back to where he had last seen him and called again. 'Haaarfooord!'

'Help... Briton!'

Everley scanned the land frantically to find the source of the pained voice.

'Help!'

'I've found you,' Everley said as he rushed to where Harford was lying not far from his original position. He was pinned to the ground by the sharpest broken edge of a windmill blade that had pierced his trousers and gone right through his thigh.

'Help!' Harford struggled to speak. He was grabbing at the massive blade and trying to tug it out of his leg as though separating the two would somehow repair him.

'Don't move,' said Everley as he removed his coat and draped it around the base of the blade and over the wound. He pressed it hard to stop the blood that had saturated Harford's trousers, legs, hands and the sandy grass beneath him.

Harford squealed and gurned as the severed skin burned.

'Can you hold this here?' Everley asked as he took Harford's hands and placed them on the coat. 'Hold it tightly. I will go and get help.'

Everley ran back to where he knew he had left his bike and searched in the rough for the radio. He followed the sound of the continuous call from the Watch Tower and finally found it.

'Whiskey Tango One, Whiskey Tango One. Urgent. Repeat. Urgent! Come in. Over,' called Everley.

'This is Whiskey Tango One. Go ahead. Over.'

'Request emergency assistance. Sierra Two Operative injured. Repeat. Operative injured.'

There was silence on the end of the line.

With the radio in his hand, Everley hurried back to Harford, who had his eyes closed and was not moving. His hands were out at his sides and, without pressure on the wound, blood had continued to seep out and saturate the coat. Everley was sure he was dead. He put his head close to Harford's pale face, turned his ear to his bluey lips and listened. There was no soft sound of breathing. Everley lowered a shaking hand onto Harford's chest to feel any rise and fall at all. As soon as he pressed it there, Harford lurched forwards and coughed blood that splattered onto Everley's cheek and ear.

'My leg, Everley!' Harford pleaded with a whimper.

'You're alright. You're going to be alright. I've called for help,' said Everley waving the radio in the air and attempting to comfort Harford with a shaking smile.

'My leg!' Harford groaned, once again grasping at the blade.

Everley cradled Harford's neck with one arm and held the coat on the wound with the other, pushing hard. He could feel the wet blood on his palm and fingers.

257

'This is Whiskey Tango One. Come in. Over.'

'Finally!' said Everley to himself as he wondered which hand to release so that he could pick up the radio and respond.

Harford was out cold. He had slipped into another agony-induced unconsciousness again. Everley gently placed Harford's head back to the ground and took hold of the radio.

'This is Operative Everley. Request emergency assistance. Sierra Two Operative injured. Repeat. Harford injured. Over.'

'Report nature of injury. Over.'

'Blade landed in his thigh, at the top of his left leg. The leg is badly cut...' Everley lifted an edge of the coat and could see the skin concave where the blade had entered. 'It's cut right through...' Everley said, gagging a little. 'Request emergency assistance. Over.'

There was a short hiss over the radio before the Watch Tower replied.

'Capital order to leave Harford and return to Point F. Repeat. Return to Point F. Emergency Health and Fire Operatives have been deployed. Over.'

Everley paused. He couldn't leave Harford here to bleed out and die. He wouldn't.

'Do you copy? Over,' the Watch Tower insisted.

'Harford requires assistance. I will stay until Emergency Operatives arrive,' Everley asserted.

'This is a Capital order. Do you copy? Over.'

Everley did not respond but continued to hold the coat down tightly. He looked up and listened out for any sign of the Emergency Operatives.

After a time with no noise on the radio, a voice called out that Everley recognised.

'Everley, this is Raines. Do you copy? Over.'

'Raines?' he replied quickly. 'Harford is hurt. A fellow Op. Are you nearby? You must help... Over.'

'Everley, I need you to follow the direct order. The Speed Line arrives soon and you must return on it. Emergency Ops are on their way. I will see to it *personally* that Harford is helped. Do you copy? Over.'

'Roger,' said Everley as looked down at Harford, who appeared as dead as ever.

'Confirm the order, Everley,' Raines commanded. 'Over.'

'Wilco,' Everley said, begrudgingly. 'Over and out.'

Everley wrapped his coat a few extra times around Harford's leg and the blade, and then tucked the sleeves underneath the bloody bundle so that it was as tight as it could be. He turned back to Harford and patted him lightly on the arm before standing up and leaving – just as he was ordered.

For every five steps to the station, Everley looked back in the direction of Harford and listened for any desperate call. As he arrived at Point F just in time to place his bike back into the designated rack and wait the short minute for the train, Everley felt regretful for leaving a fellow Op in a time of need. The regret bit at his brain. It didn't feel right to leave him, and he suspected that Harford was still alone, having not heard or been passed by the Emergency Operatives. But, an order was an order. He consoled himself with the hope that they had reached Harford from another direction. Yes, maybe.

In the Service Room, BritNews was just about to start. A bright square blinked as the tall wall illuminated with the projected image of the News Operative sitting patiently behind a desk with a handful of papers. A tuneful *PA PA PAH* signified the start of the broadcast, so the Ops quietened themselves to listen.

'North Brito reports productivity has plateaued at 98%. Higher Operatives are investigating to establish any sources of purposeless acts. Britons, you are welcome to report all inefficient behaviour to an Enforcement Operative or Higher. Your own continued efforts sustain our safe land. Remember to do your Brit for Brito!'

'For Brito! For Brito! For Brito!' shouted the seated audience to the television.

'The Health Centre has recorded a spike in cases of Operatives being infected with the InOperative virus. Remember, a live InOp can pass the virus but a dying or dead one cannot. If you approach a living InOp, be sure to kill it to prevent the spread of the virus. Symptoms in Operatives include: fever, abdominal pains, bleeding from any orifice, swelling pustules, darkening of skin to green or black, death of skin tissues and the falling-off of fingers, toes and/or nose...'

A chorus of disgusted noises sang through the Service Room.

'Now for the banishment announcements. Brito is pleased to report that no Operatives have broken the oath today. Let us thank ourselves for pledging our lives and giving ourselves entirely for our One.'

'For Brito! For Brito! For Brito!' they all stood and shouted again, Everley included. He held his arm up rigidly to salute and stamped his foot on the floor to strengthen the affirmation.

'Lastly, North Brito reports our nutrition tablet supplies are limited but replenishing. Your blood helps Brito to...'

Everley's attention was drawn to a figure who had approached the Night Watch Operative at the front desk. The Night Watcher pointed over in Everley's direction and the figure turned to face him. It was Raines.

'Command!' Everley saluted as Raines approached.

Raines nodded then nudged Everley's neighbour, who was sitting in the only other seat at Everley's table. The neighbour

260

immediately noticed the silver pin, silently saluted and backed away to find another seat.

'Alright, Everley?' Raines said as he sat down.

'Sir, you have come to visit me *here*!'

'I don't *have* to go about in the middle of the night you know, son! I am a Command!'

'Of course!'

'I don't need to sneak and hide like your pretend friend, Selby!'

Everley nodded. 'How is Harford?'

'Harford...?' Raines wrinkled his mouth, stared at the table for a moment and then lifted his eyebrows suddenly as his mind recalled the earlier event. 'Oh yes! The Op in the field today. Bad thing that happened there, but you did your best. These things happen from time to time.'

'Did he... die?' Everley said, rubbing his forehead and looking down at the floor. 'I should have...'

'You followed a direct order, son. There was nothing that could be done, I'm afraid. We tried but he was a goner... Why, don't look so sad! Harford was a single piece in our One. He was a cog in our machine. And what do we do with broken cogs?'

Raines was right, but Everley still felt uneasy about it.

'Anyway, I can't stay long. I'm here to give you something. A little proof of that Selby being a danger to your future career... *Capital!*' he winked on the final word.

Raines slammed his hand on the table in front of them and slid it towards Everley. He slowly lifted his fingers from little to big until a folded sheet of paper was revealed underneath. With wide eyes and a nod, Raines signalled for Everley to collect it.

'Put that in your pocket, boy!' he whispered. 'I also have interesting information about this Selby character...'

Everley snatched the paper and put it straight into his pocket. He looked at Raines silently, waiting for the news.

'I saw him in the InOp area, just like you said.'

'Yes, sir. What did you see him doing? Was he killing InOps?'

'Nope. He's *with* the InOps.'

'With them?'

'He gave them *stolen* nutrition tablets... That must be why Brito is low in supplies,' Raines pointed at the broadcast continuing on screen.

'So, if he's giving them life... he's not the one killing them, then?' Everley was confused. Perhaps Selby really did stab the woman with the scissors because he thought she was Lyndon.

'He could be. I used to deal tablets and other things in old Britain, you know. But I would always get something in return. Cash, sex, drugs, contraband...' Raines stopped himself as he noticed Everley's face screw up in bewilderment. 'What I mean is a trade. One thing for another thing. Like... my silver pin for your... shoes, you understand?' He looked under the table and added, 'Where are your shoes?'

Everley was sitting there in his socks. He didn't offer a reply, knowing he couldn't tell the truth; Lyndon was still wearing his white shoes that he had stained black.

'Anyway,' Raines continued, 'if my old customers didn't pay up, I mean, *make a trade*, then me and my mates would make them suffer... Put it this way, if one of those InOps didn't give Selby what he wanted in return for the stolen tablets, then he may very well have killed them!'

'Hmm...' It seemed to make some sense to Everley, when he put it like that.

'When you read the note, you'll see,' Raines concluded as he stood. Then he said so loudly that others could hear, 'Best Evening, Briton! Thank you again for your outstanding productivity score!'

Everley grinned, saluted, noticed he wasn't standing, stood and then saluted again.

Raines smiled as he marched out of the room.

'The time is 10.30 after dark, and your entertainment now follows.'

On screen, the News Operative saluted and the image faded with a *PA PA PAH*.

BUZZ BUZZ BEEP BEEP BEEP

Everley moved slowly out of bed. It had been another night without sleep and his energy levels had reached an almost debilitating low. As he pulled the sheet onto the bed, even the pads on the tips of his fingers ached with exhaustion. The lids of his black-bagged eyes only fully opened when he was in the shower and its sharp shots of water hit his skin. The usual massage it provided was replaced with a relentless dig into each muscle and nerve, and the glumness that was pulling Everley's face downwards said it all.

Everley had read the brief report provided by Raines, which had revealed that Selby was not a Capital. After that, he couldn't sleep. Sick of staring at the ceiling, he had remembered the paper previously saved from the InOp area and hidden above his clothes-hanging shelf. He had spent the whole night studying the news from the past. It had been written far back in history – long before Brito – and was punctuated with lost words, uncanny commentaries and extraordinary stories.

Folded between some of the sheets were other scraps and flattened packets and notes. One of the notes was handwritten and, upon reading it last night, Everley had cuddled it to his chest and cried. So completely did this one piece of long-forgotten paper express the deepest feelings within Everley that it was as though his own heart had drafted it by beating perfect words onto the page.

Everley arrived at Point A much earlier than the train. He wanted the time to find Lyndon and speak to her, if she would allow it. He knew his way by now (under the poster first, of course) so turned his coat inside out and headed to where he hoped she would be.

Not far into his search, Everley heard the familiar sound of the wild child that had always thoroughly annoyed him with its giggling mischievousness each morning at the station. This morning though, he was pleased to hear it.

'Little Lyndon?' he called out in as kind a tone as he could summon.

In no time at all the begrimed, barely-clothed boy skidded to a halt in front of him.

'You're Everley. Everley the human!' the boy repeated tauntingly while pointing a grubby finger upwards at Everley.

The child jumped about from one foot to another with such hyperactivity that he may well have had eight legs. Everley wanted to stamp on him like he would a spider, but instead he held himself rigidly.

'Where's Lyndon?' Everley asked.

'The human! The human!' Little Lyndon laughed with a sneer.

Everley very much wanted to kick the child, which would have shut it up straight away. He felt his knees twitch as his muscles desperately tried to lash out and level the young InOp, but he was restrained by the sustained image of Lyndon in his brain. He took a deep breath and smiled awkwardly at the young being. The corners of his mouth quivered as he held the look.

'Do you want to play with me?' the child said innocently.

'Play?' Everley questioned with a shrug. 'What is the purpose of play?'

'It's nice to play! We can play *Ops and Mobbers*, yes, and you can be an Op and I will be an InOp and you've got to chase me until you catch me. That thing there,' he said, pointing to a chair (without a back) whose seat and four legs provided a small cage-like structure, 'can be the PRORA, and if you catch me you have to put me in there. And if you don't catch me,' he carried on, breathless with excitement, 'then I will fetch my mob of InOps and they will attack you!'

'That doesn't sound like a nice game,' Everley said.

'Let's play! Let's play!' Little Lyndon was bouncing about.

Everley bent his knees and lowered himself to the child's height. He tapped the child on the shoulder and held his hand there in an attempt to stop his hopping and focus his attention.

'Can we play *Find Ma*?' Everley asked. His lips curled inwards and the corners bent upwards into an unusual grin that silently said *'Please?'*

'I'm here!' came a voice from a mound of rubble away.

Everley saw it was Lyndon and shot up onto straightened legs.

'Ma, can we play *Ops and Mobbers* with Everley the human?' the little one begged as he ran in Lyndon's direction.

'Everley doesn't have much time this morning. Maybe next time,' she said, looking over at Everley and flashing a knowing smile as she repeated 'Next time. Now, go and play over there while I speak to... the human!'

Everley was still standing almost to attention but without the salute. His pupils were the only thing on his body that moved as Lyndon approached. His face was hot and he felt himself shaking as she stepped towards him with a slow pace.

Lyndon stopped a foot away and looked up at him. Everley scanned her face to figure out her emotion but was unable to detect her mood. At least she no longer looked at him hatefully.

'You... you aren't angry with me anymore?' Everley asked, breaking the silence.

Lyndon responded by screwing the corner of her mouth into her cheek. It was as though her face was saying *'I'm trying to decide whether I'm angry or not.'*

'I didn't do it, Lyndon. I didn't kill that InOp. That is the truth. I think I know who did it though. I think it was Selby. You know, the man who was in my room. I found out that he's not a Capital... and I have proof!' he whipped out the paper Raines had given him and offered it to her. Although she didn't take it, Everley continued, 'Maybe that's why he didn't mind when he saw you under my bed. I also found out that he steals nutrition tablets to trade. Maybe the InOp had nothing to trade and he killed her. Maybe he meant to kill you – to take you away from me! But it wasn't me, Lyndon. It really wasn't me!'

Lyndon looked away, coy but smilingly.

'What is it?' he said, unable to understand her body language. 'You do believe me, don't you?'

'Just then, when I saw you with Little Lyndon... how you were kind to him... I knew it couldn't have been you.'

Everley breathed out in relief, smiling and sniffing at the same time. He rubbed his eyes with the folded paper he was holding, then remembered it was the report and handed it to her again, crumpled and spotted with tears.

She took it this time, but didn't read it. Selby not being an Operative didn't seem to matter much to Lyndon because she believed Everley, evidence or not.

'You *have* changed... into a human! Like the little one said,' she smiled again and looked up at him, taking his free hand in both of her own. 'I trust you.'

'Thank you!' Everley replied with unquestionable gratefulness.

Lyndon let go of his hands, reached around and held him.

'I'm loving you, Lyndon,' Everley said into her hair.

'What does that mean?' she said into his chest, not letting go.

'I have found a word that explains how I feel about you. It's loving. It is the opposite of hating. I found it in an old note from the past. Let me give it to you, so you can understand.'

They released their close, loving hold of each other and Everley delved into his pocket once again. He pulled out the little page, beige with the passing of time. It had a torn edge and was crinkled.

'Do I have time to read it now?' she asked, conscious of him having to leave for work in any minute.

'We have time,' he replied, keen for her to read it. He had imagined this moment in his mind many times since discovering the lovely note, and wanted to watch her read so that he would know whether she felt it too.

As she read, her cheeks glowed a dewy pink beneath their natural blotchy blue. She bit at her lips and scratched bashfully at her now-short hair. Slowly, she looked up at Everley and then, as though pushed from behind, she shot forward and kissed him.

It was as beautiful a bliss as Everley could have wished for.

The ground beneath them grumbled with the approach of the Speed Line, shaking them both unhappily free of each other.

'You must go,' Lyndon said as her lashes flickered over eyes that were otherwise fixed on Everley.

'I must,' he replied, kissing her one last time. 'When I am a Capital, I will find a way for us to be together.'

'A Capital? We won't be allowed. We aren't now! Being a Capital would make it worse, wouldn't it?'

'I will find a way,' he said decidedly as he rushed away. 'I'm loving you!' he called back with a wave.

'I'm loving you, too!' she called over to his beaming face before he disappeared behind the poster and into Point A.

Lyndon looked down at the note, read and re-read it. She wanted to be able to recall every word should she ever be parted with it.

'Loving You' for PB by RDM, 18/04/20

There's something rising from inside,
An emotion I can't hide,
My eyes will show you that it's there,
My flushed red cheeks and nervous air,
The feeling's burning through my skin,
From the yearning deep within,
It makes me ache down to my bones,
It speaks to me in unknown tones,
I'm scared it will rip through my chest,
Am I cursed or am I blessed?
Alone it drags me to my knees,
With you I fly above the trees,
Thoughts behave like crashing waves,
At once delighted, then afraid,
There's nothing that I wouldn't give,
And I would die for you to live,
I can't sleep and I can't eat,
Time moves slowly, days incomplete,
But if I must wait a lifetime more,
To know the joys that are in store,
By loving you,
I'd do it.

Selby pressed his thumb to the '0' on the control panel as he positioned his face for the camera. He rushed in before the metal door was fully opened and quickly descended the brightly lit stairway. His shoes clip-clopped as he galloped down the steps and into the old military base that was home to The Hidden.

He passed through a warren of corridors and stopped outside the last closed door. He stopped, straightened his clothes and then knocked.

'Come in!' called the Official inside. 'Thank you for coming so quickly, Servant,' his manager said from behind a desk as Selby entered the windowless room and closed the door behind him, adding, 'This won't take long,' before he had chance to take a seat.

'Madam,' he said as he nodded, with both hands behind his back.

'Command Raines has given the order to have you expunged if you are an Operative, or destroyed if you are an InOp!' She raised her eyebrows to suggested she found the statement humorous.

'That does not surprise me, madam,' Selby said, shaking his head and holding a half-smile. 'We had a small interchange where I gave my name and what I believed to be a likely role, but he obviously had my record checked with Brito and found me to be... not who I said I was.'

'Indeed,' she sighed. 'Raines has caused so many problems over the years and I fear this may be the end for him.'

'It's his time... *in my opinion*,' he added humbly, careful not to tell his manager what should be done. 'For some time now he's been looking for a way to The Other Place, and I believe he is now more desperate than ever to get there. As such, his behaviour is becoming less predictable.'

'In that case, let's get him there if that's what he wants!' she grinned. 'He's certainly been on our radar for a terrifically long time. I will cite it as...' the Official hummed as she tapped the nib of her pen into an empty box that was marked on a form.

'A danger to our Organisation?' Selby offered.

'Yes. Fine,' she replied, scribbled into the box and handed the form to Selby. 'Would you kindly hand that in to be actioned.'

'Of course, madam,' Selby took the form. 'Will there be anything else?'

'No, you may leave. Thank you,' she said as she returned to a ream of paper on the desk. 'Oh, Servant SV23!' she called to Selby as he started turning the handle.

'Madam?'

'Good job on the Operative you had here for tests. The analysis is impressive. You'll have him in for follow-up tests, yes?'

'Everley. Yes. I'll bring him back, without a doubt. Thank you, madam.'

XVIII

T'was the night before PRORA and all through the zone was nothing occurring; all Ops were alone. All went to bed early, clothes readied with care, in anticipation that they'd soon be there. Having worked without question, giving blood, sweat and breath (in sacrifice to Brito they'd work to the death), each slaved for ten days, bribed by promised reward: untold delights, the best Brito could afford. PRORA was the gift for one and for all, 'Do your Brit!' was the order, or banishment calls. These imprisoned Ops lay in bed with a grin, unable to sleep waiting for adventure to begin. So with a last chorus of 'For Brito' to all, to all the Best Night because PRORA soon befalls.

- Handwritten and rolled into the belt buckle of Building 7's Night Watch Operative

Every evening after work for the few days that followed, Everley had been graced with the presence of his secret visitor. Lyndon had perfected her route into the building and they had refined their routine to get her back out. In a flash of inspiration that was born out of their paranoia of being found out, Everley had broken his toothbrush in half and used the sharp edge to cut his bar of soap into a triangular wedge which he forced under the door. It worked surprisingly successfully as a lock.

On one particular evening, both were glad of the invention. There had been a knock at the door. It was a late, official knock that could have been Raines, Selby or any one of a hundred neighbours or Enforcement Operatives. Everley and Lyndon had frozen in fright and made no movement except to stare solidly at the door. In the pounding of their heartbeats against each other's chests there was a knowing that the door wouldn't open, but a horror that it just might. The handle was slowly turned, the door was lightly pushed, then the black shadow of Brito boots in the lit hallway begrudgingly walked away. Thank Brito.

One day before PRORA, they both awoke to the sound of a shuffle at the door. Two pieces of paper were pushed through the gap underneath and slid into the room. Everley waited until he heard the faraway clunk of the lift before climbing out of bed and fetching them up from floor. Just like last time, one was the size of a standard BritPost telegram, and the other was a small strip of paper wound tightly into a ball.

'What is it?' whispered Lyndon as Everley came back to sit on the bed.

'It will be another order from Selby, requesting that I attend the hidden place for more tests and miss the PRORA.'

'It looks official though,' she said, taking the telegram and thumbing the words that had been stamped onto the sheet so forcefully that the type could be felt on the underside. 'You're right, it says *You are welcomed to remember social cont.*' That must be short for 'Contribution', yeh?' Everley nodded as she continued reading. 'If he's not a Capital, how does he get hold of these?'

'I don't know,' Everley said as he whipped it from her fingers, tore it in half and threw it on the bed along with the second strip that had arrived with it.

Lyndon looked up at him with a face washed with concern.

'What are you going to do about the PRORA?' she asked.

Everley pressed his bottom lip into his teeth with his forefinger and chewed on the thin skin. 'I'm going to go,' he finally answered.

'But, Everley!' Lyndon sat up, grabbed and squeezed his arm, 'I've told you what happens there! If you go, I'm frightened that you won't come back *the same*. I'm so scared! I don't want to lose you but I will if you go there!'

'You won't! You've told me about the blue liquid and I won't drink it. I really won't! Don't be scared,' Everley said trying to lift her hanging head that was now pressed into his armpit.

'But what if it's more than just the liquid? There are bad things going on there, I know it. Can't you just say you are going to Social Contribution – you've got the telegram to prove the order – but stay here instead? Or come to the InOp area? Or we'll go somewhere else? I can get Little Lyndon and we can find—'

'I have to go,' Everley said with a calming tone, 'because Raines will know if I don't. He said I will be by his side, so I will get to see what it's really like.'

'You'll forget me!' she said so loudly that both of them paused when the Op next door groaned as though pulled roughly out of a dream.

'I'll be safe,' Everley hushed, 'I'll be aware. I'll keep my mind filled with thoughts only of you. I remembered you last time, didn't I? And now that we are... closer... I *can't* forget you. It's not possible. You are part of me now.'

'But what if—'

BUZZ BUZZ BEEP BEEP BEEP

'Blame it! You won't have time to shower. You'll have to leave right away,' Everley said as he reached over to the hangers and passed Lyndon her Operative disguise. 'If I can get closer to Brito... become a Capital... then I can find a way for you, me and the little one to be together without these fears. *That* is a purpose.'

Lyndon looked at him sceptically as she shuffled her little legs into the long trousers, buttoned the shirt and tied the shoelaces.

'Hold on,' said Everley as he grabbed the tiny tin of polish and took out his rag, 'there are a few spots of white coming through.'

Lyndon silently watched him as he kneeled in front of her, took each foot at a time and delicately dabbed the shoes until they were thoroughly black again. Though she smiled, an excruciating pain started within the furthest back of her head and the deepest pit of her stomach. She was truly scared. Sad, too. A kind of knowing was growing. A sense of grief before a loss. A foreboding finality.

'Finished,' Everley said as he gazed up and added, 'For Brito, the only purpose of my eyes is to see the beauty of you.'

Without a word, Lyndon bent at the middle and rested her head on Everley's shoulder.

It was time to go.

That evening after work, Everley had tidied the few objects in his room and was wasting the time before Lyndon's arrival by brushing the sand from his work trousers. The yellow grains made a tinkling sound as they scattered all over the floor. It didn't matter because the Clean Keeper would mop up in the morning. There was very little else for Everley to do while he waited, and he was too excited to simply sit down. Yet, this night his excitement was not only attributable to Lyndon. It was PRORA tomorrow and, despite her warnings, there was such a great thrill tickling his tummy in impatience for his hard-earned reward. Although he couldn't remember exactly what happened there, he knew without a single doubt that the two days would be the finest treat for himself and his fellow Operatives.

Too fidgety to sit, Everley stood cross-armed in the centre of his room and felt his right leg jiggling up and down. Time always flew in the presence of Lyndon, as though the clock outside was taunting him by turning minutes into seconds and stealing the moments away. But the prospect of such time travel was pleasing tonight, for being with Lyndon would speed this long wait for the PRORA.

At the sound of a soft *tap-tap-tapping* at the door, Everley's leg stopped wobbling. He took two strides and swung the door open quickly.

In front of him was not Lyndon.

It was Selby.

Everley stood there, open-mouthed. He hadn't expected this and felt entirely unprepared for it. His plan was to go to the PRORA and not to meet Selby at six o'clock sharp. No longer did he trust this pretend friend, but the sight of Selby there reminded him of the friendship lost. The loss made him gulp.

'Well? Aren't you going to let me in?' Selby asked with a smile.

'I... No.' Everley didn't know how to begin. He held both hands on the door frame and blocked the way with his body.

'What?' Selby laughed, baffled by the response.

'I know what you did.'

'What do you mean?'

'My room. The scissors. The InOp. Did you think she was *my* InOp?' Everley whispered the last part as the poked his head closer to Selby's and into the corridor.

Selby moved his head back quickly and squinted.

'You lied to me!' Everley's emotion erupted. He looked away and shook his head repeatedly at the wall.

'Lied? What are you talking about?' Selby reached forward and took Everley by the shoulder. He patted it a few times and then left his hand resting there.

'You're not a Capital,' Everley said, softer now and calmed somehow. Still the sadness showed and he couldn't look Selby in the eyes.

Selby paused and tutted. *'Raines,'* he said to himself but aloud.

'How do you know about Raines?'

275

'Please let me in and I will explain everything,' Selby said, squeezing Everley's shoulder with one hand, taking his chin in the other and turning it to face him.

Everley so wanted to trust him. There was a closeness between them that he felt helplessly drawn to. And he did want answers. He let go of the door frame and stepped to the side to let Selby enter.

'Let's sit,' Selby said calmly as he sat on the bed and gestured for Everley to join him.

Before doing so, Everley replayed the very same moment when Raines was in his room, sitting on his bed and wanting to talk. Selby's mild manner was so different to that of Raines, who seemed to be one word away from a ferocious outburst at any given moment. The difference between them was so distinct in a situation so similar that Everley couldn't help but notice it. For the first time, he not only realised but was also able to directly compare one behaviour to another in a life when everything had forever felt so alike between Operatives in Brito.

'There are things I can tell you about Brito, if you'll listen and try to understand?' Selby started.

Everley nodded and sat on the bed.

'I have not lied to you, but I'm not what Brito would call a Capital...'

'Did you kill the InOp?' Everley interrupted. It was the only question he wanted answering. 'Did you do it because you thought it was the InOp in my room? The one I told you about. The one my feelings are for?'

'No. No! Why do you even think that?'

'You–'

'Is this what Raines has told you?'

'You took the scissors. He said you were in my room, so it must have been you that took them and made my room all messy.'

'What? Scissors?' Selby took a breath while considering the question. 'I do remember that there were scissors in here, that's right, because I did wonder why you had scissors in your room... but I did not take them. I couldn't have! Raines found me in your room, so I said I was an Enforcement Op and I left. I didn't want him to find out about the Special Project. When I left your room, *he* was still in here.'

Everley was silent.

'He'd have stopped me taking the scissors, wouldn't he?'

Everley shrugged.

'I don't kill InOps! I'm the one keeping them alive!'

'You trade nutrition tablets with them. And if they don't trade with you then you kill them.'

'What?' Selby laughed, unable to help himself. 'Who told you that? Raines? He doesn't know a thing about it. Everley,' he grabbed him by both shoulders and shook him until he lifted his sulking head, 'I don't *trade* with InOps. They have nothing I need. I *give* the InOps life!

'So you didn't kill the–'

'No! Never! And I certainly wouldn't try to kill your InOp–'

'Lyndon.'

'Why would I try to kill her? You and me are friends, Everley, aren't we?'

Everley's watery eyes looked intently at Selby. All he wanted to do was hug him. His friend. He believed every word.

'Do you want me to tell you about Brito, the Special Project, Raines, Capitals and the PRORAs... or do you want me to leave?'

The voice in Everley's mind had craved this moment for some time, so he made his choice.

'I want the truth, please,' Everley said, exhausted by the thought of more lies.

'Then the truth you will have,' Selby said and smiled comfortingly.

Selby shuffled back on the bed but maintained their mirrored position.

'We're the same age, you and me. We have been born to Brito. Neither you nor me have seen a time before this and all we know of pre-Brito is in the history books. But Brito has been built on the foundations of the generation before: the generation of old Britain. *Those people* are getting old now. The likes of those that created this,' he pointed around the room and then drew a square in the air with his fingers, 'want to keep us contained with all measures maintained so they leave their dated legacy. But it's not a good legacy, Everley. There are things wrong with Brito, and that's because there are things wrong with the old Brits that designed it.

'We have to change Brito. We have to take it from the corrupted hands of our creators and make it better. If we don't, we will forever have this simple beginning. The old generation will leave us with Brito "Version One". There must be a version two, three, four and more for a better Brito.' Selby shook a clenched hand and thumped each number against his own thigh. 'I know there may be some words in what I am saying that you don't understand, Everley. You don't understand them *yet*, but you will... when you work for us.'

'Us? I work for Brito.' Everley was trying to follow Selby's quickening rant.

'As do I. But I work for a Brito Organisation that we keep hidden. You've been to our workplace in those secret passages that are underneath Point A. We have to be hidden, otherwise the likes of Raines would sniff us out and destroy us. We work for Brito. We lead it. We govern it from within... Governing it in hiding.'

'Govern... ment,' Everley said, recognising the word from the papers he had taken from the InOp area that told of the time before.

'Yes, similar, yes! How do you know about government?'

'I can't remember,' said Everley quickly. 'Isn't government bad though?'

'No. Government is necessary. It would be impossible for any land – even Brito – to exist without somebody... or some *body* in control. The history books... and I mean a history that goes back hundreds of years, not the edited and recent history that is taught in Brito's schools.... well, the real history books are littered with tales of all those socio-economic orders... I mean, *ways of organising society* that have failed. National Socialism, Fascism, Communism... even Democracy. They all failed. In the end. These radical sorts – like Raines – believe that they took part in creating a new type of nation using the best (and worst) of those ideologies: a society that took all of the tyranny but made it self-governing. Self-governing! Can you really believe that, Everley?'

Everley looked blank. There were so many words that he couldn't comprehend.

'There *has* to be a government or else there would be chaos!'

'But there is no government in Brito. We all took the oath and we follow it,' Everley said innocently.

'There *is* government. That is what I am trying to tell you. You might not be able to see it or touch it, but it's there. You can't see a figurehead, a person in charge, a group of people or a political party, but there is a system at work here and it's one that dictates how you live and behave and operate. There is leadership in Brito. An establishment that exists to maintain order. But it's underground, in a hidden place. The hidden place you've seen. Raines and his peers might like to think that it's not there, or that they are in control, but they're wrong.'

'But there is order in Brito, isn't there? We are dedicated without question.' Everley couldn't imagine a construct. All he knew and could see was a choice to either operate or be banished. To be purposeful or wasteful. To have purpose or be pointless. 'We Operatives, by willing choice, duty and responsibility, give ourselves efficiently, productively, for the good of all Britons and in defence of our Brito.'

'That's the oath, Everley! That's what you're *programmed* to think! You think that you *want* to work for Brito. You think that you

279

want to work at the windmills. You think that you *want* to work twelve hour shifts and volunteer in the evenings. You think that you *want* to go to the PRORA!'

'I do want to go to the PRORA!'

'These things are not *your* choices, Everley! These decisions were made *for* you, not *by* you. They were decided long before you were even born. These are the walls around your mind. Your free will... that is, your personal choice... is in a box. You are in a prison, but you just don't know it yet.'

'A prison is like this room only the door can't open because it's locked. And you can't go out for years and years and years.'

'That's right! Who told you that?'

'Raines.'

'You see, Raines and others from his era want to keep Brito exactly the way it is. They want us all to be trapped inside this way of life without ever changing it. Have you ever questioned why the elderly Ops are sent to The Other Place?'

'No. They deserve to go and rest until the end of their lives. They deserve to experience its beauty for giving their lives to Brito,' Everley said, certain of the truth in his response.

'No, that's not why. As they get older and more tired, they are more likely to be dissidents. That is, to become a person who rebels or rejects the system. This is particularly common in the elders because they remember the freedoms of old Britain. They are sent away so that they don't compromise the order or seek to change it.'

Everley looked perplexed. For so long he had thought of The Other Place as the ultimate reward: the PRORA of all PRORAs, where you'd spend your final years in as wonderful a place as your brain could imagine. He closed his eyes and tried to revisit the daydream that had played in his mind on so many mornings, but now the light blue sky of his imaginings seemed grey. The fields of grass were burned and spoiled. The vision was ruined.

280

'But change is good,' Selby continued. 'We can take this version of Brito – version one – and improve it. We are reformists really, I suppose. That is to say that we believe in the principles that underpin all that is Brito, but we want to change it to make it better. Make sense?'

'I'm not sure.' Everley opened his eyes and looked out of the window at the clock that had always been there, on the building that had always been there. 'What is wrong with it?' he asked as he pointed out of the window.

'You'll see. For now, you don't truly understand because your mind is in a cage. Well, most of it is. Part of you has been freed, Everley, otherwise you wouldn't be feeling things for InOps and having one in your room. And you wouldn't have done so extraordinarily well in our tests! If you join me in The Hidden, then I will help your mind *fully* escape. You will be free, like me. And then you can help Brito from within.'

'Could I bring Lyndon with me?'

Selby paused. He felt compelled to continue in the same way that he had started, and he had started by promising Everley the truth.

'We have InOps for a reason. We need them.'

'But you said... But the oath says... But they are the waste!' Although he was loving Lyndon, Everley felt that she wasn't really an InOp. She had started life as an Op, after all. Everley knew the InOps to be the disease of Brito, for that was all he had ever known.

'That's what you are told to think. The InOps are just people like you and me. I suppose they have been found to be less useful to Brito for whatever reason. Maybe they did badly at school. Or they are less physically able. Or they have some impairment that they were born with or something that developed over the years. Well, we take these people and turn them into Brito's 'Other'. There always has to be an Other because Operatives are driven by a joint cause against a mutual enemy. If there were no InOps at all, what would be your incentive? How could we scare you into pledging your oath if we didn't threaten you with the alternative? You keep working because we *show* you that not working brings banishment and an InOp existence. That's a life without clothes, warmth, a bed. Showers even! You see how dirty they are. We even tell you they are diseased!' he laughed.

'We? So that is you and the hidden people?'

'That's just the way we govern Brito, Everley. We keep the InOps alive because they are part of the system. You Operatives operate because you don't want to be an InOp. That's true, isn't it?'

Everley pushed his bottom backwards to create a distance between them. He shifted to the side, extended his legs and pressed his feet to the floor. Rubbing them a little to wake them up, he then stood and faced Selby who had not moved. He let out a sigh and, with hands on hips, finally made a single statement in the plainest of terms.

'I don't see how you are any better than Raines.'

'Everley! We have to keep order somehow!... But your thoughts – these thoughts – they show how much you have grown! You'll be an asset! Why don't you come–'

'I want you to leave,' Everley said loudly.

Everley felt more self-assured than ever. His time with Lyndon had opened his eyes as well as his mind and, while he only understood some of what Selby was saying, he knew him now to be part of something that took good Operatives and purposefully put them in poverty.

Knock. Knock. Knock.

Somebody was rapping their knuckles on the door. This time those official knocks could not have been Selby, for he was already here. And they weren't the delicate taps of Lyndon either.

'Lyndon!' thought Everley as he glanced over at the clock. It was later than usual. Perhaps she had heard talking from inside his room and was hiding somewhere.

The door swung open and Everley immediately identified the owner of the hand that had knocked. It was Raines.

'Command!' Everley saluted. 'I have asked Selby to leave.'

'I know you have, son. I heard you. Very good.'

Raines took two steps inside the room, revealing two other figures behind him. Both stood statuesque with wide legs and straight arms held behind their backs. They were only shadows under the bright corridor lights.

Selby stood up immediately and looked around desperately. There was nowhere for him to go.

'Everley, take your PRORA clothes then go and stand outside the door.' Raines commanded as he stepped closer to Selby, who was now trapped in the corner between the head of the bed and the wall of the room.

Everley did as Raines commanded. No sooner had he passed through the doorway did he hear the thwack of a powerfully thrown punch hitting a jaw. Then there was some coughing, a spit and splattering sound, a groan, a thud, another thud and a clang of boot against metal bedstead. He didn't turn around to watch. The sounds were revolting enough that the nature of the violence was clear without having to see it. Everley swallowed deeply. He felt sick. This was not what he wanted.

'Dogs! Get in here!' Raines called to the two Operative heavies that were guarding the door.

Both brushed past Everley as they entered the room. A second later, Raines emerged, wrapped his arm around Everley and led him down the corridor towards the lift.

'We are going to go to the PRORA tonight.'

Everley couldn't respond. His eyes were drawn to Raines' resting hand on his shoulder. It was wet and glistening with Selby's blood. A little dripped onto Everley's light grey t-shirt. The red blotch expanded into a big circle as the blood soaked in. The blood of what had once been his friend. A friendship he no longer understood.

'You'll get to see it before anyone else!' Raines was gibbering excitedly.

Everley's thoughts returned to Lyndon. He realised that he wouldn't get to say goodbye. The PRORA would mean two days spent missing her touch, smell and kiss, but he would be sure to keep the image of her in his mind so that she couldn't be forgotten. Neither blue liquid nor a brain washed with soap and water could remove her from his heart.

XIX

Date: Day 15, Year 02 AE

Dear Operative Newton,

As many males have died during The Waves or departed our nation prior to Embarkation, it is the responsibility of the living Britons to engage in the breeding programme and ensure a steady birth rate for Brito.

Tests have verified that you are well qualified for this purpose and we request that you accept this honourable duty.

You have been assigned to the twelfth district of old London, comprising thirty-three women who have been tested and selected as appropriate hosts.

Should you feel unfit for the task at hand, you must attend the Health Centre for further tests to obtain a Certificate of Impotency.

Total refusal to accept will be considered a traitorous act.

In return for your placement in the district, you will become a Breeding Operative with an open route for promotion. You will also receive a purple pin.

In due course, we will send a list of the persons to be visited by you. You must begin your fruitful work at once and report to this office on a monthly basis.

With best greetings from Brito,

The Himmler Life Source Breeding Programme

Office of Population Growth

Ministry of Demography

- Kept on file, under lock and key in the Cardinal Archives

By the time that they had waited for the midnight train, spent two hours standing within one of its cold carriages (with not a single seat to sit on), arrived at the station one stop short of Point F, walked the long stretch to the golden gates and arrived at a block of bedrooms, Everley was exhausted.

He had wanted to be excited – and he knew there would be something special about being at the PRORA before anyone else – but Selby and Lyndon had been playing on his mind. So much so, Everley had completely zoned-out while Raines regaled the most unbelievable stories of old Britain to pass the time. There had been few other Ops on the night train, which was empty in the front carriage but for Everley, Raines and the two guards that had appeared at his door. They were as still and as well-built as machines. Neither spoke along the journey and neither moved (except one, to rub Selby's blood from the back of his hand onto the side of his thigh).

Raines had chattered incessantly on the train. He had spoken of a thing called "food", which he missed, and a "match", which was a game where men would run around with a ball and try to do a "goal". When Everley asked if this was *playing*, Raines had told him in no uncertain terms that it wasn't just for fun. Old Britain seemed very strange to Everley.

As well as telling historical tales, Raines had talked of Brito. He explained how the PRORAs were his own creation, and how the Cardinals were so happy that they made him a Command. And how he wanted Everley to learn from him and take over one day because he still thought Everley was good, even though he knew he wasn't the bin man. And how his body was weary and it was time for him to be rewarded with The Other Place.

Raines had tired himself out some way there and fallen asleep while standing. His arms cuddled the metal pole that propped him up as he loudly snored against it and Everley had watched him sleep, looking at the age in his brow and hands and wondering whether Raines was really as bad as Selby wanted him to believe. He had pondered whether there could be anything wrong with Raines at all if he had been the mind behind the PRORA.

They had arrived in the early hours of the morning but the moon was still shining a bright light that bounced on and off the glossy black piazza floor. A nervous Capital had come to greet them and, after Raines had shouted at that same Capital for not opening the doors of the main building soon enough when it started to rain, Everley had been escorted to a room in the blocks. In a tired daze, he had fallen asleep fully-clothed as soon as he lay on the bed.

Now that it was morning and the natural daylight had woken him by spilling in through curtains that were open all night, Everley was awake and studying his new surroundings. This was not his bed. The tiny room was smaller than his home quarters, but had a door to a private toilet and shower within the room itself. There was only one place he could be: the PRORA. Although it felt familiar, he was sure that this was the first time he had ever seen a "Superior Lodging".

Everley went to use the shower but it didn't detect him there and did not switch on. After a minute or so of waving at the holes in the ceiling, he gave up and got dressed again. He estimated it to be past nine o'clock in the morning. Although that was far later than he would usually sleep in, he definitely needed the rest after the events of the night before and he hoped it would give him some extra energy to enjoy his reward. Feeling a serene satisfaction, Everley looked out of the window to study the new view. Three building blocks circled around him. Two were tall with lots of windows and one was wide with none.

Without warning, the door flung open and an Operative entered holding two glasses, a bottle in a bucket and a tall piece of hard paper.

'Oh! Excuse me!' said the Operative, quickly plonking everything on the table and backing out of the room. 'I wasn't aware—'

'I am a guest of Command Raines,' said Everley. 'Where should I go to meet him?'

'His office is in the tall room that faces the entrance... But you should wait here. I will ask a Capital to take you to him,' the Operative said, leaving quickly and adding 'Best Morning!' before closing the door.

Everley moved over to the items on the table. He examined the tall sheet of hard paper that stood upright on the table from being folded vertically in the middle.

Dear Briton,

For the next two days you will be commended for giving yourself to Brito and achieving exceptional productivity scores with the gift of a programme tailored especially for you.

Your chosen programme is... THE PERFECT BRITON...

For your pleasure, you have access to the best Brito can provide.

Your agenda is as follows.

Brito thanks you.

DAY 1:

1. *Exploring Ecstasy*

2. *Collective Contemplation*

3. *Anti-InOp Protection Training*

DAY 2:

4. *Best Body Building*

5. *Oneism Wisdom*

6. *Purposeful Principles*

Everley handled the programme and frowned. It was scruffy at the edges and frayed as though it had been picked up and put down several times. The black print was grey and faded on the first side, presumably from facing the sun day after day. The back was stained with the smudges of what had been many fingers. What Everley found most disappointing of all was that his name was nowhere to be seen. It was very clear that the "Perfect Briton Programme" could not have been tailored, chosen or especially for him. After all, the Operative didn't even know that Everley was occupying the room.

He replaced the card on the table, sat on the bed and scowled at it from a distance.

With a few light knocks on the door, Everley was interrupted. He stood to attention and called for the person knocking to come in.

'C-C-Command Raines requests the pleasure of your c-c-company in h-his of-fice, sir.'

'It is I who should be calling you *sir*, Capital!' Everley said politely as he saluted the nervous-looking individual who shook a little as he held the door open.

The Capital silently led Everley onto the piazza that was directly outside the entrance. They crossed it diagonally and entered the opposite building. Inside, they walked some way up a flight of stairs and down corridors of grey walls and grey carpets, flaking paint and falling ceiling tiles. It was cold in there and had the sort of musky odour of a wet coat that had taken too long to dry. It felt old, but in a forgotten way and it did not have the newness that Everley expected.

'Everley!' Raines said in a chirpy tone from his seat as they entered his office.

'Best Morning, Command Raines,' Everley said as he saluted.

'Very good, son!' Raines said as he pointed to the empty chair in front of his desk and gestured in such a way that welcomed him to sit down.

The bright eyes with which Raines looked at Everley seemed to switch straight to black when he looked back at the Capital who was standing to attention.

'Well? Fuck off,' he said with absolute disdain to the Capital, who turned his eyes to the floor, followed the instruction and left.

Raines brightened again as he faced Everley, leaned back on his chair, put his feet on the table and cracked his knuckles.

'The first rule of authority, Everley,' he grinned, 'is you've got to be *commanding* if you want to be a Command.'

'And I should use your words, sir?'

'Oh, no! Best not do that! You'll get into trouble. I'm from the old times so I'm allowed, but not you. You just need to be... assertive,' he said with a pointing finger.

'Yes, sir,' said Everley, assertively, and nodded.

'I've got a lot to show you today,' Raines started, 'and, if you do well, I shall report back to the Cardinals tomorrow that we have found not only a new Capital... but also a candidate for a future Command! How's about that then?!'

'Sir!' Everley didn't know quite what to say. 'May I ask, sir, why me?'

'You see the calibre of Capitals round here don't you, Everley? They're not going to achieve anything! They do exactly as I say. Well, I suppose that's what I've taught them to do... but they do it with no... *oomf!*' He punched the air. 'No passion, I mean. You have a passion. Remember, I've seen you kill, Everley!'

Everley swallowed and looked remorseful.

'You killed that InOp by the windmills with a real...' Raines pause to grin, 'a real anger... A blind rage! It was great! I do question why I allowed this lot to be Capitals, but I had to pick some and, you know, you Ops are all the same! But not you, Everley. You've got something, and I think that something is going to shine over the next two days.'

Everley offered a small smile and nod.

Raines stood and walked to his window with his hands behind his back. He continued talking, but more to the air than to Everley.

'If you are the next *me*, then I can be free. Yes. Just got to sell that to the Cardinals... Oh, Everley, they are arriving. Look!'

Everley hurried from the seat to the window and pressed his head to the glass. He could see what looked like an enormous worm crawling slowly down the hill. The vast mass advanced at an even pace. As it edged closer, Everley could distinguish dots of different colour faces with different colour hair from the otherwise identical-clothed front line of ten Operatives (with forty lines of ten behind). It was daunting to witness the weight of the unified Operative body. With a march so smoothly synchronised, they may well have been tied together at the hip and foot.

As the sea of bodies swept ashore onto the piazza floor, their lines widened and they stood further apart. From the towering position of Raines' high office, the Ops looked as tiny as insects. They seemed less of a force in their separated smallness and Everley couldn't help but feel dominant above them. A sort of power that pleased him, much to his own surprise.

'You could almost flatten ten of them with your foot from here,' Everley said without realising he had opened his mouth.

Raines giggled villainously and slapped Everley on the back in agreement. He was still laughing as he turned from the window and moved across the room. With a few coughs to quieten himself, he said, 'It's time to go down. Bring my speech from the desk, will you?'

Lyndon had taken the stairs all the way up to Everley's floor, but as she arrived on the landing and turned into the corridor she had seen two stocky and machine-like men standing in his doorway. She had backed into the stairwell and waited there with neck strained upwards and ears pricked outwards to try to follow what was unfolding within.

She had been frozen in fright and unable to look. Then, when the talking had turned into mumbling and then into silence, the bad noises started. It had started with a pounding sound. Then there was a crack, another crack and a yelp. Each noise had made her jolt. Each jolt knocked single tears from her eyes. Each tear scratched as it fell down her face, and each scratch made her want to leap out from this hiding place and save Everley. Well, she had thought it was Everley until the moment she sprinted into the room (a second after the door had been slammed shut, the lift had made its dinging sound and the corridor had fallen silent).

Lyndon had flown across the dishevelled room and thrown herself onto the body inside. Lifting him by the head, she breathed in relief that it wasn't her Everley. But it was a man she recognised: the Capital that had been in his room.

'Selby?' she had said whilst cradling his heavily bloodied head. 'Are you Selby?

Selby had peeled his bruised and bulging eyes open and looked up at her. With energy fading, he had managed only three words.

'Everley. In danger.'

For Brito, for Brito, for Brito!

In unison, all present spoke the vow. On the final word, glasses were lifted, lowered and drunk. But Raines didn't have a glass and nor did Everley. As four hundred wide-eyed Operatives whooped and clapped and sang, Raines left the stage and approached Everley, who had been dutifully standing to one side.

'You haven't drunk have you?' Raines said, noticing Everley's hands were empty. 'Wait here for me,' he said as he clicked his fingers in the air and then walked to the other side of the stage to give the nervous Capital another telling off.

Everley did not want to drink the blue liquid. While he did want to impress Raines, he did not want to compromise his memory of Lyndon. She had been very worried about the liquid making him forget and he didn't want to risk any part of that being true. With Raines momentarily preoccupied, Everley darted down the stage steps and rescued an empty glass from the floor where it had been thrown after drinking. He held it carefully at the base, raised it to the air and returned to the stage.

Everley watched Raines fixedly and waited for him to finish berating the Capital. At the very moment that Raines turned his head towards him, Everley lowered the glass, licked his lips then threw the glass to the ground and smiled.

'Oh. Oh dear,' Raines said as he rejoined him. He held his head and looked about as though his plans had been scuppered.

Everley immediately regretted the pretence but had to continue with it.

'Did I do something wrong, sir?'

'No, no. You didn't know... You will want to go and join your fellow Ops now Everley. Enjoy the rest of the afternoon and I will see you this evening.'

Raines cut through the crowd effortlessly and headed back to the office building. As he disappeared, Everley wondered whether to follow him but was distracted by the increasingly roused crowd. He looked jealously at the Operatives dancing, singing and laughing with each other, and he wanted to be part of it. He had diligently done his Brit and did deserve to enjoy his reward.

Toying with a rare opportunity to decide between joining in, joining Raines... or spying from the side, Everley chose the latter. He walked down the steps and stood so that the border of the stage concealed him a little. He found himself next to one of a few wide speakers that stood tall at each corner of the piazza through which "We Are Together" had been playing over and over since the oath. The music was now changing. There were still remnants of the song, but the tone was transforming into a slower, offbeat sound that pulsed in and out while the volume moved up and down like a heartbeat.

After no time, the motion in the music was giving Everley a sickly feeling. He watched the crowd as they continued to dance rhythmically though entirely out-of-step with the strange sound from the speakers. Everley was sure that they were dancing to the memory of Brito's song because in no way did their swaying match the odd noises that were added to the track in layers and clashed unnervingly. Very suddenly, the rumbling of the Speed Line surged from it all. It made Everley jump and cower next to the stage as he heard it, convinced that the train might be about to plough through the piazza.

The Operatives seemed to embrace it and were delightedly shouting 'Speed Line' or 'For Brito' with arms up into the air, yet their language was becoming less and less articulate. They seemed to be struggling with their tongues and chewing their own lips. As the rumble of the Speed Line came again, Everley felt truly sick, held his stomach and swallowed to keep it down.

'Join together,' called the sweet song through the speakers again. It was just the two words, bitten out of the original song and spat into the cacophony.

The Operatives instantaneously took hold of each other, as though the call was an instruction. They still danced, but now in pairs or more.

'Join together,' the speakers said again.

The Operatives rubbed and stroked, squeezed and kissed each other, and Everley could barely watch. They were starting to do things that he had only done with Lyndon in private.

'Join together,' the music spoke, louder this third time.

And with that, the Operatives scattered. Some ran towards the lodgings hand in hand. Some were falling to the ground and shedding their clothes. Everley watched as a number of PRORA Guide Operatives dragged those on the floor to nearby spare rooms, and then collected discarded trousers and tops from all over the piazza.

Some Ops were still dancing. They were dancing near Everley, and he knew it wouldn't be long before he would have to join in or be found out for not drinking the blue liquid. He edged a step or two closer to the impassioned party and was promptly picked by one female Operative. She had selected him as simply and as easily as a pair of shoes from a shelf and began walking toward the lodgings with his arm firmly gripped by her hand.

Everley stumbled behind her, wishing to tear himself away but also not wanting to draw attention to his sobriety. His legs fell over themselves as he pulled against the will and clamp of her pinching fingers. She hadn't realised. She kept marching into the building.

The Operative (who Everley had so far only seen from behind, and who was of average height and weight and with the same Brito haircut as all others) pressed her palm to a control pad beside the ground floor door of room 10. The door did not open.

'Welcome all guests to use the control panel,' came a voice from at or around the door.

The female Op turned around and, with glazed eyes, motioned for Everley to identify himself to the screen. He struggled against her at first, but the more he did so, the more she fell about, grasped at him and tried to kiss him. With the added pressure of a corridor filling with other Operatives, Everley finally pressed his palm to the pad and they both fell into the room as the door quickly opened then shut behind them.

Inside, more music was playing through speakers above the bed. Again, it was the kind of repetitive beating that felt oppressive and ever-more nauseating the longer it reverberated throughout the small space. The curtains were drawn, the lights were dimmed to a suggestively pink tint and there was an opened bottle with a label affixed that read 'DRINK'.

The woman wasted no time and snatched the bottle from the bucket it was resting in. She jeered as she flung herself onto the bed, kneeled and then poured the liquid from the bottle directly into her open mouth. Everley had never seen such an appalling sight. He watched with wide-eyed disgust and his back pressed against the door. He felt with his hands for the handle and yanked it up and down, but the door was locked and he was trapped.

The wanton Op peered over at Everley, gurgled and giggled before offering him the bottle. When he didn't take it straight away, she slammed it on the bedside table so clumsily that it teetered on the edge. She paid it no attention, trying to focus her rolling eyes on the buttons of her top. Unable to coordinate fingers and thumbs, she gave up on opening her shirt and instead tugged the top right over her head and threw it in Everley's direction.

The shirt fell at Everley's feet and he stared at it. He could hear her making lewd noises and see – in peripheral vision only – the movement of her arms and hands over her own body, but he didn't want to look. Although he had seen many a naked Operative, this was different. This was improper. This was wrong.

She called for Everley in garbled tones.

'No!' Everley insisted. He felt it to be a misdeed to stand in the same room as another woman, and a wicked betrayal to even consider touching her. Even to look would be to commit the greatest disloyalty, for he was loving Lyndon and wanted nobody else. He tried the door again but it did not open.

Sick of waiting, the female Op vaulted forward and forcibly grabbed at Everley. Her clawing fingernails caught the collar of his shirt and, as she fell onto the floor, ripped the first two buttons and scratched his skin beneath. With a bang she hit her head on the table leg and was no longer grappling, babbling and haggling for sex.

Everley took a second to slow his panicked heart rate and then moved towards the woman on the floor. He checked for blood from her head but there was none. He checked for breath and there was snoring. She seemed to have excited herself to sleep. Everley carefully lifted her up and flopped her onto the bed. She rolled as she landed, made a moaning sound and then continued to snore.

Everley untucked one side of the sheet and folded it over to cover her nakedness, then stood next to the bed watched her chest move up and down as she wheezed in her sleep. Her silence allowed for his reflection of the real PRORA experience.

A thousand notions of what he instinctively knew, had been taught at school and had learned recently about sex flashed through his brain like sliding sentences in front of his eyes. He questioned endlessly why Brito would want Operatives to have sex and what purpose it could possibly serve. He could think of no reason why sexual mixing would be so encouraged by Brito that PRORAs would be used not only to promote, but to *force* it... And force it every ten days with no lingering memory of these encounters in between.

A lasting, difficult question dawned on Everley: *Had he really only ever had sex with Lyndon in all of his life?*

He was sure the answers would be here in the PRORA. Determined to seek them, he turned to try the door again. While it was still locked, Everley could clearly see a switch on the wall adjacent to the handle which looked similar to a light switch only was lower down and dark in colour, making it difficult to detect in the dimness. With nothing to lose, he flicked it downwards. As he did, he heard a clunk within the door and knew it had unlocked. He supposed that in their blue-liquid-induced haze an Operative would be capable of neither seeing nor operating it. The PRORA was full of little traps, he noted to himself as he daintily edged into the hallway.

Everley crept towards where he knew the entrance to be, but the hallway was a far different scene than it had been an hour or so earlier. It was a messy state. Ahead of him was a pool of vomit slowly soaking into the carpet. There was a shirt beside the spew and a shoe – just one shoe – a few feet away. As he passed the foamy puddle and continued to the front door, he noticed a second lone shoe – presumably the partner of the first – wedged into the doorway of Superior Lodging 08. He pried inside through the gap and was confronted with not one couple, but two. All were on top of each other, moving about blindly with eyes closed, mouths open and body parts tangled. Repulsed, Everley looked away, but not before noticing a fifth person in the room who was staring unblinkingly at the floor and pointing to a tuft in the carpet as though she had found some miniature being amongst the fabric loops.

As Everley reached the main door and pushed it open cautiously, the daylight shocked him. He had forgotten it was day because everything inside the building imitated an evening time, after dark.

To reach the entrance of the building opposite that housed Raines' office, Everley would have to get across the piazza. There were Operatives all over it: PRORA Ops. None of them were showing any signs of being afflicted by the blue liquid and all were preoccupied in a tidy-up operation. Everley recognised the nervous Capital busy directing the picking up of glasses and the mopping up of liquid from the glossy floor, so hoped a dart across would go unnoticed.

After a mental countdown from three to one, Everley made a run for it. With light feet and no looking back, he sprinted from one corner to the other and stopped only when he reached the outer wall of the Command building. Knowing that there would be no chance of getting in via the front with all the PRORA Ops flitting in and out, he skirted the wall to find a back door.

At the rear of the building and facing out to sea was a huge shutter that was the height of at least two floors. Past this shutter, Everley couldn't see a door. Instead, there was a number of wide windows that filled the wall space from waist height to ceiling.

Everley brushed past the shutter, along the wall and crouched as he reached the first large window. Desperate to discover the *real* PRORA, and undeterred by the fear of being found, he peeped into the room from the bottom corner of the ledge. He held his hand over his eyes and against the glass so that he could see beyond his own reflection.

The room inside had a wall of tiny televisions with screens of black and white. Although the images were distorted by the distance, Everley could make out the layout of the lodgings on the screens. Cameras must have been positioned in each of the rooms above the beds. A handful of Administrative Operatives (perhaps six) were drifting between desks, looking up at the screens and holding pens and hard boards with paper clipped onto them. Some sat casually on chairs with feet on tables and chins propped in palms in disinterest. The live, sexual play on the televisions, though unspeakably offensive to Everley, appeared to be wholly uninteresting to the Admins. They seemed to be seasoned to such sights and waiting for something more significant to take note of.

Everley moved along the length of the wall of broad windows, careful to keep his head down. He noticed that the room inside was in fact just one vast area. The collection of small screens swept across the wall either side of one enormous display in the middle. In this central screen were illuminated words and arrows. Everley edged further along the window until he was directly opposite and was able to read the text in focus.

LIFE SOURCE BREEDING PROGRAMME

YEAR: 26 AE

CURRENT PRORA ROUND: 08

OPERATIVE COHORT: Point A Building 7, Quadrant B

AGE RANGE: 25 - 29

PREGNANCY RATES YTD:

34% Conception

87% Ongoing Pregnancy

11% Early Failure

2% Terminated

0% Expunged

RESULTS OF GENETIC TESTING MUST BE USED TO ORGANISE AND MONITOR THOSE MOST LIKELY TO SUCCEED

There was a red arrow pointing down next to the word 'Conception', a green arrow pointing up next to the word 'Terminated' and the word 'MUST' was flashing yellow.

Everley peeled himself away from the stark reality of the scene. It was simple: pregnancies weren't created in the Health Centre and injected into selected female Operatives, like Lyndon had thought. Pregnancies were created in PRORAs. Everley sank onto his bottom, rested his spine against the wall beneath the window, bent his knees upwards and buried his head into them. Another rush of questions without answers layered themselves like stacked sheets of paper in his mind.

If he had indeed participated in sex each time he had attended the PRORA, Everley considered, then any number may have resulted in a pregnancy. Of those, he would never know how many were early failures, terminations... or successes. The biggest question of all was *'Have I created any children of my own?!'*

Everley closed his eyes and pictured the face of Little Lyndon; he was the only child that he had ever conversed with (let alone, acknowledged). This was an infant not only so grubby and scruffy that he almost shined with soil and slime, but also so irritating a being that Everley had previously imagined a hundred different ways of tying his tongue. But now that Everley had uncovered a truth about how the children of Brito were generated, he felt a new kind of fondness for the little one.

Everley didn't know how many children were being created by the forced coming-togethers at PRORAs, and whether there was a child (or children) in Brito with his face, his eyes, his efficiency and proper ways. He hoped his bloodline would inherit the ability to *feel* and build character from within the fixed order of Brito; a regime rapidly revealing itself to be a system of mental manipulation, hidden organisations, supervision and control.

Everley squeezed his head against his knees to shield himself from the terrifying truths that were surfacing. Fighting a rising panic in his chest that told him so desperately to run back to the station, find Lyndon and escape, he patted the back of his neck with his arms. It did little to calm him.

'Hate! InOps! InOps! Hate!'

Everley was shaken from the safety of his curled ball by the sharp screeches of a semi-clothed Operative who was whirling around on the pebbled ground between the Command building and another, much smaller structure. Two Capitals were struggling to take and keep their hold of her as she shouted, thrashed and spun

300

about. Everley watched as an Admin Op exited the Command building and joined the Capitals in an attempt to contain her. In a flurry of hands, the three officials managed to lift her to her feet.

They had only dragged her a short distance before she screamed out again and shook herself free from their hold. With one heavy movement, one of the Capitals booted her in the head, muting her immediately. The three then lifted her limp body and dragged it into the separate building block. Then all was silent again.

Resolute to learn what else was lurking underneath the fine facade of the PRORA, Everley checked he was alone, checked again, took to his feet and dashed in the direction of the curious cabin that was roughly built and painted all black, but for a red door. When he reached the structure, he searched for a window to look through. He trailed the wall on all sides but found not a single spot to spy from. As he turned the fourth corner, the Admin Op appeared directly in front of him, having opened and stepped out of the red door.

Everley froze.

'Operative, what are you doing here?' the Admin asked.

Everley was paralysed. He wasn't sure whether to say he was looking for Raines or to search for some other excuse.

'Operative?' The Admin stretched forward and clicked her fingers twice in Everley's face and so close to his nose that he could feel a puff of air on each *click*.

Everley did nothing but blink.

The Admin stepped back to the door, pushed it ajar and called, 'There's another one here,' before walking off and leaving Everley standing alone.

One of the Capitals emerged and, without even looking at Everley's face, took him by the arm and through the red door.

As soon as they entered, Everley was flung onto the floor roughly. In front of him was the unconscious Op they had just dragged in, and in front of her was an Operative sitting on a stool facing a desk. They were in a queue, of sorts.

'Give me his arm,' said one Capital to the other.

Everley watched the Operative on the stool flinch when the Capital produced a handheld object with a red flashing light coming out of the end.

'He's scared of the light, look,' they teased whilst waving the object in the air and pressing a button that switched the red beams on and off. With force, they took the Operative by the wrist, turned it over to the side lined with visible veins and shined the light at it. Something on the screen made a pinging noise.

'Operative Bristow,' read the Capital from the screen before writing the name on a square of paper and placing it into the front of an open-topped silver box containing many other square papers.

Everley thumbed his wrist and wondered whether his name was in his skin there, somehow. He knew he would have to find a way to escape before they shined the clever red light at him and discovered his identity.

From the floor, Everley assessed the area within, which was much larger than it had seemed from the outside. Although a single room, it had been split into three sections. The first was the office space with the desk and some cupboards. The second was a large metal cage where some Operatives were locked. The third was an area obscured from view by a dark and marked sheet hanging between two poles that were screwed into the floor.

One Operative peered through the gap between the bars of the cage. He panted breathlessly, turned his head slowly in wonderment and gazed from side to side as though following the wings of a fly. His watery eyes kept blinking. His quivering lip showed he might burst into tears at any moment. Lost, afraid and childlike, he seemed to stare straight at Everley and straight through him at the same time.

A second Operative was standing in the centre of the cage. He appeared to be trying to take one step forward. His left leg convulsed with such struggle and extreme shake that he looked like he was

302

battling against an intense wind. Though he shuddered with all of his might, his foot was fixed to the floor.

A third locked-up Op was wildly twisting her neck round and round in fast and disturbing circles. Everley could see that her hands had been wrapped into two bundles of bandages. He assumed it was to stop her from scratching her face, which she continued to attempt through the material. She scraped her head against the bars when her hands failed.

It was a horror of a sight.

'Come on, Bristow,' said one of the Capitals whilst heaving him from the stool and towards the cage.

The Capital twisted a key that was sitting right there in the lock and opened the gate. Any of the caged Operatives could have easily reached through to the key to unlock the cage door, had their brains been strong enough to consider it, Everley thought. He asked himself what was wrong with these Operatives, and how these cogs in the Brito machine had broken down so helplessly.

Bristow, who was stammering the word 'k-k-kill' repeatedly like a faulty television, was slung into the enclosure by the arm. As he skidded forward, he knocked into the one whose leg had been shuddering, and the two tripped over a body lying in the cage. Everley hadn't noticed the woman stretched out on the floor.

'We've lost one,' shouted the Capital to the other at the desk.

'Sure?'

The Capital took the leg of the woman and lugged her out, carelessly clipping her head against a bar at the bottom of the cage. The Capital checked for a pulse and prodded her face a few times, then replied, 'Yes,' with indifference.

'Okay,' said the Capital at the desk, removing a square piece of paper from one box and putting it into another. 'Name? Name?' the same Capital asked as he looked up and directly at Everley.

Everley didn't reply. The other Capital was dragging the lifeless woman towards the hanging sheet and he was far too distracted by the big reveal of what was behind it. With one side unhooked and the sheet dangling from the other corner, the contents of the hidden area were now clear to see: a heap of limp limbs and ashen arms. It was a stack of bodies, and Operative bodies at that. Some were clothed, some were blue with bruising, some were open-mouthed and most were open-eyed. One set of eyes were fixed on the red door as though focussed to escape, even in death. Everley willed them to blink or show any signs of life. There were none. He swallowed bile back into his throat, unable to look away from the faces of his fellow Operatives.

Seemingly unaffected by such a harrowing sight, the Capital casually hoisted the woman onto the pile, replaced the sheet and walked towards Everley.

'I found him outside. He must have wandered off. He's not totally awake *in there*,' said the Capital, pointing to Everley's head and then waving a palm slowly across his eyes.

'Well, at least he's quiet,' said the Capital sitting at the desk and tapping fingertips on keyboard buttons.

'Do you think it's the cumulative effect?'

'No, it's only round eight. We'll be seeing a lot more cases later in the year as the doses add up.'

'I thought they were going to change the ingredients to stop that.'

'There was a bout of sickness – some had fits, too – so they had to go back to the old recipe. Maybe the liquid is just not agreeing well with him. It does behave differently depending on the body.'

Though the conversation continued as though he was not in the room, Everley was listening intently and understanding completely. Seeing imprisoned Operatives held in a cage was visual confirmation of all that Selby had told him.

'Should we ask Command Raines to take a look?'

'No. Raines will only tell us to stick him in the cage with the rest of them. He's quiet enough. Leave him there while I do the

304

paperwork for that one,' the Capital said, indicating that he meant the Op who was awakening from her kick to the head. 'Drag her over.'

With the two of them trying to position her on the stool, now was Everley's chance. Without hesitation, he planted his fingertips and feet on the floor and propelled himself upwards, skidding out of the door and running back to the lodgings without slowing or looking back.

XX

'Menticide'

Noun: The systematic destruction of a human's mental independence.

The replacement of individual values, beliefs and behaviours with an opposed psyche by use of artificial techniques to reform thought.

The use of torture, hypnosis, drugs and/or other assistive methods to ease mental manipulation and reprogramme the mind.

- The Dictionary of Brito Management Terms (Available from The Education Centre only on the request of a Command Operative, or above)

Lyndon wetted a strip of cloth with her spit. She held it to Selby's brow and rubbed gently to remove the red blood that had congealed where it had been dripping from a slit in his scalp. He sat upright but swayed slightly with dizziness. His bottom rested on the newspapers of old Briton that carpeted the InOp wasteland, and he looked at her through bleary eyes beneath barely-opened eyelids.

'Where...?' Selby began to ask.

'We are in the InOp zone. Do you remember? We walked here.'

And by 'walked', Lyndon meant that she had taken him by the waist, pulled him up onto his feet, wrenched his arm over her shoulder and dragged him out of the building and all the way to the InOp area in the dead of night. His legs had stumbled some of the way but, for the most part, were floppy, dangling and scuffing all the way.

'Thank... you,' Selby said, regaining a little more consciousness with each passing minute.

'I recognise you. Not just from Everley's room, but because you give us nutrition tablets.' She dribbled into the cloth and raised it again to his brow. She was surprised when he didn't flinch away from the inevitable contamination of her InOp saliva. 'We trust you, can't we?'

Selby stretched his eyelids wider and saw that not only was Lyndon there, but also a child and a man behind her. He nodded to them.

'He's not the child catcher, Ma!' said Little Lyndon, pointing a grubby finger at Selby.

'You sure,' said the man to the child, 'he didn't take my baby? He didn't kill my...' he faded out and turned to hide his upset.

'The man with the scissors was an old'n. Grey and old. Angry looking. This isn't him,' said the child.

'Raines,' Selby spoke down into his chest.

'You know him?' Lyndon asked with a tone of anger at the association.

'He did this to me...' Selby said with the pain of last night's attack audible in his voice, if not entirely visible all over his body.

'Everley's with him now! Will he be alright?' Lyndon said, worried.

'I don't know,' Selby said as he struggled to stand. He groaned as his weight loaded onto his clearly-broken ankle and Lyndon moved forward to help steady him on his stronger side. 'I must go.'

'What about Everley? You were his friend, isn't that right?'

'We can't save him from here. We need to wait for him to return from the PRORA... and see whether he still recognises us.'

Everley was pacing the short length beside the bed in his assigned lodging. He wanted to confront Raines, but he had seen his explosive anger before and wasn't sure whether he would survive the blast. He also knew that he would be outnumbered if he tried to fight or escape. So, he settled on a plan to see as much of the real PRORA as possible and learn what he could. He would decide what to do with the information when he got back to Point A, whether that meant escaping and living an InOp life with Lyndon or joining Selby's group and trying to change things from inside. But, if the latter, the treatment of the so-called InOps would be the first thing he would challenge.

Everley collected the agenda from the table to find out what was next in store: 'Collective Contemplation' followed by 'Anti-InOp Protection Training'. He blew his cheeks out and rolled his eyes away from the page in his own private contemplation.

A high-pitched tone played out of a speaker in the ceiling so sharply that Everley dropped the paper and grabbed hold of his ears. As soon as it stopped, an official announcement requested that all Operatives return to their own quarters. Thankfully, Everley was alone and already in his own.

Without him moving from the spot, the shower switched itself on. Everley watched water dancing on the floor through the open door between the bedroom and shower room. He observed solidly and did not move. He wanted to resist the urge to follow the sound of the spray which was wordlessly calling him. He wanted to *want* to wash, and not be mentally manoeuvred to do it.

The shower clicked off and the dryer cycle started. Everley smiled slightly, as though he had managed a small and freeing victory from within Raines' cage.

'Your chosen session begins in three minutes. You are welcome to proceed to 'Collective Contemplation' in the Golden Room,' came another announcement.

Everley headed into the corridor. Other Operatives were slowly emerging from their own rooms, falling about themselves and using the wall as a guide to the exit of the block. Most were squinting or shielding their eyes. The dim lights of the corridor were far too bright for them, it seemed.

The Golden Room was a very large space in which hundreds of black plastic seats had been carefully arranged into lines and fixed to the floor. In front of the seats was a raised stage with a podium standing alone in the centre. As Everley paused to admire a thick and soft-looking curtain that was huge in size and hanging from ceiling to stage, he was shoved from behind; docile Operatives were marching in lines towards the next empty seat. They moved automatically and had continued to push past Everley while he was sight-seeing.

Once all were seated (Everley included, finding a space at the end of a row), the lights were switched off entirely. A Capital hurried onto the stage and stood behind the white podium. She pressed a button on its side, turning on a glowing light from the podium's front. With all else so perfectly dark, the brightness of the single light was dazzling.

'For Brito!' saluted the Capital.

The light on the podium changed to blue. The blue transformed into a green, which melted into yellow, orange, red, pink then purple. It whirled in ever-quickening revolutions in a way that made Everley's eyes spin. He squeezed his lids closed to shade his eyes and protect him from the hypnotic summoning of the colour wheel.

'Please make yourselves comfortable young Operatives and relax, and take some deep breaths as you enjoy now relaxing and descending into this relaxation music,' recited the Capital in the most sickly serene tone.

Music started. It was more of the same strange *dings* and *dongs* of electronically-created song that had been played during the opening ceremony. Deep beats, low hums and swerving sounds pulsed around Everley as he kept his eyes closed.

He visualised Lyndon's face and held it there in the very front of his imagination. But, try as he might, the distorted and disturbing harmony was circling his brain and seemed ready to latch onto it with clawing fingernails at any second.

'Are you all feeling relaxed, Operatives?' asked the Capital. 'Nod with me, if...' she paused, 'You are.'

Everley felt his chin drop as he involuntarily began to nod. He lifted his hand and held it strongly and firmly under his chin so that it could droop no further as the Capital continued to ask the crowd to nod in affirmation to her numerous statements.

There was a clunking and a shuffling sound in the direction of the stage. Everley cracked one eye open to see what was happening. The curtain was crinkling upwards from the centre to reveal a view right across the coast. Everley caught a glimpse of the shutter he had seen earlier rolling upwards and into the ceiling, leaving a gaping hole through to the outside. A soft kiss of night air rippled across his face and he opened his other eye to appreciate the magnificent view.

The waves of the sea reflected the sparkle of the moon and stars with every rise between falls. A row of windmills stood like queuing Operatives in a straight line from the building out into the sea. With bases planted deep into the water, their blades rotated slowly in the air. They picked up the light from the moon, then dropped it again as they turned. They were waving at Everley. Beaconing him, perhaps.

'Behold the beauty of Brito! This is your existence...' the Capital continued.

Everley closed his eyes. He could bare the beauty of Brito no longer, for it wanted to steal him away. He could feel its pull.

'In thanks, take your right hand and place it on the shoulder of the Operative next to you,' she instructed.

Everley felt a hand on his right shoulder. It made him shudder. The very sensation of it made him feel urgently tired. He could feel an uncontrollable sleeplessness taking hold. It wanted to remove him from reality. He wanted to stay. He *wanted* to stay awake. He forced his eyes open and saw the shadow of heads hanging low. His fellow Operatives were asleep. He took the hand of the Op next to him and slid it slowly from his shoulder.

Everley watched the Capital on stage switch off the podium light and signal to another Operative at the side. There was a rattling sound and the metal shutter came back down, juddering all the way until it landed on the stage with a thump, taking the last bit of light with it. The curtains were drawn and the Capital departed.

The room was now so dark that Everley wasn't sure whether he had lost the power of sight altogether. He breathed deeply, hoped for his eyes to adjust and resolved to sit it out until the end of the session.

'You are a child of Brito,' came a voice within the music which was low in tone and startled Everley. *'You have a natural inclination to selflessness. You find yourself acting only in a way that is purposeful to the One, for Brito.'*

The Operatives in the crowd mumbled through almost-closed mouths, 'For Brito... for Brito... for Brito...'

Everley sat open-mouthed and shocked by the authority within the voice. There was a power behind it. It was attempting to dominate the mind and Everley could feel it leading him away from his own desires. He wanted to plug his ears to stop the voice from spilling in, squashing his wants and replacing them with the voice's own, but he was already committed to discovering the dishonest dealings that took place at Raines' behest.

'Your body knows how to operate, and does so efficiently. You are efficient. You see yourself as a cog in the machine for Brito.'

Again came the muttered reply of the assembly.

'You have no will but that of Brito. You follow only its will. You follow all that it commands. You carry out all that it asks. You operate tirelessly for Brito.'

Using the vision of Lyndon as protection, Everley allowed himself to continue listening to the spoken statements. He said to himself that they were as powerless as written words in a history book and had no ability to infiltrate his mind, but he *wanted* to listen, so that he could understand the manipulative methods of his once beloved Brito.

'You never question Brito, for its want and your own are the same.'

Everley knew that Selby was right. He had seen enough evidence to support it. He had heard Brito's call with his own ears and listened as it wiped minds of self-wants.

Beneath the first voice came a second. With both talking at the same time it was difficult to isolate one from the other, but Everley tried.

'You accept all that you see and hear. You believe all you are told.'

'Yours is not to make reply.'

'You see yourself as a perfect Briton and accept no lesser standard.'

'Yours is not to reason why.'

'You question nothing. You embrace everything.'

'Yours is but to do or die.'

'You give all you are and all you have. To the end. For Brito.'

Everley could take no more. The words were piercing into his brain so painfully that he may well have inserted a pair of scissors into his ears. He slid from the chair and crawled on all-fours in the direction of the door.

Feeling his way and finding the door not too far behind him, he nudged it open with one hand (the other held a finger in one ear).

312

He scuttled out quickly and stopped, watching for anyone who may have detected him. There was nobody there.

Everley stomped down the corridor in the Command building. His strides were more purposeful than ever. His shoulders were back, his head was high and his eyes were fixed in determination. He felt a tingling, if not burning adrenaline pouring through his veins and fuelling his next move. He didn't need to hear anything more. He didn't need to see anything else. The PRORA practices were clear and Raines was the crooked creator behind it all. Everley was disgusted, angry and resolute to confront him.

'Y-You c-c-can't go in there,' said the nervous Capital who was standing to attention outside Raines' office.

Everley walked straight past him and pushed the door open so hard that it swung wide and caught the wall behind it, causing plaster to clatter onto the carpet.

Raines *was* in his office. He looked to be near the climax of a carnal act all of his own. And, despite Everley barging into the room, he wasn't about to stop himself reaching his peak.

Raines had an Operative pinned between himself and his desk. The young male was bent at the waist and face down on the tabletop with his arms stretched out in front of him. The Op was clothed, except that his trousers had been jerked down to expose his backside. Raines was wearing nothing but his shirt, although even that was fully unbuttoned to reveal the wiry hairs of his belly and everything below it. His hands were positioned on the very top of the helpless Op's thighs, which he was using as handles. With every rough thrust, Raines let out a grunt. He eyeballed Everley and grinned, then threw his neck back and barked towards the ceiling. With one last plunge into the Operative, Raines howled, shuddered and stopped.

'Sorry, I didn't hear you knock,' said Raines nonchalantly as he bent down to pull up his trousers. Once his shirt was tidied and

313

tucked, he turned to the drowsy Operative on the table who seemed confused, was moving a little and wiping his eyes. 'Go. We're done here,' Raines said as he slapped his back and walked towards Everley.

Everley was still standing in the doorway. Behind him was the nervous Capital. Both were digging top teeth into bottom lips and saying nothing.

'Well? Don't fucking stand there!' Raines laughed. 'I assume you're feeling a bit more alert now, yes?' Raines said as he poked a finger into Everley's chest.

'Yes,' Everley replied, trying to refocus and recall the start of the interrogation that he had recited in his head. It had momentarily gone, as had the moment to raise his challenge.

'Come on, we'll be late for the next session,' Raines said as he brushed past them both and walked down the corridor. 'Everley, I could have taught you a bit more but you were in a bit of a haze while enjoying your reward. Now that you're more... with it...' he chuckled, 'it's time for you to learn, alright? Next on the agenda is 'Anti-InOp Protection Training'. This is a pretty essential part of the PRORA.'

As Raines continued to talk, Everley followed him out of the Command building, round the back and towards the small structure with the red door. Everley could feel his heart rate quicken at the thought of the cage inside. He knew that if he went in there again, the Capitals would recognise him. They would tell Raines and Everley would be done for and end up on the body pile.

'We are going to make sure Brito's Operatives know how to treat the InOps,' Raines continued as they approached.

Everley stopped walking before they reached the red door.

'C-C-Command,' the nervous Capital said as he jogged to catch up with Raines, tapped him on the shoulder and pointed back to Everley. 'He has stopped.'

'Son? What are you doing?' Raines called over and asked impatiently with his palms out.

'I can't...' Everley started, then simply said, 'I'd like to discuss something with you.'

'Later boy! No time now!' He paused and watched Everley's face fall and his brow crease in the middle. 'Fine, fine, you wait there. We'll be back in less than a minute.'

Everley tapped his temples with his fingertips in relief that he didn't have to suffer the horror of the building with the red door for a second time. He watched as Raines and the Capital walked towards it, but stopped short of that door.

Raines stood cross-armed while the Capital bent and reached for what looked like a circular piece of metal on the ground. As he wrenched the thing upwards, it lifted with it a wide sheet of wood. Raines did nothing to help the nervous Capital, who shook under the weight of the thing as he heaved it onto his shoulders and then pushed it over. It landed on the ground with a clang.

Raines stepped forward and then slowly descended into the earth, disappearing step by step. There must have been a hidden stairway in the floor, Everley thought, somewhat frustrated that he hadn't noticed the wooden door before. A moment later, Raines emerged. After pulling a man (probably an InOp) cruelly up the stairs, he tossed him to the dirt as they reached ground level. Raines patted his legs and then walked to rejoin Everley, leaving the Capital to replace the wooden covering.

'Right,' Raines said as he approached Everley, 'let's get over to the piazza.'

Everley was still fixed on the Capital, who was tackling the task of lifting up the man onto what Everley could now see was only one leg.

'Don't worry about that idiot, he'll manage,' sniggered Raines as he led Everley by the arm. 'This next part is really important, son. What we are going to do is *train* our Operatives to attack the InOps as soon as they see them. They will want to kill them. Rip them apart.'

'Don't we already think we want to rip them apart?' Everley asked, wondering whether Raines would pick up on his choice of words.

'Well, yes! But only because we keep training you to think that way! If you didn't practice, you might forget... Or worse, start thinking for yourselves!'

'C-C-Command?' the Capital called, holding the man by one arm. The rest of his body was just a heap of naked skin on the ground.

'Oh, for fuck sake! Do I have to do everything around here?!' Raines exclaimed as he took a few steps back, then halted. 'Everley, you wouldn't mind helping that useless prick, would you?'

Everley raised an eyebrow as he tried to compute the command, then nodded and compliantly approached the Capital and the one-legged man.

'I c-c-can't carry him.'

Everley grabbed for a part of the man and found the other arm.

'Please...' moaned the man as he was lifted onto his only foot. He looked up desperately at Everley.

'Harford? Harford!' Everley couldn't believe it. Harford had survived the incident at the windmills and was tottering there alive and in front of him, albeit on one leg.

Harford gazed at Everley.

'Do you recognise me? It's Everley,' he said, patting Harford on the chest with one hand. He shifted his grip of Harford's arm to hold him around the back and under the armpit to support him. 'Are you... alright?'

'C-C-Come on,' said the nervous Capital as he continued to tug Harford forward with the same disregard as one would yank a chair up to a table.

'Let go of him!' Everley said with a raised voice as he pushed the Capital away with his free hand, making sure to keep Harford steady with the other.

The Capital looked affronted, but didn't challenge. He let go of the arm and stood aside.

Harford span into Everley, wrapped his arms around his middle and squeezed hard. With his chin on Everley's shoulder and his face hiding in his nape, Harford wept hysterically. Stained with the events of previous days that had passed without washing, his broken body heaved up and down in Everley's arms. Everley held him tightly, comfortingly rubbing his back and repeating, 'It's okay.'

'What the absolute fuck is going on here?!' Raines shouted as he marched to the site of the scene, showing the extent of his infuriation with straight arms and solid fists that swung at his sides. 'Well?' he said, along with a series of other illegal words.

'This man is an Operative, not an InOp,' Everley said firmly.

'What?'

'This is Harford, the Operative I tried to help at the windmills. The Operative that *you* said was dead!' Everley said with disdain.

'I bloody know very well who he is, son! How well do you reckon he's going to operate now? Hey? Now that he's only got one leg?!' Raines pointed with a forefinger and continued to rage. 'You've got a lot to learn, boy!'

'He has operated for our One, *sir*!' Everley replied with a sneer. 'He has worked his life so far. He has even given his leg for Brito! Shouldn't he be rewarded? Why isn't he sent to the Other Place?'

'How dare you question me, boy!' Raines screamed, lashing his arm forward and landing a palm on Everley's cheek.

Everley wobbled on his feet but didn't let go of Harford. Instead, he held his hand around Harford's head as though cradling a baby and shuffled backwards.

'Where do you think you're going, son? Where do you think you're taking him?' Raines continued as he moved a foot forward with every step that Everley took back.

'Help me,' came Harford's voice faintly into Everley's ear.

'What are you going to do with him?' Everley asked Raines, flinching in expectation of another slap.

'Why... are... you... FUCKING... questioning... me?' Raines replied, convulsing in extreme anger on every word.

'You said that I had a lot to learn, sir,' Everley replied, quickly and cleverly trying to talk his way out of the situation for both himself and Harford. 'You said that I could be a Capital or even a Command one day. I need to understand things to do that.'

Raines frowned and glared with dark, almost black eyes beneath those bushy brows of his.

'C-C-Command, we don't have much t-t-time before the session starts,' interrupted the nervous Capital.

'Fine!' Raines said to Everley, still shaking in fury. 'Listen to this and listen good because you'll need it one day: Brito survives because we are fit! What is the purpose of those that are unfit? WASTE! Wastefulness is the disease that compromises the survival of our whole. Wastefulness *must* be eliminated. A weakling will *waste* Brito's resources. Nutrition tablets. Clothing. Bedding. A space in the living quarters. A place in the PRORA. A weakling will drain these things but add no value back to Brito... But maybe, in a small way, these *invalids* can be of some minor value. That is what you will learn. You'll learn by watching me!' Raines blasted, grabbing Harford's arm and tussling with it.

Harford squeezed Everley even harder and squealed 'No!' over and over.

'Leave him alone!' Everley shouted as he shook away, pushed back and then, without thinking, defended them both by forcing the back of his arm outwards violently.

Everley's elbow clipped Raines on the temple. He flew backwards and landed with on the ground with a crack of his back. He yelled out in pain and writhed around.

'You fucking bastard!' Raines spluttered into the grit. He grappled with the top button of his shirt, reached inside and awkwardly produced a shiny item that had been hanging from a chain around his neck. 'You rebel! You fucking rebel! You need to be reprogrammed!' he continued to curse before holding the shiny object to his lips and blowing hard.

The sound was a high pitched whistle. Each time Raines drew breath and blew into it, it whistled again. It sounded like a piercing alarm and Everley knew it signalled trouble. Still supporting Harford's weight with his whole body cuddling into his chest, Everley edged away and scanned the area to seek any potential escape.

It was already too late.

From every building and every door came a flood of Administrative Operatives, Guide Operatives, Tech Operatives, Enforcement Operatives, Watch Operatives and PRORA Capitals. They invaded the open ground from every direction with such a rush of urgent and trampling charge that the land quaked and Everley was immediately encircled.

Raines had rolled onto his front and a small group hurried to his aid and lifted him back to his feet.

'Take that one to the piazza for the anti-InOp session,' he instructed, fingering Harford.

A number of the henchmen held Everley hard while others prized Harford from his protective hold. As soon as the two were parted, Everley felt a boot behind his knee, which sent him immediately to the ground.

'Stop! Stop! Harford!' Everley pleaded whilst being aggressively forced down by the shoulders. He felt the tight skin covering his knees tear open against the sharp stones of the dirt. He felt the warmth of wet blood soaking his trousers but there was no pain; he was focussed only on saving Harford. 'He's an Operative! Listen to me!'

'Everley! Help!' Harford's begging wails quietened as he was hauled out of sight.

'No...' Everley cried, downcast and defeated. Beneath his low head and tear-filled eyes, a pair of boots appeared. The curved toe of one lifted, was pressed underneath Everley's chin and raised it, cricking his neck back so that, as he looked upwards, he was met with the black and beastly eyes of Command Raines.

'Harford is going to give more than just his leg to Brito! And you're going to watch! *That* will show you how things are done around here. Everything has its purpose, Everley, make no mistake. Once we've got our low value from Harford, then we will go about *correcting* you.' The 'rr's rippled over his tongue.

Everley was dragged by two abettors under the command of Raines. His blood-soaked knees grazed through the grit of the ground all the way to the polished black gloss of the piazza floor. Held solidly by the scruff of the neck, he had no option but to watch a terrifying torture play out in front of him.

'Dear Britons, you are welcomed to your final session for today after dark: Anti-InOp Protection Training,' began a Capital.

With a clunk, four or more enormous lights switched on, flooding the piazza with a light brighter than day.

Standing in orderly lines in front of the Capital, Everley could see one hundred fellow Operatives whose faces were those of the neighbours in his building and co-workers on his shift. In the space between the Capital and the crowd was a lost and naked Operative Harford. He had been given a stick to prop up his legless side, but was otherwise exposed. In panic, his head was turning left and right. In misplaced hope, he was imploring the faces that he too recognised to set him free. The faces didn't respond in any expressions of sympathy, reassurance or slight pity. The faces were simply blank. They may well have been sleeping. Together, they may well have been a painted poster of Brito's perfect unity.

'You will now practice all that you have learned. You will protect the future of Brito by protecting your fellow Britons,' announced the Capital.

From somewhere beyond or behind him, Everley could hear the sound of chains chinking and then dragging, and then chinking and then dragging with regularity. They were approaching. Into view walked at least ten, maybe fifteen InOps. Everley knew them to be InOps because they had long or short or straight or curly hair. They were fat with folds or thin with nearly no muscle. Not one had the body or the haircut of an Operative, except for Harford, and all of them were chained together at the foot. All of them were nude, sallow-skinned and marked with long lines across the back as though their skin had been torn with a cutting tool. All of them were shivering from fear and clasping hold of one another for protection.

'This,' the Capital aimed her finger at Harford, who was furthest out in front, 'is an InOp!'

Every head in the gathering turned. Every set of shoulders stiffened. Every pair of eyes squinted down and locked on their prey.

'NO! HE'S AN...' Everley started, only to feel the winding impact of Raines' boot into his belly. It took every breath from his body. He curled over and coughed.

'Hold him up,' Raines said to one of his army, 'make him watch.'

'InOps we hate! InOps we hate!' shouted the crowd, who were slowly edging forward. Some turned their hands into claws. Some snarled. Some even licked their lips. 'Waste we will cull! Waste we will cull!' they chanted in an ever-maddening frenzy.

'Britons,' the Capital continued, 'recall all that you have learned. Protect each other by *destroying* the InOp enemy!'

At once, the sea of believers surged forward. Harford had been engulfed, as had the chained InOps. There were tearing sounds and snaps and screams and a horrible, terrible bloodstream spilling across the piazza floor.

Everley wriggled, twisted and jerked his way free from the hands of his captivity. He launched himself at Raines, who was watching the debacle and had his back to him. Everley threw punches wildly, each landing in a different place on Raines' old body. He kicked and smacked and bit at him until the two of them were on the floor. Raines couldn't attack quickly enough. Instead, he held himself into a ball with his hands shielding his head. And still Everley continued. He hated Raines for Harford. He hated him for every Op who had ever attended the PRORA. He hated him for the InOps.

'I've got him!' said one Capital to another, straining to pull the two apart as both continued to jerk and thrash and shout.

'Get me up!' demanded Raines to the Capitals. 'You've made the biggest fucking mistake of your life!' he said to Everley as he regained his balance, then spat at him and added a last but weak-footed kick for good measure.

'What shall we do with him, Command?'

'Hold him down!' Raines raged.

A flurry of hands held Everley down on the ground.

'Hold his nose!'

A hand pinched at his nose and squeezed it so hard that Everley felt blood shoot into the back of his throat. With his mouth wide open, he coughed out and struggled to draw air in.

Raines patted himself free from dirt and dust, straightened his hair, then reached into his pocket and pulled out the miniature vial of blue liquid that he saved for what he called 'special occasions'. He unscrewed the silver cap and held it above Everley's open mouth.

'Goodbye Everley, you slippery little bastard.'

XXI

ARBEIT MACHT FREI

Selby was waiting for the Speed Line to arrive. He felt apprehensive. He had tried leaning casually against the wall but found himself hobbling back and forth in impatience. With an ankle broken (amongst other injuries), he had been provided with a walking stick and its clack echoed throughout Point A as he traipsed. His body was restless and brain unsettled by circling questions: *'What had happened at the PRORA? How close had Everley and Raines become? Would Everley return the same? Different?'*

'Alive?'

Tutting at the thoughts, Selby stopped his pacing, kicked the wall with his good foot and told himself that Everley was strong of mind and all would be fine. As he looked up, he noticed a figure crouching beneath the painted poster at the side of the platform. It was Lyndon. Selby raised his hand to wave, but did this slowly and close to his chest so that it could easily appear to be a mere scratch of the chin.

Lyndon nodded in return and dropped the poster to conceal herself.

With a loud screech of the Speed Line's breaks, the silver train arrived into the station. Selby moved to a better position for seeing Everley in the line when they passed through the exit. He chewed on his own cheeks to stop them twitching with nerves while he waited.

The front doors opened and the returning Operatives alighted in one long and continuous current. Face after face went by, but not one belonged to Everley.

With no more than forty left to debark, Selby was driven by an anxious desperation and stepped forward into the torrent. The next Operative in the line halted immediately to salute at Selby. This caused the one behind to collide into her back, and the one behind, too, until there was a pile-up of people. With the stream barricaded, Selby set about examining each face, saluting and waving them onwards to proceed and leave the station.

Just as hope had left him, Selby motioned for the last in line to step forward.

'Everley!' Selby said with relief, taking hold of his arm and shaking it kindly.

'Sir,' Everley saluted. His eyes were fixed straight forward.

'Everley?' Selby said, this time with worry. He tugged his arm and wiggled it but Everley's focus did not fade from the station exit. Selby moved himself into his line of sight and blurted, 'It's me!'

'Capital,' Everley started whilst continuing to salute. His stare was unbroken. He seemed to look through Selby's brow and out of the back of his head. He was focussed exclusively on the exit, with his next purposeful task only to return to his quarters. 'How may I be of service?'

Selby stood solidly and looked into his eyes. His brain willed and begged Everley to recognise the face of his friend, but both remained still and silent. In suspended movement, time had all but stopped. Selby felt a deep sadness rising within him: a grief at the decay of a mind and destruction of its memories. He felt the instant anguish at the confirmation that their bond had been blotted out of Everley's brain.

Selby shook himself from his sorrow and stepped aside. As he did, it was as though a button had been pressed and, without a word, Everley resumed his march home.

'EVERLEY!' yelled Lyndon as she scrambled out from underneath the poster and raced over.

Everley did not stop, slow down or turn to look.

As Lyndon swiftly drew near, Selby blocked her path and took hold of her. She passionately pleaded with him to let her go but Selby held her securely. Losing balance, his walking stick skated sideways and he screamed out in pain as his ankle folded on the floor.

'Why didn't you let me go after him?! Why did you stop me?!' Despite crying, Lyndon took hold of Selby and helped him to his feet.

'It's too dangerous for you,' Selby replied as he steadied his weight against hers.

'He doesn't remember, does he?'

Selby's shoulders slumped as he simply said, 'No.'

'I'm going to go to him tonight and make him remember. He *will* remember me,' Lyndon said, rubbing a tear aside with the back of her hand and accidentally making a clean patch across her cheek.

'There's no way tonight! All of the Operatives will be excitable after their time at the PRORA...' he broke off. 'Thanks,' he said as Lyndon passed him the walking stick. 'But Everley arrives at the station at seven twenty-two every day. It'll be quiet and empty here if we try to catch him tomorrow.'

'I'll see you in the morning, then.'

Lyndon closed the cupboard door having checked that the little one was soundly asleep. Approaching her InOp friend who had lost his baby to the child catcher and his partner to a murderer with a pair of scissors, the two sat to watch the sunset over the wasteland.

'I *have* to go,' Lyndon said. 'I can't bear it. I can't wait until morning.'

On the agreement that she would be cautious and consider Little Lyndon before risking her own life, Lyndon prepared to leave. She fetched her Operative disguise, lifted her InOp frock and tied the trouser legs and shirt sleeves around her middle. As soon as darkness fell, she took the riskiest route and ran towards Everley's building.

Lyndon neared the security light that was making its bright and circular passes from left to right in search of misbehaviour. It was always more dangerous after dark because Surveillance Operatives would attack first and asked questions afterwards if they found a person bounding over the forbidden ground in the shadows.

The red triangular flag that denoted the border between zones was billowing in the evening wind. Usually she could hear the flapping and fluttering of it calling her closer to the crossing point, but tonight it was inaudible over the roars of revelry. Selby was right: there was a heightened heat and fever in the air. She should turn back, she thought, but the urge to see Everley was too great, as was her belief that their unity had the power to shatter the shackles that were enslaving his mind. She was *certain* that their devoted connection had the clout to push out the voice of Brito and bring back the human that was hiding there inside him.

Lyndon waited as the bright light made another pass and then, as soon as the open road fell once again into darkness, she launched herself forwards and ran on the tips of her toes. It was not courage that powered her steps, it was purpose, and she managed to cross undetected.

At the corner of the building with the giant bin beside the back door, she found a secluded space to catch her breath. Still panting, she slid her Operative disguise down from her waist, dressed in it hurriedly, rolled her own clothing into a small ball and hid it in between the two back wheels of the dustbin. Filling her lungs with one last shot of dusty air, she stepped into the walkway.

'Best Evening!' merrily sung three Operatives as they crossed her path.

Lyndon jumped backwards and stared fearfully at the group.

326

'Best Evening!' one repeated as she swung around Lyndon and smiled into her face. 'The best of all evenings, isn't it Briton?'

Lyndon nodded up and down hectically, as though her head were on a quivering string. Before she was able to find any words to reply, the three intoxicated individuals staggered away and disappeared into the building. Lyndon was left alone in the walkway, shaking her hands with arms outstretched in an attempt to drop her nerves to the ground.

Carefully, she edged towards the back entrance and pressed at the door. It didn't open.

Shouts of 'InOps we hate! InOps we hate!' screamed so loud and by so many inside the building that it made the night air pulse with a rancid loathing. The Operatives were united in belting out about their mutual disgust of the wasteful class, and Lyndon was in no doubt that they would use her body to realise every conceivable method to kill if she was found on this night (of all nights).

If she could just get in through the back door, she thought, she would be able to get to the relative safety of the stairway, where the lights were dimmer and the human traffic limited. Going in the front door was out of the question: her shoes were showing more white than black, her hair had grown since the first cut and her face was dirty. Although she hadn't seen her reflection for a few days, she could feel her own filthiness.

'We-e-e are to-o-gether just one!' came another small crowd singing down the side street.

Lyndon cowered. She had nowhere to go. She tried the door again, but it still did not open.

'We-e-e are to-o-gether just one!' they sang, closer now.

Beyond the locked door was her only route to Everley. Behind her was the safety of the InOp area. Lyndon tried the door again, beat at it desperately with both hands and shoved. It wasn't moving.

'Best Evening!' said a voice that had emerged from under the shadow of the neighbouring building.

'To-o-gether,' continued the singers, turning into her path from the other side.

Lyndon retreated foot by foot, then turned on her heels and sprinted back into the InOp zone.

Everley's eyes popped open the instant he awoke as though in response to a clicking finger. He turned his head to the gap between the bottom of the blackout blind and the windowsill, through which he could see the large clock face on the building opposite.

Yet again, it was five to six.

For five, glorious minutes, he daydreamed of The Other Place. He imagined taking the Speed Line to the end of the line, resting his feet on the new land, feeling the warmth of sunshine and the tickle of a gentle wind on his face. He visualised running through flowered fields of all colours towards quaint buildings and people dancing and singing. He envisioned a soft air and haze of smooth blues and pinks that lingered low in the sky like small clouds that, if touched, felt like the inside of a fresh pillow issued by Brito on the first day of each year. It was the serenest of dreams.

BUZZ BUZZ BEEP BEEP BEEP

Getting up and out of the bed immediately, Everley took the cover sheet by one hand and pulled it straight upwards to make the bed in one movement. He patted down any creases efficiently and, only once satisfied, went towards the window. With a quick jerk on the material, the blind clattered upwards and was fully open. He squinted his eyes against the morning light and peered down to the tarmac, twelve floors below, to see the Night Watch Operatives leave their posts at the end of their shifts.

Turning to get on with his day, Everley took a second to notice the morning sunshine on his picture of The Other Place. He frowned. For no reason known to him, it had been torn right through the centre of the painted countryside. With the top corner hanging away from the wall and folded over on itself, the tag line now read, *'be forgotten!'* Everley thumbed the page so that he could remind himself of the start of that sentence. He would find some way to repair it later, he told himself.

With a shuffle, a folded piece of paper was pushed under the door. It flew across the floor and landed close to Everley.

TELEGRAM

TO: OP. EVERLEY

FROM: BRITO

FOR EXCEPTIONAL PERFORMANCE IN PRODUCTIVITY YOU HAVE BEEN SELECTED TO VISIT YOUR MOTHER IN THE OTHER PLACE STOP YOU ARE EXCUSED FROM YOUR WORKING SHIFT TODAY STOP BOARD THE SPEED LINE AT 0900 TODAY STOP

'The Other Place!' Everley called aloud, waving the telegram in the air as he erupted into joyous tears. 'Mother!' he spoke excitedly into his palms. It had been so many years since he had seen her that he wasn't sure whether he would recognise her face. Today was the day, and Everley's heart felt fuzzy with the best kind anticipation.

While reading and re-reading the telegram with one elated gasp after the other, Everley could hear movement in the corridor. It was filling up with his neighbours heading for the toilets and showers. He really hated to be anywhere except the first in the queue, but knowing that he now had an extra hour before having to leave, he prepared slowly for the momentous moment he would see the wonders of The Other Place, and Mother, too. He unhooked the hangers holding his Operative trousers and shirt and lay them delicately onto the bed. Slowly smoothing down any crinkles with his hand, Everley noticed that one sleeve had a several specks of sand stuck to it. He returned to the hangers to retrieve his replacement shirt, but it wasn't there. Also missing was his coat, another pair of trousers and his white shoes, which was puzzling.

Once the others were finished, Everley had a shower. He scrubbed extra-hard with his nub of soap, brushed extra-well with his toothbrush and took extra time to pull any hair on his cheeks and chin out from the root using the hair remover. He looked a little longer in the mirror than usual and smiled at himself in thanks for all of the hard work he must have done to receive such a prestigious reward. He dressed at a slow pace, mindfully drawing each button through each buttonhole because it seemed important to value the details of the day. Contented, he took the door handle with a happy hand and set off downstairs to chat with the Day Watch Operative before strolling to the station via the longest walking route.

As the eight o'clock Speed Line shot out of sight and the station emptied of Operatives returning from the night shift, only two beings were left standing on the platform.

'He wasn't here!' Lyndon said as she walked over to Selby with palms open in unknowing. 'Where could he be?'

'I don't know... Operative!' he said as he looked her disguise up and down with a half-smile.

'I lost my InOp clothes in the Operative zone last night,' she said, then bit her lip. Selby would now know that she had defiantly tried when he'd told her not to.

'Did you see Ev–'

'You were right,' she interrupted, 'it was too dangerous. I didn't get far.'

Selby nodded in the knowledge that his warning was warranted.

'Where could he be?' Lyndon repeated her initial question.

'He could only be in his quarters... unless something has happened and he is at the Health Centre?'

'Oh no! What if–'

'Let's check his quarters first. We'll walk together, just in case... Who knows what response you'd get if someone saw you looking like that!'

'Is it *that* bad?' Lyndon stared ashamedly at the torn trouser legs and scuffed shoes.

Selby pressed his lips together to stop a small snigger from spilling out. 'It's... it will be alright if we walk together. I'll talk our way out if anything happens.'

'Okay,' Lyndon agreed, turning to head in the direction of the InOp area.

'This way,' said Selby as he took hold of her arm and pulled her towards the main exit. 'We'll take the shortest route.'

On the way, Selby shared his plan to distract the Day Watch Operative while Lyndon sneaked in the back entrance. He reminded her to be careful, what with an Enforcement Operative doing the rounds, and they arranged to meet in Everley's room.

'Best Morning, Day Watcher!' Selby said breezily as he waltzed up to the front desk of Building 7.

'Well, Best Mornin' to you, Capital!' Operative Boone said as she looked up from the BritPost mail she was opening at the counter.

'I bet the Operatives have been in fine spirit this morning, yes?'

'Oh yes, sir! Ya should 'av seen 'em, sir! They've been raving 'appy since PRORA. Even this mornin' they seem more brighter!'

'That is good news,' Selby said, peering into the Service Room to see whether there was anybody there, or any sign of trouble. 'No illnesses last night or this morning, no?'

'No, sir! I'd 'av 'em recorded 'ere in my book, sir. Nothing for quite a while as I recall. The last little *problem*, shall we say, was...' she moved her head humorously close to the book and read through a very short list on the page, 'forty-three days ago, when the television screen fell off that there wall,' she pointed, 'right in the

331

middle of that entertainment broadcast they 'av with the InOps fightin', and, well, the Ops were so excited that they started throwin' the chairs about. One smashed, and—'

'Very good,' Selby cut her short. 'Have you seen young Everley this morning?' he asked casually.

'Yes, sir! He was so 'appy, and he looked so smart!' she spoke into the air with a grin. 'He was going to The Other Place, sir! Would you believe it?!'

'What?!' Selby stared at her, his face creasing with concern.

'What luck! What reward! Sir, he was so 'appy indeed!'

'When did he leave? When is he going?'

'I can see you wish it were you going there as well, eh, sir? He was so lookin' forward to seein' his mother that he were beamin' from ear to here!' she pointed to her temple.

'It is good news, yes, but I do need to speak to him before he leaves. If you could tell me–'

'You'll 'av ta be quick, sir! He's going on the nine o'clock train!'

Selby slammed a hand on the desk to gesture his thanks then ran towards the lift.

'He's already left, sir! He ain't upstairs!' Boone called after him.

Selby didn't reply. Instead, he hammered the button for floor twelve and fidgeted on his feet as the doors slid shut painfully slowly.

Selby flew into room B12.13, finding Lyndon standing in the centre of it.

'Where is he?' she said.

'He's...' Selby puffed, unable to catch his breath from bounding down corridor. 'We have to stop him... getting on... the train!'

'What train? The train's gone!'

'No!' Selby wheezed, then took hold of Lyndon's arms tightly and looked into her eyes. 'There's another. Nine o'clock. If he gets on it, he's...'

'What?'

'He's... We just *have* to stop him getting on that train!'

Lyndon turned and looked out of the window. The clock on the face of the building opposite read twenty-five past eight. 'There's still time if we go the short way back. We'll need to hurry,' she said.

'You'll need to go by yourself,' Selby started, 'and try to stop him getting on. I know that's dangerous for you but it's the only way. I will try to stop the train from leaving at all.'

'I'll go alone,' Lyndon said quickly and with no thought for herself, 'but how are you going to stop the train?'

'I'll go to my work. I'll tell the Controller it must be stopped.'

By the time that Lyndon arrived at Point A (thankfully, still with her life), the station was filling with eager Operatives who were queuing for the special train. She cautiously shifted along the platform and closer to the hanging poster so that she would be in a position to escape beneath it and into the safe InOp land, if attacked.

She spotted Everley from a distance. Although there was a gap between himself and the waiting crowd, it was not that which singled him out. He seemed to shine a light from the visible delight in his facial expression. He stood as stiffly as a painted Operative on a poster. He was a model of the best of Brito, with hands held behind his back and the rims of his work boots poised at the very brink of the platform's edge.

Lyndon's heart lifted as soon as she saw him there but, with an ever-growing congregation, the likelihood of stealing his attention seemed impossible.

'Ma!' Little Lyndon had scurried out from beneath the poster and was tugging at her trousers.

Without thinking, Lyndon swept him into her arms and cuddled him. She kissed his cheeks and ears with little pecks that tickled him and made him giggle.

'Traitor! Traitor!' was being shouted from somewhere behind her and, as she turned to face the source of the squawking, Lyndon realised that she was the focus of their fury.

'Oath breaker! InOp defender!' the calls continued as the crowd drew closer.

Lyndon bent her knees and slowly put the little one's feet onto the ground. She whispered into his ear, 'Go back home quickly,' as she pushed him away and signalled her head in the direction of the poster.

'I want to play!'

Little Lyndon raced past her quicker than she could grab him. His petite feet danced through the assembly so fleetingly through each hand that tried to take him, each foot that tried to floor him and each fist that tried to hit him. He giggled all the way and tied the Ops in knots.

A small number of Operatives began circling Lyndon and reeling-off lines from the oath through tensed jaws and chattering teeth.

'I was trying to get him!' Lyndon blurted, looking beyond the group to catch sight of the boy as he flashed across the platform in the direction of Everley.

'Kill the InOp! Kill the InOp!' they warbled in unpleasant song.

'I'll get him!' Lyndon shouted in return, not knowing whether they wanted to kill only Little Lyndon or them both. Not wanting to find out, she tore away and followed the little one's path.

Little Lyndon was standing not quite four feet from Everley at the platform's edge. As Lyndon's sprint took her closer, she could hear the little one calling up at him.

'Everley the human! That's you! Everley the human!'

Everley initially ignored the interruption, remaining in deep daydream and staring out with the same high-spirited expression. But then, as though his neck was the pivot in the central dial of a clock's face, his head rotated to the side at the slow speed of a second hand. Stopping only as his chin reached his shoulder, Everley's eyes were the last thing to leave the tracks and look down upon the child.

From this position, Everley raised one arm and withdrew his fingers into his palm so that his hand was squeezed into a ball with knuckles sharply protruding. Though ready to strike, an unseen force appeared to be battling his arm so that it neither advanced nor retreated, but simply stayed there in the air.

Lyndon skidded up behind the little one and fetched him up.

'Run! I'm serious!' she ordered as she plonked the child back on the ground and watched him scamper back to the painted poster at the side of the platform. The small horde that had cornered her before we also watching as she let the little one disappear.

Lyndon turned to stand and face Everley. The previous bliss that had so far been his painted expression all morning fell immediately from his face. He froze.

'Everley,' Lyndon whispered, looking into his eyes searchingly, 'it's me.'

His mouth opened, wanting to say something but being gagged by an invisible master.

'Traitor!' came the distant cry of the horde, who would no doubt now seek to destroy her, but Lyndon was not distracted. She looked at Everley with loving eyes and smiled comfortingly.

Everley tried again to speak but there was no noise. He stared at her, swallowing deeply and blinking rapidly with the rising panic of this paralysis and the growing knowledge that his thoughts were impossible to articulate.

'Traitor!' came the cries again.

Lyndon ignored them. This could be her only chance to save Everley from the seduction of Brito, she thought, and his eyes told her that he wanted to be saved.

The train was coming. The ground began to lightly tremble as its carriages rumbled down the tracks towards Point A. The closer it came, the more the platform quaked and its whistle intensified. In no time, it would be there.

Everley's mouth moved up and down. Again, there was no sound; something was stifling him.

'You are Everley... the human,' she smiled.

And then there was a noise from Everley. It wasn't a word; it was a whimper. He freed his fingers from his fist and held his opened palm over his eyes, looking at her through the gaps in between.

'She's an InOp!' shouted a voice next to her ear as the hand of an angered Operative clasped the neck of her shirt and tore it down to reveal the scratched, beaten and filthy back of an InOp.

The Speed Line's brakes screeched as the train charged into the station.

As she was being dragged to the ground, Lyndon watched Everley unwaveringly. He was shaking in terror beside one of the silver sets of doors so close to the platform's edge that it was a wonder he hadn't been knocked over. His leg seemed to be lifting and falling, wanting to step forward to help her but locked in a suspended reality. His eyes were fixed on hers and she could clearly see a hopeless loving, loss and sorrow erupt inside him. His eyes closed and a visible stream of tears poured down both cheeks.

He was inside, Lyndon thought, he just couldn't get out.

'Operatives, get onto the train!' said a commanding voice that stopped the attacking crowd before they caused her harm. Following orders, the mob stepped away, reformed their orderly lines and marched onto the train. A hand helped her to her feet. It was Selby.

'Everley? Everley!' Lyndon called urgently, no longer able to see him amongst the faceless mass of Operative drones.

'Did you see him? Where is he?' asked Selby with alarm.

'He's on the train!' she cried, just as the silver doors slid closed.

Both raced to the nearest door, poked their fingers into its join and tried to force it open. Lyndon hammered along the next set of windows, and the next, and the next, peering in and calling Everley's name.

'Everley!' Selby shouted, pointing to one wide carriage window.

Lyndon dashed over to it, finding Everley's frightened face there with his helpless hands pressing both palms against the glass. Lyndon thrust her own hand forward and held it to one of his, wishing the glass to not be in the way so that she could feel the warmth of his touch. She looked desperately up at him and called his name again.

From the other side of the glass, Everley mouthed three words.

'I'm... loving... you.'

Selby grabbed Lyndon's waist, stripping her from the glass just as the train lurched forward and blasted out of the station leaving the two lying alone in an emotional muddle on Point A's platform floor.

The Speed Driver moved a lever gradually upwards to take the train to its maximum speed.

'I don't think you are allowed in here, Command.'

Raines glared over at the young Operative and then turned back to the view from the wide windows of the cabin at the front of the train. The horizontal beams between the tracks shot past so rapidly that they seemed to merge into one another, as did the buildings on both sides until all that could be seen was a wash of greys and browns.

'You should get in the carriage,' said the driver, motioning to a closed door between the two areas.

'How dare you question me?' Raines snapped. 'What is your role? What do you do for Brito?' he asked with a condescending and impatient tone.

At first the driver was quiet, then said, '*I* am the driver of the Speed Line.'

'Then drive the fucking Speed Line and leave me alone!'

Raines eased himself back into the nice, feather-filled seat, took a lung-full of air and grinned at the thrill of the journey and all that would be waiting for him when he arrived in The Other Place.

He thumbed the long-awaited notice in writing from his Highers.

TELEGRAM

TO: COM. RAINES

FROM: HEAD CARDINAL QUARTERS

FOR EXCEPTIONAL PERFORMANCE AND DEVOTION YOU HAVE BEEN SELECTED FOR RETIREMENT IN THE OTHER PLACE STOP BOARD THE SPEED LINE AT 0900 TODAY STOP THANK YOU FOR A LIFE DEDICATED TO BRITO STOP

He congratulated himself for a job well done: not only the Everley situation, which he had to admit went rather well (although not entirely to plan), but also his thirty years' service for great Brito. Of course, there had been a few minor misdeeds over the years, he remembered. There was the malpractice and bad beginnings, the rather ghastly goings on during testing and experimentation to get the PRORA's processes right, and yes, some unnecessary deaths along the way (including that nervous Capital this morning because, well, just because taking his life was a last little treat). But Raines reminded himself that he had done a lot right by Brito and its beings, too. There was so much that he alone had contributed to the death of old Britain and the recreation of the new order. And Brito was now good. A legacy indeed.

Raines nodded in agreement with himself.

He tapped his silver pin. Looking down at it on his collar, he felt a slight bitterness that he had never been promoted to Cardinal or received a gold pin, but told himself that perhaps it was for the best. He was certainly feeling tired these days, and old. His grey hairs, wrinkled skin, increased irritability and lack of self-control showed him that retirement was really what he needed - and justly deserved.

Raines hadn't packed a bag for The Other Place. He had no possessions to put in it for a start, but he didn't bring a change of clothes either. He had also left his little notebook behind, deciding straight after receiving the telegram (but before killing the nervous Capital) that this would be a new phase in his life. Just as he had done away with Bunky to become Raines, he would now step off the train and leave Raines behind to become someone else.

The new Raines, whatever his new name, would be the best version of himself to ever be. He resolved to build bonds with others, rather than pushing people away. He looked forward to appreciating the wonder of nature and told himself that he would be attentive to the beauty of every moment of the freedom. Whether it be bobbing in the undulating water of a river, lying upon the green grass of a field or walking against the fiercest wind and hardest hail, he would respect and value it all.

In The Other Place, Raines (and Bunky) could be reinvented. He could be anything he wanted to be. He would sing, dance, request a guitar and learn how to play it. He would play parts of any song he could remember and claim them as his own. All would be well in the new life, he was sure.

A few nights ago, North Brito had announced on television the foundation of an animal farm in The Other Place. Raines remembered things like dogs and cats, chickens and rats in old

Britain. There were more but after all these years he could barely remember what animals looked like. He grinned at the idea of rediscovering them anew. Brito had also reported a flying horse with wings and a pointing horn from its forehead and Raines could hardly wait to see such a thing in the farm. The thought of it all made him jiggle up and down on the chair like a child.

'I'll be back once I've walked through the carriage,' Raines said officiously as he left the cabin. The view was boring him with its single sweeps of colour and he wanted to see whether anyone on this same train to The Other Place could be a candidate for a friendly (or other) relationship in his new life.

As he closed the door behind him, he heard the click of the lock.

'That shit!' he huffed.

The carriages seemed almost empty compared to the usual mass of Operatives on their way to work, yet there must have been at least seventy on board.

As the train whizzed through a wide area of wasteland, it came under attack. There was a series of loud breaks, bashes and bangs as a group of degenerate InOps threw rubbish at the train to scare the Operatives within it. But, though every other commuter dropped to the carriage floor in terror, Raines wasn't scared by their bad behaviour.

Raines started walking the length of the train, pulling people to their feet.

'Everything is well, dear Britons,' he began, peeling open the fingers of those who had clamped themselves to the metal poles, 'To your feet, to your feet!'

Further down the carriage, Raines noticed a man standing upright amongst a group huddled fearfully on the floor. The man hadn't moved one muscle in all the fracas. This man hadn't been scared either. He stood with legs a shoulder's width apart and, despite the natural rise and roll of the Speed Line, he was stable without holding on.

Raines drew closer to the figure as he moved through the centre of the train and lifted Operatives to their feet as he passed. As soon as he was close enough to see the man in focus, Raines stopped still.

It was Everley.

'How could it be Everley?' Raines asked himself as he felt a every hair on his own arms and neck stand on end. *'How could it be Everley?'*

Raines stared at the side of Everley's face as he looked out of the window. It was the face of a man that he had placed on the list of those to be expunged. It was the face of a man due to die today.

'I sentenced him to death!' Raines said, aloud this time, clutching his mouth with the hard skin of his own wrinkled palm.

Raines wanted to immediately approach Everley and ask him why he was on the train, but instead stood still with the dread that he already knew the answer; Everley was holding a telegram. A sickening feeling surged inside him as he saw the piece of official post in Everley's hand, just like that which he had also received that morning.

In horror, Raines slowly gazed back at the commuters in the carriage. Each one was happily holding their own invitation to The Other Place. As he looked, he noticed those that were bandaged from some sort of injury, those that were blank from some sort of brain malfunction, and those that he was sure were destined for the expunged list for one reason or other. But, like Raines, every single one was cherishing the paper, for it was their ticket to a reward of unimaginable delight. These were golden tickets. These were the winning lottery tickets of Brito, and the faces of those holding these tickets were of joy. So, though Raines couldn't read Everley's telegram from the distance, he was sure he knew what it said.

Raines swallowed to suppress the contents of his stomach from spraying out of his mouth. He had ordered Everley's death. He had written "EXPUNGE" against Everley's name (and a long list of others, too). To cease life was the command, but now he and Everley were on the same train, on the same day that death was directed.

He rubbed his throat as another wave of sickness lurched from deep within his stomach. The reality hit him with a smack: Brito had lied to him for thirty years. Just as he had lied to the Operatives. Just as they were lying to themselves.

There was only one option; he had to get off the train.

Raines raced back to the door of the front cabin and pounded against it.

'Let me in!'

'Not far now, sir,' came a jolly call from the driver inside.

'Fucking let me in!'

'I can't do that. We are nearly there though... Command Raines.'

The way the driver had added his name was sinister. Raines hadn't told him his name. The driver must have *known*. Raines turned and rested his back on the door. He felt his chest tighten as though his throat had been packed with barbed wire and netting. He wheezed when he felt the Speed Line slow. As the train swayed to turn away from the usual straightness of the route, Raines flung himself at the nearest window and looked outside. With the train decelerating, the washes of colour that had previously constituted the only view now settled into focus to reveal a terrifying reality that only the old world history books were made of.

Ahead, the mis-sold "Other Place" was no idyllic oasis. Tall concrete walls on all sides were topped with wires that had been spun in circles over metal spikes. Surveillance towers loomed above a wide, red-bricked building with a row of small, square windows. Either side of this building were two huge pillars, also of red brick but blackened at their tips. One of the pillars moaned a deep gurgle as it frothed a thick black smog from its top which spilled oppressively over the otherwise blue sky.

Raines knew the purpose of these pillars; they were chimneys. As soon as he confessed the truth to himself, he could smell the burning. Though it had been an age since he had sniffed a burning smell, he knew that this wasn't the burning of fuel, food or waste. This was the burning of bodies. And then Raines noticed that there were bodies. There were bodies everywhere. Bodies lined the ground like a carpet. Rather than the rolling hills that Brito pledged in return for time served, these mounds and slopes were made from the limbs of its people.

Raines touched his shaking fingers to his chest, where his tattoo had been lying dormant for so long. But now, caused by the quiver of his petrified heartbeat, the swastika seemed to be giggling at him. Raines was suddenly confronted by all that those straight lines represented: the betrayal of humankind. This place was a human extermination centre. Raines had never been more certain of a sight. It was as though he had stepped onto the pages of the books he had owned before Brito, or stumbled into the pictures he had torn from those same books and used to decorate the walls of his old flat. He had been cheated and had foolishly walked into an unimaginable place of terror. It was a place where there were only two types of people: the doomed and those overseeing the doomed. And Raines was on the wrong side.

The rationale dawned on Raines with clarity. Brito had taken every of molecule of energy and spirit and breath from him, and now he was useful for very little. He was simply skin. He was bone. He was teeth. He was hair. He was nails. Maybe Brito could make use of some of those remnants. Efficient and purposeful to the end.

'Stop the train!' Raines screamed at the height of his voice. 'We must go back! We must go back to Brito!' he shouted, grabbing the nearest Operative and shaking them, but being met with the same glazed and confused eyes that he had created at the PRORA.

'EVERLEY!' Raines shouted as he sprinted down the length of the train, pushing aside anyone standing in the way. Despite what he had done to Everley, he knew that he was different. He had a special mind that had triumphed over the PRORA before. He had a kind of cleverness and individuality that Raines hadn't managed to beat, frighten or programme out of him. Perhaps now that strength could save them both.

'Everley!' Raines cried as he reached him. He took hold of Everley's hand and spun him around to face him. 'You have to help us, Everley! We have to get out! We have to go back! Or go anywhere!'

Everley's blank face creased into a relaxed smile. He shook his head slowly at Raines, who watched on in extreme panic.

The train shuddered to a stop with a piercing shriek.

'Please!' Raines screamed into his face. 'We'll die here!'

Everley thrust his hands forward, grabbed Raines by both arms and squeezed. He pushed his chin out so far that their noses were as close as they could be without touching. He looked intensely into Raines' eyes.

'A weakling will waste Brito's resources. Wastefulness must be eliminated,' Everley recited deliberately and without emotion.

'What?!' Raines wailed as the silver doors slid open.

'That is what I learned. That is what you taught me.'

Knowing the words to be his own, Raines shuddered and fell to his knees, clawed at Everley's trousers, buried his head into Everley's work boots and cried for forgiveness into the black polish.

While Everley stood solidly in the doorway with Raines grovelling at his feet, the Operatives around them began to dismount from the train. The loud stomp of their work boots was soon overpowered by the even louder sounds of screaming. These were screams of fear, sudden understanding and broken promises.

'MOVE!' came a harsh bark from a voice on the outside of the train.

Raines couldn't bear to raise his head. He couldn't bear to look. Without a second warning, a blunt object jabbed sharply into his ribs. Releasing his helpless hold of Everley's trousers, Raines fell further onto the cold metal of the carriage floor. His eyes and cheeks were sodden with selfish tears, his nose blew pathetic bubbles, and drool spewed from his lips as he wept at the reality that he was facing his comeuppance.

Feeling a comforting hand on his shoulder, Raines shook himself to a still calm. He cautiously creaked his neck to raise his lowly head upwards. He saw only Everley's sympathetic eyes. Everley was softly stroking his shoulder and, with his other hand, offered an open palm to help Raines stand.

'NOW!' snarled the angry voice again. It was accompanied by another, harder blow to the side.

Raines stopped snivelling. He could hear the crimes occurring outside the train and knew there would be no mercy. With the inevitability of death, all that he wanted in that moment was the safety of an ally. The consolation of a comrade. The comfort of a friend. He knew that to look away from Everley now would be to see the evil of Brito. To see it meant being forced to believe it, and to be tormented – for however long or short the remainder of his life may be – by the fact that he had assisted in an abomination.

Solace was in Everley's eyes, and he would stay in their sanctuary.

A number of overseers for The Other Place were directing (and dragging) Operatives into one of two lines. Three of them roughly removed Everley and Raines from the train, separated the clasped hands that they had loyally linked together and forced them into opposite queues. Their eyes remained locked on each other as they were hauled to their feet and pushed into the back of the last in their line.

From the group on the right, Raines was led towards the red-bricked building behind similarly old or damaged Operatives, yet he continued to gaze across at Everley. Despite his own destructive attempts, he hadn't been able to blot out all that was good in that young soul. In Everley, Raines could see ever-so undeniably now that humanity still existed.

With a thoughtful farewell nod, Raines placed his hand on the shoulder of the Briton in front and closed his eyes.

For Everley and Raines, this is
THE END

EPILOGUE

We swear to each other this everlasting oath:

We do solemnly and truly declare that we faithfully give unconditional and absolute allegiance to Brito, the safe land that gives us life.

We, by willing choice, duty and responsibility, give ourselves efficiently, productively, for the good of all Britons and in defence of our Brito against any individual InOperative.

To this purpose we pledge our lives and give ourselves entirely for our One, for Brito, for Brito, for Brito.

Selby had been sitting in his manager's large, underground office for almost an hour. His biannual performance appraisal was going surprisingly well, all things considered, and she had been writing many a good example of his conduct on a form for The Hidden's records.

A rap of knuckles on the door interrupted the conversation.

'Yes?' called his manager loudly.

'Madam, this notice came in. I would have waited, but it is addressed to you both,' said a Servant who entered the room, handed the report over and hurried away quickly.

'Ah! Very good, thank you,' said the manager as the Servant closed the door.

Selby leaned forwards on his chair, waiting to hear the news.

The Madam hummed as she scanned her eyes down the sheet to read, then said plainly, 'Raines had to be stopped. A bad human with that much power is a risk to us all.' As she handed Selby the memo, she mocked, 'He really believed his crimes would go unpunished! The silly old fool!'

'He felt *entitled* to behave as he did. I'm not sure he even considered there to be a punishment. And I lost a fr–' Selby stopped himself from saying 'friend', then continued, 'an excellent candidate because of him.'

'Yes. I am sorry we couldn't stop the train. We were not aware of Raines' order to expunge your candidate.'

'Hmm...' Selby felt a renewed sorrow at the loss. There was another photograph pinned to the board in his office. It was another face that stared out with the dead eyes of an enslaved mind. It was another failure for Selby to torture himself with, but another reminder to never quit. 'He was so close to being free,' he said aloud to the single piece of paper that trembled under the weight of his breath.

'Don't think about that. You need to move onwards.'

'Yes, but there was something about this one. I liked him. He was different!' Selby said emphatically, and more forcibly than he would usually speak to his manager.

'There are plenty more. You need to go and find them.'

Selby stood, saluted and motioned that he would go back to his office with the silent wave of his thumb over his shoulder.

Nodding for him to leave, she added, 'Always remember, *free will* can never be truly controlled.'

Lyndon had spent another dull day scavenging. She had been avoiding Point A station and was setting up a new shelter on the outermost edge of the wasteland. It was an area that brought her the happiest memories. It was a place that felt serene.

With the night falling, she lay Little Lyndon in the cupboard, grabbed a stack of papers, unfolded them and packed them around him, layer after layer.

'There, nice and warm. Sleep well little one,' she said softly as she gave him a final kiss on the forehead and carefully closed the cupboard door.

Lyndon took a position close by and sat on the sediment of a lost civilisation. She stayed there to watch the sun flatten into the ground and the stars appear out of the darkness. She let her mind wander and think.

Before trying to sleep, it had become her nightly routine to trudge down the slope to the square area where the rubbish was at its flattest. She stared hopefully at the synthetic hillock above her. And every night, after her eyes adjusted, she was sure she could see Everley's silhouette emerge out of the blurry blackness. He was sitting there on the hill, watching over her.

'Thank you for bringing a brief moment of joy into a world so full of hatred and human suffering. I am loving you,' she spoke to the sky.

AFTERWORD
FOR
AFTERWARDS

Thank you for reading, Brito trusts you enjoyed it!

For Brito! is a story about the endurance of the human spirit and the development of character despite a regime of manipulation, supervision and control.

This novel evolved after first drafting in 2018, yet it seems more relevant now than ever as it looks towards a post-Brexit and post-Coronavirus Britain.

Start a dystopian discussion!
To access Book Club resources, more information and join the reader list, visit: www.forbrito.com.

If you enjoyed *For Brito!*, please leave a review!